£2·50
1/v

17/4 ·

The Burning Book

by the same author

DYING, IN OTHER WORDS (Harvester)

ff

MAGGIE GEE

The
Burning Book

faber and faber
LONDON · BOSTON

First published in 1983
by Faber and Faber Limited
3 Queen Square London WC1N 3AU
First published in Faber Paperbacks in 1985

Typeset by Goodfellow & Egan Limited, Cambridge
Printed in Great Britain by
Redwood Burn Limited, Trowbridge, Wiltshire
All rights reserved

© Maggie Gee, 1983

British Library Cataloguing in Publication Data

Gee, Maggie
The burning book.
I. Title
823'.914[F]   PR6057.E24/

ISBN 0–571–13417–3

For my friend Barbara Goodwin, who has always helped me, with love and gratitude

Contents

Acknowledgements

Grateful acknowledgement is made to all the following sources. My principal source of historical information on the Japanese Empire and particularly the siege of Nanking is David Bergamini's fascinating *Japan's Imperial Conspiracy: How Emperor Hirohito Led Japan into War against the West* (Heinemann, 1971). I have drawn extensively on the harrowing first-person accounts of Hiroshima and Nagasaki contained in John Hersey's *Hiroshima* (Penguin, 1946, reprinted 1982) and Tatsuichiro Akizuki's *Nagasaki 1945* (Quartet, 1981), two books I hope my readers will also read. Other sources of information on Japan include James Kirkup's *Japan Behind the Fan* (J. M. Dent, 1970), R. Jungk's *Children of the Ashes* (Heinemann, 1961) and B. W. Robinson's *Arms and Armour of Old Japan* (HMSO, 1951). Quotations and information in Chapter 12 are drawn from John Cox's *Overkill: the Story of Modern Weapons* (Penguin, 1977). Quotations in Chapter 14 are taken from T. Hall's *The Alpine House* (HMSO, 1981).

I should also like to express my grateful thanks to Grania Jones and to Musa, Nina and Rachel Farhi.

Author's Note

Throughout this novel 'miracle' is used in senses (1), (7) and (14) of the *Oxford English Dictionary*, revised edition:

'. . . ad L. *miraculum*, object of wonder: object of earthly wonder e.g. the Siberian birch-forest, the Colorado Desert, the Hanging Gardens of Babylon . . . . . . [or] . . . marvellous event (or change in the course of events) brought about by human agents . . . [or] . . . a miraculous story, play, legend'.

If all is reduced to the One, to what is the One reduced?

Buddhist *koan*

i Chapter of Beginning...

This is the story of Lorna and Henry and Angela, George and Guy. I'm afraid that since no one likes Guy, he does get left out of things. But this is the story of a family, the Ship family, not forgetting anybody. They all start different, but they mostly end up the same.

This is the story of Lorna who was born in Wolverhampton, daughter of Mervyn Lamb, who kept the corner shop. The shop went broke when Lorna was just sixteen. So she married Henry, and in a few months she was pregnant with Angela. Knitted lots of things in pure wool, like everyone else. Later she had Guy, and then George. They came in a row. They come later. She fought with her husband, who drank, as most people do.

She understood shops, so she went to work in a shop, when the children were older. A supermarket, in fact, and of course it was different. She had "an affair" with the manager, lunch-times, out at the back. She still loved her husband, as most people do, and her husband, of course, still loved her. She had been such a beautiful girl, very thin, grey eyes and red cheeks. She was just a child when they married: her hair was a burning bush. She was over forty, though, when the final violence started.

The story of Lorna and Henry. Henry Ship will be one of our heroes. He was born in Wolverhampton too, nine years before Lorna. When he married Lorna he was happy as a cricket. He would soon give up at the Brewery, boring; he was being trained by his next-door neighbour Ken to mend clocks and watches. He loved them, loved their insides. He loved Lorna, too, with that first blind passion, and she longed blindly for him. . . .

. . . his eyes, vast and blue, and the thing that he felt for the watches.

They married, like everyone else. Then the kids started coming, and they all went to London, the future, they thought, to the future, like everyone else. They went to Acton; he worked in Ken's uncle's shop. Then the uncle left him the shop. But the money went out of the watches, the money, they needed the money. So he went to work in a bar, for the money, like everyone else. And drank. And hit Lorna. And Lorna, of course, hit him back. And he fell in love with his daughter, a bit, because when he was drunk she looked just like Lorna. Or just like Lorna once used to. He suspected she had an affair, and so he drank more, like everyone else. He was over fifty, though, when the final violence started.

The story of Lorna and Henry and Angela, *Ange* at home. She cried a lot as a baby and Lorna and Henry both hit her, not spiteful, just tired and cross, like everyone else. They loved her, though, as everyone else loves their daughter. Who doesn't. *You love your own kids* (this was said by Lorna, who sometimes suspected she didn't).

Later Ange grew lanky and separate and strange and clever, but only at English. And said odd things, and *refused*. She didn't like horses, didn't like sweets, didn't like Christmas or outings. And in a few years she didn't have boyfriends, didn't like her brothers, didn't like violence, didn't eat eggs fish or meat. And she read about wars, and bombs. The smoke made her nostrils tingle, and clung like a stain in her hair. She was not, you can see, quite the same as everyone else.

But then she got happy. She found a nice boyfriend, and loved him, although she would always be selfish. The happiness made her forget; if John was there, who she loved, she happily chewed at the muscles of lambs and chickens reared in the dark. Not minding, enjoying the flavour, growing older like everyone else. But she didn't forget the smoke. It drifted across from the future. She was nearly twenty-five, and happy, when the final violence started.

The story of Lorna and Henry and Angela, Guy and George, or

"the boys". The boys were really quite different, so here are their stories in order.

First Guy, who's the elder. He was named after Mother's rich brother in Australia, who sent his namesake the wrong birthday presents, elaborate ties, dull leather-covered books, and once a Chest Developer. Guy was in the "slow" stream at school. They emphasized '*not* retarded'. The teachers said he was slow, and yet he was quick to hurt. His face had a permanent sneer. People hit him because of that sneer. He was lonely and nasty mainly because he looked lonely and nasty. He just got into the habit, and later he couldn't change it. He didn't like George or his sister and he didn't like Mam or Dad. They didn't like him; they felt just like everyone else did.

He left school early because everyone said he was dim. With a sneer like that and with no CSEs it was hopeless. He queued at the dole every fortnight, knew terrible shame every time. *What did you do with your time?* Amusement arcades, and the Party. He had joined the New Empire Party, which felt like being in the Army. (The real Army turned him down flat; weak chest, an irregular heart.) He loved the chanting, the marching, the frightening black uniform. Before he had always been frightened; now he could be frightening, too. With his uniform on, he looked tall.

He was not, in fact, very tall. He was slight and weak and he died in a underground station, in time to trouble his mother, at only nineteen years old. He had always liked to upset her. Guilt troubled her last two years. He had only been dead two years when the final violence started.

Then George. George was fat and gentle and clever and loving, as a child. People hit him, because he moved slowly and ate too much. But he loved them back, which is not what everyone else does. He loved Lorna because she was lost and tired and still pretty and Henry because he was tired and frightened and old and Ange (most of all) because she was clever and weird and loved him (although in the end she gave up). He even tried to love Guy, which was *not* what everyone else did. In fact no one else except George had ever tried to do that.

George stopped being fat in his teens and grew tall and broad and afraid of the Russians, as Guy was, and most other people were too. He argued with Guy, all the same; Guy said he was a coward, so George left school and joined the Army. Real Army for

17

George, not nutters like Guy. He argued with Ange, because she thought the Russians were people. "They're just like everyone else," she insisted, her pale grey eyes on the sky. George didn't want to think they were people. He was frightened of having to love them too. He was only twenty, and puzzled, when the final violence started, the end of the story of Lorna and Henry, Angela, George, oh yes. . . .

. . . oh yes Guy—young Guy—he does get forgotten, I'm sorry. His eyes were pinkish, like eyes of mice, when the sunlight managed to reach them. They didn't get on with each other; his eyes were not set straight. And it wasn't easy to reach them, because they were lemon-pip small. In the shade they were black as mouse-droppings. You couldn't tell what was inside. He was not like everyone else was. The mouse was too thin, almost shrivelled. So rats are dried out by poison, and children by lack of love.

He was dry as a match, I fear. And I fear they tried to forget him, his family, like everyone else (but here he shall not be forgotten).

He was still in the family home, the house which he thought was his home, he was still nineteen and miserable when his frightened heart stopped beating. . . .

That was how Guy came to be left out of the final chapter of burning.

He was always getting left out. But at least he is not forgotten.

There is comfort about a synopsis. Except that it doesn't quite fit. There are other sounds in the air. Stray giggles and drunken laughter. Someone sniffling, waking alone. Odd acts of love on cold landings. The nuclear family looks tidy, but a lot is cut off by the frame. A baby found on a doorstep . . . *not in our family, surely*. . . .

And a ghost hand waves in the distance, a pardon sent from the past. Another hand gently plays shadows, a bodiless rabbit, a bear . . . the running fauna of dreams, whose names don't fit in synopses.

No one knew Grandpa was there. Frank Ship, an old man on a mountain. They thought he had died in a home. Rose *hoped* he had died in a home. Frank and Rose were Henry Ship's parents, and parents should stay as they were. Parents hang at the back of their kids, in an organized family picture.

Rose hoped Frank had died very painfully, calling on her at the last. She hoped he had somehow made money, and left her his all in a will. His letter would find her much later: *my darling . . . so foolish . . . too late.*

She had told some terrible stories, to neaten the narrative ends. She said he had left her for drink. In fact it was *her* who drank, *glug-glug* at the VP sherry. He left her to get some air. He had packed up his life in a suitcase. It fitted in easily, then. All the best of his life was to come.

He drank thirty years of free air, all alone on the side of a mountain. He thought of them all, when it rained. Then the skies were lower, the world seemed smaller, he wasn't so sure he was free.

They crowded back into his bed, when he closed his eyes after midnight. He saw them all glazed in embalming fluid, frozen the day that he left. His wife's brassy ridges of hair: and the red wrapped lard of her cheek, which had once pressed close to his own. How lovely the Swiss sheets felt, stretched under his solitary cheek-bones.

(In fact, the lard had grown lumpy, and some had melted away. Rose was blotchy and bitter and waterlogged, and her roots and her heart were grey.)

They had both floated off from the group, where the parents receded in pairs, their hair growing white together, white heads growing backwards in pairs. Frank and Rose both stood out of line, disturbing the family picture. You could see the glint of brown glass where a bottle peeped out of her skirt. And he looked away out of focus, at things too far and too large.

Nor were Lorna's parents quite right. Mervyn Lamb had died out of turn. When his daughter left home he gave up, let the crab cells swarm up and eat him. He loved her much more than his wife, the white head which rolled on his pillow. In families excess is a sin, and untimely death is a crime. Prunella was left on her own, in a genteel frenzy of mourning.

The photographer was consoled: Prunella in black added *ton*. But things soon went very wrong. She is wearing black stockings and garters. There is lipstick on her false teeth. You could see the glint of brown flesh where a youth peeps under her skirt.

Though the front row ought to look good, the children won't

19

stand a close-up. At first glance the girl is a beauty, small features and clouds of red hair. And her name will do well enough: it's a popular name, is Angela. But *she doesn't look after herself* (that's Rose, her nose in the sherry): *she's skinny, men like a nice armful* (she folds a great ham round her own).

And George is too fat, with sad eyes, the eyes of a saint sick of chocolate. And Guy is not really a child, but a lonely old man in boys' trousers. Whoever designed this got tired. These are clumsy mock-ups of children. . . .

"Those kids haven't turned out well. Barring George, of course, in the Army. That Lorna is scatty as an alley-cat. She fed them all on Baked Beans. But I mean—in a family photo. You can't pretend they fit in."

Still, nothing entirely fits in. There is sand at the back of the camera. Fluff as the fixative dries. The light-meter says it is dark, and yet it's not long after breakfast. Something not running quite smoothly, something impeding our flow.

It is hair, old nail-clippings, droppings. The millions of cells that we shed. The daily selves that escape us, unacted, the words not said. It is doodles, time-wasting, wishes, those final letters unsent. It is small mistakes and misreadings, mistakes too late to set right.

Hairs catch the keys as they fall. People will not keep still.

But there's something more fundamental, fogging my diagrams. There are shadows stretching on down from the darkness before it began. There is something more frightening as well. There is laughter, but also screams.

The screams seem unwritable, likewise, and yet they demand to come in. It is hardly the thing, I think, to be heard in a family play. But thousands of voices are crying. They scratch at the pane like birds.

Like pigeons in a lost grey square. The buildings they cling to are lifeless. The bright tours of summer are gone. They scratch at a pane with no faces. But the truth is, yes, we are here.

Yes, we are here inside, reluctant to cope with their pain. Ashamed, I must open the windows. Those syllables make no

20

sense, but their discord shivers with grief. *Hibakusha, hibakusha*. Something broken pleading for life.

There are people not spoken about, people not written about, people whose name is a way of saying they are not there. *Hibakusha*, atomic victims—the scarred who carry our scars. They reminded the Japanese of the horrors that come with defeat.

Hibakusha, the scarcely human. More decent to cover their faces. Those great ridged keloids, please hide them. Dull purple, coming too close. . . . At night when we close our eyes the *hibakusha* come flocking. They expose themselves through torn sheets, or maybe torn skin, not mending.

Hibakusha, queuing and pleading—for jobs and money and help. Even worse, they beg us to see them. They can't imagine our terror. In time, they will vanish of course. Those who lived through the Bomb die young (though not young enough for our comfort, in Hiroshima's crowded streets).

It's as if their brains have been burned, as if they cannot forgive us. They try to make us feel guilty. Their cries will not leave us in peace.

Hibakusha, hibakusha. Let us in, let us darken this space.

There are other people so famous that they are more real than life. They have names that sparkle with toothpaste and diamonds and chandeliers cleaned with gin. They wear contact lenses of sapphire which glitter with cold blue fire. In fact, they see nothing through them, and no one outside can see in.

Yes indeed they are real people, more real than most of us are. They are proved by oceans of print and mountains of newsreel footage. These people are our leaders, perhaps to the end of time. In this novel they stay backstage, with final control of the lighting.

The leaders are booked for embalming, the finest bunkers reserved. But even if they don't get there, they have made their mark in our world. If anything human remains, their names will shine in the ruins. Our children, cripples or mutants naively looking for pattern, will find their images stored. They will stare at their runes recurring, sure that these were our gods, beings of blazing beauty or wisdom or virtue or strength. . . .

But no, they are just our leaders. Their size is a trick of the light. Their outsides are frail lacquered cases. Their sound-effects come from machines. Their scripts are written by hacks. . . .

Our children, should any survive, will try to make sense of those speeches. But they will find nothing there. There was never anything there. We give real power and real glory to dying, neon-dipped actors. They radiate our own sickness, speaking blank words through blank smiles. That blankness will not be forgotten, the deadness in our own souls. Its image may be trapped in flesh, in tons of collapsing matter.

Our children may not understand how to read these pictures of God. They will try to use primitive logic, try to make sense of our end. They will think these are love's own deities, call on their names as they mate, softly for fear of the dark and the rats and the wild men in the old sewers. In the heart of the darkness we left them, light is the paramount virtue.

The truth, however, is simple. Silver in teeth which are dead. They are real because we are rotten. In them our real image survives. The symbols are quick to read: they are greed and glitter and lying.

And those who stare at our gods will all be one with our homeless. The meek will inherit the earth, at the stinking end of the earth. They will all have become *hibakusha*, the name that means they are nameless. The people we would not speak of will triumph after our death.

Hibakusha, hibakusha—for years they have cried to come in. They warned us, as well, those bird-cries, but we were too busy to listen.

The hour of their triumph, however, has come rather late for them. There is no one left free of pain to pity the pain they suffer. No one is left to refuse them but nothing is left to offer.

22

1 Chapter of Rules and Red Hair

Lorna had always thought of herself as a very gentle person. Her mother Prunella encouraged that, because *girls should be sweet and gentle. Do as you would be done by, be done by as you did.* Her mother Prunella was not really gentle but her mother was very *genteel.* Her mother had a name of surpassing gentility, given her by *her* mother. That is to say, Lorna's grandma, whose professional name was Joanna Smythe-Fielde. A *very* genteel name, but what it meant was quite simple. Joan Smith had a mother called Field, and decided to go on the stage. Her hair was a red-gold curtain framing her face in velvet folds. The performance was lustrous eye-lids and dimples like settling honey. She played her best roles on *chaises-longues*, and there she seduced Edgar Cleaver.

She acted a virgin divinely, and he had no need to act stupid. They married weeks after her fall, deep sighs on his rose *chaise-longue.*

The fruit of their sin was Prunella, a name Joanna adored. Poor Edgar, a gentleman tutor, could only yield to such passion. Little Pruney was raised to think pink; life would be roses and cherries.

But she wasn't as pretty as she should have been. Her face was too long for lace collars. Her teeth were too big for the simpers Joanna taught her to do. She walked with a forward tilt and her sharp hips tapping behind her. At twenty-seven she met Mervyn, in a Haberdashery Shop. He sold her some stockings, holding

23

A Family Picture

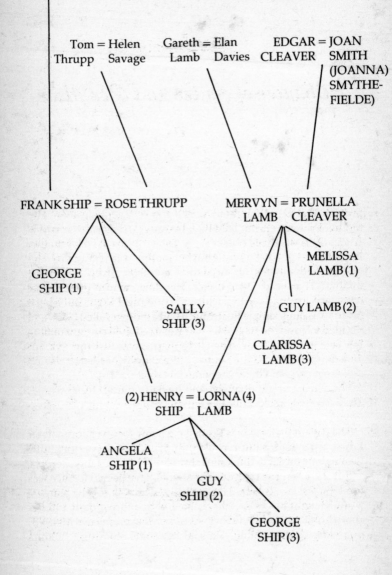

Tom = Helen
Thrupp Savage

Gareth = Elan
Lamb Davies

EDGAR = JOAN
CLEAVER SMITH
(JOANNA)
SMYTHE-
FIELDE)

FRANK SHIP = ROSE THRUPP

MERVYN = PRUNELLA
LAMB CLEAVER

GEORGE
SHIP (1)

SALLY
SHIP (3)

MELISSA
LAMB (1)

GUY LAMB (2)

CLARISSA
LAMB (3)

(2) HENRY = LORNA (4)
SHIP LAMB

ANGELA
SHIP (1)

GUY
SHIP (2)

GEORGE
SHIP (3)

them up to the long beams of sunlight falling; they were not as fine as she wanted, but his eyes were brilliantly blue. He was short and kind, too kind, with a generous imagination. He found her background romantic, and her desperation too. Edgar set him up with a shop and a suit to marry his ageing daughter. He wished his wife would go too, and the giggles and whispers and worries . . . but at least his duties were done. He would switch his hearing-aid off. Edgar settled down to a slow, dry death around dry tobacco, dry gin.

Prunella Lamb, née Cleaver, bore Melissa, Guy, Clarissa, and Lorna. She would have called Lorna Nerissa, but Mervyn Lamb put his foot down. "All that hissing, woman," he exploded, in a once-in-a-lifetime row. In any case Clarissa became Clarrie and Melissa Mel, except to their mother, who never let Mervyn say Pruney. She let him do so little it was a marvel that children were born. But she bent her rules minutely, since *all girls want to be mothers*.

Joanna gave Pruney fixed notions, hoping they'd make her secure. If she knew *her colour was pink*, she would not waver to purple. If she knew that *money was good*, she would not go wasting herself (though as time went on, twenty-five, twenty-six, as her cheeks grew yellow and her neck more craned, Pruney's mother realized she was saving her daughter for life on the shelf, cold pickle). If she married a man like Mervyn, then, she could know maternal joys: and not *quite* descend to the gutter, since Mervyn was just above it. His soft Welsh accent redeemed him, so much less damning than Brum. His nails and his collars were clean. For a forty-year-old he would pass.

Joan Smith (Joanna Smythe-Fielde) had fixed notions about class. You chose which drawer you would go in, and then you made sure you would fit. It was up to Prunella, then, to define the class of her children. So Prunella tried most of her life, making rules, *thinking pink, keeping smiling*.

(One day her children were gone, and her thoughts turned to what she had missed. She had wasted her youth, she realized, which was worse than wasting herself. So for twenty years she had fun, confusing and shocking her children. It was her fault they were confused. She had taught them fun wasn't nice, that rules were both nice and simple. *Don't go playing with dirty kids, don't ever think you'll get away with anything*. They didn't obey them

25

themselves, but they thought that their mother should. *Parents aren't really people.* Be done by as you did.)

Boys should be posh and not gentle. She called her second child Guy. He grew posh, in the end, as she wanted, with sports shops, a sports car, a chest. But he had to go to the other side of the world to be a success. In England, until he was thirty, his mother's voice scraped at his sleep. *"You don't want to waste your time. You want to think of the future."*

All his life he had a soft spot for Lorna, his youngest and prettiest sister . . . as she grew less pretty and less young, as things went predictably wrong. As her hair became split and wild, a caricature of her grandma's.

"Ooh, he loves his sister," cooed Prunella to guests, stroking his red-blond hair. If boys didn't have to have crew-cuts, his hair would have been like Lorna's. But she didn't add, equally truthfully, "Lorna couldn't give tuppence for him though," which would have made her guests stop nodding indulgently, ruching their cheeks into smiles. Prunella liked smiles in the parlour, you see, just like everyone else.

"Front room, not parlour," Mervyn said quietly, again and again, twice a day, every day, alone in the thimble-sized store at the back of his GENERAL SHOP. "LAMBS' HAVE GOT IT! TRY US!! THE SHOP FOR YOUR EVERYDAY NEEDS!!!" So the hand-printed notice announced, in the early days of their marriage. Later on Prunella insisted that all exclamations were coarse. (Still later, *she* would get coarse: black stockings, open-crotched panties.)

But at first the notice was true. They started with one of most things. A gent's umbrella, six pairs of gloves "for the paper-boys", Mervyn suggested (he was writing a story, as usual, bringing the whole world in, a dappled cast of people browsing the dim velvet pile of its detail). There were little socks (of pure wool) for six-months-old triplets, though one-and-a-half pairs sold or vanished, leaving three socks going slowly grey. There were Beecham's Powders, chocolate watches, ten fish of blue sugar, pink-finned. . . .

Young Mervyn was ruled by joy. He saw them at the seaside, one summer, just out on his own for a stroll, and brought them all back in his pockets, triumphant, to the guesthouse where she sat grimly and sensibly dressing the kids for the Prom. He burst in, short and square as a postcard with the sea air bright on his cheeks.

26

"I'll sell these for three times the price, see, Prunella. They'll love'em. Real novelty, these. . . ."

At first there were too many novelties, things which amused him, things it amused him to show her, before he abandoned hope of showing her things which amused her (yet later, she would be amused; fancy garters, sex magazines, things Mervyn would have thought most peculiar, but by that time Mervyn was dead).

EVERYDAY NEEDS, the board said, but his needs and his days weren't normal. The shop had too many novelties, really, for anyone but Mervyn's everyday needs. Which shrank and grew less in the end as life ceased to amuse him so much, or amusement hid deep inside. As some of the zest went out of the struggle to ripple her ink-ruled calm.

Her marital calm, that is, her rules for managing Mervyn. For her social self did a non-stop speeded-up switchback dance routine, from kitchen to parlour, from bottle to glass, from snickers of pantomimed laughter to shrieks of decorous shock— "Oh *no*, Mr Edwards dear, you really *mustn't* say that!" There were rules, after all, to maintain: you could think it, but oooh, to say it!

With Mervyn, however, it wasn't social. She grimly and quietly meant it. He must not and would not, eventually, say or do that. The blue sugar fish grew dull, kept under the counter. They lay there belly-upward, and the chocolate watches all stopped. In the shop front, needs became flattened. Bread and sugar, butter and eggs. His newspaper in the mornings, his pipe and slippers at night. At ten they put off the light, and the bedspread lay quiet as a carpet.

But Mervyn chuckled inside, and his gentle menageries with him. The sun made stars on the jars. Light lay on the woodwork like water, spun the high dust into spores. There was life in his shop, and beauty, and often his youngest daughter.

And Mervyn also thought of her as a very gentle person. She was gentler with her Dad's dreams than his other daughters had been. Where the others saw black and white, Lorna saw clouds making shadows. There was black and white in their play, but they twisted together in stories. Unlike her mother and sisters, Lorna preferred this to facts. One day he would take her to London, to show her shells to the Queen. They would drink champagne out of teacups with golden seahorses on. Or perhaps they would fly out to India to get some real curry for supper. It

27

came on ivory plates, with a pattern of tusks on the edges. The ivory gleamed like butter, the best unsalted kind. (The world had opened for Mervyn when he fought in the First World War. Magical names he might be sent to, places not to be killed. It was not a *serious* war . . . until his friends got killed. Names of the dead in their solemn lines, marching on cold stone walls.)

Lorna liked to play on the edge of the shadows beneath the counter. Until she was nearly fourteen she like to crouch in the little tunnel which led between her father's privileged world at the back and the routine world where the shoppers waited, in front of the polished counter. If she liked the shopper, she would peer from the darkness, blue eyes gazing up from a dim gold cloud of hair. The imaginative were startled. At ten she looked quite naked from above, except for white socks and striped wristwatch, the strap of the yellow-and-navy elastic not so much wider than her wrist. Then there were slender greenish-white arms wrapped tightly round slender greenish-white calves, and sharp knees were pressed together like knuckles, no clothes, it seemed, and scant flesh.

Quite soon she realized the effect she had on the customers, the little intake of breath . . . and then smiles and questions and compliments, and for the last few years that she fitted the tunnel, before her frail bones grew too long and her body too tender and aching, took accurate pleasure in judging the moment when she would announce herself, turning the everyday lists being dealt with above into gasps and laughter and feigned irritation from her father, which melted into great grins when the shopper announced her a beauty.

"You'll be turning her head," he would say, shaking his, reaching under the counter, though, to stroke the soft spring of her curls, and then when they were gone he would drop the pretence of crust and call her "my beauty" or "my little beauty" and tell her another story, as he polished the long metal stalks of the keys of the till with the love other men gave flowers, as he brushed the shelves for the joy of the sunlight making incense of the motes of dust.

Lorna's future was not to be a beauty, not to sit like a goddess in an alcove, exciting men's wonder and greed. But the memory of those years in the shop, with her father in priestly attendance, the rituals of sun and stock-taking and *not letting on to the customers*, the

28

sense of a special kingdom where she would forever belong—
stayed with her always, a mysterious brightness at the back of the
greyness of days.

Lorna's looks took after her grandmother's, which worried her
mother a lot. Prunella was not very clever, but her memory was
photographic (for the first fifty years, at least, before she forgot all
the rules). She never forgot one item her spendthrift husband had
bought. In a mean small drawer in her forehead the blue sugar fish
still mouldered. Since she would not help in the shop she had
plenty of time for reflection. She thought of her girlhood and the
decade after when she was too old to be a girl. She thought of her
mother Joanna, and scattered snapshots piled.

As her mother had grown older her hair had become deeper red,
and the tints on her lips and cheeks had grown lusher, in
sympathy. Her face was upholstered satin, fine skin over laughing
flesh. Her dimples were deep and contented as those on a sofa
back. The phone often rang for her mother, and she always "just
took it next door". From just next door in the hall soft shrieks and
laughter would blow. Her father seemed to hear nothing, fish-
jaws in the deeps of his drink.

Prunella's face was like his, without softness, raw bone
showing through. Joanna had melted in chairs, white honey
cupped by a spoon. Red curls poured over the cushion, those
reddening, maddening curls. Her daughter Prunella was joints
spreadeagled, angles which would not fit in: *keep your legs together*,
hissed her mother. *Don't slouch. Hold up your chin.* Prunella's hair
was vague down. *At least you could keep it tidy.*

Her hair was very important. Joanna's hair lit the stage, a torrent
of flashing electric. With hair like dust and vague cobwebs, her
daughter sulked in the wings. *At least you could keep it tidy*—tidy
that dust away. *Girls should always keep tidy*—tidy your youth
away.

Inside Prunella the darkroom waited for when she could look at
the slides. Her mother's legs weren't together. Her mother's
round legs opened wide. Her mother's back curved like a treble
clef and her hair was a nest of serpents. Her mother's voice
lounged on the telephone wires and the high notes trembled with
sin.

Yet her mother had said "Your skirt's too short. . . ." "That
colour looks cheap, oh *Prunella* . . . you don't know *men*, my

29

darling, you don't know what they will *think*."

In longish skirts and drab colours, the habits her mother had taught, the ageing Prunella remembered, the ageing Prunella *thought*. She thought, and with bitter envy, her mother had been a tart. And she thought of her mother's dimples, and the vague sly shine in her eyes, and the perfumed fur on her collars, smelling of hot sweet spice.

Though Prunella had never known it, she recognized happiness. And because there had to be logic, some reason why she couldn't have it, she saw that shiver of bliss as something set in the flesh. It came in the shade of your iris, the curve of your lower lip. *Look as you would be done by: be done by as you look.* Prunella still needed rules, but decided the rule was beauty.

Her own daughter moved like Joanna had moved, with her red curls drifting behind her. Hair which would drive you mad as the curlers snatched at your own. And the way she straddled on Mervyn's lap, one thumb pushed into a sleepy pout, her pale legs swinging and twitching, her left hand curled into his. . . .

"What do you look like?" she suddenly snapped, waking both from a TV trance. "*What does she look like?*" Prunella repeated, more venomously, to her husband. "Skirt round her waist. She's not a kid any more, *if* you haven't noticed."

Mervyn stared and sat up, and Lorna got off his knee, but she kept her hand in her father's. She always knew just who she loved, and her mother and brother could forget it (and later on in this book we shall find her first son could forget it: young Guy, who they all forgot, could forget being loved by Lorna. "He isn't such a bad kid, but well—let's face it, no beauty").

When she wanted to needle her mother Lorna spoke in a high vague voice. "I'm eleven, actually," she said. "Wasn't doing anything, was I?"

"Still sucking your thumb at eleven," hissed Prunella, hands on sharp hips, "Not doing anything, precisely. I know who won't be getting into the High School. Then you'll have to go to Hannaford Road. Don't say I didn't warn you."

"Leave her alone," said Mervyn. "Give over, Prunella. It's Sunday."

"Have you done the books?" she screamed at him, self-control snapping as a nervous little smile started playing like sun on water round Lorna's mouth, as she saw those white slender fingers tighten on his veined hand. "I bet you're scared stiff to even look at them. Call yourself a man . . . you can't even keep your own family."

It was true that he couldn't keep much, at the moment: the figures were slipping away. A man must keep his own family. Figures which danced like fleas. "It's me you're after now then is it. Well have you said enough?"

"I want to watch the TV," said Lorna in the same remote voice, not looking at her mother, not looking at the TV, her blue eyes turned out of the window, swinging her father's hand.

Melissa was sitting by the fire, knitting a turquoise scarf. She was engaged to be married to a travelling salesman. She had warts and a bulldog jaw and a live-in job in an Old Folk's Home. She was mostly kind-hearted, as it happened, but she hated her pretty little sister. She put down her knitting with a business-like click that sounded like angry teeth meeting. She pulled down her skirt, jerk-jerk, over fire-blotched fat firm knees (her legs took after her grandpa's: poor Edgar had very short legs). She was only seventeen years old, but she could have been twenty-seven.

She waved the bright turquoise wool to rope Lorna back from the garden. "You're a trouble-maker," she announced. "That's what you are, Lorna. You always make trouble. This is supposed to be my day off. I mean I've come to have a chat to Mum and Dad. Some hopes."

"You want to listen to your sister," pronounced Prunella, delighted, her spine rearing up in rapture.

"I thought you were knitting," Mervyn said mildly, his lilt more singsong than usual, as ever at times of stress. "Was it something special you had to say to us then? Precious little you've said to your father indeed the last few Sundays you've been with us, isn't it?"

"Leave her alone," shrieked Prunella. "It's your other daughter we're talking about." It changed, as events mysteriously change, from a small discontent to something frightening and serious. Her face was all rigid tendon over frameworks of painful bone. The cheeks were two furious boils of colour. The lips were pulled back from the teeth.

"This is all about nothing isn't it," hummed Mervyn, but the gaiety had drained from his voice and he dropped Lorna's hand, pushed her gently away. "What's the matter then Prunella? She'll do her homework after tea." As he spoke Lorna walked on light

31

feet across the carpet and stood three inches from the set ignoring them, staring at the programme with her back between them and the screen. The pool of light from the central light-bulb (Prunella would never have it off, not even when they watched television which was most of the time, "too gloomy" she said with a shudder, "I don't want to sit in the dark," and she didn't, even with the light on she didn't want to sit in the dark but the rules her mother had given her got between her and the brightness

don't make me ugly   *don't make me*
don't make me sit in the dark)

—the pool of light from the central light-bulb cascaded down Lorna's red rivers of hair, light like a whole sinful city glowing and burning

—never for her—

and then in a frenzy of maddened puppet-like motion Prunella was up on her flat slippered feet and had seized the thin arm and pushed her towards the door, "She'll go *now*, when I say so," and as Lorna raised a high bird wail and they tumbled together through the hallway Mervyn caught a small grin of excitement on Melissa's square face, which died in shame as she noticed him noticing

don't make me wicked   *don't make me*
I want to be good, and gentle

She was a nice girl, really, Melissa, usually kind to the patients at work, usually sweet when they couldn't look after themselves, gentle to the very old. Prunella meant all her daughters to grow up gentle, Prunella meant all her girls to be good, tumbling the small thin body as hard as she could through the hall. . . .

girls should be gentle/girls should be mothers/mothers should be gentle/
beating through her head

"Happy?" asked Mervyn, singsong, mildly, his blue eyes sharper than usual. He made Melissa blush. She picked up her knitting again, a scarf for her husband-to-be, whose red ears turned purple with pain on walks in the depths of winter. She wanted to keep him warm, and her patients secure from worry. She wanted to have small babies who would nest on her strong round breasts.

32

But she also wished she was Lorna, as slender and pale as wind.

"It's all very well," she said, her voice deliberately neutral. "But that child is spoiled, you know. Just see. You're going to have trouble."

"Some people go looking for trouble," said Mervyn, his eyes on the screen.

They did have trouble, of course, but not the conventional kind. Though others perceived her as sensuous, all Lorna wanted was love. It was not her fault that she wore for two decades a body of striking beauty. She was lovely enough to cause pain, and lovely enough to cause sin. She was lovely enough to cause grief when her loveliness dried at the edges.

She never noticed it going, though she missed the worship it brought her. In her late thirties she was quite surprised when Jack Latham failed to adore her. She never quite made the connection, as life started drying and shrinking. So many people once loved her. She just thought love had worn through.

The trouble she gave her father had nothing to do with her looks. She broke her father's heart when she swopped one love for another. She had done the same thing at school, rotating the prettiest partners. All Best Friends were the same. It was only the names that were different. What mattered was adoration and you got more of that to begin with. To her love was what you received, and what you gave back was pleasure.

When the shop began to go bust she no longer relied on her father. Henry had come in for years, a shy, wiry youth who bought rubbish. She knew that he didn't need pipe-cleaners, pepper-mints, chewing-gum, matches, combs. He came in to bring her presents, and she smiled at him more and more. His eyes were as blue as her father's. They were bluer, since Dad's had grown old. They were blue with black curtains of lash, and they stared as if he was drowning (Dad had grown heavy, of late, and his jokes were like broken toys). She knew who he came in to gawp at. She stood so the sun caught her hair. At first when she was thirteen he seemed impossibly older. But then she was fourteen, fifteen, and her breasts began to grow. By the time Lambs' crashed she was ready, assured of another protector. It wasn't her fault that it killed her father when the last of beauty left home.

It was not just chance, of course, that Lorna was born a beauty. It was not just chance that *her* daughter Angela, Prunella's granddaughter, Joanna's great-granddaughter, should be born a beauty too, if slightly *less* of a beauty (her jaw more obstinate, her nose more snub, her calves more sturdy, muscled like a dancer's). The genes came glancing like golden rain from the burnished head of Joanna. But the rain did not fall on Prunella, or her daughters Melissa and Clarissa. Beauty throws up exceptions, though it mostly plays by the rules.

So Mel and Clarissa would hog the bathroom till Pruney, enraged, thumped hard on the door. After they came out, with Clarrie pink-eyed in a turban of towels, there would be a dreadful smell of ammonia. Later Mel's handiwork would be unveiled. Flat curls, unnaturally stiff, some patches almost straight and the rest as dull and frizzy as an armpit. No wonder they resented Lorna so much, her hair which grew like a burning bush. And the gold went to Angela, paler than Lorna's, a fine washed auburn the sun bleached to blonde.

The beauty of these women was plaited together over thousands and thousands of years of growth. Each hair was a long chain of protein, as families are a chain of protein. Head after head glimpsed the bushy bronze light in the street and stopped and turned. By the time the last heads were turning, the first heads were long underground. By the time the last heads turned, more than bushes would soon be burning.

The gold did not go to Prunella, nor her daughters Melissa and Clarissa. And they blamed the world on their mother, as their mother before them had done. They thought, when they thought about anything much, it was families that set the pattern. Family life is a pattern. Family life is the rule

*(voices pelting like stones   wild stones pelting the window
out in the cold   no loved ones   rules and patterns are fiction)*

Prunella broke her own rules, and the pattern into the bargain. She rebelled in old age against the body she'd been given, long skirts over limbs like an insect's. She rebelled against her dingy bad skin with its tinges of sand and jaundice. She rebelled against her thin mouth, where the blood never seemed to reach. She rebelled against all the neatness she'd tried to instil in her daughters: it hadn't disguised her own plainness, or made her any less sour.

Instead of searching for precedents, theorems of proved

34

correctness, she stared at the items before her, and nothing would make them fit in. She saw her husband die, who should have stayed by her side. She saw her father dead and her hateful mother senile. (There was pleasure, of course, in visiting: Ma's scalp, dyed red cotton-wool.) But that wasn't the pattern for mothers. There *wasn't* a pattern for mothers. There wasn't any way you could get it right by doing what everyone else did.

She looked in her mirror and saw what she lived with. It wasn't a pattern, but her own awkward limbs, the raw disarrangement of truth she was left with. So far she had dressed it to do as she was told. Only now the instructing voices were silent. No one could help her, there were no rules.

And then she heard *him* as she gazed at the glass. The ghost of Mervyn was standing behind her. She thought he would reproach her but his eyes were kind. He said, "I am dead, and you know you must die." She knew he'd never loved her, but he wasn't triumphant. "This is all that there is girl," he said, looking sad. "This is all that there is, so you might as well enjoy it." She sat down sharply on the end of their bed.

Next day she went out and bought herself some lipstick. Her mother had worn lipstick, why shouldn't she? She tried it at home in the safety of her bedroom. It sat on her face like a sharp crimson fish. She didn't look pretty, but she did look alive. She wore it to the shops when she went to buy some eye-shadow. She got some Royal Purple, which the Queen might well wear, then she mixed it with some gold so it wouldn't look too sombre. She grinned at herself in the sunlit mirror. Her eyes looked twice as big as before.

She looked at her hair. A grey-white lichen. It would never be silky but it *could* be a colour. She bought a little bottle with a fierce, frightening smell. She read the leaflet carefully as she ate her ham for tea. Next day the scrub was feathers, thin crimson feathers. Brave crimson feathers which matched her fish mouth.

With her eyes like two plums and the little fish waving, "I feel a bit brighter," she said to herself. "This lipstick does make the new teeth look whiter."

She wore the whole lot when she went to find a future.

"She fancies herself, it's *indecent*," hissed Melissa. Of all the three girls the least shocked was Lorna. She just looked vague and attended to her baby. It didn't bother *her* if her mother looked peculiar. Lorna's whole life felt peculiar now. The baby was tiny

35

and pretty and helpless, and Henry was helpless when it came to the house. So she wasn't the youngest or the prettiest any more; and since she'd had the baby, there were changes in her figure, small bulges and pleats where it used to be hollow. These changes seemed more serious than any of her mother's. She didn't think about them much but they were always *there*. Standing at the sink, she would stare at her belly. It was strange they never mentioned it, that looks didn't last. Her mother had rules for everything, but she spoke as though everything got better.

As a little girl Lorna wasn't vain, if vain means looking in a mirror. She used to giggle and mimic her sisters, staring in the dressing-table mirror. They pulled in their cheeks as if they'd swallowed a hard-boiled egg in one go and couldn't get it back again. They pulled in their belts to waists which would kill them and then they compromised a few holes before. (So why should they be so hard on their mother? Because their mother was breaking the rules. Mothers should be decent, stay in the straight grey rows at the back of the family picture. Mothers should love their children, and always put them first.)

People do love their children, of course, and not just because everyone else does. Prunella did love Lorna, despite being jealous of her red-gold hair. Prunella loved all her daughters, her gentle and well-mannered daughters. She had done her best for them, until she grew suddenly bored. She had given them rules to live by, and plenty of nice fresh greens. *Eat up your greens and you'll grow* (but did that include growing older?).

For Melissa would divorce her travelling salesman husband, and her lover would let her down. Clarissa, who was good at mathematics, would end up cooking the books for a massage parlour, and her photograph, ugly as ever, would appear in the *News of the World*.

WE NAME WOLVERHAMPTON'S MISS WHIP

"Around here all the blokes are just dying for what we've got to give," said Mrs Clarissa Coombs, 43, of Trysull Road. . . .

Which seemed at the time, to the Coombses (the husband managed a bank) to bring the whole world to an end, though only her age was right. The quote was a fabrication, the photos had got mixed up. But a plain face isn't distinctive. Her neighbours were sure it was her. In fact, mostly due to her mother's rules, Clarissa had always loathed sex. But she got a lot of offers, in the dreadful months that followed.

And Lorna married beneath her, and lived for a time on the dole; had a kid who didn't look normal, and a cheap affair with Jack Latham. She would lose her looks and her confidence and her woodsprite lightness of heart. (And yet, against all the rules, she also learned how to be happy. It was more than being given pleasure. It was learning how to give love.)

Prunella was way past caring if her daughters' lives went right. She was tired of all her daughters, since they were tired of her. She was fond of young men, and sex. They were so much better looking than the others. Their skin was firm and gleaming, and so were their you-know-whats. And other new things, like make-up. A whole fresh world you could buy. With all those ravishing colours a Cosmetics Department was Christmas.

The men weren't always so young, of course, and sometimes they never came back. Some were rude and unpleasant, and some cack-handed or limp. But the bliss of the fun before it, the brandies and giggles and warmth. And the faint salt smell of excitement, of what she had missed, of youth. . . . Prunella was far too busy to grieve for her dull old daughters. Indeed they'd become like parents who she visited once a month.

She would feel quite shy on the bus, though she'd put on a modest make-up (just pale pink lips and mascara) and sensible lace-up shoes. She would go so far to please them, but she couldn't go far enough. When they asked her what she was doing, she told them what she was doing. She told them the names of the men, the names of the men she was doing. Her speech was just as before, artificially lively, social. She made her rota of lovers sound brisk as a church bazaar.

The winter that should have been hardening in the year of the final violence, Prunella was heading for a showdown, on the day of her birthday tea. She would have been seventy-five on the seventeenth of December. She looked about sixty still, with the agelessness of the thin. She'd determined to show the girls her latest admirer, an Indian, a plumpish, satin-skinned man who was sometimes the worse for drink. His marriage had been arranged, his wife brought wordless and weeping from India,

37

which she loved. Now she was heavily pregnant, and sobbed when he made her accept him. Prunella at least spoke English, the language of decent folk. And she listened to him and admired him, and praised his smooth purple penis (his wife of course was too stupid; besides, it was the first she'd seen). He liked to push it inside Prunella, her dry thin white woman's skin. Prunella positively *glowed*. This thing had gone on for *weeks*. After a month she decided it was time to present her friend to her family.

Such tensions might have been felt. Such shock-waves might have convulsed them. Melissa did not like black men, Clarissa did not like sex, Lorna would have taken his side but she wasn't coming till Christmas. Rashid was a sensitive man and might have insulted them back. And this would have riled Prunella, who might have had a heart attack. Or called him a Paki bastard (*good manners are often skin deep*). Or pushed his face in the cake (*for family may still be family*). All manner of things might have happened, a fine set-piece for this book.

But none of this was to happen. The candles would never burn. The cake would never be baked. The children would never be faced by Rashid in pearls of proud sweat.

Clarissa and Alfred Coombs would never have time to live down their shame. He had told his wife to "wait on: you'll see, people won't remember." They had giggled a lot, in the bank; each snicker might be at *him*.

They would find, however, that worse could happen than shame, and worse than living. They would find that sheets of flame were sharper than sheets of newsprint.

Lorna would find that you could lose more than your lover, your childish beauty. When her lover Jack Latham rejected her, she had longed to turn over and die. These words had rung through her days as she piled the tin cans on the shelves: "Please let me die, I can't bear it. I can't go on, let me die."

Not meaning, "Please blast me, please crush me, please blister the skin off my back." She would want to live very much, by the time of the final violence.

This family wanted to be normal. It imagined what normal might be: tiers in a family picture, smiles in a normal row. At the front the children, in glowing colour, insist it is their life now. Their eyes are on the same level, their clothing more or less matches. Together they present arms, face outwards, shoulder-to-shoulder. Behind are parents and grandparents, black-and-white, grey, then white. . . . The focus recedes demurely until they pass out of sight.

Our family was not like this picture. It ached with discontent. It was always *the others* who spoiled it, always the others who moved. There was always one of the children closing her eyes or scratching her knee. They sat too close or too far, they slouched or showed off for the camera. And the ancestors pushed for attention, would not give ground to the young. . . . Prunella with purple eye-shadow, flashing her thin black knees. . . . Henry's Mum on the bottle, his Dad on the mountainside. . . . Had anything ever gone right? Could anything worse go wrong?

They would learn that worse could go wrong. They would learn that worse could happen than defective habits of love.

They would find there was only one story, when it came to the final violence. They would find they had noticed differences where in fact all flesh is a likeness. They would die of violent shock, not the subtle wounds of the heart.

Her hair was a burning bush, but her body crackled like pork.

They would find that all hair burned, and that metaphor is a lie. They would find all their talk had been chatter, while generals talked about death. Their griefs were refusals to mourn, their "worries" fled from their worry. And while they evaded the issue, others made plans with hard edges. Just round the corner, just underground, just out of our depth, it was brewing. . . .

And people whispered, of course. *But then, people like to be gloomy. . . .*

Then suddenly something cracked, and the novel was torn in pieces.

I can hear them calling again, those voices calling for room. They have something to say about hair, since this chapter is criss-crossed with hair. The hair of Japanese women is long and thick as a blanket. It was hard for the stricken women, no heating, their clothing burned. And their heads became bald as stones on which the night-dews fell. It is cold to lose your hair and your roof and your husband's life together.

The women were not sentimental, and many of their children

had died, since it is the young and the old who die quickly from radiation. They would have been willing enough for other warm arms in the rubble.

But it's hard to find a new man when your skin has those mulberry stains, when your scalp is a ruined city of stubble and blind pink shine.

Hibakusha, hibakusha. The women chatter and giggle. Their ugliness comforts each other, and their anger against the men. The city is built again but who wants these balding pigeons. Grey and pink heads peck scraps in the freezing outlands of guilt.

"do as you would be done by, be done by as you did"

Rules have not yet been found which are proof against radiation.

2 Chapter of Humming

Consider the sheep in the fields. They maim not, neither do they kill. Yet Attila in all his crimson glory is not as deep in blood as some of these.

When Lorna was a little girl there was one thing in the shop that she hated. It was the fridge, with its grinds and bumps and its steam of frost in the light. The first time she opened the lid, she thought it a lovely game. It was nice holding on with your fingers and making the ends go white. And pain was an interesting game, and making her father cross. And the things on the top were exciting, though always too cold to be eaten.

There was chocolate and strawberry icecream, even *striped* icecream in packets, but it was so cold it was dead. It would come alive next summer. It was nice, an underground kingdom, sweet things cold as Christmas.

Then she found some packs of old meat. They were labelled in ink by Mervyn: PREMIER PIGS' LIVER. It was queer, almost *rude*, to find meat in there, next to the Vanilla and Strawberry. She didn't know they were old until she showed them to her father.

"My God, my girl," he chuckled, "that liver goes back to the ark! It's stuff I get from Fred Cartwright, you know, my pal with the pigeons." He sometimes took meat from Fred Cartwright, who worked in a butcher's shop. Kind-hearted Mervyn always paid him for it, though it "fell off the back of the counter". It wasn't easy to sell: it was more of a favour to Fred.

"What's a ark?" she said, but doubtfully, putting the black thing back.

41

"I mean ancient, girl, it's ancient. An ark was the thing in the flood."

She stared down at the ice-rimmed packages. What would they be like if they thawed? She half listened to what he was saying, imagining a flood of black mud. She pushed the fridge closed very hard. In bed that night she thought about it: ice seemed so solid and safe. But you couldn't count on it lasting. Underneath it, things going bad. Dreams lifted the gleaming lid, and the night was heavy with humming. Next time her mother cooked liver she left the whole lot on her plate. "I've got toothache, Mummy," she lied. And she never forgot the bad feeling. She knew that livers weren't meat. They were soft bits cut from inside you. She watched live animals carefully, to see if they'd had things cut out.

The worst thing was it was a secret

all the worst things are secret

The worst thing was it was a secret. The liver didn't fit in. Meat should be sold in butchers'. The rest of the shop was so nice. There were things which were old and musty . . . old toys or pencils or sweets . . . but dry and nice, like history, the sort of secret you liked. But this was a *nasty* secret locked down by a clean white lid. And the ice, which was clean like the hospital. When all their class had taken the patients the fruit from the Harvest Festival. But it only pretended to be clean, it was only temporary clean. It was only safe, she supposed, till the electricity went off. She thought of the meat in the fridge whenever there was a power-cut. The hospital might be the same. They tucked them down under clean blankets. Perhaps when the lights went off at night they would wriggle and start going rotten.

"Dad, I don't like the fridge," she whined, staring down at her feet.

"Well, I don't expect it likes you," said Mervyn, not really listening. He didn't know what he had said. For Lorna, the fridge was alive. Its humming became something threatening, obeying a complex plan. For a while she kept right away from it, hardly went into the shop.

But Lorna wasn't very old, and the whole bright world was about her. At school there were lots of people who quarrelled to be her partner. She loved running and reading and drawing pictures and making up stories in bed. And she loved her father of course,

42

or *loved being loved by him*. She was golden, morning was golden, light in Joanna's likeness. She couldn't remember for ever the dangerous machine in the darkness. She couldn't remember her dreams, about the torn flesh it had eaten.

The disguise was brilliantly clever, even better, in fact, at night. In her dreams the meat looked like ice-cubes, completely bloodless, transparent. Then someone did something awful, as her mother did for guests. It wasn't exactly her mother, it was someone who hated Lorna. She took the ice-cubes and dropped them into Lorna's pale lemonade. The lemonade turned blood-red. Something black and wet at the bottom.

But Lorna grew up and grew busy, and the fridge became merely a fridge. She still didn't like the hum, but she rustled and tapped to drown it. She tittered quietly with nerves whenever her father sold anyone meat. He only sold it to strangers, knowing how long it was there. "Got rid of those kidneys at last," he would say with a grin to Prunella. "That fridge isn't meant for meat. One day you're going to kill someone." Her voice was disapproving, but she was half smiling as well.

Only Lorna wasn't really amused; her titter was tension and terror. In her mind the packs came alive as the customers carried them home. In the carrier bags they would be stirring, softening, the blood seeping out of the plastic. So many things had been killed, and one day they'd kill a customer. Awful the thought that things had been mangled but didn't lie decently dead.

Most Sundays her grandparents came for lunch, a rather grand occasion. Prunella was cross all morning, and it was too hot in the kitchen. Her father went to the pub, with a jacket which made him look different. In pubs men always got late, Lorna learned from her mother's chatter. The house filled up with steam, and Prunella would jump at the doorbell. "There you are," she'd mutter, wiping her hands, "they're here already, and him not home." Lorna wondered why she always said it, since it always happened the same.

They would always be served roast meat, which her mother bought from the butcher. It wasn't like the meat in the fridge; it sat red and firm on the plate. Lorna wished you could eat it like that. It was the colour of the bricks in Bayko. But when it was cooked it was different, more like those cold, clear packs. It was dark and shiny and smaller, the juices were clotted with black. "I'll throttle

43

that man," said her mother, wiping sweat from her lip.

He was funny when he got back. He seemed very jolly to Lorna, always smiling and joking and vague. And he smelled very nice, like Christmas, and always put his arms round Grandma. It seemed to Lorna her mother should have been glad he was in a good mood. After all when it was just them Dad often never uttered a word. Still Lorna distrusted her grandmother, and didn't see why he had to kiss her.

Her mother's mother and father never seemed quite real to Lorna. They looked like grandparents might have looked in an out-of-date picture book. Her grandfather's voice was quiet and posh, and he wore a suit with a watch-chain. He couldn't quite hear what you said, but he wouldn't admit he was deaf. So he laughed and made the wrong answer, and tried to pinch her knee. Her grandmother's voice was a mixture, sometimes posher than his, like singing, but sometimes it got too shrill to be posh and she noticed her mother wincing. Her grandmother wore things like hats, and furs which had heads and legs. The eyes weren't real, Lorna found in the end, but the first time she saw them she screamed in surprise and ran behind her father.

She didn't know why she was sure of this, but what they said wasn't real either. There wasn't any point to them. There was no special thing that they wanted. It was a bit like the jokes that her Dad had to make to customers in the shop. Grandma Cleaver smiled and laughed a lot and squeezed the arm of her husband. But whenever she did it he looked surprised, as if she was really a stranger. And Grandpa Cleaver made remarks and told stories too tidy to come from a person. They didn't fit in with the conversation. They were complete, like her Dad's old newspaper cuttings, and they weren't in natural English. He often told the same ones, but her parents laughed each time. Perhaps it all came from a play.

Bits of Grandma *did* come from a play, a funny old book or a play. And not the right play for a grandma. She was painted a quite vivid crimson, like the actresses at the Church Hall. There were patches on her cheeks and her lips. When she ate her dinner it smudged, and there were nasty red smears on the glasses. Her cheeks on the other hand got brighter, if you *could* get brighter than that.

Both Grandpa and Grandma drank quickly, and Lorna knew

44

this bothered her mother. She caught her watching the bottle of wine as the level crept down the label. Lorna didn't much love her mother, but her mother belonged to *her*. Whereas Grandma came from outside, and took little notice of Lorna.

There was something altogether not right between Grandma Cleaver and her mother. For example, Grandma often brought flowers for her mother, which sounded like a good thing to do. But as long as Lorna remembered she'd known that the flowers weren't right. In themselves they were very beautiful, like flowers from a book about flowers, not ordinary garden flowers, and they came in stiff frills of paper with pretty lettering on. But her mother flushed dark as she took them, wiping thin hands on her apron, and never met Grandma's eyes as she carried them out into the kitchen.

She would cut off the stalks with big scissors, forcing the blades together, not carefully but violently, so the stem ends shot everywhere. Then she got a Robertson's jam jar and rammed the flowers inside, in the same tight formation they came in, so the heads often hung lopsided. She would kneel down and scoop up the stalks in a series of frenzied sweeps, muttering to herself in a way that wasn't at all like her mother.

"P'raps . . . p'raps you could have put those flowers in that vase," tried Lorna one Sunday, but carefully. "Have I got time," asked Prunella satirically, "to mess about with vases?" "Well it doesn't really take longer," Lorna whispered, but very quiet. Lorna felt for the flowers, which were lovely and never looked happy.

"Call Clarrie to help with the washing-up. They'll do well enough as they are."

There was something here whose rules Lorna couldn't grasp at all. Her mother was usually very particular about everything being just so. *A place for everything and everything in its place.* She practically measured the spot where the rugs were set on the carpet, and when she dried up the dishes she didn't just wipe, she polished. She got very cross if you ate with your knife or dipped your cake in your teacup. Lorna thought and thought till she felt quite sure that the trouble was Grandma Cleaver. It was nothing to do with logic, it was nothing to do with flowers. Grownups tried to pretend that they acted by sensible rules, but they didn't, they followed their feelings.

What Lorna felt about Grandma Cleaver was that she was too strong, like perfume (she did wear very strong perfume, but that wasn't what Lorna meant). Or like the red drinks that her mother told her father to pour, when guests arrived. The rule was that fathers made drinks and mothers put in the ice-cubes. The drinks went with fiery lemon which would make the redness transparent.

something disturbing the rules
black dreams rising through liquid

The guests would get weak and funny if he didn't put enough lemon in. So her mother could blame her father if anyone misbehaved. "You always make them too strong. I believe you do it on purpose. . . ."

something to do with the ice-cubes
bruises under the surface

Grandma was strong on purpose with her funny red hair and her hats. And dead animals draped round her shoulders from which a faint bitter smell mixed with her scent. And her voice, so posh and so loud, would sometimes go sweetish and furry, and then Lorna's Dad would go funny, and fill up her glass, and bend close.

Grandma might have got strong through age, as tea did, but she might have got strong through what she ate. She had big white teeth which looked whiter than they were because her mouth was stained crimson. They tore at each Sunday's meat like a frightening bone machine.

Grandma had long frightening fingers and her knife and fork flashed in the sun (Prunella cleaned the silver on Sundays, so it always looked its best). It was a wedding present from the Cleaver side. Edgar held his spoon up to the window: "We didn't do badly by our only daughter." Joanna always chuckled when Edgar did that but Mervyn and Prunella sat silent.

Grandma's red lips sucked the meat in pieces too big to be polite, and the white teeth sheared in skilfully, and Grandma smiled in content. Her throat was as white as her fingers, and plump where Prunella's was skinny. You could see the meat slipping down, smooth ripples of flesh against her pearls.

Grandma always had three helpings, and the joint always got used up. Prunella always looked very sour and thin-faced when the last piece disappeared. "That meat would have lasted us all week," she would say, when they'd gone. "I don't understand my mother. And we went without all war. . . ."

Lorna ate potatoes and gravy, very quickly so she could escape. She stared at Grandpa. He was drinking, not eating. He was shrivelled like raisins or prunes. The voices all mingled together, and the clash of glasses and plates, and her mother offering more, and her father laughing too loudly—grownups didn't know when to stop, whereas children knew when to stop. They would sit for ever at table, making pretend conversation. However quickly she ate, it wouldn't help her get free. All depended upon her mother, and how well Lorna judged her moment. It was all a question of timing

> *it was all a question of time*   *voices crying together*
> *help us to kill*   *kill time*

"Please may I get down," she'd say, trying hard to sound soft and casual, trying hard to sound as if her ankles weren't knotted together with misery under the table. "That child eats like a sparrer," her grandpa would gruffly remark. Lorna smiled at him like an angel, wishing him evil dreams. She did her good child's voice. "I've eaten masses of things. All that Yorkshire pudding and potatoes. But now I'm really full up. And *I want to go and do my homework.*"

The thing she minded most of all, before she learned not to do it, was the trips they made to the shop, just her Dad and Grandma and Grandpa. Until she was fifteen and refused, her Dad always asked her to come. She somehow knew that he needed her to, although he just said "Are you coming?"

What happened when he'd unlocked it and they all four trooped inside was that everyone became quite different. Grandpa and Grandma turned into thieves, and Dad turned into someone helpless, someone whose pride was hurting but who couldn't hurt anyone back.

Grandma took a big shopping basket, a great green thing of plaited leather. On the way she patted her white ringed hand on Dad's thin arm and shoulder. Edgar walked stiffly, smile craned round towards them, claws clasped behind his back, hearing nothing. They all looked very large in the sunlight, and their laughter embarrassed Lorna. She hung just behind them, looking neutral, as if she was waiting for a bus. Her own voice was perfectly normal, like Dad's, so why did her grandparents do funny accents?

In the shop however they were worse. They suddenly got very efficient. Grandpa didn't seem old any more. His expression was still vague and gentlemanly, he still sometimes hummed through his nose. But his little red eyes were as sharp as a chicken's, darting about after grain. It was things like cigars that he wanted, and treacle toffee "for me innards".

You could see what made Henry least happy was the bottles he took from the "Off". Lorna thought it was called the "Off" because there was so little of it, but Lambs' had a small stock of wine and spirits on the shelf under Biscuits and Cakes. Edgar always went there last. Each time Lorna hoped he'd forgotten. He'd always take two or three bottles from the twenty or so that were there. And he always asked, which was curious, since he always did it the same. But he made it sound as though *just this once*, now he came to think of it, *maybe*. . . .

"*If* you don't mind, old boy," he would mumble, collaring two bottles of gin. "My pleasure," said Henry, very quietly, now, holding tight to Lorna's hand. "That *hurts*," she objected, once, in a whisper, but he didn't let her go, just slackened his grip a little, and his blue eyes stared down *please* just as clearly as if he had said it.

Even then, Lorna wasn't hard-hearted. She didn't like to see people hurting. As an adult she could never refuse things when someone asked her directly. She sometimes said "Yes" and then let them down, which at least gave *her* less pain.

So after that time when he hurt her hand she always pretended to have homework. "I've got some English for Monday," she sang, and she knew her mother would support her. There had been an awful fascination, though, watching Grandma set to work. The bag looked big when it was empty, but became enormous when full. The rings flashed frenetically about, the husky voice pattered softness. But the flashing hands told the truth. Her grandma was a very good thief. She packed so much in the bag that she'd hardly have to shop all week.

She got jellies and salmon and cupcakes, marmalade, butter, shampoo. She got cat-food for Ronald and Archie, their horribly fat Manx cats: she got chocolate digestives and processed cheese and light-bulbs and bluebags and matches. . . .

When her mother nagged about the books, Lorna felt very sorry for her father. She was sure it was not his fault if the books for the shop didn't balance. It was the fault of those dreadful Sundays, the fault of her grandma's greed.

The week before she never went back any more, Lorna did something peculiar. It didn't make sense to her, not precisely remembering her fear. It didn't make sense at all to her grandparents. But Mervyn understood, and was happy. He remembered it much later, dying on his own, remembered his loyal little Lorna.

Lunch had gone off as usual, roast lamb, on this occasion, rather pale. Lorna ate the chips and the peas and a great deal of redcurrant jelly. Grandma had a big snakeskin handbag which she kept on her lap while she ate. As soon as she'd finished her crumble, but before Prunella finished hers, she took out a fluted glass spray and sprayed her round arms with perfume. She did it rather slowly and deliberately, pulling little mouths of pleasure. Her lids drooped fatly in contentment. She seemed to be staring at Mervyn.

"I want some more crumble," said Lorna, in a peculiarly definite voice. "Good girl," said Prunella. "That'll fill you out," and she spooned out a fist-sized helping. Usually she would have got angry if Lorna hadn't said please.

They went to the shop in the usual way, with Grandma complaining of the cold. "Could you just catch my fox-fur round me?" she asked Mervyn. "This horrid, horrid breeze." Mervyn had to hold it around her, which meant he lost track of Lorna. She dropped further and further behind, and her hair whipped painfully back in her face in the fierce November wind. "Are you coming, pet?" called her father, about to unlock the shop door. She stared across from her separateness at the other side of the road. They looked like three funny little puppets. Her father and grandmother were married. Her grandfather was an old man, and had nothing to do with the play. She didn't want to be in it. She wanted a play of her own. But when you were quite on your own, the world seemed too wide and too frightening.

"I'm coming, Daddy," she called, and ran over the world to join them.

She sat on the counter as they snatched and grabbed, with her feet dangling down at the front. It was a feeling she usually liked, since she couldn't do it on weekdays. Her Dad stood behind the counter and stroked her tangled hair. "We'll have to cut it off," he said, as he sometimes did, but just joking.

Her feet weren't far from the floor. She knew she was getting too big. She had a funny tingle in her ribcage as if something was going to happen. She watched Grandma going the rounds, the poor dead fox-feet swinging. . . .

When the basket was nearly full, she suddenly jumped off the counter. She ran and opened the fridge, and burrowed among the icecreams. "It's too cold for an ice," called Mervyn. "Your Mum's got some chocolate sponge." But she wasn't looking for ices. She was looking for long-dead meat. She found a packet of liver. It was black and shiny as coal. But she knew the firmness was illusion. It would soon soften up, in the bag. By the time Grandma got it home it would be all trembly and warm.

She skipped across the shop to her grandma with the liver and a radiant smile. "You like meat, don't you Grandma. You better eat this nice liver." And she shoved it into her shopping bag before Joanna could stop her.

There was always a strange streak to Lorna, although she was a gentle child. She liked flowers and lambs and affection, and people adoring her. But Lorna had impulses with people, not always gentle impulses.

Her loves were impulsive too, as Mervyn found to his cost. She left without a word of explanation, since she didn't know how to explain. She traded him in for Henry, a father swopped for a husband. By the end of Lorna's life   *which was not a very long life*   she had found that all love was different, and couldn't be traded in. She had found that although you can crush someone, just on the strength of an impulse, you couldn't bring them back to life, you couldn't erase their pain.

Having started so badly, however, she didn't learn *all* about love. She didn't learn to love her sisters, she didn't learn to love Guy. She didn't learn to love her mother, her new, sharp, purple-lidded mother. She didn't get enough time to show how much she had loved her father. She could have made him very happy, his finally grownup daughter. Lying awake long after his death she explained to him in the darkness. . . .

(hair which lit up his darkness
light which can weave through time)

50

What she didn't understand, having learned so late about guilt, was that Mervyn loved her far too well to remember her as a traitor. He didn't remember the dreadful pain of finding her bed unslept-in. The image that hung in the air above him as he drifted through thin pale hospital sun, drifted across the final drug-softened sea of waking and drowsing, was of Lorna sitting on his counter, swinging her feet and smiling. She was whispering, holding his hand. She didn't want to go home ever. Her hair was the sun in the room, love which can weave like light. In a second she would skip across the shop to the fridge and scoop up the liver for her grandma.

Mervyn was a loving man, and he'd learned to love life as well. Since most of his life was "going without", that meant that he loved his own fiction. He believed that Lambs' was unique, he believed he was loved by Lorna.

(The blue fish swam in the sea, blue sugar fish and their young. Their young were a bright red-gold and they flashed like the smile of his daughter. The paper-boys waved the red gloves in the wind, on holiday where they were free. Their pale limbs jumped on the sand, the firm dappled joy of the sand. Twelve gloved hands waved in contentment. The watches weren't chocolate but gold:

WOLVERHAMPTON HONOURS BEST CORNER SHOP

—print flickered in the evening paper.)

As Mervyn slipped to the sleep of the just, slipping the cutting in his wallet, he thought *I didn't do damage. And that must be why I've been lucky. Life didn't do damage to me.* Maybe it was all a fiction but no one could take it away.

Lorna really did learn to love Henry her husband, though it started like loving her father. "I really love you Daddy," she'd say, meaning *"I love you loving me so."* Being married, everything was different. You couldn't be a baby yourself, not with three of your own to look after. And later Jack Latham didn't see Lorna as a gorgeous, lovable baby (he saw her, in fact, as a fuck, and a fuck well past her best). And by the time all that was over, Henry didn't see her as a baby. The miracle was he still loved her. The miracle was, she loved him.

51

In an ordinary novel that would be the whole story, how a woman found out how to love. But Lorna was in the wrong story, the wrong century, the wrong world. She could only learn so much, she could only change her own heart. She could learn to be kind to some people she hadn't been kind to before. She could learn that sometimes love lasted, whereas beauty didn't last long.

But she didn't look out of the window, she didn't answer the door. She read the stars in the paper, but didn't look up at the sky. She cursed the scream of jet engines, killing her favourite record, but she didn't think about worse things, real screams, real curses, real deaths.

She did discover real love in a world which was mostly fiction. But she lived, like most of her neighbours, in a novel too late to be bought.

There wouldn't be time for this novel, there wouldn't be space for this novel. There wouldn't be time for words to do justice to Lorna's heart. It was only a heart, after all, just one more smashable organ. It was only a mind which had found, at last, how to house pity and love.

She had tried to let other hearts in, to take guests in her empty rooms. She had forced herself to clean floors, forced herself to cut keys.

But this is the language of novels, the architecture of novels. There are other and brisker languages, other lessons to learn.

Nobody told her it wasn't insurance, learning to love the light. Nobody thought and so nobody taught her how to go blind and burn. No one had taught her that she herself would be black uneaten meat. In such a confusion of offal, no one could find her heart

with such a hubbub outside, great cracks appear in my novel
other novels do better, build us a paper home
but *Japanese walls like pages*
                    miles from the flash, things smoulder
     time   *no time to remember*
                         pages of memory, burning

In the shop, the lids were kept closed. There was only the sound of humming. The meat stayed safe in its packets. It was all a question of time.

3 The Gentle Chapter

Madam! What do we have for you today then Madam? Well
for a start we have sheep's eyes neck of lamb saddle of lamb
leg of mutton lamb chops lamb's liver and kidneys Madam!
All fresh today Madam look at the lovely hue of it Madam
blooming red as rabies Madam what'll you have today?
Cat got your tongue Madam how would you like a <u>lamb's</u>
tongue Madam pink as your baby's cheek Madam what
would you like today?

Prunella went by the book, as mothers of the family go. *Girls should
be sweet and gentle, girls should not make a fuss.* But she didn't teach
Lorna much about how to be a grownup. Lorna was to be the
beauty, who would probably marry a Prince (the Prince never
came for Prunella: she loved and hated her daughter).

It was all in the hazy future, and shopping was done today. It
was Mel and Clarrie who went with Mum and helped with the
Saturday shopping. It was quite a social event; they sallied out
dressed in their best. Prunella imagined people whispering,
watching their fleet sail past. "There's that smart Mrs Lamb and
two of her lovely daughters!"

After they'd finished, they went to the Capri Grotto for coffee
and cakes. Prunella was sure they enjoyed it. They spent a long
time choosing when the waitress brought the cakes. At first it was
straight competition for who would have the cream slice. Prunella
tried to be fair, but quite often she had lost count. It was a

marvellous castle of pastry, with cream as yellow as butter and jam as bright as blood. When you cut it it fell to pieces, jam and cream foamed over the knife. At the end you had to try to scrape up the cream without Mum seeing you do it.

Then Clarissa got to eighteen and went on a savage diet. And Melissa got to fifteen and very sensitive, and just the notion of them piling into the Grotto with their carrier bags full of veg . . . once the kidneys bled on the floor, dissolving the strong brown paper. Melissa didn't say a word but she blushed as red as the stain.

Prunella would arrange the bulging bags round the little wrought-iron table. These bags protected her virtue, a stiff palisade of food. Then she would flounce off her coat with a very self-satisfied air. Melissa thought people were smiling at all the neighbouring tables. "Mum nobody can move if you put all that shopping there."

"People can move very well," said Prunella, her pencilled brows shooting up. "They have to move round it, that's all." That sounded too blunt, a bit common. She settled her skirt and rephrased it loudly, pitching her voice at the window. "They will *me-ah-ly* have to walk round it."

Melissa shuffled and stared at the floor of the deepest grotto in hell. There people moved on, blindly forward, and raw meat spilled on the floor.

Lorna wriggled out of these expeditions, establishing herself as the fey one. She thought that food was boring. She would never have to buy food. She would go off to the Park and play with her best friend Maisie. She changed her best friend every week, since she found that new friends were nicer. But Maisie was a kind of a standard. She was very in awe of Lorna (little girls can bully their friends even if they're taught to be gentle).

Maisie was plain with a round pink face and a dull brown helmet of hair. Maisie was very grateful that Lorna continued to play with her. Maisie would fetch the ball when Lorna threw it too far. She was always *It* at hide-and-seek, she was always the *Back* at leapfrog. When Lorna felt like climbing trees, Maisie always gave the leg-up.

Maisie had rarer talents too. She made bracelets out of buttercups and daisies. You made a tiny slit in the stem with your fingernail, then slipped another stem through. She loved to make bracelets for Lorna, piling them on her thin wrists. They were buttercup-gold and fresh grass-green, cunning as Indian craftsmen. And she played at *Do You Like Butter?* pressing the buttercup under her white chin.

When Lorna was in a good temper on the long hot summer days she would let Maisie plait her hair, shrieking whenever it pulled. It was rather soothing, those firm pink hands moving through and through her warm curls. And the sun pouring down on her scalp, and the smell of the grass being cut.

None of this helped teach Lorna how she ought to behave. She learned how to be a Princess, with gold and white flowers for a crown.

(Life isn't served to order; the crown didn't come in time. She ended up doling out Ostermilk to three very ordinary babies. And when babies see long hair they just want to clutch it and cling.)

Maisie was the daughter of a farmworker, and they lived out Tettenhall way. Maisie's mother was mental, sometimes, which wasn't much fun for the family. Maisie had to do her Dad's sandwiches and feed their four mangy cats. Sometimes they would crap on the floor. That made her feel sick, in the mornings. Maisie learned how to be a mother long before she ought to have done. She like playing mother to Lorna, though she didn't really know she was doing it.

Sometimes when Mum was ill at weekends Maisie went to the farm with her Dad. She got very used to animals, their warmth and smell and steam. It was the very best bit of the week, getting up when it was still dark.

Her father always talked in a funny sleepy voice, but she was too excited to be sleepy. She watched her father do the milking, which seemed very rude at first. But then she got used to it, when she realized they were busts and not wee-wees. Maisie's mother had told her one normal day that *her* chest would grow busts too. It was the day after Maisie went milking. She hoped they wouldn't look like the cows'.

When she told her friend about the farm, Lorna asked if she could come too. Of course she didn't *really* tell her about it. There were things you didn't say to Lorna. It was partly that Lorna didn't listen, and partly that she didn't talk dirty. She listened a bit, with her eyes going funny, very wide and blue and vague . . . .

(Maisie thought Lorna the most beautiful thing this side of her local church. The stained glass made Maisie's flesh prickle. There was an angel just like Lorna, dreamy-eyed with long golden hair.)

. . . then she suddenly interrupted. "Are you allowed to look at the lambs?" "Yes," said Maisie. "They're all red." "*No*," said Lorna, crossly. "They're *white*. The sweet little baby ones." Maisie never contradicted. She sucked on a piece of grass. Lorna was thinking of something.

"Next time," she said very carefully, not looking at Maisie, as she never did look when she wanted something very badly, "that you go and look at the lambs. The little white ones. I want to come too." The moment to look was *now*: you had to look right into their eyes just after you asked the question, with your own eyes as wide as you could get them, and a little trembly smile.

Maisie knew her Dad would be furious, but the tide of bliss was too hot. "What," she said determined to get it quite straight before she got too excited. "You spend the whole day with me, you mean. On a Saturday. Your Mum would let you?"

"I do what I like," said Lorna, which was true, unless Mum was in a temper.

"Course you can," said Maisie. "I'll pack more sandwiches."

It was even better than she thought it would be, because Lorna had to stay the night before. Prunella had always liked Maisie, a nice quiet decent girl. Lorna told her Maisie's father was a farmer, which sounded impressive enough. She didn't say a word about her mother; it was scary when people were mental. "I'm going to see baby lambs," Lorna told Prunella, very prettily. "Very nice dear," said Prunella. This was how girls ought to behave.

Prunella lacked common sense, and got carried away by pictures. When she thought of lambs she thought of fluffy boleros, bluebirds, daffodils, eggs. So she dressed up Lorna to fit, in a picture: white socks, little bolero of white angora, duck-egg blue dress with a Peter Pan collar. In her best shopping bag she put a box of chocolates, an Easter egg for Maisie and some daffs for her mother. Her shoes were black patent with an ankle-strap, polished to a slick of oil. Her hair was tied in two bunches, with ribbons of daffodil yellow.

"You look good enough to eat," said her father, when she went into the shop to say goodbye. "You stay close with Maisie, mind. No wandering off on your own."

Maisie was a practical girl, but perfection put her off her stroke. Perfection arrived, and she gaped. It should have occurred to her that lambs were often muddy. It should have occurred to her that farms are always cold. She herself always wore three pairs of knickers under trousers, and big rubber boots which smelled of frogs. But when Lorna arrived on the Friday tea-time, the daffodils rustling in expensive florist's paper, all Maisie felt was passion; it had actually come true. It might not have been such a wonder if it had happened during term-time, when in any case Maisie sat three desks away from her idol every day (she had never been Lorna's partner: they were the prettier girls). But this was the Easter Holidays, and Maisie was deprived.

"What's the matter?" asked Lorna, standing on the doorstep, as the hole in the round face opened. (She sometimes felt sorry for Maisie. She looked like a red balloon.) "Nothing," said Maisie. "Except you look very pretty." "Oh," said Lorna, biting her lips. "I though you were gawping at something." (She *didn't* know how to behave.)

"Come and say hallo to Mum," Maisie told her, taking her carrier. Mrs Briggs was lying in the front room, on the sofa. There were splotched velvet curtains, half drawn, the colour of ketchup or blood. She was covered by an eiderdown, but one thin leg stuck out at the side, as if it grew at an angle. She had long hair spread on the cushion, which was funny for quite an old lady. In the half-light from the window you could see it was nearly grey. She didn't look at all like Maisie: her cheeks were scooped out with a spoon, and her eyes lay in deep brown holes. It looked as if they wanted to escape from the light, to dig back inside her brain.

She stared at Lorna. "Pretty," she remarked, then turned over on her back and stared up at the ceiling. This was quite surprising behaviour, but then Mrs Briggs was mental. "This is my friend Lorna, Mum," Maisie said, with unnatural brightness. "Come to stay. I told you."

"How do you do," offered Lorna. "I've brought you some chocolates, and some flowers."

"They let *you* stay," Mrs Briggs remarked, rather slowly, addressing the ceiling, "you see, but they won't let *me* stay. Every so often they send me off to a home. . . ."

pain that will not be heard   *off to a home for the homeless*
pain that cannot be heard and kept within the family home

"They're daffodils," Lorna insisted, in her most proper, little-girl voice. Mrs Briggs sat up, without warning. She was wearing an old woollen vest with sleeves, and a crucifix on a chain. "Our garden," she said, in a voice of deep venom, staring hard at Lorna, "is *full* of daffodils."

Maisie was red as the curtains. "Mam I'm going to make Lorna some tea now do you want some shall I bring you some?" she asked frantically, words sticking together anyhow in her confusion. But Mrs Briggs had lain down again and pulled the eiderdown up over her mouth, and her eyes were closed. The two girls went out. As they were going back into the kitchen the voice pursued them, suddenly ten times louder, piercing the door like a needle piercing flesh: "How about the chocolates? Did she bring chocolates or not? I want the chocolates!" Maisie wouldn't look at Lorna. She found the chocolates and took them through.

Mr Briggs was in the bath. Great grunts and slaps of water reached the girls as they ate their Penguins (they ate their Penguins first because Lorna liked Penguins the best: it had never occurred to Maisie to eat the cake before the first course). When Lorna suggested it, Maisie's gloom disappeared. Both girls dipped their Penguins in their scalding cups of tea. The Penguins went hot and wobbly and lovely, and the tea had a taste of chocolate. Both girls pretended that nothing had happened, back there in the curtained room. They got a fit of the giggles when Lorna tried to be a penguin, folding her arms to make flippers and making high quacking sounds.

The trouble began very early next day when they were waiting to get into the Landrover. Mr Briggs had ignored Lorna, not wanting her to be there. Then in the morning he was too sleepy to notice what she was wearing. Suddenly it connected. He roared like a bear at Maisie. "If she thinks she's coming like that, she's got another think coming. She'll freeze to bloody death in that silly get-up."

A tear immediately rolled down Lorna's pretty cheek. At home, no one ever shouted. Only horrible rough men shouted

voices tearing the paper   *paper torn with that pain*

Mr Briggs sent them back inside for Maisie to "get her some normal gear. And for goodness' sake get a shift on. We're late enough as it is." Lorna cried more, but noiselessly, as she pulled on some horrible jumpers. The jumpers smelled of Maisie, and Maisie smelled faintly of mice.

Then some thick warm socks which scratched and Maisie's old

59

Wellington boots. With the socks on the boots were too tight. Lorna's tears became audible. Maisie stared at her under the lightbulb. She didn't look the same girl. Her hair was pulled all haywire and caught in the neck of her jumper. Her eyes and her nose were red, and a dribble ran from her nostril. Maisie addressed this person as she would not have dared address Lorna. "You won't have to cry in the car. Or else me Dad'll go mad."

The farm was muddy and cold with a wind blowing straight from Greenland

voices rigid with cold *frozen sagas of voices*

It was noisy: engines and mooing, and the howling, crying wind. Flaps of old metal banged. To Lorna it all smelled of toilets. She could hardly keep up with the others because her feet hurt so. Maisie didn't look round for her friend. She sped along by her father.

Squelch in the mud, then the pain. The pain, then squelch in the mud. And the cold like pepper in your nostrils. And wanting so much to go home.

Nothing was like the pictures. The cows were as big as a house. They pushed and shoved and looked fierce, and their moos were as loud as lorries. They lurched in your direction when you least expected them to. Otherwise Lorna was ignored. Maisie was helping her father. She'd become a different person, a dwarf grownup, not a child.

The fields weren't smooth and green. They were black and pitted and wild. They were edged with barbed-wire fences, not hedges and bright spring flowers. There were daffodils, of course, thick sneering banks of yellow. Lorna winced and looked away, thinking of her poor bunch.

The chickens weren't playing in the farmyard, running about for seed. They were kept in a horrible building she wasn't allowed inside. A faint high sound like telephone wires came drifting down on the air. When you got closer to the building, though, it was much more sad than electric: it was millions of tiny voices crying because they would never get out.

There weren't any horses *at all*. She was sure there were going to be horses. Horses were her favourite animal, from looking at them in books. She had ridden on a donkey, at the seaside, and thought about riding a lot. When she'd planned today in her head, they had showed her a fine black horse. He was shiny and slender and handsome. Maisie's Dad would lift her on his back. But then Lorna would have astonished them. She would have ridden by instinct, perfectly, and when she came back they all cheered. It would have been just like flying, in the dreams she used to have. Nobody thought she could do it, but Lorna knew it was easy.

However, this dream had gone wrong. No horses, not even a cart-horse. And no one was nice to her. And the wind had given her earache. It was hard to know which hurt most, her feet or her ears or her temper.

Maisie relented slightly when her father was up with the chickens. She got out the banana sandwiches, and offered Lorna her half. Lorna ate one very fast, to avoid looking at Maisie. Then she waited for Maisie to be nice to her. But Maisie didn't say anything.

Maisie was too busy thinking how awful Lorna looked. Maisie was surprised to discover how much she enjoyed that thought. Lorna started to sniff. She still had two sandwiches left. She put them down on the paper, and sniffed as hard as she could. Maisie seemed to be waiting for something. Lorna wiped her eyes ostentatiously.

"I'll have those sandwiches," Maisie said, "if *you're* not going to eat them." "Not hungry," Lorna hiccupped, giving Maisie a maddened stare. But Maisie was wolfing the sandwiches, head full of sweet banana. When she'd finished, she felt benign.

"We'll see the sheep in a minute," she offered. But Lorna was actually crying. When she cried she felt much colder, as the cold wind lashed her cold cheeks. And the colder she was the more she wanted to cry, so there wasn't much chance of her stopping.

She saw the sheep through rivers. They smelled, and looked like old car-seat covers, car-seats which bounced and jostled and blurred as the tears welled up to confuse them. The lambs were just smaller car-seats, broken-off bits of car-seat. She couldn't see one pure white. Their faces were black or dappled. And some were quite big and fat, pale yellow and splashed with mud. She had thought one would run up and lick her, and she would feed him a sugar-lump (and she would have been in her pretty blue dress, in her jacket of snow-white wool). But her dress lay in a heap on the floor of Maisie's bedroom, there wasn't any sugar, no snow is white . . . she was going to feed him, but now he was dead, the warm white lamb of her dreams.

Then Maisie was pulling her arm. "Dad says there's some just lambed." Lorna couldn't take in what she said. "It's a real baby," Maisie repeated. Lorna stepped on sharp knives through the mud.

She could never explain what she saw, being licked by the fat mother sheep. It was shiny and squashed and blood-red. It was dripping with blood and slime. She closed her eyes and said nothing

   raw softening meat   *the fridge humming*

Perhaps they had killed it already, made meat as soon as it was born. Once more the lids of the world had lifted, and she glimpsed the vile machines.

"I've got to have a bath," she suddenly said in the Landrover, sitting up wide awake after sniffing herself to sleep.

"We only have baths in the morning," said the new, self-confident Maisie.

"I'M GOING TO HAVE A BATH BEFORE I GO BACK HOME!"

Mr Briggs spoke over his shoulder. By now he was sorry for Lorna. "Course she can have a bath. Me and your Mam aren't savages."

Lorna lay in the bath for half an hour, although she knew they were waiting. There was some lily-of-the-valley perfume which she knew belonged to Maisie. Her aunt had sent it for her birthday, and she'd shown it around in class. Lorna unscrewed the bottle and shook it into the bathtub. She left about half an inch so Maisie didn't complain. By the time she was dry and warm with her own pretty dress and ribbons, her own white socks and bolero and her own little ankle-strap shoes—except for the plasters on her blistered ankles—she was almost a Princess again.

Yet something extraordinary had happened. The world had turned upside down.

Mr Briggs was driving her home. "Come on, you come with your friend," he said to reluctant Maisie, who felt very shy of Lorna. "Have you got everything?" he inquired (she was much better-looking than Maisie. It didn't do on a farm, of course, but she was kitted-out a treat).

"Yes thankyou Mr Briggs," Lorna dimpled, feeling her old

magic working. Then something occurred to her. "Oh no, I've forgotten my Easter egg." The Easter egg lay by the table, in the carrier bag it came in. It was meant to be for Maisie, who had already sneaked a look. "The Easter egg for me sister." Maisie couldn't say a thing. She couldn't admit she had seen it. Lorna did beautiful writing and the label was quite clear. *"For MAISIE. A HAPPY EASTER."*

But Maisie had one more weapon which she used without even thinking. "She's got to say goodbye to me Mam," she remarked, with self-righteous poise. Mr Briggs was surprised. That wasn't a bit like Maisie. "Well, p'raps just have a look in," he apologized, shrugging at Lorna. "It ought to cheer her up, see a pretty young face like you."

With a small smug smile at Maisie, Lorna waltzed out of the kitchen. Maisie's lily-of-the-valley was all round her. She knocked on the front-room door. "I'm just going now, Mrs Briggs. I want to say thankyou for having me."

She was expecting to see the same old invalid, but this was a different person. She was sitting up in the sunlight, and her hair looked pretty and fair. She had a flowered cotton dress on, and her face was thin but not gaunt. The only odd things about her were long bare feet, very white: they stretched out like two sleeping animals in the long pale beam of sunlight.

"Your name is Lorna," said the lady. Her voice was perfectly friendly.

"Yes. I've been to the farm. I saw the cows, and the lambs."

When the lipsticked mouth spoke again, her voice was still calm, still friendly. But as her speech developed, it became a mad high scream.

"And you like the little lambs do you Lorna, you love them. Yes you would, they like animals, all little girls. But do you understand me. You must understand me. They say I am mad, but no I am sane. You don't understand what they do to them on farms, I tell them all but nobody believes me. That farm is not for growing, that farm is for killing. They lock up the animals out of the light and later they kill them, I tell you. The lambs are just for meat, you buy them down at the butcher's, THEY TEAR OFF THEIR FUR AND THEY HACK THEM INTO PIECES. . . . " (Behind Lorna's back the front-room door opened; Mrs Briggs looked frightened, and she finished in a whisper.) "Poor little things, they're better than

63

humans. They pull off their skin and they eat their insides."

Mr Briggs tugged Lorna back by the skirt of her dress. "You'll have to rest," he said to his wife, and he made it sound threatening, more than the actual words. "You know you'll have to rest, if you get all excited."

Those long pale feet started moving in the sunlight. With a hopeless slapping sound, she stamped them on the floor. "He's going to send me away," she sobbed, quite gently, at Lorna. "Whenever I try and tell the truth they try and send me away!"

Safe back home in the family, Lorna answered questions.

"Oh yes thankyou Mummy, I had a lovely day. I had chocolate biscuits for tea and lunch was banana sandwich. I fed one to the horses. And we saw some little white lambs. I had to bring back the Easter egg because Maisie's gone allergic" (she'd learned that word in Biology, only two weeks ago. Prunella listened with pride. Growing Up To Be A Beautiful Lady) " . . . oh Mummy can I really? Yes, I'll save it till Easter Day. . . . "

But she didn't seem to want to talk much, which Prunella put down to tiredness. And then, she talks more to her father, she thought, with a trace of regret. So as she put Lorna to bed she told her what *she* had been doing. (Prunella was in a good mood. Today it was nice being mother.) Grandma had got a bad stomach, so they wouldn't be coming tomorrow. A pity, they'd got some nice beef, but still, it would last them all week. Your father had a good day, he got rid of the last of the steak. We had a nice time in the Grotto. Clarissa's come off her diet. I'm glad that you're friends with Maisie. A sweet, good-natured girl. I bet Mrs Briggs liked the chocolates. They're quite an expensive line. And Mervyn never seems to shift them. . . . One day she must come to tea. You always did love animals. I've never been bothered myself. The Co-op were out of streaky. I've just got enough for the morning.

Prunella always liked mornings, the brightest part of the day.

The voices of the women weave onwards, weaving their gentle days (some are angry, or sad, or selfish, but mostly they make themselves gentle). They think of their growing children, growing taller, growing older. They think of the people they love, how they speak, how they walk, little details. The little things they do wrong, the things that will never alter.

They plan their work, and their hours: they think how things will fit in. (Some women give up, or go mad. But mostly they keep things going.) They plan how people with different edges and shapes can be mixed together. They wish their own wishes away: "No, I don't mind what I do."

They keep up appearances, when the flood sweeps under the floorboards. (Some women weep or draw blood. But mostly they look on the bright side.) "My husband's a bit off-colour, so he's having a holiday." "We *have* got behind with the payments, but nothing to worry about." "I had a lovely day . . . and we saw some little white lambs." "Oh honestly, Dad, don't be daft— they'd *tell* you if it was cancer."

Some women show their pain on their skins, and some must be sent away. But most women take a deep breath and then keep on keeping smiling.

These gentle voices of women weave on in their dusted houses. The seeds that the gentle women plant become primroses, marigolds, daisies. The daughters they dress to be Princesses become tired mothers and wives.

The women of Hiroshima were gentle women like these. Their houses were full of light: their rock-gardens shone with plants. Their halls, packed with neatly rolled bedding, were cool blue caves of softness. Their city lay on the coast, fan-shaped, striated with rivers. To the south was the Inland Sea.

That day they expected nothing. They were keeping life going, as usual, hiding their fear from their children (*Americans raped all women—the round-eyed brutes that were coming*). Most of their husbands and sons had gone to die for the Emperor. The rest were ready to follow. The women were angry now. As they worked and slaved to make guns, they fell out of love with their Emperor. It was no good dusting and varnishing if their family wasn't there. Girls should be good and gentle, but what if fire falls from the air? It was no good smoothing things over if nobody smiled at their skill.

And yet, the days moved round and they kept on smoothing things over.

That morning the skies were warm and blue and the all-clear signal sounded. Women were cooking rice: children played on their bed-rolls. Sun poured in like a promise that everything would get better. The planes had roared over last night, just after 2 a.m. After that you didn't sleep well. But the sun said *look on the bright side*.

It was just before 8.15. Little Toshio cried for his breakfast. "It won't be a minute, little one. Here, you can have these peanuts."

And then the whole world turned white; whiter than blindness was. No noise, and then everything dark, and the universe turned on its back.

Some of the women were crushed, some of the women were blinded, some of the women lay stunned with their young and were cooked in a flash like meat. Their eyes melted down their cheeks, their gentle tongues became rigid. The lives they had woven tore, and the small growing things they had cared for.

They were used to buying and cooking the fish and flesh that their husbands loved. Their voices stayed sweet and gentle, paying the shopkeeper. Their flowered kimonos shone in the sun as they took their parcels home.

But then all the packaging split, and all that was left was blood. Blackened, their gentle cotton flowers became one more wrapping for meat. They could not look on the bright side with eyes that ran down like tears.

Hibakusha, hibakusha—their voices tearing the wind. And they are no longer gentle, teaching us how to behave.

Gentle, gently, gentleness didn't help them to stay alive.

4 Chapter of Babies

After the Alamogordo atomic test Churchill was handed this message: *Babies satisfactorily born.* What if Babies kill babies?

Some kids like to play Soldiers, some play Mummies and Daddies. The categories seem clear, and the rules of the game no problem. The Soldiers kill other Soldiers, and the Mummies and Daddies have Babies.

But what if people who are Babies end up being Mummies and Daddies?

If Mummies and Daddies play Soldiers?

What if soldiers are butchers, and babies are just raw meat?

The weekend with Maisie taught Lorna something, but the lesson sank deep inside. It didn't surface again till she left the family home. Then she had to remember *something*, since her mother's lessons weren't useful. She remembered what happened to animals whenever she went to the butcher's. It somehow connected in the end with Mrs Briggs, who was mad. It connected to clean white fridges with a throbbing core of blackness. It was all about frightening truths, where nice things turned into horror. It was something to do with peace.

Peace wasn't actually anything at all, it was just going on as normal. But sometimes it turned into war, and then everyone got killed.

Nothing was perfectly sealed. Mervyn thought that his love was perfect. She was glossy and whole as an apple, the apple of a father's eye. She would never change, his Lorna. He would keep his baby for ever.

But the dark leaked in at the edges. The colours rubbed off those fish. They lay in the drawers, not leaping, and the rainbows died on their sides. Sugar flowed quietly from bags, silting his papered shelves. Spiders and mice crawled out. Only ice kept the fridges safe.

Lorna looked *good enough to eat*, in her duck-egg blue and yellow ribbons. She was always good to her father, a good little girl to her Dad. She minded when things went wrong: she would stand like a ghost at his back. But sometimes he had bad dreams, where she was moving away into the shadows. *If things went wrong for Lorna . . . for even good girls go wrong. . . .*

(the shadows would print her neck . . . what my Dad would have said. . . .)

You couldn't keep ruin away. The damp seeped in when it rained. And whatever he spent on the roof the water found a way in. And the money trickled away. The prices rose at the warehouse. In the shop he kept them down, so the customers wouldn't complain. It was LAMBS' FOR LOWEST PRICES. But the ship settled down in the water. His debts grew deeper and deeper, and the business began to die.

She whistled while he did the books, as if to disguise the bad news. That winter, he grew much older. He had pains in his back, and headaches. He'd grown fat, but not healthy fat. And now suddenly much much thinner. Deep lines drove between his eyes, so he always looked pained or puzzled. She watched him staring at the fire, and her mother drumming on the table. There were rows which stopped when she entered (her mother knew how to behave). It was her mother's voice hard as a machine-gun. Her Dad hardly spoke at all. His voice sounded soft and hopeless.

He didn't tell jokes any more, although he still told her he loved her. He said it whenever she went out. "Be good. You know your Dad loves you." One day he said it when Henry was there, and Henry thought it peculiar. "He always says it," said Lorna. "I'm the apple of his eye, he says." No one would love her like that, though Henry would love her intensely.

When Lambs' Family Store broke down and the black flood of

debts pushed in, she thought it was simple enough to escape and be warm with Henry. And then of course they'd have babies, and make it a proper home. There was nothing safer than families. Every little girl knew that.

Or else they weren't safe at all. The weekend with Maisie said so. Nothing was what it seemed. Life didn't last for ever. Good things came to an end, and lambs were born looking dead.

People didn't last for ever (what if her father died?). There were worrying things in the darkness, things which were waiting and growing. There were worrying things in History, terrible things like Wars . . .

People had died in the War. Her grandmother's brother had died there. Or maybe in the one before, she wasn't very good at History.

Henry helped her with History. He knew too much about History. In the last War Henry's brother had died, and George was his favourite brother. He would tell her all about George. They would name their first son after George (*what if their baby played Soldiers? . . . babies shouldn't play Soldiers*).

Maisie told Lorna her mother had only gone mental because of the War. Lorna thought she was just getting out of it, and she didn't like people fibbing.

"Your mother didn't fight in the War," she insisted. "Women don't fight in wars."

"I didn't say *fight*," said Maisie. "It's because Mum was very . . . *synthetic*."

"Sym*pa*thetic, you mean," corrected her friend.

"Yes, she says we burned Japanese babies. The Americans and us. When we'd won the War already."

Even more of a fib, thought Lorna. She couldn't quite forget it, though. She knew the *War* had been true, at least. You sometimes saw people crippled, on seats near the door on buses. Prunella had always said *don't look*, but she couldn't look away.

Bodies being broken, twisted. It connected to that weekend.

It had something to do with her father, whose body smelled in the end. It was much too late, of course, by the time that Lorna visited. The guilt and the panic prevented her, till Henry insisted she go. "He *was* your father," he said. "And I mean, he must've loved you." "But I loved *him*," wailed Lorna. "Ever so much more than my mother. It's just that she's going to go on at me. And

69

Clarrie and Mel as well. They've got it into their heads that it's all my fault that he's dying."

But the guilt was inside her too, that she had run off with Henry. "You chose your moment," Prunella had hissed, the first time she had phoned home. "In your father's hour of trouble" (her voice was tremendous, biblical), "and I hope you may be forgiven."

Of course they had known for years that the shop wasn't paying its way. But the crisis had come that spring, and Lorna had gone in the summer. She couldn't stand it, Dad silent and ill, the CLOSED sign up and the heat. She ran off with Henry one night, leaving behind her pyjamas. He was dead within the six months. She imagined the fridges, switched off.

When she went to the hospital to see him he couldn't say very much. His skin was a weird yellow colour although his eyes were still blue. He just said "How are you, how are you. My precious Lorna, how are you." It wasn't a question though. He just wanted to hold her hand. She could feel his bones poking through at her. He was a body now, not a person. Every time he tried to smile, and he tried to smile all the while, his lips pulled away from his teeth. All round him was poisonous breath. The smell was of rank, rotting liver. "How are you, my precious Lorna." She remembered that smell for ever.

She'd moved into Henry's flatlet, a room with a kitchenette. He had decorated it with magazine photos, of crystals or stars, not girls. There were pictures of watches, and clocks. Especially unusual clocks. And a sunset behind high mountains, and the tallest tree in the world. There were butterflies too, and maps. Lorna thought they were dull, the maps. She wanted to take them down, at first, and put up her pictures of Elvis.

Then Henry explained about his father, who had vanished eight years ago. His father had been a globe-trotter, his mother had pinned him down. But Henry adored his father. Lorna then sobbed for hours. Henry fell in love with her deeper and deeper, hearing her helpless tears. She was crying, of course, for all fathers, and all wicked runaways too.

They managed on tears and laughter at first, and sex (a disaster) and beer. She had never drunk anything but wine, on Sundays, and beer got her giggly very quickly. They had their whole lives to tell, though of course she did more of the talking. He couldn't believe his luck, that this red-gold girl was his wife. That she

70

should wait for him every day, there in his poky room. That she should go out each morning and bring back food for his supper.

Once Lorna was married of course she discovered she had to do shopping. She didn't know much about that, since a princess-to-be doesn't shop. At first she thought it was fun. Henry gave her money: she spent it. She bought whatever she felt like on that particular day.

He couldn't have cared that their menus varied from merely unwise to mad. There were plenty of chocolate biscuits, which she would pile up on two plates. She bought nine different kinds of jam, though she often forgot fresh bread. And was scared to throw out the *old* bread, fantastic blue growths in the breadbin. She thought cheese was nicer in packets, those pretty wrapped triangles. He hinted that he liked chips, so she dutifully cut up potatoes. She cut up *three pounds* of potatoes, because he liked them so much. Her peeling was not to be faulted: the chips were cut very straight. She dropped the whole lot in a saucepan, and then she put in some lard.

"There couldn't have been enough lard," she wailed, as they scraped out the pan. "It's not the right kind of pan," said Henry, but very gently. "You need that big frying-pan, when you're going to fry a thing." "I'm not stupid, Henry," sniffed Lorna, her wide eyes filling with tears. "It was just that that pan looked so *flat*. There was such a *lot* of potatoes."

They soon had a kind of routine, however, and she did a kind of cooking. She remembered that sausages were her favourite supper at home. She knew they were a proper first course, and they hadn't any blood or any bones. She cooked sausages and eggs, sausage-on-toast and sausage sandwiches. This would be followed by jelly (her triumph) or chocolate biscuits, or chocolate cake. And with it they drank so much beer that they had to lie down for a cuddle. They went to bed, which was warmer, and talked, and listened to the wireless. They had their whole lives to tell, and a great deal of love to make.

They had to make love very often, since Henry couldn't do it for long. At first Lorna thought that he did it just right, but then Henry told her he didn't. Sometimes he got depressed, but he said it was just because he loved her. "Before—you know, with them girls—I used to go on for ever." She wasn't jealous at all. The factory girls were so common.

71

One night he did it five times. The last time was four in the morning. She lay there peacefully, as always, and in a few minutes it was over. Henry got very depressed. "I'm just no good to you Lorna." "Oh go to sleep, Henry," she said. But she could hear him lying there sighing.

He usually brought her some tea in the morning, but he got up so late that he couldn't. "You've forgotten my tea," she called huskily, just as he ran out of the door. But he didn't come back and make it. She was sore, and a little fed-up. When she looked in his wardrobe mirror, she imagined she was getting slowly fatter. She went back to bed with a comic. She didn't feel like going to the shops. Perhaps Henry didn't really love her. She ate half a Mars bar and fell asleep. She had an awful dream about her father. He was lying in bed and crying. "I just can't do it, Lorna. I'm just no good to you, Lorna."

When Henry came home she was quiet. For tea there was only sausage. There were only three sausages left, and nothing at all to go with it. For afters there was half a Mars bar. Normally Henry would praise her, and call her his clever little poppet. Today he pushed away his plate with three-quarters of a sausage still on it. Both of them had got very spotty, but Lorna didn't notice hers. She felt quite severe about Henry's, though, under the fluorescent in the kitchen.

"You have got spotty, Henry," she told him, as he silently stared at his plate. When he looked at her his eyes were desperate.

"Look, we can't live on sausages, Lorna. I know you're doing your best. But they're not really good for you, sausages. They haven't got vitamins in."

At once her eyes filled with tears. "You said that you *liked* my sausages."

"I do like sausages pet. But—not sausages, *sausages*, SAUSAGES!" He flipped the thing into the bin. The tears spilled as soon as he shouted. "Oh don't cry, please, never mind. It's just that you have to have meat. Especially being a man. I'm not any good without meat."

Next day she stopped the old girl who lived on the floor below. She was padding down to the toilet, in a bright pink dressing-gown. Wonderful smells of cooking used to hang about on her landing. Mrs Price was very flattered to be asked. She thought they were a heartbreaking couple. The easiest thing was a joint, she told Lorna, who wished she had known before. You just had to stick it in the oven. It cooked itself on its own.

Lorna got the best joint she could see. It cost her half a week's money. She used the word *joint* to the butcher. *Joint* was better than *meat*. She washed it, stuck it in the oven, and left it to cook itself. There was a pleasant smell of fat frying by the time she took it out. It hadn't gone black and shrunken like the joint used to do at home. She felt rather proud of herself. She had got some fresh bread to eat with it. She left it in the tin on the table while she got her husband out of bed. He only slept in on Sundays, but Sundays he needed his sleep.

It was bloody and raw and appalling. The juices which spurted weren't gravy. It lay in a bath of blood, bright red on a blood-red plate. "She said it would cook itself," sobbed Lorna as she made a jam sandwich. "That horrible old Mrs Price. She wanted it all to go wrong."

"We just have to put it back in," said Henry. "It needs some more time in the oven."

"Don't touch it!" screamed Lorna, clinging to him. "Don't touch it. It's going in the bin. It reminds me of something horrible. Oh Henry . . . I want to go home!"

But they went to bed, instead, and Henry lasted much longer. And slowly she learned how to cook, and how not to cry so often. She taught herself how to behave, which her mother had failed at so badly. Mainly by loving Henry. Or else he might die, like her father.

They looked out for little terraced houses, and drank less beer, and saved up. And soon she was pregnant with Angela. "It'll do her the world of good," said girls who had been to school with Lorna.

It'll spoil her figure, they thought. It'll make her normal, like us. She always thought she was different. It wasn't really true in fact; it was men who though Lorna different. Lorna just liked to feel loved and safe, exactly like everyone else does. "Talk about fancy herself," they said. "Just because of the colour of her hair." Women aren't really sisters, no more than men are brothers.)

She knitted lots of things in pure wool, and her eyes were heavy with contentment. Her round belly made her giggle. She liked Henry to stroke it at night. She forgot to go to the clinic, and she did

73

most exercises once. She didn't learn how to have a baby. She didn't believe that she would. She felt she would just be a pregnant Lorna, with a belly like a warm full moon. People would make more fuss of her, since pregnant women were special.

One morning everything went wrong. Henry went to the Brewery as usual. She had a bad tummy last night, and he said that she ate too much chocolate. But she didn't feel very well. She supposed the baby was wriggling. When she got out of bed the pain came, worse pain than she'd ever had. She still had six weeks to go, and she hadn't finished her knitting. She thought she would go back to bed and wait for him to come home. There wasn't a phone in the house; the nearest was down the pub. Outside there was freezing rain, the blackest kind of November. She pulled up the blankets and wished. There was usually plenty of time. . . .

> *time to get over the pain*   *all that we need is time*

But there wasn't plenty of time. The pains came quicker and harder. She dragged herself down the stairs and called for Mrs Price to come. She took one look at Lorna and wrapped the pink dressing-gown round her. Then she put her mac on over her nightie and was off down the pub like a sprinter.

The waters broke when she was still on the stairs, soaking Mrs Price's dressing-gown. Lorna began to cry. Like wetting your bed as a baby. The pink towelling was soaked, all spoiled. And Mrs Price had been so kind. She dragged herself back upstairs. She was sure the doctor would come. She was sure nothing *really* bad would happen, just as everyone else is. . . .

But the phone in the pub was out of order, and the doctor was out on call. And Angela pushed her way into the world as Lorna sobbed on her own. She was utterly sure she was dying. Whatever it was was a monster. It pushed and shoved, enormous, at the tiny space in her body. It would have to tear her in two to have any hope of getting out. It wasn't meant to be that size. She had simply got one the wrong size. If the doctor came in time he would be able to put everything right.

But the baby was stronger than hope. She had to get out, or strangle. She pushed herself into the light, and Lorna's flesh tore to let her. The pain was suddenly eased, and somebody else was howling.

Lorna looked down, and saw horror. Shiny, and squashed, and

blood-red. It was dripping with blood and slime, and it must be nearly dead. Many bad dreams flooded back, memories of fears and dreams. Things she hadn't learned from her mother, things she'd never told to a soul. She knew in that moment, lying there staring, that all those things were real. People didn't like to talk about it. She remembered poor Mrs Briggs. Perhaps she would go like her, and nobody would come and see her. Lorna didn't touch the monster. She had never felt so alone.

It grew quiet, outside the window. The driving rain had stopped. But the monster had gone on living. She saw it was terribly small. With a human face, all crumpled. Its crying sounded like the pain in Lorna, the fear of dying on her own. The tears ran down Lorna's cheeks, and she reached out her arms to the baby. After all, the mess came from inside her, and joined their bodies together. She didn't care about the mess. She saw it was a little girl. She clutched it, and started to love her.

Of course when the doctor came he called Lorna "a very clever girl". "Oh we *are* a clever girl aren't we. Doing it all on our own. And this little lady, what a monkey. Ladies always *are* in a hurry. Let's get her cleaned up a bit, shall we, and then we'll see who she takes after."

Soon there were millions of people; Henry, distraught, and her mother. And her sisters, offering advice, and her schoolfriends, "to see the baby".

It wasn't quite convincing, to Lorna. The world had turned over again. She had seen through the back of the mirror, and what she had seen was fear. She saw things without their clothes. She saw that people were meat, and other people were killers. She saw there was love, as well, but the two sides didn't balance out. What they did was pull you in two; you didn't know what to believe. But she didn't believe she was safe, and she knew that her babies weren't safe. Bodies weren't perfectly sealed: they could split and bleed like hers had. Or rot from inside like her Dad's. And so you were never protected. And most people didn't eat chocolate. It was only her who did that. Most people ate fresh meat. Most people weren't to be trusted.

The rawness would go in time. She tried to explain how she felt. The doctors called it depression, and said it was perfectly normal. As long as she didn't brood too much it was sure to go away. Angela was a good baby, who slept much more than she cried.

With the other two kids she was extra careful, and the horror was never repeated. She had her gas-and-air, and stayed a few days in hospital. And the rawness went, as they said. She learned how to cook meat black. She avoided frightening telly, and rarely went into the butcher's. If you bought meat from the nice new supermarkets, it hardly felt like meat.

She taught herself how to behave, and be a pretty good mother. She never forgot Mrs Briggs. She knew you had to keep cheerful. Brooding too much didn't do. . . .

There was plenty to occupy her mind, however. There was never half enough money. She was all on her own once they moved to Acton, not even her sisters for company. Guy and George came so close together that all she could think of was nappies. Then Henry started to drink, real drinking down at the pub. And when he was drunk something happened that you would never have expected.

They didn't get on so well, with the house all crowded with children. He couldn't seem to get near her, all those other bodies between. And the shop was slipping downhill, the nightmare that happened to Mervyn. His *life* was slipping away, and nobody cared but him. He was losing his sense of the future, his sense of a growing pattern. . . .

Then a new black pattern began, irregular, horribly shameful. He drank to escape his thoughts, and when he was drunk, he hit Lorna. *My husband hits me*, thought Lorna, astonished. This wasn't, could never be, true. And she learned to hit him back, from a sense of outrage, not anger. Her Dad would have been so upset. She winced to think of his sorrow.

There were other things on her mind. She had learned to love that baby. She loved her daughter painfully much, but Angela grew up queer. She moped about on her own. She wouldn't talk to her mother. She didn't seem to like men, and she thought too much about war. . . . *I suppose it's her age*, thought Lorna, thinking the thought of a mother.

The worst drinking began when Henry got the job in the bar. You'd have thought that he'd have been happier, bringing in all that money. But Henry had loved his watchmaker's shop just like Mervyn had once loved Lambs'. Lorna should have understood, but of course she thought of the money.

The last few years had been impossible, with five mouths to

feed. HENRY R. SHIP: TIMEPIECES. Replaced by INVICTA COMPUTERS. She knew that the sign still haunted him with its evening pinks and golds. But she tried to look on the bright side. The bar must be better for *him*. It couldn't be good for a man to go on being a . . . *failure*.

If this was success, he loathed it. He drank every day after work. Weekends he tried to get off when he could, but he didn't stay home with the family. He'd never had mates before, but now he insisted he did. "Don't go on at me, Lorna," he grumbled. "There's people I have to go and see."

It seemed he was drinking with *someone*. He mentioned some vague men's names. She worried he was being unfaithful, but the drunkenness worried her more. She looked at her husband dispassionately, and knew he was no Errol Flynn. His eyes were wonderful, piercing and blue, but those specs turned him into an old man. . . . She felt she knew him so well, even when they weren't really talking. The violence was never quite *Henry*, it was just *Henry drinking*.

If she'd seen him down at the pub, she wouldn't have thought she knew him. His voice was jolly and loud, and the glass of his lenses steamed up. He laughed to the (yellowing) roots of his teeth; later on he would swear like a trooper. *Time please, gentlemen, please.* He heard TIMEPIECES, *please*, TIMEPIECES. . . .

 time *they needed more time* *peace, they would find it*
  peace

In the pub that evening it was bright, the jangling brightness of piano; bulbs blooming out in the mirrors, in the glasses, in their eyes, which were looking at nothing. Bright beery eyes growing redder, going darker as the evening wore onwards and the mirrors grew dim.

"Sheep, that's what we are. Bloody sheep. Off we go to the slaughter."

"Not off anywhere next time. That was your old war, wasn't it. Off in your nice shiny uniform. Great big goodbyes from the missis. Then if you played your cards right you got a bit the other end as well."

"Got dead, if you didn't, though, didn't you. All my great-uncles copped it that way. Got their heads shot off at Wipers, back in the First World War."

"Well at least they saw a bit of the world before they kicked the bucket. Us, we just sit here like sheep. Sit here and wait like sheep. Just think of Berlin, and Cuba. We didn't know what was going on. Wake up one morning and there you are, WHOOOSH. Not even a 'Bang you're dead.'"

"For fuck's sake stop depressing me. You lot fuckin' bleatin' on and on. It's Saturday night, I mean, isnit. Buy you both another fuckin' drink."

They could never quite remember the last few hours, but they tasted bad, of black things, of bile and coal-tar and fear. Of the dregs in the glasses, the lights going out. "Time, gentlemen, *please*."

"Come *ahn*, yer stupi' fucki' legless bastar."

"Tha' bugger fucki' push me. Fucki' killim. Fucki' Henry. Wai' an' see. FUCKI' BASTAR!!!"

In the end there was Henry on his own, not unpleasant, the moon going in and coming out, more out than in, in and out, and his legs going on of their own accord, mouth sour from the vomit but not doing badly, it was nice to be going home, going home *nice*. . . .

What happened happened so quickly he couldn't make sense of it after. No breath, trying to breathe, no air, the pain of breathing, sick jar to his jaw and then frightening wet in his mouth, not right, something broken, lying on the pavement, *no please*, something coming again and again for his chest like a hammer, very clear and enormous, there it was yes the toe of a boot swinging in the moonlight, then darkness. "*No* . . . no please."

He woke up to a taste of iron and burning drouth in his mouth. "Lorna," he tried. In their bedroom, but he could hear all the wrong sounds. The TV, was it, downstairs. Just a needle of light through the curtains. Hurt. Close them. He must have some water. "*Lorna.*" Felt his face. Swollen. Horrible, something horrible. Half of his face felt dead. Panicking. "LORNA! WHERE ARE YOU! COME HERE! I'M . . . I'M DYING!"

The door opened, the sound hurt. He curled back, shocked, into the pillow. She stood against the light. He couldn't see the look on her face, but her voice was enough, dead cold. "Look at you, Henry," she said. "You should see yourself. Stupid bloody bastard." She had never said that before. Too tired to work out why. "I'm . . . dying," he said. "Wha' happened? Tell me what happened. Someone bloody try to murder me. Gemme some water, please. *Lorna*."

"Murder *you*," she hissed. "*You?* Don't you remember? No, you never do." She made something agonizing happen: a flood of white light from the bulb, cutting in through his lids like acid. He stared at the light, and remembered.

(Came home, and tried to hug her. With blood on his face, from the fight. And she had called him *disgusting*. Trying to rile him, yes. And he . . . . He winced. The horror again. He had hit her, out on the landing.)

"*No*," he said hoarsely, limbs convulsed, squeezing up his eyes against the light. "It's my eyes, Lorna. It hurts." It was really the fight that he meant.

"Hurts *you*," she said. She came over under the light and he noticed her clothes were old. You could see the threads, worn white. And her stomach, he noticed, too. Wasn't like that once. His Lorna. He reached out, half out, with his poor sore hand. Automatically, she flinched back.

"Look at this," she said. Pointing (red nails, he didn't like them) to her cheek. It was blue, the wrong colour. And a bad dark purple. "And my *neck*. Look at *that*, you bastard. Want to strangle me now, Henry, do you?"

He looked. Dark marks on her neck. And he loved her neck. *Lorna*. "What," he said "What, *I* . . . ?"

"*You*," she said. "That's right. You were drunk. You . . . *pig*. And the kids. They all heard. They were frightened. Guy came out. Had a go at you too, your own son. See the scratches on your cheek. That was Guy. They're all worried to death. I'll leave you."

"Last night. . . . " he said, lying back. Sick. "I'm sorry," he gritted, tongue sliding over the new rough space in his mouth. "Must be mad." His voice was quite flat, unexpressive. All said before. The same shame. But the pain was always surprising. "Drunk," he added softly, half hopefully, as if this was new information.

She had gone over to the window, stood with her face turned away into the curtains. Her fingers clutched at the hem. She was making little sounds like an animal.

"*Sorry*," he said. "*Please*. Don't. Cry." The sounds quietened a bit and she turned back to him, face slippery with tears in the light.

"I shan't," she said. "Not any more. Not for you. But I hate you though, Henry, don't forget it. Hit a woman. It's not right. Wh my Dad . . . would have said. . . . "

"Mistake," he said. "I was drunk. You know how I get. I was drunk."

"I *should* know," she said, more normal. "What am I supposed to do?" In the silence, he heard the TV. Guns firing, then yells. That was Guy joining in. Must be tea-time. "What time is it?" Silence. The guns. She pulled the curtains back fiercely.

"It's tea-time," she said, staring out. "Will be dark soon. Wasted a day. A whole day. There aren't that many days. We could have spent it together. Some hopes." Her voice was too tired for anger.

> *a day*   *not that many days*   *we could have spent it*
> *together*   *if Mummies and Daddies play Soldiers. . . .*

A whisper, too tired for anger.

"Lorna," he wheedled. "Come on. I'm sorry. Can't I have some . . . *water* . . . ?"

Her daughter saw Lorna walk down the landing past her open bedroom door. Ange had stayed upstairs, today, not even coming down for dinner. She didn't want to talk about *that*. She wanted to be left alone.

Her mother walked past again. Ange felt pity and irritation. Back straight, eyes down, mouth down, like a nun. Her long draggled hair like a nun's dead habit. She held the glass of water in both hands like a candle, cupped on her stomach (she ought to do exercises), staring at the water as if something was growing there. A flower, perhaps, or poison (in fact, it was something like love). Then their door closed dully behind her. But peace didn't come to Angela. She stared through the glass. Blank sky.

And her brothers were hearing it still, the names they had heard last night. "*Drunken sod*," she had screamed. "*Fucking animal*." Things that they cringed to remember. Guy had run out on the landing when he heard a heavy body falling. He was too scared to lie in the dark, listening to what sounded like a murder. It was Dad though, slumped on the carpet, and his mouth was covered in blood. One hand was confusedly pulling at the hem of his mother's torn skirt. Both of them were panting like animals. Red marks on his face and neck. Then Henry swung at her again and caught sleepy Guy on the nose, catching the long tender tip and the base where the twisted nostrils were rooted. The blow stung hot tears of pure rage and without even thinking Guy clawed him, dragging his nails down his cheek. Long terrible stripes, like rock. Now he twitched with the guns on the telly. He wanted to kill them all. . . .

Angela was thinking of it too. Her Mum said they loved each other. They might be doing *that*, next door. Under that dirty blue quilt. She didn't want to be like them. She wanted to be on her own. But things had got in to disturb her. The window wasn't blank any more. Thrown on the night like a screen she saw hump-backed bodies under bedclothes, swelling and stirring, no faces, two white shoving mounds like sheep. And she couldn't even feel angry. Pity was so much more painful. With an effort of will she saw clouds. No suffering. Still white clouds.

Her mother had wanted that too, but life didn't go as she thought. Still probably things would get better. It would all come right in the end. . . .

Lorna taught herself to be deaf, she taught herself to be blind. Each time that Henry was violent the full tide of horror returned. She never told a soul about it. She told her own soul that he loved her.

But love came in different parcels, and no one would love her like Dad.

You could say nothing good keeps for ever. Blood seeping, the smell of bad liver.

(Mervyn was the lucky one, actually. He died *in time*, on his own. He had time to look back on his life, time to consider his dying. He could lie in the vague kind sunlight that swam through the hospital glass. He could live his life through again, in the morphine's gentle shining. He had lived his life to the end, and a whole can be seen as a pattern; a pattern of feeling, fishes flying through waves of golden water. Something with rules and water-babies, where goodness might turn to gold. A Victorian frieze of sunlight, framing his baby daughter.)

When the first successful atomic test was performed at Alamogordo, Churchill was handed this message: *Babies satisfactorily born*. The uranium bomb which smashed Hiroshima was also a child, *Thin Boy* . The military grow up fast. They dropped *Fat Man* on Nagasaki. While all these things were happening, billions of babies were born.

In 1945, Lorna was a bouncing toddler, a glorious late-born baby having piggy-backs from her Dad. She was three years old, and plumper than her friends, since the Lambs didn't live off rations. You always knew where to get hold of some extra, if you kept a shop.

These were the things she liked: Daddy and flowers and sun. She liked being tickled, and cuddled. She liked Mummy brushing her hair. She was spoiled, if children can be spoiled: she cried when she had to go to bed, and went to bed later and later. She once bit her sister at breakfast, because she was "overtired". But it wasn't much of a bite, and all she really knew was being happy.

Sleeping in the afternoons, waking up wonderfully rosy. Sitting on the steps in the sun, and the customers giving her pennies. Sitting on the grass in the morning, playing with the dimples on her knees. Sitting on Daddy in the sun on Sunday, looking at his pink shell-ears.

"'Oo's my darling ickle baby den. *Oo* is, *oo* is, *oo* is!"

She didn't know anything then, she was curled in the palm of time. She slept with her thumb curled into her mouth and her knees tucked up to her chin. She had just got her first proper bed, but she still pretended it was cot-sized. Her cheek on the pillow was an apple, and her hair spread round it like sun. Her eiderdown was pink roses, faded to the sky before dawn. The planes came over quite often, but she slept as they carried her down.

Yet outside the pink-striped bedroom, history was a stain in the carpet. Outside the Lambs' little house, history was blackening the sky. They thought this was the year of a new day dawning: now everything would get better. People had been terribly shaken, but things had come right in time. And now Japan was knocked out of the war, in one clean blow, this summer. . . .

It wasn't just *them* they thought of. As they toasted the neighbours, tears flowed. "It's not just us," they agreed. "It' . . . the good of the world. And our babies."

They were right, babies should be protected. And spoiled, if they can be spoiled. Mervyn held her and held his future. The future was warm, and smiled.

In the garden he put her on his shoulders, and Prunella screamed from the house. "Be careful, Mervyn, you'll drop her!"

He would never drop his baby. Her legs were wound round his neck, her fingers were entwined in his. There was a distant hum of engines, but it would be one of ours.

In the end, things had to go right: you knew it, looking at Lorna. "Gallopy, gallopy, gallopy," sang Mervyn, being a horse. "Oh *does* her Dad love her, *does* he! Of *course*, of *course*, of *course*!" In his heart of hearts he knew it: babies *ought* to be spoiled.

They dropped *Thin Boy* on Hiroshima. They dropped *Fat Man* on Nagasaki. These things must not be forgotten. Near Urukami Church the stream was a vision of hell. People lay heaped in the water where they had plunged to cool their burns. A pregnant woman had given birth, and lay drowned, still linked to her foetus. It wanted to be a child, but it wriggled and died like a fish. A naked father and daughter lay locked in each other's arms. They had planned a day in the fields. The water was dark with blood.

Babies satisfactorily born. Babies should not be killed.

5 First Chapter of Brothers

Families pose for the camera with the children hand in hand. Outsiders see them as all of a kind, lined up under their surname. Together they are the Ships or the Lambs, the Smiths or the Fields or the Cleavers. Sisters and brothers look after each other. Brother fights beside brother. "*Of course* the children love one another—what a peculiar question!" That is a mother telling a lie, just like everyone else does.

But sometimes the lie is true: bright truths hide in convention. Sometimes the world flashes love like a miracle, leaving words dim as stone.

Henry remembered his dead brother George with unqualified adoration. He had a sister as well as a brother, but only his brother counted. He would shake his head sadly at his own two sons, as sour skinny Guy poked fun at fat George. "You ought to try to get on," he said. "It's very important, a brother." George listened gravely; it wasn't his fault. George Junior had a sweet nature. Guy didn't take any notice. It was just his peculiar father. That was the thing with him. Kept quiet as a mouse for days on end and then crept out and talked rubbish. His Dad would sneak up behind him when he was troubling nobody, playing by himself in a corner, scribbling in George's new book, for example.

"*I* used to really love *my* brother George," Dad would whinge, sounding sad, not angry.

And Guy would cringe with embarrassment, his thin mouth twisting with rage. You could never exactly prove it, but grownups told lies all the time. They all pretended to love one another, but Guy would never be fooled. Nobody seemed to love Guy, for instance (he drove his pencil point right through the page).

And Henry could never exactly prove how much he had loved his brother. That was the torment, peering back to that terrace in the dim thirties. What he had was the living shadows of memories, but the words, *my brother*, had died. He had sworn he would never forget his brother, sworn to keep time alive. It was like the most precious of his watches, which he would take out very rarely. Left them to sleep in the dark, so their magic would not wear out. Stare and stare at the intricate mechanisms, hands which had stopped like a bird in flight. Winding them up to prove they still worked, the minuscule flutter of a bird's heart beating. . . .

The thing about Henry's big brother George was his great gentleness. He would smooth the dark feathers of Henry's hair, cup his hand like an eggshell. Henry was six when war started, and George was only twenty. He was called up to fight among the first, and he didn't want to go. He wasn't a coward, though. You had to go and kill Germans. Or else they would come and kill you. Or even his little brother (his stomach tensed with anger). You couldn't deny it was justice. It had all been explained to him ages ago. The logic of it was perfect, only one of the words wasn't right.

The word was *kill*. He knew what it meant. It was the thing that happened to Rose's chickens. She strangled them, out at the back; that day George always went out. It was the thing that happened at work when the foreman fell into molten metal. Pushed, someone said. The machines went dead and the news spread round in whispers. People looked green and sick. Later you lay there in bed . . . *don't think about it, don't think*. It was the thing that the next-door children did to snails, when they were bored, with a knife. Digging down into their shells. It was living things cracking and tearing and panicking, crying, fighting for breath.

George thought about it in snatches; he couldn't think of killing very long. In the weeks before war was declared he woke up often in the middle of the night with a sense he was dying, lay there locked in a trance of cold sweat, unable to move or cry out.

Railways for him meant his father: trains were things that you loved. It was nice that their house was near the railway line, it meant that nights weren't boring. Trains were safety and smells that you knew, day-trips to Ironbridge in summer. But now the midnight shunting of the trains had turned into monstrous evil, grinding of vile machines in the dark. Far away, but now closing in. And he would lie dumb and be eaten.

He was gentle, unlike their loud sister, Sally, unlike their red-faced, hard-handed mother. George was kind like Daddy, thought Henry, but softer, and more often there. The Friday that George was called up he came to meet Henry from school. He was supposed to be off sick with a poisoned finger, but the summons made him feel sicker.

He was standing by the gate in his old blue great-coat: beaked like a chicken, with cheeks cold as ice, he bent from a very great height and kissed him, the little boy running like a rocket gone amok from the moment he saw tall George in the distance, charging his stomach with a squeal of delight, round cheeks blazing, eyes bright with joy.

"I'll leave you this coat for an extra blanket," he said. "Would you like that, Henry? For you, not the others." "What will you wear then? " said Henry, clutching his hand, trotting hard to keep up. His brother's long legs were hardly moving at all but his were going like pistons. This was seventh heaven, being met by George. He looked up at him, the sharp pink nose that he loved, it looked like a bird but when he laughed it wrinkled, the kind blue eyes which didn't look down, the mouth which today wasn't laughing at him.

For some time there'd been talk of George going away. Mam told him it was for a holiday, *abroad*. "What will *you* wear then? If it's cold, George. Mam says there's mountains abroad. They're cold," his words coming out in little breath-groups of hurry. Nothing was so interesting as being here with George. "Wiv *snow* on top," he explained, very anxious. Then he looked across the road at a sparrow hopping in the gutter, and instantly forgot what he had asked.

"Not yet," said George, and his voice was so peculiar that Henry stopped watching the bird and gaped up at him. "Don't want to think about that yet." The joy inside Henry started to falter. There was something frightening, something not right.

"You got to take your coat George you will get cold," he insisted, dogged. "You know what Mam says. We always got to take our coats. Even on holiday," he added to make sure, though he'd never been on holiday *(he had been on holiday, he didn't remember, flown across waves and mountains in Rose, wrapped in a lost soft part of his mother)* "especially a . . . a-*board*." That didn't sound right. Words were an enemy, laughing at Henry.

"I'm not going to go away from *England* for a bit," George explained clumsily, dragging it out. "I've got to go and . . . *learn* things. In a special camp. I can *take* my coat, as far as the camp."

Henry cheered up a bit, hearing the "camp". So it must be Scouts, or something like that. Their feet sounded nearly together on the pavement but with George doing one for every two of Henry's. That was nice to listen to. "Fetch me next week?" he asked, squeezing tightly on the hand that held his.

"Shan't be here," said George, high above, into the wind. "I know you can't write much but will you . . . send me a drawing or something . . . or get Dad . . . to write down your messages . . . when Mam and Dad write?" He seemed to find talking hard; he must be out of breath from walking so fast. All the same his voice made Henry feel scared.

"You're not *going* for long. I don't *wanter* write. You don't have to go for very long, George. It's holidays. They're not very long," (he was almost shouting, getting more urgent) "you've not to stay long, please don't stay long."'N'*if* you do . . . I won't write you *anyfing*." George went to interrupt several times as the little voice grew more miserable and stubborn. The little hand gripped like somebody drowning so his right hand hurt like his bandaged left.

"I got to wear a uniform, Henry," he said finally, patting Henry's hand against the wool of his school jumper, squeezing his great arm round little bones too small to be shoulders, surely (and it flashed, very briefly: broken bones, little children. There were *German* children . . . breaking little bones.)

"It's not quite true, what Mam said. It's not just a holiday, really. We got a spot of bother in Germany, a war. Our country will win, that's obvious, but . . . " (voice wearing at the edges: the stupidity of it) "I've got to go and fight, that's all. And first I have to learn how to do it."

And then they marched on without saying anything, George very grateful that Henry had stopped asking, past houses where lights were just blooming into eyes, gentle light budding through open curtains, light on women's hair, light on white tablecloths, music from wirelesses, children screaming (with laughter? with laughter), the odd open window or door in a kitchen through which you could tell for a second that someone had sausages, someone else haddock, and someone was baking a cake, delicious, just perfect, burnt-sugar, then starting to burn . . . by the time they got home they were running.

George left the next day, in too many clothes, too many clothes to feel him. Too many clothes and too many bags. Underneath it might not be his brother. They were Rose's shopping bags, full of baking. He smelled of soap, and toothpaste, and newness, not like his brother at all. Things were going wrong, very quickly: his face and his voice were queer.

"I'll be joining you, lad, before long," said Frank, and they clutched arms as if they were fighting, George towering over his Dad, and his eyes were bright, too bright. Rose stared at her husband in poisonous fury. "Oh yes," she said. "Don't talk so bloody silly, don't think you're running off so easy, Frank Ship. Who's going to help *me* with three children? You may think you're gointer go for a joy ride, but you're too bloody old for it, in any case." He let go of his son. "*Shut your face*," he said suddenly, quiet as a knife, something unspeakable, never said before. "You're not decent, are you. The day the boy's going. Will you shut your face."

George stared at his father in dreadful appeal. He had never been able to bear arguments. Today he felt he could stop them, for once, with the power of departure upon him. "*Dad*," he said softly, with nothing coming after. "*Dad*, I'll have to be going now."

Henry had his arms clutched tight round George's knees, except they just felt like stupid thick blankets, as he burrowed his face hard into the thickness so he needn't hear anything and George needn't go. When he dared to look up, Rose's face seemed to have shut, as if something had jammed and the blood had turned dark purple. Her mouth was pulled tight like the stitched-up wound Billy Rees had got on his calf and then showed the whole class: all puckered and sore and perhaps full of poison.

The day was September going on winter, the wind blew sharply down the road and a flurry of leaves blew off the thin plane trees, spinning for a second against the blackened bark. Everything here was blackened, bricks and walls and faces. For a second George thought, would France be different, might it be green and fresh? Might everything smell like it did up Cannock Chase on a Sunday with Henry? Playing at tracking with his daft little brother, away on their own in the grass . . . pretending tomorrow needn't come ever and they never had to go back home . . . now everything was coming out different and the past was blowing away. Watching those yellow leaves spinning, blowing, blowing away.

George was turning into something quite different as his boots marched away down the pavement, slowly turning into a tall tree-man, baggages trailing from wide wooden shoulders. . . . "That's not my brother, not going away," Henry whispered to himself, half closing his eyes. He wanted to close them completely; if he didn't see it, it mightn't be true . . . but he couldn't bear to miss the last glimpses, so he opened them wide but looked through his fingers, *call good luck*, George was willing them silently, *wish me luck, go on, I'll need it* . . . hope fading fast as he marched past door after peeling door till there were no doors left and he told himself *well, I didn't really need it*, rounding the corner, *goodbye* they were calling, that was Mam's voice shrieking, *go on Mam, say it*—she didn't, what she called was "Hold it!": flapping with a camera, the sun coming out—"Smile!", she was yelling, and he waved, unsmiling, *goodbye*, the bricks cut them off, *goodbye*.

There were many little groups of tense bodies like this one, frozen on the pavements along the dark terraces, clustered round bodies hung with baggage like George, mostly young bodies stiffening to corpses already, rigid with the weight of the wind and the cold and the weight of the future pulling at their shoulders . . . drawing them away to the drab brick camps where hoarse men teach them to march like soldiers, and now they are losing their different colours, now they are wrapped in autumn brown. . . .

On the station platforms a few months later the same groups clamour, hundreds of groups, none of them noticing the pain of the others . . . small crazed movements of identical insects, all of them thinking their pain is unique . . . then whistles shrill in irritation, doors slam a ragged drumbeat, stuttering to nothing as the bigger rhythm starts to shunt, sad metal pistons setting up their discipline, sad metal bits drilling deep into the countryside, moving the corpses towards Dover, *goodbye*, the smoke blows grey and oh not like the wind blowing greenly on Cannock Chase on a Sunday, no, towards Calais, the *Continong*, not for a holiday, no, not for Rose's fantasy of mountains and oranges, yes there is snow but the black-and-white crosses as yet are just kisses crossing the sea on the first long letters, the last long letters before there is no more time for letters . . . *yes I'll go home and write to him now, right away, and say all the things we forgot* . . . walking home, hearts brimming with words not spoken, goodbye, *not my brother*, goodbye, goodbye. . . .

"I got a brother in the Army," said Henry, briskly, at school the next day. And he it said again and again in the months that followed; "Me brother's away, in the Army," proudly. It wasn't *George* though who had gone away; it was somebody else, my brother-in-the-Army. The George he adored was still here but hiding, safe in his heart for a rainy day.

But hearts have no walls to protect anybody, love doesn't work against bullets. *Because it's my brother, he can't get killed.* The logic seemed perfect to Henry. This was just a play that George had got into. Reality stayed here at home. What George really was was *my brother*, which was separate from things like dying. (Henry was right in a way, George would always remain his brother. What he as a child didn't yet understand was that you can have brothers who die.)

Rose had her photograph at any rate, though he didn't stay for a second. What if it didn't come out? Always in a rush, those boys. And he didn't seem to be smiling. She wanted to run after him, make him pose again, but didn't, on her big stiff legs. Her running days were gone, *not gonna come back*, and she didn't even say good luck, no time, couldn't think, that was Frank's fault, sticking his nose in, making things up about going away. . . . And he'd said not to come to the station for the final departure to France. He was always thoughtful, George; they would only upset themselves. He didn't want that, in front of everybody. So she wouldn't ever say it, just say "Good luck, love," she'd meant to, planned it, something like saying she loved him, which she couldn't, she knew, having tried it, often . . . it never came out. And now nothing came out. There was nothing left. He had vanished.

Rose loved her elder son, though she shouted at him like the others. He was tall, which she wished Frank had been, and good with the young ones, and helped if he noticed (who else did) that she was down. So the day before he left she was grimly sewing, initialling his hankies, effortful initials in yellow, G.S. (Oh George, I love you), G.S.: and baked with the same black fervour great batches of misshapen biscuits, ginger and cinnamon, their surfaces bubbled and pitted, shortcakes which came out like butterscotch, angel-cakes with thick snapped wings. She rolled and rolled till her eyes stood out of her head with strain, knowing her pastry was always too heavy, everything always too heavy, knowing it ought to be thin. She was making mince-tarts from a cook-book. They had to have lids shaped like shells. The shells were a triumph, quite beach-like, but there were brown sticky leaks on the side. "I don't know, George, not *ree-ee-lly*," she pondered, her brows shooting up to her turban and back again, climbing the grid of her frown, "if you ought to take many of these. They're not watertight, see, not exactly. It might get over your things." "Look Mum," he had said for the umpteenth time, "I've been telling you. I can't hardly take any of it. I mean thanks, you know, really. But well, you don't wanta go mad."

In the end though he took nearly half of it, lovingly buffered in greaseproof paper, very neat, for his mother, tied in wool, "It's softer than string, string'll crush things," her best set of George V cake tins the outer armour. "Are you sure you wanta send me off with these, Mum? I mean, they're not gonna come back."

Things would be crushed, things would leak, things would shatter, shells would fall blindly, flesh would turn black and the surface be bubbled and pitted, bones would snap drily like insect-wings and the cripples come home misshapen for ever, and far too many, we can't take all these, most of them never came back. . . .

The eight weeks of training killed Rose; the feeling that *she could still stop it* . . . still bring her son back home. Like the war that wouldn't begin. They'd *declared* a war, why not get on with it? She burned with contempt for the men.

If it didn't start soon she'd go crazy, itching to sort things out. It was all a mistake, it was crazy. She imagined the cakes running out.

Why couldn't they give those boys time off to come home and

see their families? Soon enough they wouldn't be able to. She shivered, thinking of the sea.

The worst thing of all was the parcel, although she knew to expect it. Three days after they waved him off, the postman knocked on the door. All news was bad in those days, waiting for the planes to come over. Her heart began to thump automatically. But he was just standing there clutching a parcel, a huge brown parcel tied up with string. George's writing, addressed to her. The knots were so neat, he was always so careful.

She slashed them through with her kitchen scissors, wrenched at the thick brown paper. She was hoping there would be a letter. There was, but it was more of a note.

> Dear Mam, my togs as you were expecting. It is quite hard work here. I'm fine and the other fellows not too bad. Who knows people say it may still blow over. "Here's hoping!" How is Henry?
>
> from your loving son George
>
> PS. Please let Henry have my coat for a blanket I *promised* him that before I went. Don't forget!

He might have mentioned the cakes, she thought, told me how they were going. She laid the thin piece of paper aside, then folded it, put it in her pocket. When she came to look at the clothes, the tears pushed up and hung trembling. Clothes that she knew so well, but . . . cold and dead, in a parcel. It was as if he was dead already. She shoved them away and put on the kettle. Thinking that way was unlucky. *Look on the bright side* (sucking her tea). He would be back, and she had her snap.

But *not gonna come back*, she remembered it, biting her lips for her temper with his father, not quite believing it, stooped with his baggage, the tall dark tree-man walking away: always turning, three times, four times, and waving, five times, six times, special ones for Henry, a gesture that might have been kissing his hand for his mother, *could* have been, maybe, but the street was getting shorter, seven times, eight times, rounding the corner, he's forgotten me photo, calling him, wanting him there by the plane tree, Frank in the background hissing *"get on with it,"* panicking her so she almost forgot that she hadn't wound on but she caught him there in her viewfinder, tiny and solemn, why don't he smile, *well that's that*—last glimpse of the sun behind him, wind catching her throat but she still yelled (louder than all the others) 'GOODBYE' and forgot *good luck*.

That bloody old bitch, thought Frank, as George disappeared round the corner, shouting her horrible mouth off, drowning us out, that horrible slag, fucking cunt, old biddy, old hag. He shot her a look like a flame-thrower but she was deflated, eyes fixed on the pavement, veined slabs of flesh, *gone away*, *not gonna come back*. And she stayed all mopey for the next eight weeks while George was away in the barracks.

Too much was stirring and wrenching in Frank for him to be able to bear her. She wanted to talk about it, she thought he should cheer her up. How could he cheer up his wife when he was planning to leave her? He only came home to sleep, sat at work writing endless letters. He wasn't too old, he would show her. He *wouldn't* grow old, like Rose. And he found out when George's regiment was leaving, never said a word at home. There was something he had to say to his son, something that had to be said. Without bloody women poking their noses in, shrieking and making a fuss. He had it all planned. It was Sunday, the one day he wasn't working. Somehow they got up late, and she was slow with the breakfast. But still, there was *plenty of time*. He would *put it all right in time*. "I'm going up the allotment," he said, and was off before she could complain.

There was no need to run, except his heart was beating. There was a good half-hour before the train. Frank should know, as a dedicated railwayman, the footsteps of the numbers imprinted on the pages of his forehead, turning them, turning them, turning them round in the cramped ticket-booth of his days. But he ran all the same, because George was leaving England, his son was leaving, perhaps for ever. If it was his son's last morning, it was the last morning of the world.

But what kind of world was ending?

There was one part of Frank, a tiny part he didn't like to look at at the moment, not decent, a rainbow-coloured part, very small and very brilliant, a distant country he might have once travelled to (or if he had a mother, she might have travelled to) which sent out messages, signs made with sunlight through foam or feathers, the flashes of wings or waves—that part was in ferment, delirious with joy, for peace-time was ending (for Frank peace was murder every day just averted out in the dank dark kitchen), the era of staying-at-home (which was not home for Frank) was crumbling, doorsteps the men trod each morning with their lunch-time sandwiches were cracking and heaving, tremendous evils and upheavals snaked up from the depths beneath . . . but also the concrete shifting freed thousands of bird-beaks tapping and pushing, little live things which must have been sleeping below— one part of Frank which had been waiting and dozing under its forests, waiting in the night with its muffled bird-calls, now sang like a drunken plover as the lights came up, the lid lifted, the wild birds shot free as hope across a nakedness of sky. . . .

(are wars really romantic? birds can be burned or blinded)

He felt good, running heavily but fast up Order Street, up Bengis Street, away from the women and children, a man on a crisp cold morning running, running alone. He was thudding uphill now, hearing the blood pounding hard in his skull. Too fast, he was not really used to it since youth and football, and his heart kicked out at his chest. *Slow down.* But the rush of blood was like love.

He caught sight of the station, now, in the distance, and a scattering of Georges, brown skinny tree-men, every one George most probably, every one making his heart thud harder, then a little bit nearer it was obvious that none of them was George, they were nothing like George as he trotted up the forecourt and the thin sun strengthened, there was young Alf Bridges, "Morning Mr Ship," even skinnier than George, poor bugger, *poor buggers*, keep on the move with his eyes straining on through the crowd until suddenly he saw him, that's funny, he'd been looking for a figure on his own but what he saw through the railings of the station platform was someone that could only be George, yes it must be, a very tall crab moving fast for all its encrustments of webbing and knapsacks but someone was with him, wrapping itself round him, a flossy pink bundle of dress and blonde hair that Frank didn't know, a Dad *ought* to know, and why were they hurrying, where was he going . . . then it struck him, and "GEORGE" he bellowed through the railings and was sprinting through the forecourt, there was plenty of time, the train shouldn't be leaving, it shouldn't have come and *"George"* he cried like a prayer and doors slammed in rhythm, *no time, no time* . . . as he tore through the booking hall his friend Ted Gilly stared shocked through the glass for a second, the whistle, oh no, not possible, a blackboard with scribble on, capitals, no time to stop, there he was *right up the front* of the longest train in the world (which should not have existed) and that vile pink dress hanging down from the window, *get her off*, just let there be time enough to say what he'd come for, touch him, squeeze his hand once and say what he'd come for, *good luck*, wish him luck, and he yelled at the loved bony face just a dozen feet away now "*George*" and drew up blowing and stamping like a buffalo, gouts of phlegm hanging from his nostrils, his son's face comically slowly responding, a great black O of surprise and the pink girl stepping back frightened as he began to pant "George I've just come to say sorry about your mother she does set me off but I wanted to say. . . . " and George shouted "This is Daisy, Dad, from the factory," at just the same time, then the unbelievable started, the sound of shunting, yes they were moving, tantalizingly slowly but moving, trying again "Look George, I just wanted to say, I'll be joining you! Never mind *her*, I'll be coming! And . . . " (cutting across what he wanted to say the thin face was shouting with equal urgency) " . . . Henry! Look after Henry Dad won't you! Give him my love, don't let him worry . . . ", slow puffs now shaking the whole mass forward, his son was no longer facing him now but craning back round at him, something forgotten, *why don't he smile so I know it's all right, so I don't feel a fool for coming*, but all he could see on that face now slipping away, now five yards, ten yards, was grief and confusion, then he heard the girl calling like a cat miaowing in his ear so he couldn't hear whatever George was shouting through the stamping of the engines but it sounded like *Henry* again and he tried so hard to lip-read the face as it shrank that he didn't remember again until after the last carriage passed him *oh* and the blank dark back of the train, *no time, too late*, he was barmy, he couldn't have, run all the way through the town like a madman and still didn't say it and suddenly the pink flossy thing was right up next to him, her silly voice squawking "Well it *is* nice to meet you, Mr Ship, did you just come to wish him good luck? . . . George promised to write every week," she babbled, and he saw a black insect crawling underneath her eyes which was an eyelash, how could George put up with it, they were animals, pink greedy animals covering it up with paint. "He's not much of a writer," said Frank, turning to go though his limbs felt bloodless and weak after all that running, the blood had all gone to his cheeks and his temples, throbbing in tune to the sound of the wheels in the distance, running away.

"I made him a card with a lovely black cat," she continued, he must get away or else he would hit her but he cast one last glance in the direction of the noise, that last plume of smoke which was all of his son now remaining . . . and that drab squashed feather looked so hopeless, promising nothing, no time, shrinking fast, that as he turned back to his dour way home he took in her empty grey eyes and said suddenly "Never mind love, he's gone."

George sat on the train on his own, though the other brown bodies pressed round him. He didn't feel himself any more, lost in a shell of equipment. However he moved, it hurt. He wasn't just *George*, or human. They had all been turned into clumsy machines, labelled with clumsy labels. All of them with the same arm-flash, all of them in the same brown. He felt too young, and too weak, to carry this heaviness. He remembered Rose's bags, and half smiled. If they were just carrying cakes . . . if this could all just be a dream, if this could all just be a mistake.

But he knew there was no mistake. He knew there was no escape.

There wasn't any time, no time to escape, no time to explain all the things that he meant to explain to Henry, no time to help him any more with his reading, and he'd wanted Henry to be reading properly before he got into Old Pinder's class, Old Pinder who had terrorized George all those years ago and oh how could there ever have been *so much time* when now there was none left at all and the train pushed him into the future, no time for dreaming or wishing, the train muttered urgently *come on George, come on and kill us, come on and kill and be*—what?

"They say that me brother got killed," Henry said, always sounding doubtful, years after. He never said straight *George is dead*. Until in the end hope died.

"Wish me luck as you wave me goodbye. . . . " George died among the first, when the new war songs were still quite thrilling to the girls from the dance hall who heard them, no time to have got tired of it, no time to have got used to it, no time for the hero to write more than a letter or two to Daisy and four letters home with a message in each for Henry, *oh please Dad, please read it again* but Frank couldn't bear it . . . no time to do more than understand, in the end, what had given him nightmares before leaving, no time to do more than take in what it meant to kill human beings, not so

96

different, he'd thought, to killing kittens or chickens *(which was vile)*, no worse, he had thought, than killing spiders or snails *(which was vile)*, and he burrowed deep into his pillow, those weeks before leaving, and stifled in feathers his fear of their pain so the thought never finished but in the cold French night finished it, time to concentrate, nothing to drink to forget it, no silly Daisy to spoon with, no little brother to kick up a ball with, *come on then Henry, yes, run . . .* unable to bury his face in his own kind bedroom, unable to stifle the midnight whispers coming closer, now, closing in, *come on and kill us, can you kill us, kill and be . . . what?*

Time to discover the ending, *kill and be killed*, enough time to discover he *could*, in the dark, by mistake, it was not real killing, just shooting, but suddenly dog-like howling, something choking on phlegm, far away, *please God*, but coming closer, closer, will crawl back out of the dark with its guts spilling out, pus weeping and pouring, to touch him, *it's time, it's time. . . .*

. . . time before dying in fragments of bone and flesh to guess what it meant to kill hundreds of humans, thousands, not dog-like but human, not quite like mosquitos or hens but like him or like Henry, *no please*, all round him he knew men were dying like flies *(like him or like Henry*, like flies. . .).

Not quite enough time (please God) to know thousands of human beings, millions, in fact, would be crushed against walls like mosquitos, have spines broken crudely like hens, would be poked from their shells like snails for the pleasure of children, would burn, split, mangle, or burst, would be cooked in hot bricks, molten glass, molten metal, each pain, all those billions of pains, as acute as the pain of the single foreman who screamed and then died of the agony, pushed in a vat of red steel and the whole factory stopped in horror, in *England*, at *peace*, long ago. . . . George hadn't much time (he was only twenty) but enough to know that killing was just what he thought, beyond him, beyond him, but the great steel wheels ground down and compelled him, *come on George, kill and be killed. . . .*

Time to imagine with pity and terror the grief his brother would feel.

The morning the telegram came was a Saturday. It was the first day of spring. Henry and Sally had quarrelled over who had the milk jug at breakfast. The milk spilled over suddenly on Rose's clean tablecloth, Rose's red hand struck out at her son and the row somehow turned into one between Rose and Frank, which was normal, and yet . . . horrible, scary, Henry *never* got used to it. He held his breath, wondered how long you had to hold your breath before you could die. He wouldn't mind a bit, just as long as it wasn't too painful. Nothing worse could happen to you, after you were dead.

Dark milk, soggy sunlight on the lace. "As a matter of fact, Rose Thrupp, you make me sick. . . . " *Don't think don't breathe and don't look* Henry told himself and forgot not to breathe through thinking *please God, please let terrible things not happen please God, please stop it, please God,* and his head was still full of the prayer when the thing he had surely been praying for happened, the doorbell rang which would be Mrs Potter from next door coming round for a chat with his mother, and all would go back to normal, his Dad would pretend there was nothing the matter and go and get drunk at the pub. He wriggled like a greased fish under the table, was up the other side and out in the hall in seconds, "I'll answer it Mam," and when he opened the door there was a tall thin man in uniform looking embarrassed, *like George* was his first sharp thought looking up at the face, *like George* and he smiled up to welcome him, yes he looked crinkled and kind and embarrassed and God sent him just in time—but he just handed Henry a thin brown envelope and said in a sad voice "Telegram, give it to your mother, son, give it your Mam," and Henry was left with the rustling envelope and the nice tall man had gone. . . .

On the daffs, the spoiled tablecloth, sun. You could never go back to the beginning. The row had stopped dead like that. Now Mam was sat howling with Sally. And Dad stood out on the lawn like someone else, someone mad. And everything had changed now, utterly, because the telegram man had come.

Only Henry himself felt the same. He decided he would stop time. He sat half under the table with a rag book he wasn't trying to read, and the telegram hidden inside. He was planning to tear it in two, the stupid great letters meaning someone thought George was dead which he couldn't be, twisting the pages of the book and trying (now no one was looking) to stop breathing for ever, so time stopped dead, which would show them, make them stop quarrelling, make them bring George back home . . . he crept out from under the table and tiptoed upstairs to his room.

Henry took down his brother's blue coat from the door where it hung on a peg. He'd touched it for luck all winter whenever he had something difficult to do, like a sums test which he always had to come top of, or else he couldn't bear it, not being able to read: he spread out the coat on the bed and lay down on top of it, pressed himself on to it, hands flat, cheeks flat, knees digging into the old blue wool that was George. In a bit he unfolded the paper, and stared at the ants very hard. They were dull kind of letters, sort of faint and squarish, no interesting squiggles and delicate bits. They were made with a machine, like the letters in books, but it wasn't a clever machine. He opened his eyes very hard and pushed his eyeballs at the writing, pushed until the letters changed shape and shivered and blurred, willing it to turn into reading, but all that happened was that his two eyes felt like great bruised holes at the front of his head, so he gave up and let the lids fall.

It ought to be easy, he thought, since he knew what the telegram said. All he had to do was read it different, make it say something else. Make it say George was still here, and would meet him from school tomorrow . . . but his effort was turning to tear-filled sleep, staring through a smoke-filled tunnel, the grey letters turned into George standing waving at the faint bright end of the dark, "Come on, Henry. . . . " But he couldn't move, and George vanished away. He woke up crying quite hard, with the hot drops splashing on the great-coat, his breath coming out in hiccups like a pop-gun and not like crying at all. He had torn up the stupid scrap of paper in his sleep, so he couldn't see the stupid grey letters any more, just the dark-blue wool, all matted with tears, and flecked with grey snow, still winter.

For years he would dream of being with George, held in his brother's strong arms. He was always his six-year-old self again, the exact small boy he had been. For that self George was real as ever, his kind, gaunt face against the sky that day . . . but he hadn't been able to *feel* him properly, out there saying goodbye. With that stupid frightening quarrel starting and the other bodies getting in his way. And the hateful thick uniform, hateful. Changing the shape of his brother.

He wanted to be there just once more, sitting on George's knee. If his body was given a good leg-up he could put his face right close to George's. He could peer right into his kind blue eyes and see the tiny smile lines spreading like ferns . . . blue-green eyes which had all Cannock Chase in them, Sunday mornings in spring . . . *Come on Henry, can't you run faster*, in the dream he was trying to catch up with his brother, the long legs not really trying to escape him, and then when his lungs were on the point of bursting George would turn and scoop him up higher and higher, flying up into the blue free sky . . . hold him there tight, so their hearts beat together. "Who's a little pickle then? Who's a pickled Henry?"

For years he would hang up the coat each day on the door so it looked like George, looked the most like George he supposed that anything did on earth. At night he curled under the warmth of his elder brother, listening to the planes in the darkness, shaking with fear of the bombs, but George's body would protect him. Clutching the sleeves in his arms all night he imagined they smelled of his brother. Lying in George's firm embrace till the strong dream arms flapped open. . . .

Henry could not stop time. His heart was sworn to be faithful; but other loves always crowd in in the end, other pains make you forgetful. He fell in love with watches, had a passion for keeping time. You could wind them up, or not. You could make them stop, or go forwards. . . . And he fell in love with pale pretty girls that he was too shy to speak to, girls with pale flower-like names. Daisy was just like that; she *must have been*, George had described her. . . .

Frank Ship wasn't keen on photos (they would trap him there in the bosom of the family) so the brothers were not recorded together, except in the colours of dreams. Even dreams fade, or come back less often: "They say me brother got killed."

In the end Henry had to admit it: "I had a brother who died." The coat went into the cupboard, its threads wearing down into the future.

One of his greatest sorrows was not having a decent picture. What if his memory was playing him tricks? Or one day he couldn't remember? The poor brown photo that Rose had taken was all that was left of his brother.

6 The Broken Chapter

Henry had buried his grief in a shell where it quietly grew, like a pearl. The watches moved quietly on, and the coat wore away in the shadows. It seemed things were going to plan, that once again there was pattern.

Henry spent all his life yearning to find that pattern. The world was a complex timepiece, immeasurably slow and vast. But you somehow had to build it yourself, and it had to be built through time.

He knew he had to grow up, not stay and grieve for his brother. *Little boys have to grow up*. He would find a wife, and love her.

In fact he found girls (like girls, not flowers) the girls who worked in the Brewery. He found their bodies (like flesh, not petals) gave shudders of dizzy pleasure.

A pattern to bodies, as well. He would soon understand completely. . . .

And then his father left home, when Henry was just eighteen. The wind howled in from the frightening dark, the jagged broken pane. The scar for his brother opened. He shrank down under his skin.

And then he found Lorna, and fell in love: deeper and deeper, then loved her. And soon he was the father of a family, and the pattern began again.

But Henry was afraid of his father's blood in him. A tree of dangerous blood spread out in him. He'd loved his father, like everyone else does, but then his father had vanished away.

His father had not understood; his father had smashed the pattern. There must be another way of living and being free. There must be a perfect pattern, thought Henry, which also allowed you freedom. And *he* would find that, with Lorna. He would fathom it out, in time. . . .

In the meanwhile he hid, and followed the rules. In the end they would both be free. For the moment he would be a man: *be a father, be tough, make money*. And he would pretend to grow old, though youth sometimes blazed beneath his glasses.

(They were Frank Ship's eyes before him, the eyes of his runaway father. Frank had those blue eyes still, far away on a high blue mountain. *Try not to think about Frank*, he disturbs the family picture. White lashes flutter beneath white wings, eyebrows flying for the snow-line.)

Henry was an odd-looking adult, though he had been a beautiful boy. Though Lorna lost most of her looks, she was still thought a very pretty woman; so they made a peculiar couple, their bodies saying different things. His was stiff and delicate, thin and particular, his soft bright parts all in-turned. He wore his skeleton on the outside, a shell which jerked like a crab. Very long looking would search out his eyes. Still luminous blue, a locked ocean.

Lorna was loopy and nervous and warm, with limbs that just stopped themselves hugging you. Once she had not been nervous: once she was always being hugged. Once her hair was a clear bright red and her skin was pale and veinless. As her beauty stretched and wore thin, she had to reach out for love. But her shyness usually stopped just short, each looping movement aborted.

Their lovemaking got better with time, but it never got into the text-books. His frenzy was a triggered mechanism, jerking itself to the bell: as he came he was human again, moaning he loved her, weeping and spurting. They lay there afterwards separately. His silence hung like a sound. Could this be all that there was? If he'd say that he loved her *after*. . . . But in sleep they lay curled together, peacefully curled like kids.

They'd been kids, of course, when they married, and played at keeping house. In a way they stayed kids to the end: they remembered to want to be happy. But most of the time they hadn't a clue where the other's happiness was.

Henry knew when *he* was happy, with watches or with his wife. He loved tiny, intricate things, like the small half-moons when she smiled. He loved gentle, secret things, like her rare short gasps of pleasure: things that would come again, rare moments which made a pattern. There must be a shape to it somewhere, his hope built out towards that. There must be a perfect building, with towers gleaming red.

It yearned in silence and darkness. All watches would mend in time. The heartbeat would be restored. Jack Latham would die or wither. She would come for him again, and the missing beats would fly home. But the hope was placed beyond time, in the deep dense shade beyond seeing.

Henry had a problem with words. Orgasmic, he would growl, "I love you." He had sudden flurries of words, like leaves falling off in autumn. It seemed he had less and less, as he grew more woody and gnarled. Yet the women, it seemed, his mother, his wife, used words as easy as breathing. It seemed to Henry there were very few words which buttoned the loops of his meaning. He clearly perceived the loop, the absent sense of something. But the buttons were cheap and small. Great brilliant displays had got lost. He remembered them clearly, then almost clearly, then only the shape of their absence. He had never possessed them, of course, but once he believed they were *there*.

As a child, he had longed for such languages, which burned behind grilles of letters. A world of such light and ease. But the screens were fantastic, distracting, barbed, and they shut little Henry out. He could never grasp the screen as a whole, each coil seemed a separate fossil. But if he could never pass beyond each shell, he would never reach the faint bright ocean. Staring up at each curl of the screen, his forehead rigid with trying.

Not reading until he was seven, he was put in the "Backward," stream. But knew he wasn't "Backward". *Backward* was something ugly and horrible and most of the children were too. They were big and heavy like his mother, red and slow-moving like Rose. Their movements hadn't any pattern; jerky and casual, crude.

Henry's toys were always very neat. He arranged them in crescents or squares. He was quite unable to sleep if his cars were not quite in line. His favourite things were toy bricks, much better than Bayko or Balsa. The bricks had a magic about them; they were somehow numbers, disguised. Some were square, some oblong, some flat and round, some pointed cones for roof-tops. They were all different sizes and weights, and ranged from rose-red to leaf-green. All pointed cones were not green. All rose-red cubes were not little.

Henry built magical houses, which he and his brother would live in. He and his tall shining brother . . . *blasted to bits by a bomb*.

(*Never show what you feel*. His brother, and later his father. . . .)

The builder did not accept the truth. Each knock might be George, returning . . . and then he did accept it, and built for himself and a ghost. And soon he became a teenager, too old for model houses.

Time to grow up, be a man. Go out and earn his living. Rose kept telling him how lucky he was to have a good job down the Brewery. "You're a man now lad," she said, almost reproachfully, thinking *not half the man George was*.

He was lucky to have blue eyes. The girls at the Brewery made him a mascot, which was easier than being a man. Gentleness and blue eyes. "I melt when I look at his eyes." And the way he didn't flirt with them, but helped them with the machines. He didn't talk much; no jokes, no spiel, which the other men did non-stop. But he looked as though he was listening, with his pale grave face that watched you. You could see yourself in those eyes. Words fell into deep wells . . . and his hair was glossy and black, thick silk that they wanted to stroke . . . wings like a small bright bird. "I wish that we got more young ones."

The older men fancied themselves, with their shiny pink scalps and hair like wire wool. They winked and their faces wrinkled up, and laughed loose mouths of stale smoke. Henry hadn't started smoking, and his teeth were small and white. He had long pale fingers like sapling twigs which would never go stiff like the rest of him. There were white half-moons on his nails, not yellow with failure yet.

Rose washed his shirts every day. He had a wad of pound notes every week. He didn't feel trapped, or bitter, since he knew this place was not the future. He helped Ken Minder every evening he could. "You'll ruin your eyes with those watches," said Rose. "You kids have no time for your mother." (It was just that she missed his father. He wasn't a kid any more.)

104

For the first time people made a fuss of Henry. He found that his shy smile charmed them, he found women loved his blue eyes. In those seven years young Henry bloomed; his chest and his smile expanded. He never learned to talk much, but he learned to be loved for listening. He never learned to make the running but he learned it was fun to be caught.

The "girls" in the factory weren't girls. They called themselves girls, but they weren't. Their faces were lined and cheery and shiny and their arms were thick and veined. They had sharp careful eyes saying *sex*, which blurred when they got to know you. With most of them, the sign blurred in the end and turned into unguarded fondness. He reminded them of their sons, he recalled their favourite kid brothers. There was one particular "girl", however, who didn't fancy being Henry's mother.

This was Elsie, a cello-shaped blonde, with a deep fruity laugh and slim ankles. She had the figure to pose for a corset although you could see that she never wore corsets. Under her straining overalls the flesh was tight and full. She made endless jokes about sex, and her blacked eyes swerved over Henry. From a distance her eyes looked large. Close to, you could see they were not. They were pale green, greedy eyes, laced up with mascara-ed lash. But her lips were generous and plump with blood, and they never quite closed together.

To Henry she seemed pretty ancient at first, though her paled spiked eyes were exciting; and the way she posed her hips on the table by his arm, and the way she smelled of lavender and armpits. She must have been thirty, he supposed. Or twenty-eight at the least. She had little lines fanning from her eyes when she laughed and the rings made her fingers look bony. "'E *dotes* on me, does Graham. . . " purred Elsie, and flashed him her jewelled band.

"You're very good with your *hands*," she said, watching him, and pulled at a strand of bleached hair. "You're very good with your *hands*, young Henry. Ye-es, I really think you have talent."

Henry lived in fear of meeting Graham. That he should have Elsie *all the time*! At first he felt gut-searing envy. He would be big and handsome and loud. He was only a fiancé, not a husband, but it was rumoured that he stayed all night. To hold Elsie in his arms all night, her big bouncy breasts and rude words . . . he broke out in a sweat at the thought. She would only have him in before dark, and as soon as they finished she got edgy. . . . "People will be talking," she said. "I'm not really that kind of girl." But it was *her* who asked *him* round to tea. "You'll love my sister Shirley." Only Shirley wasn't there for him to meet. Instead he made love to Elsie.

He didn't have the talent she expected, but she loved his pale body, no paunch. And the first few times were so exciting that his face shone and trembled with tears. Though Graham often said she was good enough to eat she had never been called "beautiful" before. He only said it once, but unforgettably. It shot from his mouth like a startled bird. It was the first time she ever took her clothes off for him, and the first naked woman he had seen.

But she didn't understand him, quite. What he saw was a dazzling machine, the most delicate symmetry. The skin on her body was pale and young and she was slimmer than she looked in her clothes. It was all overwhelmingly strange; that she had allowed *him* to see it. . . . Her head sat on top of her body like a bright ball caught in a tree. It was at once too small and too old and too bright, and belonged to everyday. Whereas the rest was secret and rustled on the quilt, silver-birch limbs on blue satin, blue sky. . . .

They grew sick of each other, of course. He didn't learn as fast as she hoped. He didn't call her beautiful again. He never even said that he loved her. And *he* got sick of *her* first. Once you knew how it worked, where was the wonder? Up close, her pores were enormous. He didn't like the taste of her lips, and the eye-black made stains on the pillow. He didn't like her rushing him to go but he didn't like the way she looked after. She looked older, puffier, defeated, all the fun and the acting disappeared. And her body smelled of his sperm. This made him somehow ashamed. It wasn't different and exciting any more, once he had made her smell like him. Next day he would watch her, astonished, her tight cheeky face back in focus. Once more she was Elsie the tease, her wrapped flesh pert and voluptuous.

She lived twenty minutes from his home, a walk through the gathering darkness. It was true that his body felt marvellous. And he looked at the fellers he passed in pity: what wouldn't they give to be *him*. . . . But sometimes there were long empty stretches of road and his feet sounded sad and defeated. A little fellow swam through shop windows behind him, suspicious eyes under black hair. His overcoat was too long, his legs and trousers too short. He had just been murdering someone, or stealing a little girl's purse.

But the worst thing wasn't that they might find him out, that Graham might beat him to blancmange. The worst thing of all was what *he* had found out, the emptiness after the party. It was finite, and sweaty, and smelled of warm fish, this machine he at first thought was beauty.

There were other girls after Elsie, but Henry never changed his routine. He expected the mysterious transformation would happen one day on its own. There was something which would blaze from the road without warning like sunshine on petrol and rain . . . but it always rained, in his bedrooms, and someone was always coming. Cars passed and choked in the distance and everything was over too soon. The tenderness was always solitary. The tide surged and melted within. The words that burst out were just animals roaring, great mouths which yearned at the bars.

And the thing he had once been building was lost behind bars of rain. Days fell straight down the calendar, long wasted bars of days. Did he really dream of a rainbow city where hands of watches were birds . . . ? The plans had gone grey like the daily papers, the daily lines of rain. . . .

. . . until he fell for Lorna, a flame-haired child of thirteen. Magic blushed back into his plans, invading pale corridors and attics. Dimly remembered arches and columns now bloomed with dense watercolour washes. When he saw her everything burned red: he would carry her away to red towers. The roof of the tower was incredibly precise, red hair on a cloud-white dress. They sat in elaborate gardens, stone lions, a dazzling glasshouse. . . . His future glinted and beckoned again. He would have to woo her with marvels.

She wore Indian bangles on her wrists. Wrists so thin and so white. The bangles were too big, rather clumsy. They were set with emeralds of glass, however, the details picked out in gold wire. Where he had seen only flat light for years. Fluorescent days at the Brewery, her sudden intricate beauty planted kaleidoscopes, periscopes, microscopes. Red rainbows on her white cotton. She must be a *Claire*, a . . . *Regina*. . . .

Henry brought her cakes and sweets, which he meant to be pearls and feathers. At first he gave them to her father, making it a joke between adults. Mervyn Lamb was sympathetic; everyone fell for his Lorna. Professional envy might have fouled things up, since the shop sold cupcakes already; but Mervyn knew they were usually stale, and the lad was bright-eyed and fresh-faced.

The one really good thing about Rose, Henry's mother, was the wonderful cakes that she baked. Whereas George had been a very big eater, Henry ate like a sparrow. But she went on baking in great grim batches, long after George was dead. And batches of sponge cakes sickened and died and the bodies were fed to the birds

(they did not fed them to us   we are hungry, feed them to us
Frank Ship, off on his travels, was shocked to find so many hungry)

So Rose was pleased and surprised when Henry asked her for biscuits, "would you bake some gingerbread men," "would you pack us some butterfly cakes." It made her feel useful again, which she hadn't done since Frank. He pretended he'd eat them at the Brewery, and she popped in some more for his pals. She didn't know her son even vaguely; he didn't have what she called *pals*.

Things don't rise to our recipes, life isn't served in order. Those crumbling butterflies with butter-iced wings flew dumbly from Henry to Lorna.

To Henry, Lorna was posh. To own a shop was quite something. It was posh to leave your hair long and loose and have sisters whose names were all hissing. And Lorna said she had drunk *wine*. "Grandpa brings us some, every Sunday. And then he nicks all our gin!" *Melissa*, *Clarissa* and *Lorna*. Would she ever look at a Henry?

But Henry had confidence, then, He was twenty-two, and nice-looking. He had spent six years at the Brewery as the darling of all the girls. If the Lambs had known about Henry at the Brewery they would have locked up their daughter. But he looked the innocent one; and in all but fact, he *was* innocent.

The shop wasn't quite on his patch, being six or seven blocks away. He was out for a walk one Sunday evening, just wanting to hear himself think. Rose had been tipsy all day, and her sister had a girlfriend round. They were giggling in the bedroom next to his, sounding just like the women at the Brewery. A whole Brewery week stretched ahead. It wasn't so much fun any more. He had to have a break before it started. Elsie picked on Sandra, his latest. And *she* had hair on her breasts. It wasn't right. He felt queasy. The window in his bedroom was warped, you could only open it a crack. He had never had a woman in here, but he started to imagine their smell. It felt there was no air left. They laughed through the wall like witches.

All day it had been drizzly and warm, but the last few hours had brought thunder. Now it rained a real grey rain and the outside air streamed clean. He half ran and skipped down the road. All the others were skulking inside. He sometimes still felt very young, though he'd been out of school six years.

That was one of the things that was wrong, you were shoved from one drawer to another. The process would go on for ever, *keep changing and never go back.* Inside he felt like a boy, but the women assumed he was a *man.* The women who wanted him all seemed to think that *all men wanted was that.* They assumed he would like it all the time, at least while he was still keen. . . . They didn't expect things to last, although they got sniffly and hurt. They expected men to get bored in the end, and go somewhere else to find it.

It didn't fit in with his sense of pattern, his sense of what was right. He didn't feel like *a bit of a lad*, or like *one of the lads at the Brewery.* It was hard for him to understand, that they thought him at all like the others. Henry felt one on his own, with his two deep wounds and his dreams. The Brewery was only a sideshow, for him: it didn't touch what was inside. He was only there for the beer, and of late the beer had gone flat. He was waiting for the coming of perfection, the rainbow on the wet road.

He really went into Lambs' General Stores because he got tired of walking. He had been this way before on a Sunday, perhaps two years ago. He was sure that the shop wasn't open, then, or he would have gone inside. Henry always used to buy small treats when he took himself on an outing.

Mervyn would have got out those long-ago novelties, if he had known who was coming. But nothing seemed novel to Mervyn, now. Sunday opening was desperation.

Henry just wanted to lean against the counter and look at the colours of the sweets. He wanted something sickly to squash with his tongue so the sugar would go to his feet. He wanted an interesting wrapper to shorten his journey home. . . .

Instead, *she* was under the counter, wrapped in a pale yellow frock.

It was stiff as the paper on a sherbet fountain, with fine white caster-sugar lace. Thin tender limbs, white liquorice. But the fountain, the fountain was her red flood of hair, burning gold in the light of the bulb. She stared up at him like an elf, with wise child's grey-white eyes. She was just a kid, he realized. Stick arms with a young woman's bangles. Then she hotched back under the counter, and the auburn sun went in.

"Have you got any sherbet fountains?" he asked. That must be her Dad. He looked like the father of a family; old and fat and defeated. "One sherbet fountain," Mervyn said. Then he grinned, showing long grey teeth. "Not wet enough for you then?"

"What do you mean?" asked Henry, then realized. What a stupid joke. Fountains and rain. Old men made jokes that weren't jokes. You couldn't laugh at things like that. But she rustled under the counter. He stopped on the way to the door.

"What's she doing under the counter?" He smiled his most beautiful smile. White wrists and gold-and-green bracelets. Mervyn changed his mind about this customer. "That's my girl Lorna," he crooned, his voice a lilt of Welsh love. "And that's her best frock she's got on. Her mother'll kill her after. It's like a den for her see."

Certain things burned their way into his mind. The shop bell ringing behind him, ringing for his last flash of gold. Then the clean cold ring of the rain. The skin of her legs, matt white (Sandra's was pinkish, muddled). Then when he got home, something else: washing a glass for some water. He was thinking of that hair as he took a teacloth and pushed his hand round inside. There was a faint cool ring like a bell. The grey-white ring of her iris. From then on Sandra seemed dirty.

Such things he noticed then, when he was too young for tired jokes. Each day cut fresh for him then, cross-hatched with sharpest gold wire. And his heart was coiled like a spring. Before he was the father of a family. And Lorna was the perfect image, the thing he had been waiting for. Peacocks blazed from the crown of the road, sun through a prism of tears. His longing etched her in gold, that razor-edged teenage beauty. Such things he had suffered then.

Later you become what you do, and things dull down to their outlines. Inside he would never accept it, never agree to grow old. But he grew a thick layer of dumb dead cells, obedient wood to protect him. The woodiness muffled his secret heart, which went on stubbornly beating. Stubbornly ticking like the watches he loved with their small shy hands and faces. No one quite spied out Henry, since he lived so far inside. And no one perceived the form that he yearned for, the city he never completed.

He tried to be a man with all that he had, and the father of the family too. He always worked very hard, as a decent father should. But he never made very much money, which shows that rule doesn't help you. At first, when he worked in the Brewery, the money wasn't too bad. But now that he had a family, he couldn't do the watches, evenings. The Brewery was hell, without watches. So Henry wasn't very happy. It was silly of him to think so. *Fathers can't expect to be happy.*

Henry dumbly didn't agree. He thought he ought to be happy. So when he got the chance of the watch-repair job he was off like a shot to London. Hiked them all off to Acton, *the future, the sparkling future. . . .*

Rose said, "It's expensive, London."

"It doesn't matter, Mum," he insisted. "Thing is, I love the watches. And Lorna wants to go too."

Henry never stopped loving watches, which many people thought odd. Fathers should really attempt to give up all curious habits.

There were other odd things about Henry, things which nobody noticed. A list which wouldn't start to be seen as a list until its shape became clear.

Very rarely, Henry broke out, and became another person. It was always when it became unbearable, being the person he was. A few days after the telegram which pretended that George had died, he had taken his bricks outside and thrown them at the lavatory window. He had to throw hard for a very long time before one cracked the window. He would have been stopped in time, but Rose was sobbing upstairs.

One day he had a fight with his sister and left her bruised and screaming. She had teased him all that morning: "Back-*wud*, Back-*wud*, Back-*wud*!" He knew that Sally was stupid, he knew that *he* was bright. But he didn't have the words to prove it, and the knowledge hammered inside. "I'm a teacher," she shrieked, excited, doing a teacher's face. Her mean little mouth pursed up, and her voice went high and peculiar. "Hen-ry Ship is Back-wud!"

she announced, to the miserable grass on the lawn. "Hen-ry Ship you are Back-wud. Henry Ship will *go down*." Inside him the blood boiled up, boiling up to a crescendo. Sally hadn't noticed anything, since he had made his face wooden. Provoked, she tried one more time. "*Now* you'll believe me!" she muttered, climbing on the coal bunker. "You'll fall," he said automatically, *be a good boy to your sister*.

She was standing on top reaching up to the sky with a garden cane in her hand. Then she pointed it at him like a gun. "I'm tall, very tall," she informed him, and her voice was an attempt at a growl. "I'm George, and I'm dead, I know everything, and I know you are VERY VERY BACKWARD." He didn't remember what happened after pulling her down on the lawn.

Other odd items, now listed, as the end of the list comes clear, as drink and frustration pour through the stencil and leave the word on the paper: a radio that Frank gave him, from which some parts had been pillaged. "It's on its last legs," said Frank, "but it's good enough to play with." One day he found it lying in pieces on Henry's bedroom floor. "It fell off the table in the night," said Henry, but he knew the lie sounded feeble. He had strained for hours, night after night, to pick up a country where George was. The pointer flickered uselessly up and down, the crescent of light was deceptive. All that he got was a hideous crackle and mocking bursts of music.

A china poodle of Elsie's. It stood up on its hind legs, and it had a little frill of pale blue net which Elsie said was a hat. "Do you think it's a boy or a girl?" she giggled. It was watching them, lying in bed. "It'll tell on us to Graham." The thing was a present from Graham, like her garish cuckoo clock. One day she started calling it "Poopy". "Poopy's peeping at us!" While she was next door sluicing herself the dog crashed down and was shattered.

"That's very odd," she said, coming back to find him dressing. "Are you sure you didn't just catch it with your sleeve? I really do think that's *odd*."

And Henry began to *look* odd, odder as he grew older. When the Brewery girls all fancied him he was a tender youth in his teens. Later he got the glasses and wouldn't meet anyone's eyes. His body grew slowly wiry, too wiry, tensed like an angry hand.

In other ways Henry was defective, also. Not only too slight, but too short. *Fathers should be big and slab-like and serve as an oak front*

112

door. But Henry's front door was frail and rackety and painted some very odd colours. Pink, then two shades of green. Bright gobstopper pink, of all things! The neighbours talked for a week.

Every year it was a different colour, when the inspiration came. Painting houses is not inspiration, not normal family houses.

There was more to it than the colours. He had to be different, Henry. He grew dog-roses over the door, which was not quite the thing in Acton. They grew too long and too straggly and the winds snagged thorns in your face. It was mad to grow roses in Acton, those innocent pink briar roses. You only had to breathe in Acton and your nose went black as soot.

Their petals were sometimes flecked with soot but the plant grew strong and survived. It was wiry and gnarled like Henry, but the roses came out each June. For him, the flowers were like watches, something perfect which marked the time. In the Brewery there were the hooters for getting in and going home. At first it was all a game, when he was young and alone. But then he realized it wasn't a game, like Elsie without her make-up. He wasn't so young any more, and he knew the Brewers meant business. It was a horrible sound like an air-raid warning, drilling a hole in the morning. It was like all the other ugly machines, grinding down on his brother. He felt such joy on the day that he left. That noise had no power any more

It wasn't to do with the air-raids. It was just the way he behaved. I hated seeing them run like ants when somebody shook the powder

(That time it was Henry speaking. I don't want to listen to Henry. I'm trying to tell a straight story, just like everyone else. But voices keep interrupting, cries thrown back from the future. And others shout from the present, a crazy anthem of need. And Henry is much too elusive, will not conform to my plan.)

Perhaps Henry saw too much, though he said less and less about it. His irises behind glass shone as pure and unclouded as Frank's. He didn't have his father's body, though (it's easy to write about bodies). His lines were twisted like bark. His father had been quite straight. Well his father had *looked* quite straight, but his soul inside was a maze (I hope we can keep the soul of Frank Ship right out of the family picture)

(That blurred bit there in the corner—has someone spilt wine on the gloss? That shape like a plane-leaf caught on the cross or a bird blown crooked by the wind. . . . Shades of the cloud-ships
    passing, dying   as the air blows down from the mountains)

That is fanciful, of course, You can't catch a soul with a camera. Henry tried not to think of his father, as he strained to perceive a pattern. But something of Frank was there, flecking the film on his iris. Atoms of Frank or dust of Frank, those floaters in the thin sunlight

*(atoms and dust could be anyone   bodies of nobodies,
    rustling)*

The flecks of uncertainty floated across when Henry stared at his children. It should have been touching to show them together, the father's arms around his kids. It is what we like to suggest, in today's photographic studio. But Henry found touching difficult. No wonder; he hadn't been taught. But he did the best that he could, and I'll do my best to describe him.

He managed all right with Angela, till she was into her teens. It was easy to cuddle a moppet like that, and the spitting image of Lorna. Indeed there was nothing nicer, and then it was somehow too nice. Inexplicably something changed. He realized he mustn't touch her. Then all he could have were those soft dry kisses she put on his cheek at parting.

He wasn't too bad with George. They were both as shy as each other. George was shy because of his fatness mainly, which made him painful and clumsy. He hated to be so fat, and not just because it was hateful. He hated to be fat in case it made Dad feel skinny. Henry wasn't bothered about being thin except in the bedroom with Lorna. But he did feel awkward with this red-cheeked giant and he timidly patted his shoulder. That should have been manly enough, but under the shirt there was blubber. And yet he loved George's insides, that kindness like his own brother.

With Guy he was a disaster. At least Guy was *small* as a baby, since no baby isn't born small. So Henry could hold the baby. But afterwards he was appalling. Guy was mean and whiney and

114

lying, and his features spelled it all out. In fact, the features came first. People read faces as words. Guy soon found out from their answers what words he was doomed to say.)

So Guy has to be forgotten, as far as fatherhood goes. As a child Guy got in a red-faced rage when he wanted them to show love. In life you never get love by shouting HELP ME I'M HURTING. Guy couldn't even do that; what he shouted was *MA MA MA*.

It was nothing to do with Henry, to *DA DA DA*'s relief. Guy loved his soft pretty mother—to him she was gloriously pretty. He wanted to hold her long hair, which drove her wild with anger. He wanted to touch her soft breasts, which made her brusque and uneasy. He didn't think much of his father, shrivelled and smelling of beer.

He saw what was there as *the truth*. There had never been another Henry. There had never been a nervous boy in his teens, eyes that black birds' wings shadowed. He had nothing to do with the roses. Around him, no shadow of doubt. He wasn't much of a father. His son had found him out. He was bones and peculiar specs. He was *DA*, and he was no good.

Henry stared at his red son bawling, the hatred pinned in his eyes. Sons ought to love their fathers. Fathers should love their sons.

This isn't a model family. I've tried to make them behave. They shouldn't have tried to have children while they were still children themselves. There are too many children wailing. The noise shakes the window-panes. It's no good drawing the curtains. There's not enough love to go round.

I'm sorry, I'll write that again. I can hardly hear what they're saying. The noise of the pain is so great, a wordless opera of hunger. I think they are saying

> *not love   it is novels that hunger for love*
> *we need to have something to eat before we can think about love*

They say that they have no homes, no food, no family, no story to tell. Their stories lack incident, the kind that we like in our stories. The only thing that happens of note is that every so often they die.

It is something wrong with the wind, a freak effect of the airwaves. No reason for them to be here. My unities will be shattered. They can neither write nor read, they don't know what "character" is.

I think it's because of Henry, perhaps, the fact that Henry rebelled. A little leak in the book and the ocean rushes in.

I don't really know these people, although I know they are there. I don't want to think about them, because they make me feel guilty. I know I am writing a novel, and novels are not for them.

I know that novels need detail, the vivid detail of life. . . .

It sounds so innocent, put like that. Perhaps it is not the whole truth. The vivid detail of novels is mostly our vivid wealth. These voices that come on the wind have a misery lacking detail. Their faces resemble each other, drawn to extremes of hunger. They have very similar bone structure. Novelists write about that.

But bone structure really means something else when skin is pulled tight over bones.

And then, there are far too many of them. You must keep your canvases small. A couple, a marriage, a family—yes, my nuclear family. But how can I keep my eyes on the page when those faces move like the sea. I wish that I knew who they were. You'd think that they might try and help me. But they cannot define themselves, except as a focus of pain.

And yet, they do look a tiny bit like something I've seen in a novel. Looking at them again, I know what it is they mimic. They are horribly like a family, but far too *large* for a family. Skulls insist on a likeness, when they press too close to the skin. A family of the hungry, the dying and dead. And no one is here to protect them; a family without a father.

They are not all there any more: absences ache in the shadows. They are all those people who died and their names are not recorded. The families in novels are usually good at tending their family trees. But these people died in paperless camps or wars or famines or prisons. They died far away from their children, or their children died before them. Because their names and details are lost their voices can never stop calling. They add their terrible volume to the cries of those who survive.

The shadows stretch forward as well. There is something I can't understand. They are saying they will have children (they looked too sad to have children). They are crying that they will have children, and they will inherit the earth.

116

The bodies will cover the books, if it comes to the final violence. The bodies will have their revenge on the novels which left them out.

Sometimes I catch a single refrain from the wordless cry of that opera.

> something you have to learn   something the rich will learn
> paper and skin both burn   all men will be like us
> men will lie blind as books when it comes to the final violence

7 Chapter of Flight

You wouldn't have guessed from the facts that Henry had wanderlust. His honeymoon was at Margate, he had been no further than France. Travel was always in the future for Henry while he still thought he was young. As he grew less young he became less sure there were seas and skies in his future. But his life was all secret compartments, haunted with detailed ghosts. They were ghosts of time and space, locked in a room in a city. The ghostly ticking of watches, the ghostly motion of trains.

It was all theoretical though, and his ghosts weren't things he could speak of.

When Angela was thirteen and she and her Mum were still speaking, she went and asked Lorna about a discovery she had made. "George looked under the lid of the TV seat, and it's full of old geography books. And loads of posh magazines called *National Geographics*. So where do they come from? And a smashing old globe, it would look nice in my room, can I have it?"

"They're always poking about, those boys," said her mother, face closed, not raising her eyes from the sand-yellow bowl she was mixing in, stirring and stirring. Recently she'd started to make cakes. They never would rise in the middle. The cake phase wouldn't last long. She went back to cornflake cake. There was a pause, in which the wall-clock ticked. "Look Ange, I haven't got time." Why were there so many clocks at home? Why didn't grownups have time?

Angela knew better (in those days) than to pursue the matter any further. However, she knew cunning as well. With a charm she was soon to lose she put two fingers into the deep S-bend of her mother's thin spine, tickled briefly, then pretended to undo the knot on her apron. Lorna stopped mixing with a shriek and her cheeks went pink with pleasure as she swung round to cuff her daughter, cuddled her instead, their thin bodies almost one body. "I love you, Angela."

"I love you, Mummy," said Angela, one of the last times she'd manage to say it (inside her hedges and thorns were growing: too many dramas, too many demands).

"You *do* love me, Ange," smiled Lorna, her wide pale eyes with the sunlit window in them and an extra dazzle, opening. "Yes," said Angela, more doubtfully, growing shy, not knowing what to do with her hands which were still stuck round her mother.

"Funny old things," said Lorna, clutching Angela's fingers and starting a sketch of a dance, sliding on the freshly polished floor like a skater, a sketch of the dances they did when Angela was little, and didn't much these days, wouldn't much longer. Joints seizing up. Love running dry

> (*love can grow back in time*   *all that it takes is time*)

Lorna stopped and her face became grownup, wearing signs saying *serious* and *helpful*, as she did, not often, when deciding to play mother (Angela frowned, but she wasn't very kind: how else could Lorna be a mother?) "They're your Dad's," she said, very solemn, a mother teaching her girl. Angela waited, pretending she wasn't annoyed by the pose, though her fingers were clenching. Why did she do it?

Lorna rested her thin red elbows on the window-sill, either side of a sick geranium. It poked up under her chin. She gazed at the blue of the sky as if *there* all true things were written. "That'll scratch you, Mum," said Angela. The flowerhead was mostly brown and spiky, with a few red petals going black. Lorna frowned for a second then ignored her, recalling herself to her script.

"It's to do with your grandpa, you see. Your grandpa that was. Henry's father. Your ex-Grandpa Ship. Well for you kids, I suppose, he always *will* be your grandpa."

This was thrilling stuff. Ange almost stopped breathing, her anger forgotten. No one spoke of that grandpa, not ever. As a very young child she had asked Grandma Ship why she didn't have a husband, and Grandma had gone nearly purple, and Daddy had sent her out to play. They must each have at some time wondered, and asked, and never been told. Last year Ange thought she found the answer, listening to the big girls talk, at school. They talked about homosexuals, and then they talked about bastards. With her heart turning over with pity, Ange realized her Dad was a bastard. So Grandma Ship had three bastards, and Grandpa Ship had never been!

She gave herself thrills of excitement and sorrow in bed for nights after that, lying thinking and thinking, her grandma did wear very short skirts. Those big red legs and tight skirts. It must be what Aunt Mel meant when she moaned about Angela's skirts: "If you wear your skirts up to your armpits, men will get the wrong ideas." Grandma Ship was young once of course, though her waterlogged, vein-blotched skin made it hard to imagine. She must have always worn her skirts like that. It must have given men the wrong ideas.

And if men got the wrong ideas, they would put in their penises (they must do it very quickly, or else you could stop them, she thought) and then you had babies. Still three seemed rather a lot to get past her, and Ange looked at her grandma (sitting on the sofa, nodding at telly, her red legs spread in the direction of the fire) and felt quite kindly but basically severe. For a week, until she forgot about it, she was extra affectionate to Daddy.

Now suddenly the question had come up again. "You're a big girl now, so I can talk to you more. Only—don't tell the boys until they're older. Oh Ange, I'm so happy that you're growing up now!" (spinning round, her voice painful with pleasure . . . the geranium toppled and crashed as her Mum's thin arms locked round her) "and we can be friends, real friends, like mother and sister. I mean sister and sister. Do you love me?"

Ange jerked away slightly but tactically resigned herself. Her jaw was squashed painfully by Lorna's collarbone. "Uhhn," she ground out, "of course I do. You knocked over the geranium. No one ever talked about Grandpa before."

Lorna was satisfied, and picked up the geranium. The earth straggled over the tiles (she ignored it) and the last black petals were gone.

"Frank Ship was a railwayman . . . " she began. By the end of the story Ange forgot to resent her. They were chattering like birds, both close again, really close, making milky coffee and forgetting the mixing, faces very similar, like sister and sister, pecking at their biscuits, sun rubbing out the lines.

Frank Ship had been a railwayman. "It wasn't just a job though, know what I mean, it was like your Dad and the watches. . . ."

Lorna didn't *really* know the meaning of Frank, the ghost which peeped through the window. . . .

Frank had loved the railways, everything about them, the figures of light at the points as the smooth metal arcs swung across, the steam making castles of cloud in the sun, the smell of mixed metal and coal. The fresh coats of arms on the coaches, the detail smart as paint. He loved the new carriages, the tweed of the seats hard and bright and the firm pale leather of the window-straps, lovely, still smelling nicely of cow.

He loved the *old* carriages too, with the out-of-date ads behind glass and the string of the luggage-racks broken and knotted till they looked like the webs of very old, very tough spiders. He loved the old paint grained with black and the brass growing layers of dullness. He loved trains by day-time, their bright wheels and windows signalling back at the sun. Loved them at night-time when their long chains of light flying over the fields signalled something more urgent, the future—

future, the future, the future   the future was running away

And timetables, all kinds of timetables. Local ones, comfortable, straight, all the names that you knew written fair and square on the white, the times magnificently precise in a world with no points failures, everything oiled, and drivers who never drank tea. He could read them for hours, on the ticket window, on long winter days when the trains were mysteriously empty . . . Frank Ship didn't understand it—why didn't the whole world use trains?

There were also the long-distance timetables, the cross-channel timetables, tables of numbers which leaped across thousands of miles. "Their power almost scares you. . . . " he once confessed to a workmate, a pal, in a pub, after three pints of bitter. It gave Frank the creeps, just thinking of it, though he "wasn't the emotional sort".

"A bit like a spell, get my meaning. I daren't hardly read them too often, it kind of works on your mind. To think of it, starting off here they run all those thousands of miles. It's *Paris*. It's *Rome*. It's *Milan*. It's the Alps, and those great long tunnels a million feet up and there's holes in the sides for the sky, I've seen 'em" (his long hands were black with print from the timetables, drunk with the thrill of the rails in the sky).

He had taken Rose once on a holiday, when she was pregnant with Henry. She had got very low, being sick every morning, Mrs Simpson to do for and the men to look after. Rose's way of showing depression was shouting and dropping the plates. She was sick of Frank doing overtime, and George going on he was hungry. He had been an enormous baby: she dreaded her second birth. She had been a big girl to begin with and both times her ankles swelled. It was always the women who suffered. And just so that men could have pleasure (she forgot how she liked him touching her, making her groan and whimper). She had hardly got over the last little beggar (she had a long memory: twelve years' getting over) and here she was having another.

Each morning the smell of the gas and his fried eggs cooking made her heave and rush through the back door to the damp dark privy in the garden. By the time she came back the whites would be burnt to black lace

> whiteness burnt to black lace
>> they were sick all day in the darkness

and the fat smoked vilely, blue-black. All she felt like doing, coming back, was throwing up hugely again. Frank never complained that his breakfast was burnt, ate looking down at the tablecloth, frightened of connecting with her misery, frightened of having to cope. Rose stood heaving and glaring at his two dropped eye-lids, his blank lowered plate of black hair. As he left, calling "Bye then," too squeamish to kiss it—the big red miserable face that might bite and the sour smell of vomit—the china would crash, every day, in the sink. Each week there would be replacements, ghosts of the price-tags sticking.

One morning she followed him down the hall, the drag of her floppy slippers behind him. Feeling it coming he kept on walking.

When he tugged at the door it stuck, *bloody hell*. As he turned to pull it, her belly pressed in. He smelled the sick. "You better kiss me, Frank," she said, and her eyes were a bright glaze of murder. "Better kiss me, Frank. Or else never come back."

never come back   *he may never come back*
kiss me quick   *we may never come back*

That day he made a few calls after work. He came home looking strange, eyes shining with love. "You're drunk," said Rose unbelieving. "You won't believe this," crowed Frank, "and nor do I. But we're going on holiday, Rose" (he never called her Rose, not once since George had arrived, but today she was Rose, he must be mad, drunk, dying. She stared at him fascinated. Lock him away.) "I've been and asked the Thomases. They're having George. And I've asked Jim Gross for a couple of quid. I've got twenty left from my overtime. We're off to Geneva next month."

Rose gawped, and sat down. Her mouth opened again, not controlled, jaw sagging. "You gone off your head," she gasped. "You never borrowed money in your life, Frank Ship. You never asked Gross for that money, you didn't." The blood was dark red in her cheeks, almost pretty. There was thrill in her voice as well as the shock. "Is Geneva in Italy?" she asked him, hands twisting her apron, staring at her apron, staring at the bright printed oranges on it, unable to bear his bright blue stare. Aprons were normal, aprons she knew.

"No, Switzerland, it's much nicer," he said. "It's mountains and flowers and miles of snow."

That night, although they thought they shouldn't, Henry's mother and father very gently performed sexual intercourse, the first time since she'd been told she was pregnant. Frank came with great bliss but in a whisper, lest Henry should hear as he swam in her belly and wake in the dark and be afraid. He glimpsed sun on red snow from the brochure, a boat on a heaven-blue lake. He floated fast asleep into the sunset as Rose still lay there awake. She saw snow behind trees full of oranges, the fruit printed bold on the white: *ooh Frank it is lovely, Geneva.* . . . Henry kicked and shook the fruit off.

It was one of her complaints when they got there. "I'm sure you said oranges," she said. There were apples and peaches by the road, there were fields of wild flowers, but no oranges. *One* of her complaints. There were the trains, which were bumpier than English ones, she said: he didn't agree. There were the breakfasts in the little hotel, "Not enough to keep a sparrow alive," she said. He didn't agree, spreading blackcurrant jam on pale butter, the bread crisp and warm in his hands. But he went and bought her chocolate to make up for it, exotic bars of Lindt for the baby. She'd have walked twenty miles for it at home: *truffes* and *praline, ananas, framboise*.

"Doesn't taste like bananas, not a bit," she said, pulling faces at the fir-trees. "It isn't," he said, "take a look at the wrapper." The wrapper showed fat wheels of pineapple gleaming with sugary wet. He was hungry if she was not. "Don't push that thing at me," she shouted, so loudly that people turned and stared. A fat American playing with a dog favoured Frank with a filthy look. "I'm pregnant, I deserve consideration. It *isn't* bananas, doesn't matter what it says on the wrapper. I *like* bananas, I'm homesick, I'm hungry, I want to go home."

He didn't agree for the first three days and for the other seven he did. Walking wordlessly along the esplanade, by the bright blue waters of his dreams, a resentful red face was always with him. The thing he avoided in the mornings at home bobbed along at his side like a tug. He would catch their reflection in shop windows full of pretty things she said "must be dear". No one else that they met looked as unhappy, except perhaps the very very old, being pushed in dead bath-chairs under blankets. But *he* wasn't dead. Nor old.

On that holiday Frank understood. She could only see the pattern on her apron. He hadn't travelled anywhere yet: you could only ever travel on your own. The last evening he packed himself into his suitcase, his knowledge, his longings, his dreams: folded down to the size of a suitcase the whole intricate criss-cross of tracks and timings which soared in his skull like the black-and-white glass-and-steel vault over St Lazare (he'd seen pictures, *one day would see more than pictures*), wrapped around it a sheet of assumed indifference, and filled in the spaces with time. From the outside he looked just the same. He would wait till the children were older.

"I'm packed, dear," he called down the landing, to Rose in the WC. She emerged in a flurry of clothing and bellowed "You got no manners, have you. Don't talk to me when I'm *in there*." Waddled

124

back down the landing, wriggling at her knickers, her snub pink nose in the air. He watched her, precise, scientific. She didn't know he was *no longer there*. "Not as if they had proper lavvies here, is it. You'd think in a *hotel* they could manage it, wouldn't you. At home we've got better, well haven't we, admit it?"

"Yes," he agreed (yes, one day I'll leave you). As she tugged her purple coat on in the mirror, frilling out her ugly mouth at the glass like a meat pasty wrapped in mauve paper, he picked up his life in one hand, tested the neatness of it, tested the weight.

"I'm not ready yet," she snapped at him, pouting at herself, tipping the silly hat forward. "Nor am I, my dear," her husband agreed, not looking at her, smiling at his secret. Smiling at its satin lining, smiling at its bright little locks.

They went home: she went home, and he pretended, and Henry swam home inside Rose. As soon as she got back she decided Geneva had been wonderful, and broadcast the fact to the road. It was 1932, in Wolverhampton. Only soldiers had ever been abroad. "He's a man in a million," she crowed, now sitting with her belly in her hands. "Other side of the world, it was, nearly. And just 'cos he thought I was *tired*. You can't imagine it, not having been. Mountains and chocolate and orange trees."

She couldn't see into the future, or else she wouldn't have crowed. She had pulled her apron right over her head, but Frank looked out at the world. He knew there was not enough time: each day he waited was wasted. But he knew he would go *in the end*, and the knowledge helped him to bear it. We shouldn't crow over Rose. Nobody knows our future.

Rose couldn't see that he meant it. Frank backed his loves with his life. Frank didn't understand theory: Frank had the world to explore. They were codes, the maps and the timetables. The message was simple—*get away, get away*. Internally he nodded: *yes, one day.*

Rose thought Frank was like herself, content not to be contented. She thought he would always be there, just like everyone else is. But Frank was in love with the future, with steel drawing in to a point. Lines that made sense on the far horizon, where the parallels met without pain. He would follow them into the distance, and the steel would curve up into mountains. Peaks and blue air waiting, the naked spine of the world. The air would glitter like glass, and there would be cool plants growing.

125

Frank really wanted that fearful freedom, which is not like everyone else. You can't blame Rose for not seeing it. She lived life by the wrong book. Though I scattered the page with warnings, she never heard what I said

always say goodbye nicely   *turn for that final look*
there is always someone with a secret
someone who never comes back

When war broke out, Frank volunteered, to her admiration and fury. He was "one of the lucky ones": just over age for the draft. But "I'm going, that's that: I'm not *old*," he said. She was losing her son in any case. . . . And Frank had to up and go too, *like a great big overgrown schoolboy*. That was what she said to her husband, but the neighbours heard he was a hero. "He *will* go, Frank. I can't stop him. He was never like anyone else. He's a man in a million, Frank. I know he'll come back a hero." She didn't believe he was serious until after the news about George. "I *said* I was going *months* ago, I gave you plenty of warning."

Fighting was better than rotting at home, but he knew he wanted to live. He didn't try any heroics, since he didn't know who was right. He knew what they said in the army, but then, they wanted you to fight. There was something wrong with it all; at a signal, the world turned over. . . . So he didn't come back a hero and he did come back in one piece. He was brown and quiet and confident and he hadn't come back for long. He certainly hadn't come back for his wife: he moved into George's old bedroom. He would stay till Sally was properly grown, then he and his hope would be gone.

But he sometimes looked at Henry and his heart turned over with grief. If he could have told the boy, if he could have taken him with him. His eyes were just like his Dad's, there was nothing of Rose about him. He was solemn and eager and interested, and loved order, like Frank, and plans. After George had been killed in France, Henry was all of his sons. He would kneel and stare for hours when Frank spread his maps on the floor. He expected Frank would always be his father, just like any son would. The eyes that he fixed on his father were not meant to cut him like wire.

Frank knew he was committing a sin, the sin of smashing the pattern. To find his own kind of pattern he had to smash what was there. He had to erase all the long shared days, the roots digging

126

into his heart . . . you got used, in the end, to anyone, they came to seem part of yourself. Frank was getting away from it all, but you can't get away from love. He would make a new life for himself, but he couldn't quite leave the old one

> *he would leave his life very suddenly, the new and the old together*
> *all time is true together*   *if all time comes to an end*

However far Frank would run, he was still in the family picture, a whisper of wind disarranging their hair, a wrinkle on their composure. The hatred eating at Rose, bile puffing her up like a bullfrog. Thwarted love stored in bottles, the drink which kept her wounds wet. A question in Henry's eyes, an absence expecting nothing. All his life he expected to lose, having lost his brother, his father.

For the son there was loss, and fear. *You can never deny what you do.* Frank had to shut out these suffering ghosts as he lay in the far-off mountains. They came in the middle of the night, of course, and he told himself he must sleep. Henry would be a big tough lad. The last thing he'd need was a father. Frank never did have a father, so Henry would do fine too. It was better as decades went by: he could think, Henry's really a *man*. *Men*, after all, were independent: *men* didn't brood or mourn (in the middle of the night Frank brooded, but *that* was Frank, and not *men*).

Ineradicable loss, and fear. Henry's fear was of his own self. The times when he broke, and tore. What if one day it went further. . . . Frank used to say "You're like me son," and then sigh, and turn away.

What if one day it took him the same, this need to be up and gone? What if he upped and left Lorna?

After they moved to their first little house he never unfolded the maps. (One day they would go *together*, but money meant *not quite yet* . . . .) They were still his most treasured possession, after his tools and watches. He hid them in the TV seat, where they were well out of the way. Frank had taken some of his maps, but he left the globe, and the rest. A globe wouldn't go into his kit-bag. And he had the real world now . . . .

But how much of the world do we have? growing darker, growing smaller. To Frank it was wide, and painted with light. Frank never looked in the paper.

In the first few months after he left, Henry stared at that globe with such passion. He was sure that it held the secret, that Frank must have marked his route, just from the weight of his finger moving, moving over his future. Patterns of clear bright colour, the crimsons that made power clear. But loss didn't figure in power. Frank wasn't lost in an Empire.

(On a footpath somewhere, keep running. Eating bread under a bent blue pine, the sky spinning down through the needles as his blood drank the rough red wine.)

The globe span stupidly, empty. A globe is too small for a man. A man must have enough room (but the earth is slowing now, aching. Play with a thing too much, and it turns to a toy of tin. Spins like a red-stained toy of tin, the stains of empire spreading . . . .)

A man must have enough room, or his skin will chafe at the corners. But if the pain is too great, is it right to tear the walls down?

Henry was all of eighteen, Sally sixteen, looking older. Frank had waited and waited, until they were almost grown . . . .

The wind still roared through the house. The sky looked enormous and dark. Little dolls as the dolls' house tumbled, the empty airwaves howled . . . . They sat together in the kitchen, hunched round the kitchen table. Rose had cried for three days and nights. She served grey toast on grey plates.

(Frank went running up the mountain road, the high banks wild with colour.)

All voids are filled in time, they say, *kind dust covers the crater. Widows can't weep for ever. Orphans have kids of their own.* It's easy enough to dispose of time when you're dealing with other people. A day of pain is too long. Time burns when the pain is your own.

(But novels are full of the pain of time. What of the pain of it ending?)

The void would echo on down, as long as time echoed on. Henry never stopped feeling cold, and even his children shivered.

George was in love with past time. What it carved on the present was certain. That was why Guy wasn't trustworthy, lacking the carving of history. And history meant there was hope. Most things would come right in time. There were lines of right behaviour you could find if you kept on looking. Not only arithmetic dealt in truth. There must be equations for goodness. There was logic to everything, George was sure, and a sequence for history and love. The family tree had an order, spreading its shade at his back. Lorna would learn to love Henry, Henry would learn to love Lorna. Ange would stop crying so much on her own, and sometimes eat her dinner.

George didn't want to escape: he wanted to be secure. As he grew, however, the numbers went wrong, and time taught George about failure.

It wasn't till George was nearly seventeen that Henry told him all about Grandpa. He didn't tell the story very well, and George felt curiously angry. He should have been sorry for his father, but he was too cross to be sorry. He should have been told long ago. It was one more straw in the wind. The wind smelled badly of burning, wind that was shaking his pages. He had never been told enough truths in time, and the world he had built didn't do. He had strained and strained to think out what was right, but the world wasn't good enough to bear it.

His anger turned heavily outwards. There was empty darkness to fight.

But the darkness couldn't be empty. George saw the Enemy.

What are these patches of darkness, stains from a thing we can't see? Something has passed in the night, and it may come back at sunset. We look about and see details, the encyclopaedic light. Our history is here, and our purpose. But the wind is shaking the set. For the first time we see it is finite. Loss bellies up underneath it. Nothing has been repainted (the last red petals turn black).

    black petals lost on the blackness   *please bring the details back*

George didn't want to get away like Grandpa, he wanted to bring him back. He wanted a pattern, and meaning. He wanted everything safe. He didn't just want to be one on his own, he wanted his roots behind him

Lorna told Guy one long bored day when she was helping him write for a job. He had got so bored with them all, she just wanted him to show interest.

It hadn't any interest for Guy. He lay in bed and reflected. One boring relative the less. You didn't need families at all.

Guy had no truck with ghosts. Behind him the air was quite empty. His own thin life was quite hard enough, he dreaded that there should be more. He hated having a brother and sister who shared the little he had. George of course was the worst, sucking up praise and love. He lay and heard the pig snoring, gorging air in the next-door bed.

Guy wanted so badly to leave them all, to get away on his own. With tall blonde girls and . . . a *motorbike*, and nothing to make him angry. He wanted to be on a . . . yes, on a *plane*, with *air hostesses* all round him. The sky was enormous and *blue*, that was easy, they were all in uniform.

One day the trap would just open, and he would come into his kingdom. The girls would spread their silk thighs, sighing, the General would slap his back: *George would be chucked out of their bedroom*—he never forgot to wish that—and the house would get larger, magically, like coming out of a tunnel (funny the house was still there: escape wasn't quite so easy). His mother might still be there, but she would be just *his* mother—which was strange since Ange was still there, and was just *his* sister too. They both lived. . . . up in the *attic*, and only came down when he called them. They brought him his favourite puddings, and Angela didn't read books. She dressed in proper . . . *dresses*, and his brother officers stared. His mother had got short hair and never left off her *stockings*. Both of them laughed at his jokes and admired the cut of his jacket. In later versions, Angela spent her evenings *polishing buttons* (that was a touch of genius: he was very proud of the buttons). The house was exactly like theirs, but infinitely higher and grander. Guy *did* know he hated Acton, though, so the house was always *abroad*: somewhere far and summery, full of sky, where the warm air banished pimples.

The detail was always vague. He could never escape what he knew. Guy had no hope of escaping, locked in his own warped shell.

130

He dreamed on the long empty platform, on one of his last afternoons. It blew and blew like a dream coming true, the warm air coming through the tunnel. He was picking his nose and court-martialling George, as he waited for the Acton train. Away from it all in the sunlit future, he would never use the Tube again. . . .

never use the Tube again   not one of the family would use it)

. . . he would get away from it all (he moved slowly, with all that luggage). Guy pushed on towards his future, the train crashing on through the tunnel.

Till Angela was nineteen she had never been abroad. She didn't like to admit it was her very first time on the ferry, sniffing the sea and cigar-smoke and staring at the waves on her own. She said she couldn't go below with the others because she always got seasick, but really she wanted to stay on deck and watch her childhood drown. The cliffs got smaller and smaller. No trouble could touch her now. Whatever happened back in Acton she was sailing out of sight, out of hearing. . . .

She realized this world was hers, that no one had been here before her: this was her life on her own. No one could take it away. And hope was salty and cold and different, a swell never felt before: the ship might never reach land, they might float on green salt for ever. Seagulls blew back from France as she had known they would blow. The deck gave her a white feather. She cupped its sheen in her palm. She thought about *other* White Feathers. How could anyone want to fight? How could anyone bear to die? The birds danced across, wings strong as the waves, one spiralling up against the light. Joy prickled through her whole body, tears surged up like cold wine. She wept for that dazzling second of life, wept for the dazzling future.

Feelings don't come in families, feelings can never be shared. She thought that second of life was unique, her solitary self and the water. She would have been very surprised to know the same tears had been cried by her grandfather. She wanted to be her own person, but the nerves grew down in great trees. She didn't know Frank was still alive somewhere, and most of their nerve-ends matched. She thought she had got away from it all, but you can't get away from time . . . .

131

past time isn't the problem   *keep us away from the future*

Frank on the side of the mountain, refusing to read his paper.

Once the world was enormous, and mostly composed of doubt.
There were continents still obscure enough to hold the long rivers
of dream.

There were mountains, too, to puzzle, beckon, fatigue. Which a
dreaming man all his life could not manage to understand, his
hopes in the end going down like the sun on the pines that he
never reaches . . . . (and yet his whole life was a climb,
transformed by the wind from the snow-line).

And Frank did get there: tiny, a laughing and waving man.

This was a world where mirages stayed real beyond the skyline,
things that one shipwrecked sailor testified he had seen: his
two teeth catching the sunlight, eyes in their brown seams
blazing . . . unstrung islands of pearl-shells, crazy lyre-feathered
birds . . . .

The seas were too many to poison, the mountains nameless as
waves. And lives were lived under trees which no one had ever
counted

(someone is counting them now, counting away my pages
if we can't count on time, please don't count it away)

This was a world where people could die on their own without
doctors. The pain was the same perhaps, but if they saw flowers
and leaves . . . .

(others will die without doctors   *others screaming and burning*
whiteness burned to black lace   *sick as death in the darkness)*

There will be no islands to run to, all named, all counted. All of
them count as nails in the built-up battened-down world

pearls   *wild pearls which were islands*   *now nailing soldiers' charts*

All continents will be mapped. They are scabbed and scarred
with missiles. The world will be one world only, with all holes
blocked. Winches of steel and steel hooks will have disciplined the
high peaks. There are man-made caves underneath, but not deep

enough to hide us. Mountains lie blind as bulls' eyes, flattened by soldiers' maps

nowhere at all to run to, if time runs straight

(Frank still high on his mountain . . . ecstatic, a man's silhouette)

The world still shines like a garden, but its distances grow darker. Cloud-shadows run too quickly, breed with the shadows of planes

all that we need is time   *space might return with time*

Time pressing on too fast, the train pushing on through the tunnel.

8 *Chapter of Lovers*

Couples cleave to each other, to reach the end of the story. Getting away from it all, they still want to cling to each other. Human beings who come in ones ache to be part of a couple. Rose ached rawly for Frank: Henry ached for his Lorna: Guy ached for nameless air hostesses, and Angela ached for John. Back at the beginning of the century, Joanna ached for her brother.

It sounds well organized, but other chains make it less so. For a time, Lorna ached for Jack Latham, who itched to have someone younger. Frank ached for Rose for three weeks, and thirty years later left her. Guy was to die a virgin. The vicar gave Joanna a lecture.

Novelists write a lot about love, meaning the love of a couple. It seems the world was well lost for love *(is it well lost for hatred?)*.

Joanna Smythe-Fielde was thought fast as a girl, and fast as Mrs Edgar Cleaver. First, she was very pretty: and went on the London stage: and married a man for his money: and "went in the fields with men". This last was hardly the case, though there *was* a lot of truth in the rest. They were boys, not men, in her mind, friends of her twin brother, Joe. She had always adored her Joseph, but now he was courting a girl. Valerie was silly, yellow curls. . . . He hadn't much time for Joanna any more, and it left an aching hole.

Girls fell in love with boys, of course, so she fell in love with them all. They had all been children together, before all the glitter of London. Now she was back in the country she would be a child again (but the child had flaming red hair and her lips were pouting satin: bored already with dusty old Edgar, aching for young brown skin).

She didn't know what she wanted: she thought she just wanted fun. And "Surely Edgar," she wheedled, "you'd trust me with my own brother. It's really a family party. If you didn't so hate parties. . . . " (In fact, she'd omitted to ask him. He'd never had a chance to like parties. At first Edgar ached very badly: later the pain ran down. The clockwork rusted and stopped. He chose to hear nothing, see nothing. Hard to see nothing painful in those summers of endless sun.)

She dressed in her best white satin and lace, a very smart dress for a brother. The lace had a pattern of daisies: she wore daisies on a great hat. She had made them a picnic again. They would fish, and play French cricket. ("I feel I have to be nice to them. They're going off to the War.")

The shadows were long on the grass. Harry Richie was a friend of her brother. Of course he told her he loved her. They had one kiss as the willow flamed, weeping on the bright water

(all the water this chapter weeps won't put out the fires of the future)

"I know it's madness to talk like this but somehow we'll be together. Wherever I go, I'll return." They heard Joe and Valerie coming. The girl had a silly giggle, yellow curls, a plump white neck. "You're the loveliest girl in England," Joe whispered to Valerie, worrying, aching. *How far could you trust a woman? Would any of them come home?*

Joanna went home well-pleased. Valerie had got bitten. It was right in the middle of her round white cheek, and she looked very silly, very cross. Her own beau Harry had made a sharp comment, and then told Joanna he adored her (*her* cheeks would never get bitten: *she* would never get cross).

She lay that night beside her husband, playing it over and over. That song they sang by the river, inspired by the great moon-daisies. What was it called, "When the fields are white with daisies . . . "

135

> I stood once in a harbour when a ship was going out
> On a voyage to a port beyond the sea
> And I watch'd a blue-clad sailor as he said his last farewell
> To the lassie who loved him most tenderly. . . .

She was very glad she was a woman, that *they* didn't go like the men. All the same, she felt part of history, with her tender romance with Harry.

Harry Richie, though, ached with guilt. A *married woman, Joe's sister*. The night before he went off to sea he confessed his sin to the vicar. The vicar was young and indignant and had often stared at Joanna. She brought temptation to church, in her sparkling eyes and trimmings. The following Sunday he took her aside (after prayers for the men who had gone. She had prayed especially fervently, wringing her gloves in her fingers. Big tears came to her eyes; the moon coming up by the river . . . .)

> I saw the teardrops falling as the last goodbyes were said
> 'Tis the sorrow of a parting all must share. . . .

He stopped her and asked her to see him alone. She blushed, and her green eyes shone. She'd thought life was going to be boring, now, but he was tall and handsome. His blue eyes looked very fierce; that was a sign of passion. She was nice to Edgar at Sunday supper, patting his aching shoulder.

Blue eyes spoke of the sea. Harry had had blue eyes. But Harry had kissed her and gone

> And I heard the sailor promise to the lassies now in tears
> When the fields are white with daisies I'll return

Of course it was true she loved Harry, but the vicar was so well-spoken. Did love always return? Her brother loved Valerie now. Silly to think of her brother. The fluting tones of the vicar. Fluting into the marital bed as Edgar snored beside her. *A man of God, and a Cambridge man* . . . (And yet it was Joe she ached for. They used to go hand-in-hand, even when they were in their twenties. He used to tickle the soles of her feet and put buttercups under her chin. What if he died in some foreign field? Mud in his red-gold hair. The sheets were unbearably cold, all at once. She tried to think of the vicar.)

Delicate feet on his long gravel drive. He'd be watching her from some window. So she stared at her little black patent feet, demure underneath her white satin. "Who is he going to marry you to?" asked Edgar, risking some humour. At least when she visited the vicar he didn't have to stifle the horror. Visions of her laughing and naked, which made him wince in his chair. "What's the *matter*, Edgar," she would ask him sharply. "Rheumatics, I expect, my dear."

Crunch went her feet on the gravel. White lace and satin looked *pure*.

Nothing quite goes to plan. The housekeeper opened the door, and showed her into his study, whose windows faced the wrong way. She offered her hand to be kissed, but he squeezed it limply and dropped it. (Lace which fluttered like cloud, a great complicated white cloud . . . once things used to be clear, but now everything was changing. If good and evil should change, in the course of this awful war?)

Much as he burned for the hussy, he lectured her about sin. (He would have liked her to tell him in detail about what she and Harry had done.) The maddening silvery sheen of that satin, flowers on her big hat bobbing. It was not that he didn't love virtue, but how things were shared wasn't fair . . . he was only twenty-seven. Why should *he* be shut out of the garden? Her cheeks with their heavy roses, the blowing scent of her hair.

She saw he had an erection and laid her hat on his sofa. Blood in her chest like a drum. Abroad the boys would be dying. Harry, but Joe, her Joe. . . . "Oh Joe, my darling," she moaned, minutes later, the springs digging in her soft back.

After it happened he cried, and left the village in autumn.

When Joe was killed she turned hard. It was no use loving just one. They grew up, left you, were murdered. That homesickness for her twin. Her heart couldn't bear to be homeless, and she made a vow for the future. *Always have more than one lover, and love will always return.*

Love is a powerful medicine, though nothing can heal charred flesh (red hair burns like any other hair: each cell was twin to Joanna. He had darted back into the flames when the bomb set fire to the building. Someone was trapped inside, a brief pale face, yellow curls . . . he had darted back in after Valerie's ghost, but dying he thought of his sister).

Couples cleave to each other though custom keeps them apart.

They would never manage to fit their love inside the family picture.

He had buried her image inside him, forced himself to turn cold. "Oh don't be silly, old girl. We're much too old to hold hands." Now love was buried inside him, in the stupid choking rubble. When they were both fifteen they swore they'd be buried together. His body was never recovered: black in the speechless dust. But Joanna was left to burn alive, all those years of trouble (then suddenly quiet, the fires went out, shrivelled and small in a wheelchair. Staring hopelessly up at the light. *I've still got my nice red hair. . . .* Little stick woman with crimson fluff. Peace came too late for Edgar.)

Couple love's powerful stuff, as all good novels will tell you. It makes them quiet and in-turned like Joe or a babbling brook like Joanna. It makes women swell like the moon, transforming the flow of their body, stretching their skin into miles of thin silk which will furl a pale tent for a baby.

But love can't make a new world. Worlds don't swell out of bellies. World's don't grow like Japanese flowers when dropped in this chapter of water.

Lorna started work in the supermarket at the age of thirty-four. George had started his barman's job, so it wasn't just the money. Thirty-four is a dangerous age (*so are all ages dangerous. All numbers ice-skate over the void. Screaming, dying, all ages*).

To a woman going to work for the very first time, all ages are *not* the same. It felt like her very first day at school, but she felt like a very old schoolgirl. It had never quite hit her before, that her schoolgirl beauty had gone. But she looked in the mirror that Sunday, trying out the clothes she would wear.

Her hair was its natural colour again, she had let her own red return. The perm had affected the texture, though. In the sunlight it looked kind of dead. The veins stood out on her hands, but men didn't care about hands. She still had a lovely smile, she thought, smiling at herself in the mirror.

Was there something different about it? Somehow too bright, and anxious. A flutter on all her features. Her cheeks had got very thin. She'd always had good skin, very fine, Henry called it

138

transparent. She'd never had to worry about that, but now daylight made her worry. It was better not to have transparent skin if things weren't quite perfect inside. You could see tiny red things floating, like miniature fish or weed. Minute heads of blood in the fierce cruel light. In a soft light that was "good colour". But she realized that day it was age. What if heads were followed by bodies?

She had always felt like a lake or a sea that feelings or days swam through. Now other things swam in the water, blue fish flew under her eyes. She fluffed on some sand-coloured powder. The soft light touch of her father.

Lorna said she was going out to work, but really she was looking for love (Angela had turned out odd, and Henry had started to hit her). She was looking for her history, too, since for her the word "shop" meant her father's. They advertised as a *Superstore*, but she turned it back into "shop". She had seen an ad in the local paper, for General Staff and Cashiers. The cashiers got more money but she was frightened of numbers. She wouldn't have thought of another kind of job, though she knew that women should: but "shop" she said to herself, and a voice deep inside said "childhood, Daddy" . . . a voice deep inside her wanted it back, the gold cloud under the counter.

The idea settled and grew. She imagined bringing back the money. She imagined herself in a smart new dress, giving kind advice to the shoppers. (She somehow forgot the overalls: they didn't fit into the past. In the past she had worn pretty dresses, and the sunlight gilded her hair.) She found she would have to "wear it up, the main thing is to look tidy." "You've got pretty red hair, Mrs Ship," said the manager, smiling at her. She blushed very red, and trembled. She wasn't the same person any more.

When Mervyn's customers admired her, she had preened herself and flirted. But a million miles of life had gone by, and the confidence had all left her.

Nothing was like she expected. She wore too many clean jumpers. It was hot under her mauve nylon overalls, and they made her figure look lumpy. "My, we *are* all wrapped up," breathed the manager, brushing very close behind her. She looked like a mauve nylon parcel, but her ankles were slender as before. She was learning where everything was, and how to put price stickers on. There were cities of foodstuffs here. It bore no relation to Lambs'. More food than she ever imagined, more food than could ever be eaten

they did not feed it to us   *we are hungry, feed it to us)*

She felt lost among so many brands. She hoped she would be able to manage. "Managing all right?" he leered. She distinctly felt his hand touch her, through all the layers of clothes. Just between her shoulder-blades, briefly. Remembering it, she wriggled. He was big and handsome and tall. She stared at the storeroom wall.

What Lorna learned was that falling in love is a good way of wiping out history. She had loved Henry Ship twenty years, but ten weeks of Latham seemed longer. Poor Henry shrank into the shadow, and Jack blazed bigger and bigger. The supermarket was huge: it was an empire, he was the emperor.

She shivered like a leaf when he touched her, wonderful, the first time she let him touch her. Jack liked to see someone excited. It made him feel more of a man. He had taken her out to the pub, meeting her discreetly round the corner. He had asked her to come every day for a week, and at first she thought he was joking. Then she was scared he was not, and wondered what she should answer. It was being unfaithful already, going out to lunch with a stranger. She knew that she'd have killed Henry if he'd done the same thing on her.

He poured two pints of cider into her, telling her about his plans. He put her in the category *sensitive*, since redheads often were. So he told her he loved Nature, and wanted to be a tramp. He loved the World of Nature, he said. One day he would leave, with a knapsack. He offered her another peanut, and smiled so the sun caught his teeth. "You look rather wild yourself," he said, and his tone became—well, *cheeky*. (But wasn't it romantic too?) "You look like a bit of a Gipsy."

She felt a little downcast. She thought she was a woman of the world. With the "Glittering Impact" of her eye make-up and her ladderless tights (Pale Chocolate). She had sat and batted her eyelids at him and hardly looked at the nuts. She didn't like talk about *leaving*: it made her think about Frank. And that made her think about her husband (she would *never* leave Henry. Would she?).

"Drink up," he said, "it costs money, you know. And we'll go

140

for a spin in the woods." A little thrill shot through her tummy. "I've got to be back," she said. "I was only off till 1.30. Mrs Timmins will give me hell." "She won't," said Jack, flexing his muscles, his manager's muscles in their fitted shirt. He ran his hands over his thighs. You could see their convex bulge. She felt her breath going funny. Imagining *them*, on *her*. . . . She followed him out like a lamb, half dead with lust and terror. A little tired lamb to the slaughter. She didn't know a thing about men. She didn't know a thing about the future. She felt apprehensive, all of a sudden. A stranger was going to kiss her.

Going to do more than just kiss her, thought Jack, driving into the woods. He stole a sideways glance at her. She was biting her nails, and flushed. But her eyes were bright from the cider, and her slender legs weren't crossed: "I think you're romantic, like me," he lied, as they drove past a fire of red berries. "Your cheeks are much redder than that." "Go on, Mr Latham," she sighed. "It's Jack, I've told you, when we're not . . . back there," he said, slowing down to a halt.

All of a sudden his lips were on hers and his big tongue pushed like a dog. It didn't really feel romantic, but his hand thrust hard at her nipple. "You've got lovely titties," he panted. "You don't really need to wear a bra." "I thought it was respectable for work," she gasped, half fighting him off, half pressing against him. "You'll make ever such a mess of my make-up, Jack. I think we'd better drive back." He liked a bit of resistance: it was what he'd expected from her. "I like you a bit less respectable," he smiled, tugging at the top of her knickers. They were amazing. Cotton, little daisies. Came up to the waist, like a schoolgirl. And a married woman. Bloody hell! But the innocence made it better.

She felt so thin he could snap her, but she still had decent tits. There was flesh in her cheap skirt too. It was vulnerable, like a bruise, when he finally got to her belly. A soft pale blue-veined swelling. Underneath it, a bush of red hair. He had had a bet with the storeman, that she was a natural redhead. "It's nice that you're all red *there*." She was crying and he was grinning, clench-teethed, as he thrashed and groaned to a climax. Afterwards he looked at his watch. "Three o'clock, we'd better get moving."

He drove with a little smile on his face and his lids looking fat with contentment. She didn't know what to say. "I shouldn't have done," she burst out. "Of course you should," he replied. "I think

141

you should do it much more." "I don't like you talking like that," she said, tight-mouthed, sore legs pressed together. Her heart said *Henry, Henry. Oh Henry, will you forgive me?* Jack changed his tune, which was easy.

"I just want to tell you, you're special, Lorna," he said, "there's something about you. You're . . . a *lady*, not like the others. I thought it as soon as I saw you." "Well it didn't feel much like a lady," she sniffed, "in the back of a car, with a stranger."

"I've never felt we were strangers, Lorna." His brown eyes stared into hers. She had never seen eyes so direct and honest (you could never see Henry's these days, with him wearing those horrible glasses). "From that very first day when I met you, I felt that you . . . understood me." (He made it sound like a million years. It was only a month ago, though.) "Are you trying to say that you didn't feel anything, that afternoon in my office?" His voice was indignant now. He was looking away. She had hurt him.

Angela would have seen through it, but her mother swallowed it whole. Twenty years she'd been dying for dialogue, for a man who would play The Lover *(but dying is not so easy: all lovers dying together)*. The square-built figure in *True Love Stories* with all the right words in his bubble. His gaze was serious, tender. The story carried on down.

She opened her compact and looked at herself as they drove back into town. She was looking absolutely awful, black streaks where the tears had run down. "You're beautiful, Lorna," he suddenly said, and it echoed from years ago. Her father had often said it, and his pals, and her girlfriends too. Henry used to say it every day, when there were just the two of them in his flatlet. He hadn't said it for ages, she couldn't talk to him now. Since the shop going bust and him drinking. Nobody said it now.

It was wonderful talking to Jack, such a clever man, and *sensitive.* He'd noticed at once she was different. He saw she was "understanding". . . . "You do understand me, don't you Lorna," he pleaded, his finger slipping in. "You feel so welcoming today. I knew you'd be a good little worker."

The affair with Lorna lasted longer than most: by an irony, she did turn out special. Her combination of excitement and fear made him stiff whenever he got near her. He liked her snooty little voice going soft as a child's with love. He liked being able to take her in, the way she still blushed and sparkled (already losing that sparkle. Those two little lines of strain). And making her take him inside her. He liked small women: they made him feel big. The way they mixed pain and pleasure. He liked to see her grey eyes closing in bliss or pain as he entered. (They closed to shut out her husband, at first, and later to shut out fear. Fear that Latham would leave her. The veins on her lids stood out.)

One day near the end, it was getting boring, he teased her a bit as he fucked her. They were lying on the grass, in the sunlight. She had worried that they would be seen. He told her not to be silly. He *liked* the idea of being seen. Being seen would help him get going. Being seen being good at it. "Is this as good as you get it at home? Am I doing it as well as Henry?" Her face (which had got too thin, he thought: you could see the stretched skin round her eyes) turned suddenly into a ferret, her eyes blazed reddish, she fought him away (she couldn't disentangle his penis, but she battered his smooth heavy chest: his penis went on regardless, fun to be fucking a ferret). "You filthy *bastard*," she panted, scratching him. "Don't you dare talk about Henry!" He was strong and young and greedy and he held her till he had finished, coming more quickly than usual in case the scratch-marks might show. He pulled out of her and sat up. She refused to look at him. She was scrubbing at the sperm running out of her, scrubbing the filthiness away. "What's the matter, are you in love?" he asked, pulling at her head by the hair. He didn't understand what had happened. Her anger suddenly melted. She pushed her head against his shoulder, and he could feel hot tears on her cheeks. "Oh yes Jack, yes, yes I *am*."

Lorna Ship was in love with Jack Latham, Lorna was aching for Jack. Who already ached for someone younger, the blonde who'd started last week. . . .

In the sun you could see all the stretch marks, and the lines which ringed her thin neck. It was spring, and time for an ending. He couldn't stand this all summer.

She was never anything but thin, and as winter passed she's got thinner. Henry said less and less, but he watched and worried over her. At first he thought it was doing her good. Now she looked like something from a camp. "You're working too hard, Lorna," he finally said one tea-time. "You've hardly touched your tea. You're getting as thin as a rake." "It suits me," she snapped, to his surprise. She never used to talk like that. "When I started, you

143

said I looked pretty. When I put my overalls on." In the 100-watt light she looked old and ill. He remembered her transparent beauty. "You never used to worry what you looked like, Lorna," he said, with a twinge of pity. "It suits me, it does," she said desperately, staring at the flowers on her plate. *Jack loves me, he does*, she screamed inwardly. But they'd done it less often, of late.

"It's none of your business, Henry. It's the fashion, being slim, you don't understand. I mean what do *you* know about fashion?" It was something he couldn't really answer, sitting in his old grey flannels. "I only wear these for an evening at home." "Thanks very much," said Lorna.

They sat in a cold, busy silence. "I'm just going out for a jar," he said. "I'll put on my decent trousers." He went, got drunk, came back after midnight, too sad to fight, fell asleep.

When he'd slammed out she went into the hall and looked at herself in the mirror. Same as the day before it all started, trying on clothes in the sun. She ought to be looking much better, now, with her job, and some money, and her—*lover*. (He'd never quite *said* that he loved her. But all of the rest was recorded: she was special, and a lady, and *beautiful*—and—the *best*, and a lady, and special.)

It didn't add up to as much as all that, not playing it over this evening. He was a *feeling* man though, Jack Latham. And only *she* Lorna understood him. Henry had never said that, though she knew she did understand him (very deep inside her, buried not dead, a voice saying *Henry, Henry*).

He didn't appreciate her, Henry. His silly remarks about her weight. He never really looked at her body (but it did look thin in the mirror . . .). They just weren't close any more. She supposed they never would be again

(all things return in time   love returns in its flame . . .
all things are done and undone at once, at the burning end of time. . . .)

When you say two people are lovers, you say nothing at all about love. Jack liked power, and orgasms, and slim ankles, and red hair. For a bit he liked anything different, and an older woman was different.

But Lorna had definitions. She thought she was a decent person. She wouldn't have had an affair, not *Lorna*, if she hadn't been in love. Only deep and desperate love made a decent woman do *that*.

Love led to marriage, in the definition. It led to Jack marrying Lorna (his plump young wife and thin tired Henry blew off the page together).

It led, in fact, to disaster. He didn't mean to upset her. She had given him power, and orgasms, and done it whenever he'd asked her: she had opened her long slim legs, and shown him her bush of red hair. All this seemed enough to go on with. His shopping list was crossed off.

"People are starting to talk," he said one day in the pub. They went to a different one each time, and he filled her up with cider ("I expect you never touch beer," he said, the first time, and got her cider.) A cold hand touched her heart. "I think I'd prefer . . . white wine." They looked at each other, warily. "You don't want to mix them," he said. "I know what I want," she said, stubbornly. *"We used to drink wine at home."* He got her some warm white wine. "I'll have to go back in a minute," he said, tapping his digital watch. "It's been noticed, see, you and me. I'm not supposed to have favourites." (It was noticed at the very beginning, since he told his crony the storeman. The bet he had had with Freddy was a couple of pints of beer. It was worth a couple of pints of beer, the red of her pubic hair. Only a couple of pints of beer, the burning red of her heart.)

The publican shouted "Time." It was time to make a clean break. . . .

"I love you, I love you, it's true!" screamed Lorna outside on the pavement, half running to keep up with his firm cold strides, hair blowing wild, didn't care what she looked like. In the end at the cross-roads she caught him by the arm and Jack turned and shook her off like an insect. "Listen to me. Will you stop, or not. If you won't stop this rubbish you're out of a job. Now wipe your eyes or go back on the bus!" "I love you, I said, *I LOVE YOU JACK!*" "That's *your* business. I never asked you to."

> *I saw the teardrops falling as the last goodbyes were said*
> *'Twas the sorrow of a parting all must learn. . . .*

There was a policeman looking nosy on the other side of the road. "All right, now stop," Jack said, his voice softer. "I loved you too, in a kind of a way. Only it can't go on, us . . . *loving each other*" (he squeezed it out quickly, past his distaste). "I'll never forget you, honestly, Lorna."

I heard the sailor promise to the lassie now in tears . . . .

"You can't stop seeing me. I'll just go crazy."

"It's just at the moment. There's been so much talk. If we let it quiet down, well who knows what will happen . . . .

when the fields are white with daisies perhaps I'll return . . . .

(That was clearly how you did it. She was quietening down now. Already it was memory, skin touching skin.) The sobs were irregular, she straightened her hair. "I'll be quiet if you take me back in the car." He patted her bottom as she got in. She got out her compact (he hated those plastic ones) and looked at her scrawny little face in the glass. "My God," she said flatly and brokenly," my God." She was thinking *no wonder, no wonder he's leaving me.* But she rubbed at the mascara for a second with her hankie, and bit her lips so the blood came back. It wasn't so bad. *At least he touched me.*

Lorna was sure at any rate that her pain and rage were unique. Those carving knives in her heart, the blazing red of the slices. She had loved him with all her heart, and now she had turned into meat. No pain could be like that, there had never been pain like that. For a while pain was all she had, and she pressed her heart on the blade. Her pain was her precious secret, the thing that was purely Lorna.

She'd never liked Henry's mother, red-faced and bitter and blowsy. She wasn't a snob exactly but Rose was exceptionally common. And *ignorant*. Lorna wasn't a scholar, but at least she could spell and do grammar. While the thing with Jack had been on, Lorna could hardly bear to see her. Thank God that Wolves was so far away, and the sort of home Henry grew up in. They had never really got on, but now Rose symbolized something. How could Lorna be the manager's lady with a mother-in-law like Rose?

When people look at each other, they only see how they differ. Lorna would not have been pleased to know that her perfect pain was shared. She would have called you a filthy liar if you'd said it was shared by Rose. *How could a pain so slender and fierce apply to tipsy old Rose?*

It was cooking sherry, Rose told herself, carrying home the brown bottles, litres of cheap British sherry. They gave a little lift to the

146

trifle, or a big one to Rose when she was down. It had started when Frank came back from the war and moved into George's old bedroom. The funny thing was it was only long after he was gone that she started to realize. The fact of it was, *she loved him*, as soon as it was too late.

She wasn't sentimental, she told herself, but in the long dark nights in the shelter . . . she started to remember the good times, going dancing with Frank in his first-ever suit, and the bright pink, tight-blossomed roses he bought her when she had George. Then it went downhill, of course . . . but then, things *do* go downhill. But he did say "I love you" once when he was doing it, years after George, a kind of new beginning, and shortly after, she fell pregnant with Henry. The beginning went wrong, and the holiday.

She thought about all of it, why she never answered, she was pleased he had said it but the words didn't come, sitting with her eyes closed in next door's Anderson (there wasn't really room and they didn't really want them, but Rose had a very thick skin). She would certainly rather be here with the Potters than under the table in her kitchen in the dark. The table was as strong as an eggshell any way, it shook something awful when Frank carved the meat.

When Frank carved the meat. That image was another one she polished till it gleamed, in the long dark years he was away. He was hardly ever home after that holiday abroad, but he never missed dinner on Sunday. It had to be a meat and three veg, and they had to make an effort to look nice. He got furious once when she sat down to eat in the pinafore she cooked the lunch in. He himself always wore a clean white shirt, and his hair glossy wet, slicked down. (In the dim distant past which smelled of carbolic, all the small Franks had been dressed by rote . . . but Rose never liked him to speak of his past, she felt that it let them down. It reflected on *her*, on Mrs Rose Ship, if her husband had been . . . she swallowed, forgot it. *The Ships were the equal of anyone in England.* And her husband had *standards*. He was almost a gent.)

He would keep very quiet, very concentrated, the steel shearing down though the meat with a great pink sigh like a hand stroking silk, each slice curling smoothly and then lying down, as if it was still alive. When Rose cut the joint on her own, and she tried to when they were first married, she ended up with scruffy lumps

147

and tufts of this and that, hacked chunks where she'd just lost patience. On the other hand, useless lace hankies of flesh, frilled things nobody wanted. With Frank they were regular as leaves of trees (telling her something; *in the dream they fell . . .*).

The truth was, saying it, saying it at last, telling the darkness, *she loved him*—telling the darkness with him far away, *on a voyage to a port beyond the sea.* The damp cold nights were full of fretful movements, you didn't have to think about the mice or the spiders because it was a man's job to see to the vermin and Frank—*she loved him, the truth was she loved him, oh Frank, Frank*—was away. Would he be back, *when the fields are white with daisies?* His dream image promised *I'll return.*

She had never been able to get out the words even when they were teenage sweethearts, somehow. She didn't have to: *he* had the words, he was full of words, bursting, then. Full of whirls and tumbles of words and wild passion, telling her of things that she couldn't take in, beaches and islands she had never seen. (And she couldn't believe that *he* had, either. His past to her was an uneasy dream. No one else in this town had been a sailor. No one else had grown up . . . *where he had grown up.* How come she had married an . . . *oh, go to sleep.* She just wanted life to be normal.)

The funny thing was she half liked what she hated, his hidden strangeness, not being like the others, the mad things he told her, sometimes, in bed, all the time at first, then more rarely, never, pictures of things which came into his head which were not like anybody, never knowing quite what to say in return, so "Give over, I'm trying to sleep," she would say, though half of her wanted to hear more wonders, more details of the snow which he said he could see which was all black and white like Mrs Simpson's chessboard and the little pieces were people, naked, who were suddenly crying and falling off the board

(yet the board had been perfect, his vision of the future, a radiance chequered with dark life and detail, black lines of glittering wire ran across it which was people laughing and talking and crying, words from one side of the world to the other, and other dark lines which were rock curves diving, the glittering cold black back of the world writing words which were "endless" or "stillness" or "peace" on the white which was sun breaking light into whitenesses, bleached white peacocks spreading their tails, blazing white rainbows in frozen fountains

the board had been perfect, his vision of the mountain)

But people were crying and falling off the board: "What into," she asked, "where would we fall to, Frank?" and he said "It's just dazzling blue, all round it, at night it looks black but it's blue when we fall. *If* we fall, Rosie. In the dream we fell." That she never forgot. *In the dream they fell.*

Though it wasn't her vision she saw it as her own, long long afterwards, thinking of her husband, thinking of the way things were coiled in his brain, of the blue of his eyes, how it darkened or was empty, but it always called her, that absent blue. It somehow linked up with the way little Henry stared out of the window for hours and hours, after the telegram came about George: and it linked up with how she would stare out of the kitchen, mornings, after long nights in the Anderson, blue after the blackness, the square taped panes, glad to be alive, to be still on the chessboard, wondering where was he, how free and how far. *(Where are you, Frank? Do you know I love you?)* Wondering if his blue eyes saw the same blue.

In which case, she thought, it connects us, doesn't it, the hole he once dreamed we fell into. Maybe George is there too, maybe Henry can still see him. It all melted together, as she stood at the sink with her mop in the air, standing dreaming who never stood dreaming before . . . he was probably right over there, perhaps waving, behind ranges and ranges of waves and then hills, that dim purple colour, they melted together . . . . "I love you, Frank," she replied, years later, saw mountains, oranges, dazzling blue.

The image turned into a man, dog-tired and tense as a telegram, black and strange against the lamplight, *not Frank, not Frank already.* . . . Come knocking one night with a pile of baggage that swiftly turned into dirty washing, *not Frank, it couldn't be, couldn't be Frank* as her plans for a proper arrival some two weeks later became waste paper, yellowing paper, as imagined speeches became stupid ghosts which sighed in the silence in unchanged sheets *(didn't know you were coming)* sad pillowcases *(I'm sorry)* dirty washing *(I'm sorry, I'm doing my best)* crumpled silences, dead dreams: dead tired, *he's sorry*, he's back, dead tired, with the washing and thinking, going round and round, I remember each

149

letter, I remember every phrase—*he's sorry he's back*, his back in our bed, dead soldiers, sorry, dead letters, dead dreams.

Where there was love, it would find a way, she told herself, staring in the bathroom mirror. He stayed seven nights in their bedroom, and didn't make love to her once. She was shy, and after three nights she was angry, having looked forward, kept herself pure (*and enough of them didn't, Frank Ship*, she thought, forgetting in her virtue that nobody had asked her).

The first six nights she didn't put her hair in curlers, to please him, which meant she looked a sight all next day. Flat as grass, and depressing. It was all for nothing, since he merely mumbled something he wouldn't repeat, a tired hopeless mumble, turning away. The seventh night she compromised, wore her best nightie but curlers as usual, and *Summer Fieldes* perfume she had hoarded all war (it smelled a bit strange but it hadn't lost its strength). It was nice going to bed smelling like a garden.

He went to bed early after sitting all evening staring through the window, brushing her away when she went to pull the curtains, "Give over," he said, and his eyes didn't see her. "What's the matter with you," she said, but flatly, holding herself back, not like in the old days, you had to make allowances, they said that on the radio, said it was hard for the men coming home. *And what about us?* They sat there, dark.

"Give over," he said, once again, in bed, in the tense early hours of the morning. The last trains shunting, shunting down the line. She had waited, heart beating, her dry eyes open, listening to his breathing, had he gone to sleep? She would give him till for ever, till two o'clock even, giving him a chance to get his nerve back, maybe . . . she would wait until three, if he didn't fall asleep. *I'm not old, Frank*, the voice inside her whispered.

She had powdered her nose before bed-time, though the shine would have worn through by now. The moon poured through the cheap checked curtains, black-and-white check, it was really for table-cloths. She got it in a Summer Sale, just before the War. . . . *Just before the War.* You could never see the future. She had him all the time, and she really didn't care. But now he was exotic, and filled her with desire, lying there separately, chequered with moonlight.

The clock ticked horribly, mocking her, and his breath came quiet, too controlled. *If he's not asleep, why doesn't he touch me?* the

150

loneliness inside Rose screamed. Once his foot shot out and touched her, but he pulled it away in an instant. "I'm not a bloody German," she whispered, near tears.

When the clock chimed three she nerved herself, forced herself, stretched out her big right hand and after an unbearable number of clock-ticks landed it gently, very gently, she was sure, on his arm which was lying on his tummy, and started to stroke him, his body, her body, her Frank. He was suddenly rigid, like a switched-on machine.

"Did I wake you . . . *love*," she said, and to her her whisper sounded wonderfully tender, and the "love" came out almost natural, astonishing her, who had never called him "love" in his life.

"Can we love each other," she whispered, then forgetting the kids and everything in the world except the sharp new thing in her throat which would choke her if she couldn't express it, she said in a tense thin voice they had neither of them ever heard before "Can we love each other, Frank, can we be with each other, I'm dying for you Frank I am. I have missed you, Frank. *I . . . love . . . you*." But her hand had stopped moving when his body went rigid and she waited with her breath trapped tight.

He took her wrist and for a split second she thought it would be all right. Then she understood the movement and her heart lurched low in her ribcage, *no*. But he lifted her arm from his body, dumped it back on her own, moved over to the furthest part of the bed and then burrowed down into it away from her, as if he would tunnel through the mattress and then through the wall and be gone. *"Give over, will you,"* he said, the words muffled. *"Give over, I can't, I just can't."*

In the end when his breathing deepened to snoring she let the tears flood into the blackness, *People can die on their own*, she thought, *you can die from being too alone*, and the thought made the tears flow more thickly, *don't let me die on my own. . . .*

By the time it started to get light her tears had grown cold on the pillow. She felt there were no more left. It was going to be a beautiful day, which was an insult, the blueness, the beauty. What good was beauty if life was empty. It was the hole you fell into, the hole in his dream. The aching blue of the hole you fell into. It didn't join them, then, after all. You were one on your own again, after the fall. The endless emptiness of waking alone.

151

But is it worse to die on your own than to die as the whole world dies? Screaming and dying together. Love driven out by fear. Tumbling over each other as the whirlwind shakes the garden. Is fear stronger than love?—climbing on top of their loved ones. Climbing on top for air, and not for the act of love.

Angela grew up aching for perfection, sure she would never marry. She *had* to look for perfection, driven by shame for her mother. Everyone knew the truth. To go with a man *like that*. . . . She would rather be alone. Being alone wasn't bad. No, she would never marry, though she *would* find perfect love. . . .

(couples cleave to each other, to reach the end of the story)

In her first year at Bedford College she decided sex wasn't so bad. The first time it hurt like mad, on a sofa after a party. She was full of dope and wine but her nerve-ends were still alive. The man was a married tutor who wasn't excited by virgins. He failed to fall in love, or telephone the next day. Or telephone the next week, and so in the end she called him. By then five weeks had gone by. "It's good to hear you," he said. "We're just off on holiday. Taking the kids to the sea." The following Monday she saw him in the distance, walking to work through the Park. She veered off down by the artificial lake, trying very hard not to cry.

She looked at the tall white swans, their progress, impossibly stately. Their two necks bent together, making shapes with meaning, white words. With her silly scuttling walk, and the wind tying knots in her hair, and the water cold on her cheek—she felt stupid, and painful, and young. She wished that she was a swan. Or she wished that she could die. What if he'd told other lecturers . . . don't think about it, don't think. Empty blue sky, that ache . . . she must have been the oldest virgin . . . wincing, holding her ribs. You could trust your own arms to protect you. All the same , she shivered in the wind. You couldn't keep yourself warm.

"You look freezing," said a voice behind her. She jumped: it was Andrew, a man from her year. She felt he must have heard her thinking.

Yes, she would go for a coffee. Yes, she would go to the cinema that evening. And went to bed with him painlessly.

152

Lying in bed with an aching head and his heavy arms around her, she thought some more about love. It wasn't a search for perfection. It was trying to keep out the cold. The cold blue wind from the edge of the world which shivered with loss and unknowing. It was trying to keep out emptiness, the aching blue in the Park. It was trying to make the pain of glimpsing perfection less pure and sharp: swans on their blazing images, bliss of their bright beaks meeting. Very very far from that meaning, his heavy arm kept out pain. She wondered about her mother. It was probably time to forgive her. What kind of pain had the man from the shop made bearable for Lorna?

Couples cleave to each other to reach the end of the story. The student Angela met in the Park stayed with her just over a year. When she knew it was all going wrong she started to think that she loved him. She wept as she wrote him the letter, walked to the post like the end of the world. However, reason prevailed . . . she mourned him for only four days.

On the fifth day she felt a lot better and went to work in the library. It was always too hot in the library. She slept with the books piled round her. Her cheek was pressed on the blotter. She dreamed she was having his baby. In the dream she cried with contentment. To her horror she woke up crying. The man in the next-door carrel was staring across at her. "Are you all right?" he whispered. He had beautiful sun-green eyes, and a generous sweep of black lashes. Angela recognized *soul* (though *beauty*, of course, didn't matter).

John was an honest man and did have a soft spot for beauty. Her less-than-ethereal calves were safely tucked under the desk. What he saw was a pale startling face, sandy lashes dusted with sunlight, the whole at an angle of ninety degrees, resting in the crook of her elbow: on a red-gold nest of bright hair. He watched her asleep for several minutes. The mystery of strangers sleeping. . . . Tears trickled down the bridge of her nose. They stayed in separate drops on the desk, little floating worlds of love. Islands of sun and mercury, and *he* was falling in love. . . . He wanted to put his arms around her and stroke her soft thick hair. He would wind himself in her hair, he would rest his head on that softness . . . and he wanted to keep her safe. He wanted to make her his own. Her freckles like golden dust-motes, her arms with their velvety down. On the blotter she had written ANGELA, in

153

bold blue childish writing. Next to it *Andrew*, small. In his chest
something started to hurt in the darkness, the distant aching of
drums.

But some people get what they want . . . that's what makes it
confusing.

I love you. I'll love you for ever. I'll love you for ever, you only. It was like
that for John and Angela; they managed the trick together. They
longed for each other equally and their hearts beat out the same
time. Both of them wanted *for ever*. Both of them wanted *you only*.

Four years after that day in the library Angela woke in bliss. His
head would be back on the pillow. He had been away two weeks,
in the Austrian alps for a conference. With the new black mood of
the papers she had felt intensely alone.

Lying in the dark afraid. *Soon they might both be dead.* She longed
for him every night, lying in their attic flat, not switching off the
comfort of the light till the night outside grew lighter. Staring at
her things, her obsessions, staring at the peopled wall. Wishing
she could see the future (what if he had gone for ever?)

She shouldn't have felt so alone. The flat was full of her family.
Great-grandma Cleaver's old dresses. Grandma Ship's old fur
(Rose said she'd never wear it. "You don't want that funny old
thing." But it smelled sweet and sad, lost flowers, lost summers.
They used it as an extra blanket.)

The family were there on the pinboard too, a very rare family
photo. They were all lined up for a wedding, one of Aunt Clarrie's
plain daughters. (Clarrie was delighted hers were all married and
so far Lorna's wasn't. "Petula was married at Angela's age." "But
Angela's going to be a doctor." Lorna was improvising wildly. She
wished her daughter would get wed. It was hard to explain to the
family that they were just living together. "A doctor, is it, then,
now. I thought she was going to be a writer." "Not that sort of
doctor, ignorant. There are *philosophical* doctors.")

The family were drunk enough to be natural and the lines
slewed wildly crooked. Some faces were out of focus, some of
them moved or blinked. Her father and mother were cuddling.
Guy had his back to the camera. Prunella was showing a mile of
black leg, and shaking it, too, at the camera. Rose hadn't even been

invited but she always had a thick skin. She was there with a fortress of bottles, lined up under her chair. She thought she had been discreet, but the sun had come out and caught her.

Ragged as they were, the despair of the photographer, there was something there that moved Angela. There were absences, there were differences (Guy pulling George's hair) . . . but also , there was a likeness. Something linked them all, some pattern. Something comforting, like the weight of past time, said that nothing final would happen. That time would always lurch on, that there would be time to grow in . . . *all that they need is time. Families can grow in time.* She might be part of the growing . . . dreams of having John's baby. . . .

Her typewriter waited on the table with neat rows of books against war. Goodwin's *K/V Papers*, Akizuki's *Nagasaki 1945* . . . Hersey's *Hiroshima*, Cox's *Overkill*, *Four Minutes to Midnight* by Nicholas Humphrey, Thompson's *Protest and Survive*. . . . Angela knew she should protest more, but she sometimes felt frozen with fear. And fear gave a glow like virtue, *nobody felt it like her*. . . . She was trying to write her book against war, but *oh—she just wanted John here*. The book might never get written, and sometimes she didn't care. *Just to have his arms around her*, something to squeeze out fear . . . *What could you do in four minutes? Next* year she would do more. . . .

There were other things on her pinboard, other things leaning against it. *Dying, in Other Words* by Maggie Gee, open at the last few pages. Things which helped her to write; things which *would* help her to write, if the writing really started . . . two poems by E.J. Scovell, "The Evening Garden", "Strollers in a Park". Pictures of those she admired, a haunted Einstein, Russell. Virginia Woolf, near the end, when the planes were about to come over. Beckett, tense as a bird. A poster, *"For Life on Earth"*. The picture was a great blue eye. The iris turned anxiously skywards. Close up, the iris was the globe, the lovely fragile blue world. Continents and seas gleamed blue against the black of the lashes. In the corner of the eye, a small tear.

But how did you make people care? Staring up aching, afraid. Soon they might *all* be dead. She *knew* she ought to do more.

No use seeing what was happening if you didn't cry out against it. . . .

The truth was she'd cried in the past two weeks but the tears were just for her. She felt guilty but it didn't stop her. It had always been the same. People saw wars erasing their world but they grieved for just one name. A postcard she loved on the pinboard went back to the First World War. It showed a sailor in his blue uniform, saying goodbye to a girl. Behind them the wide blue seas, that empty, aching sky. Inset in the top right corner was the lovers' dream of the future. They walked in a field full of daisies. Millions had died in that war. Yet they kept on dreaming of love, cared more about that than survival. She'd found it in a cupboard at home. Perhaps it had been Joanna's.

One of their walls was covered with black-and-white photos of them together. She longed for his real live body, seeing them locked in print, the sharpness of sun on his browbone, his bare arm under her chin. Here they lie under a weeping willow, black-and-white waves behind them. That must have been in Kew Gardens. The day they went there with Mum. She was like a child with her shoes off, sniffing the flowers and dancing. Happy to be on her own, while they lay close and watched her. She was healed from Jack by then, and Ange from hating her mother. (*Wholeness returns in time. All that they need is time.* . . . She was only twenty-four, and in time would have grown less selfish. . . .)

Ange has Joanna's old dress on, grey-white lace and satin. He'd said, "You look like a bride." Sometimes she wished things were simple. A beautiful dress, vague stains on the silk like shadowy love affairs clinging. . . . It was luxury, it was memory. Lorna took their photo lying on the grass. "Oh Mum, you haven't got it straight." "It's you two *not sitting straight* . . . " They are printed on white like a word. The sky is complicated cloud.

That criss-cross grid of their images charred its way on to his absence. What was the use of such ghosts? Memory is not a comfort. . . . Lorna would have agreed, when the memory of Jack was her world. Living in a world that had vanished, staring out of Angela's window. That much Rose would have granted, tipping the cheap brown bottle. Looking for the ghost at the bottom, in the bitter-sweet gust of dregs. All they could see was emptiness, the endless road of the story . . . wishing the story was over. Wishing the end had come.

Wishing their love would come back, so the heart would have a home.

Lovers, of course, may live to rue that they longed for the end of the story. Bodies longing for bodies may find that they lie in a row.

The fearful lack of meaning in their final nakedness. Aches which melt in a blaze of pain, the final homelessness.

Four years after that day in the library Angela woke up one morning. One eye first, then the other. Sun on big cotton daisies. The burning gold of the centre, the pool of light in your iris. Petals as white as snow. (He had managed to fix an afternoon off, and climb up above the snow-line. "I know how much you love heights . . . one day we'll go together.") Opening both eyes now. (He had brought her back a small chess-set: small enough for a handbag. "You can take it all over the world." "We had one at home, Grandma gave us one, but nobody played . . . will you teach me?" Lying there thinking, *I'd like to learn*.) The light was a blessing this morning.

The warm kind colour of skin. His sleeping hand on his sleeping cheek, his sleeping body beside her. A great tide of warmth rippled through her. *Back in their place one morning*. He was smiling a little as he slept. He looked so young and so naked. The trust of sleeping with someone, letting them see you sleeping. Letting them see you stir in dream, the smile of the very last secret. A secret you don't even know yourself when the watcher wakes you up.

"John." He twitched, then rolled over. His breathing went back to normal. Beautiful breathing animal, now lying sprawled on his back. Having pushed away the daisies, his bare chest swelling and falling, no hair on the smooth gold skin. She loved him for his hairlessness. So much more naked, smooth skin. *Skin touching skin, hearts beating*.

She touched him very gently. "John." He was suddenly wide awake, and in a split second was holding her. "Hmmmmmallo, beautiful Angela." His smile was a total smile, as a cat smiles with its whole body. He seemed to wrap himself round her twice, so they were locked in each other. Her head was pressed to his shoulder: she kissed the curve of the bone. He was licking her neck, very gently. The sun poured on to his back. In a minute he reached behind her and pulled the sheet over their heads. Light poured brilliantly white through the summer cocoon which held them. "I'm ever so glad you're back," she mumbled into his shoulder. "I hated saying goodbye." "But you knew I'd be back in a fortnight," he whispered through her warm hair. "Want to be with you all the time," she said, and tears pushed up with meaning it. Happiness blurring the view, the miles of brilliant snow. Happiness blurring the view, the miniature figures falling. . . .)

He wound himself in her hair, rest in a soft world floating. The thing he had always wanted: some people get what they want. The bedspread stretched on the floor, miles and miles of white daisies. A postcard had fallen beside it. The sheet wove round their joined bodies. The bodies lay in the snow, the stainless, innocent snow.

> I stood once in a harbour as a ship was going out
> On a voyage to a port beyond the sea.
> And I watched a blue-clad sailor as he said his last farewell
> To the lassie who loved him most tenderly;
> I saw the teardrops falling as the last "goodbye" was said,
> 'Twas the sorrow of a parting all must learn;
> And I heard the sailor promise to the lassie now in tears
> "When the fields are white with daisies I'll return."

The Japanese called the pleasure quarters of their cities "floating worlds". On the edge of the everyday city, acres of crowded streets . . . lanterns winking all night at the gilded tails of the dragons, girls who swung like fireflies in their tiny summer cages . . . through the lattice-work gates you saw delicate pools where laughter and incense floated. Islands of earthly love . . . if you closed your eyes, it was heaven.

When the Americans came to Japan after the Japanese surrender, the MPs were sent to post OFF LIMITS signs in the pleasure quarters of Tokyo. Yoshiwara was forty square acres of shimmering, floating world. But when the MPs got there, they found only black shells of buildings. The floating worlds had been charred to nothing by steady incendiary bombing.

Girls were shipped to the Yanks in trucks, since the floating world was gone. New centres of pleasure with different names sprang up for the GI lovers. The *Big Tits* bar in Yokohama, the *Hard On* cafe in Tokyo . . . love was mostly for Americans, marching on down the tunnel.

They never saw the *hibakusha*, creeping back into this chapter.

And Japanese marriage-brokers refused to deal with *hibakusha*. If your skin had been scarred, you could never touch skin again. Women stopped menstruating, the little fish died in semen.

But some of them did have children. Love produced mutant children. Some of the children had heads so tiny there wasn't room for a brain.

There was only one world after all, only one narrowing chapter.

Loveless children push blindly on down the narrow tunnel alone.

9 Chapter of the Loveless

Guy didn't know about love. Guy had never *had* any love. As a child he had tried to get some from his mother, but she had run out, run dry. In the weary process of growing up he had tried every member of the family. Porker sometimes pretended to like him, but Porker didn't count.

Guy ached for tall blonde air hostesses in sparkling uniform. He always ached for vague plurals because he couldn't get *one*. No girl had ever been nice to him (he had never been nice to a girl). Girls were silly and nasty, and much too big for their boots. They ought to be kept in uniforms: the boots were a good idea. They would have to salute when they saw him, and bring him cups of tea. Later, the fantasy grew into a Concorde full of tall blondes. By now they were all older women with sleek short golden curls. They had to be older than him since he wasn't sure what to do. Their job would be teaching him, humbly, gratefully, doing it one after another.

Guy felt the nearest thing to love (hot cheeks, chest swelling with longing) for Big Ray, and his son, and the Party: the New British Empire Party. For a future free from coloureds. It made you feel strong, hating coloureds. There wasn't enough for him in this rotten snivelling little country. In his rotten snivelling home. So how could there be any spare for *them*?

Guy was in love with being strong (which he wasn't), then

people would have to obey you. He could make them love him, then. His hopeless mother and sister. Not that he'd need *them* then. But their faces somehow lingered. He would keep them just long enough to make them . . . *worship* him. Then he'd get rid of them, quick.

In any case, they weren't satisfactory. His sister's bare feet, and weird clothes. His mother all vague and scruffy. He had given up hope of his father. You couldn't call his father a father. He wasn't what you'd call a man. All skinny and quiet and weedy, and . . . the *awfulness* when he was drunk. So you wouldn't be all that surprised if that filth about his mother were true. But Guy still couldn't accept it. Not possible, not his mother.

When he thought about that, he felt sick, and a queer desire to cry. She was getting on a bit, his mother. To let another man see her . . . he was ashamed that a man outside his family should see how her tummy stuck out.

Imagining them, doing *that*.

Guy thought about *that* all the time. He didn't enjoy being young. He wanted to be big enough to *show* them, to make them take notice of him. No one took notice of Guy, and no one made a fuss of Guy. Looking in the mirror as a very young child, Guy could quite well see why.

His nose bent over to one side of his face like a funny thin banana. One day he thought it looked less crooked. Then he saw his whole *face* was bent over. And his skin was a yellowish colour. And his eyes were too close together. The worst thing of all was his mouth. He wished he could have changed his mouth. His mouth was set in a permanent smile which his nose turned into a sneer. It was just because of the bend, coming where you didn't expect it. Awful to be born looking bent. He wished he could get himself straightened. He would close one eye and half close the other, and pretend in the glass he was straight. It wasn't very easy to do, but sometimes he thought he had managed. He actually looked pretty handsome, once sight was blurred to a crack. And he might grow straighter with age. Like George was growing less fat. He was sorry that George was growing less fat since that made him harder to get at.

George was to grow very tall, some seven inches taller than Guy was. "An inch or two," Guy grudgingly admitted. He didn't grow suddenly straight.

161

There was only a year between the brothers but they were never in time. Guy was obsessed with sex when George was obsessed with religion. George was busy growing tall while Guy grew bandy and spotty. It was torture sharing a room.

Guy's body grew bigger all at once, though not as much bigger as he wanted. His mother had nailed the mirror to the wall in her usual haphazard fashion: roughly at shoulder-level, so to see your face you had to bend at the knees. This was almost ideal for looking at your penis if you stood on Guy's bed just beside it. You could get a view that was just framed penis, snug between the top of the thighs. Like that, it looked frankly enormous: it made Guy hot with pride.

He only dared masturbate twice a week when George was at confirmation. Even then he had the chair against the door, and turned the radio up loud to cover his breathing. His fantasies were always of violence. You had to *make* people do things. You had to have power over people. People never did things for love (at least they never did things *for Guy*) . . . they were down on their knees, and weeping.

It was really fantastic doing it, but afterwards he felt depressed. It left you with nothing you wanted to do, nothing to do all evening. It sometimes seemed to Guy that his penis was the only living part of his body. He wished he could live inside it. He had found a safe source of joy.

The rest of his body wasn't quite so impressive, but at least he couldn't look at it whole. The two-foot-by-one-foot-six mirror only showed him a cube at a time. His torso had grown much faster than his legs, though not quite so fast as his penis. His shoulders were broad but his chest was flat, and his ribcage pressed against the skin. He sported occasional spots so enormous he wondered if they might be cancerous growths. He felt them furtively to see if the lump under the skin was growing or shrinking. He was terrified of breaking the skin lest the cancer should creep elsewhere.

hatred will creep elsewhere   *if children's hearts have been broken*

Perhaps he hadn't very long to live. And early death would be a tragedy. His feet dug into George's bed, balanced precariously, liking the bed's bounce and sway as his penis rose and fell independently: wonderful machinery, heavy as a weapon, down

162

like a roadblock, up like a gun. Would be wasted if the cancer stopped him showing it to girls who would faint and whimper and scream. He knew, he'd been told, that girls liked large penises. If he beat the cancer, they would like his.

Girls were peculiar, though, and he couldn't make up his mind. They were either incredibly dirty or else not dirty enough. They were always very far away. And often they seemed to be laughing. One day, in the carrier bag where she'd packed her picnic for school, he found a paperback that Angela must have forgotten. *Sexus* by Henry Miller—the name made him twitch with surprise. He thumbed through it quickly and found it was just what he expected. Except that he'd never expected his *sister* would've read a book like that. He longed for her to come home so's he could get her for it.

She came home looking bored and snooty as usual, her long pale neck sticking bonily out of her jumper, not looking at anyone, making a sandwich from something revolting (she liked weird things like tomato and raw cabbage—just to show off, *in a sandwich*). She was humming, just under her breath, some miserable classical tune. When she went upstairs with her sandwich he was right behind her, staring at her pointed ankle-bones as her feet lifted one by one out of her horrible cheap-looking sandals. She never wore stockings. She never looked nice. Always secondhand clothes, funny colours. As if they were really poor. And everyone knew he was her brother.

"You've got dirty feet," he said, as she turned along the landing. She stopped and stared at him palely but didn't say anything. "You've got all mud on your feet. Only idiots wear sandals in winter." "I'm not cold," she said. "What's the matter with you?" She went into her bedroom and the door swung shut, catching his long tender nose. That released the bubble of spiteful pleasure and anger, knowing he would get her: he pushed in behind her without knocking, which normally he'd never dare, and as her annoying pale loose mouth opened he shouted "I know all about you! It's not just your feet! You're not so wonderful as you make out. You read dirty books—*really* dirty books—I saw it, I read it, it's horrible!"

But something he couldn't explain happened in the middle of his moment of triumph. When he started to talk about the dirtiness he realized he hated it, hated it, and hated to have found out that his sister was also like that: that she might be just like him, thinking horrible dirty thoughts as he balanced, grinning, on the dirty pink eiderdown . . . and his voice went funny and tears rushed hotly to his eyes and flooded on down.

Though he thought about it afterwards time and time again, clenching his fists and wrinkling his eyes in awful anger and shame, he could never understand what had happened. Ange put her arms round him: he couldn't remember her ever doing *that* before, not since she was little . . . . and that wasn't fair: she often cuddled George, and George was bigger than him. . . .

(people need to be touched, or else they grow thin and twisted . . . poison grows under the skin, when love never touches the surface . . .)

He wanted to tell her to fuck off but he couldn't get his breath back and another part of him splitting off somewhere just wanted to be cuddled and he buried his face. . . .

"You've gone crazy," she said, "poor little thing," (which stung him even as it made him sob more, quite helplessly, *yes, he was little, he was poor, nobody loved him and his sister was filthy*, snot dribbling horribly out of his nose as he gulped and laboured, *I'm only thirteen*) "what are you talking about? You must have found something the plumber left behind. Or something of George's. Oh dear, *don't* cry. Mum'll hear and think we're having a quarrel."

He kept shaking his head and looking down at the floor as he struggled for breath, *don't look at her eyes, don't look at her face, it's all soft and pitying*, big stricken eyes like the ones that she turned on George coming home with his knee all bloody or the next-door cat shut out in the rain . . . she didn't love him really, just felt sorry for him.

And he *did* hate Ange, he would always hate Ange, for not loving him when he—didn't-*not*-love her, once thought that he loved her. Talked about her to his friends. How she always came top at school and had poems in grownup magazines. And the Head Boy had asked her to the cinema, who everyone admired because he played for the County Schools First Eleven at football, but she was so stupid and—*stupid*—*hopeless*—*why have a sister who was stupid and hopeless?*—she *refused*, which no one could understand.

Raymond Perkins had started on George one break-time. George shouldn't even have been there. He was in the year above

164

Guy at school, though Guy was a whole year older. Mum had packed their lunches together, so George had come up to fetch his.

"Quinn fancies your silly old sister. But not enough to take her out. I 'spect that's 'cos she's so skinny. Why're you so fat then, Porker?"

George pretended not to hear, chewing on his chewing-gum. So Guy had to answer, of course. He never hated his family so much as when he had to defend them. His brother was a horrible embarrassment. He didn't even *look* like a brother. He was much too fat and his cheeks were too red and *everyone* called him Porker.

Raymond Perkins was a famous bully. Guy wished that *he* could be a bully. But bullies were always tall. Guy did his most worldly-wise voice.

"She's choosy, my sister," he said. "Me Dad says she's gointer be a beauty. She told Quinn she hasn't got time. I expect she'll go out with a Professor or someone. She's not interested in just *boys*."

"Your Dad doesn't know anything," growled Raymond. "Your Dad used to be a scrounger." He had stubbly red hair, yellow eyes. He was aided in being a bully by becoming adolescent at ten. He shot up to nearly six feet and his chest and thighs had filled out. In races on Sports Day he swept the board, a prefect trouncing the first years.

"I daresay Quinn just wants her to help him with his homework, actually. She's too brainy for a girl, your sister. And another thing about your sister. She likes niggers, your sister does. Your sister's a nigger-lover. That's why she doesn't fancy Quinn."

George got off the desk and walked out, bright crimson, leaving his lunch on the desk. "*My sister???*" shrieked Guy, incredulous, the thing was impossible, barmy. "You're round the bend. *My sister?* She's not interested in boys at all. She's only int'rested in books and things. I bet *you* like nigger girls."

This scene of three months ago flashed through Guy's mind as he tried to get his face back to normal. So maybe it was true what Perkins said. If she would read a book like *that* . . . if she was dirty she might do anything. He butted her away with his head.

"Stop telling fibs," he said. "I saw it, it's called *Sexus* and it's disgusting. And I know it's yours 'cos you'd written some things on it in red, that's why. So there."

She was smiling, which made him want to kill her. By

165

strangling, or beating to death. "Don't be silly," she said, "he's a famous author, though I don't think he's very good. You can read it if you want, I don't care. You might even enjoy it, who knows?"

He could feel himself doing something he only did every few years: a tide of blood swept over his face and neck and the sweat-glands pricked under his arms: he knew he must be blushing brilliant red, the colour George went so easily. She must have heard him panting next door, and the bedsprings twanging up and down. She was laughing at him, she must be. He would never, ever forgive her. He burned his love into the carpet; never, ever forget. There wasn't any love, there was hatred. The flowers were a crude bright blue.

"You're a . . . dirty bitch . . . and I'll tell me Mam . . . and I HATE YOU!" he screamed at the top of his voice, and ran out, slamming the bedroom door, just as Lorna's miserable "What's the matter *now*?" came sailing up the stairs to meet him.

Angela, shocked, eyes filling with tears.

You could never predict what would happen. Splits opened up in time. That day had seemed so ordinary, coming home, looking forward to her sandwich. Then the ordinary tore in two. Through the gap, a torrent of hatred. She sat on her bed, feeling sick. There was something wrong with that boy. There was something wrong with them all. There was poison just under the skin, though they sat there smiling and talking. You nearly forgot it was there: you would almost start to feel safe . . . then the teeth ripped up through the surface. She went and stared out through the window.

Families locked in their houses, pretending to love each other . . . none of them really loved Guy, so no wonder Guy hated them. It was dreary, hopelessly dreary. The clouds looked sad and metallic. Fences divided the lawns. Little packets that should have held love. They were sewn to the houses by flowers.

Close up there were holes in the flowers. Things had been eating the petals, wet slugs dragged round the roots. Good things were leaking away and bad things flourished and fattened. She drew the curtains heavily, heavily. *Never live in a family*.

(Ange wrote a poem that evening about the mystery of hatred. She put her whole heart and soul into it, and felt the whole world was there.

166

Most of the world wouldn't read it, and none of the world would care. Most of the world felt hatred as a physical fact, not a mystery. They felt it as bullets, or hunger, or flame: as people trying to kill them.

They thought of houses with longing, those who knew about houses. They thought of families with longing, those who had lost their families. *Two hundred thousand died at Nanking and didn't see hate as a poem.*)

What Perkins said about niggers would return to Guy months and months later, lying in bed with his aching spots in the hateful inhabited dark. It didn't matter about his sister, it was *principles* that mattered. They ought to be hacked into little bits if they went with white girls like that. Something nasty would happen to her, as well, if he could find time to arrange it. He enjoyed thinking what ought to happen to his high-and-mighty sister. He couldn't wait to be bigger (*he would never be quite big enough*. You can never be quite big enough, once you fall in love with power.) When he was bigger, things would be different. He wouldn't just dream about things. He would get some action, as well. He would . . . start to make things happen. And he didn't need *Sexus*, either, he thought, to get his machinery going (cautiously, in case George was awake . . . its sticky weight in the dark).

He was getting quite friendly with Perkins, now. Perkins' Dad was a butcher, a great six-foot-plus ox of a man who drank in the same pub as Henry. He kept two enormous Alsatians, and he *said* he kept himself fit, though when Guy sneaked a look at his stomach, pressing over the top of his trousers, he wasn't too sure about that. Mr Perkins, however, was so gigantic he could frighten you off with a look. In the shop he would flourish his blood-dripping knives, wave them about for a joke. Raymond said that every Sunday he sharpened and polished his knives. Guy thrilled to the thought of *that*. When *his* Dad was getting drunk and silly, Big Ray was polishing knives.

Guy managed to make friends with Raymond Junior by showing him how nasty he was. Guy had always had a real talent for making people feel bad. He wasn't a clever boy but in this respect he had genius. He had always felt small himself, and he learned to make others feel small.

He picked on all Raymond's enemies, which gave him quite a

large field. He could settle things with a word that would have wasted Raymond's muscle. Raymond appreciated that. He started to feel drawn to Guy. The fact he was little and scrawny didn't matter: Raymond didn't need friends his own size.

Guy gave him half of his sweets, and let him copy his homework (not that it helped a lot, copying Guy Ship's homework). "Did you and Ship work together?" Miss Baines asked timidly, still very new. "She's accusin' us of cheatin'," Guy declared, in outraged bravado. "Oh . . . no, it's not that," blushed Miss Baines, in confusion. "I . . . don't object to . . . co-operation." "She's accusin' us of co-operatin'," Guy told the class, who giggled. The subject was safely dropped. Raymond grinned, loose-lipped, at his friend.

One Sunday Guy went round to the Perkinses for lunch. Mrs Perkins was a great silent woman who wore extremely long skirts. Her flesh was heavy and damp-looking and her voice was dull and deep. She piled up Guy's plate with mountains of greasy impossible food: (warmed-up mutton for first course since "the Boss" was not at home, roast potatoes and chipped potatoes and piles of white bread-and-butter: she told him to eat up his meat, it would fill him out a bit. Make a man of him, same as Raymond. "And heaven help you," he thought he heard her add, under her breath. She had a funny sense of humour. She poked him in the ribs, sitting next to him. Raymond was fetching some squash. "You couldn't sell those to a Chinaman," she remarked, with grim satisfaction. Guy tolerated it all, smiling thinly and insincerely. He ate his pudding and potatoes and passed the bread over to Ray. You had to put up with women talking: they were all pretty stupid, women.

Around two they were both watching telly, hot and half asleep on the sofa. She had let them take their apple pie next door to watch the film. Then the door slammed hard, and Big Ray came in. He was noisier than usual, with bright excited eyes; swaying in front of the telly, he lurched and turned off the sound. "I think you've grown a bit," he roared at Guy. "Must be Mum's pudding. Make a man of you yet." Funny thing was, Guy felt really flattered when *Mr* Perkins said that.

His friend Raymond was watching the two of them anxiously, eager for Guy to make a good impression. Guy searched his brain, which didn't take long. "At home I've got a Bullworker," he said.

"My uncle sent it from Australia, and I never used it before. I think I'll start using it, now."

"Thass right thass right," mumbled Big Ray thickly, not listening as exactly as he might have done if he hadn't just taken in six pints of beer. "You gotta learn to look after yourselves. You gotta learn to look after *England*," he declaimed into the gilt-curled mirror, burping, but cuffed his son on the shoulder expertly just to make sure that he heard. "Yes, my son, it's you and your young friend here that we're talking to." He leered at himself in the glass.

Raymond thought his father was a god, but he also knew he was drunk. "Who's *we*," he said, "when we're at home." "You'll know in the end," said his father, grandly, eyes fixed on his mask in the mirror.

Funny clothes he had on, thought Guy. More like a teenager, really. Black leather jacket with a zip and pointed-toe boots and jeans. It was impressive, though, on a man so big. He looked tough and heroic. Sinister, even. And with lines in his face, kind of . . . *evil*. Thinking Big Ray looked evil gave Guy a queer kind of thrill. Guy meant to be evil too. Evil was stronger than good. He wasn't allowed to be good, since none of the good people liked him. But no one could stop him being evil. He smiled a small evil smile. Better than love was power. He would be as bad as Big Ray . . . he sneaked a look, while he thought about it, at the front of the strained blue denim. You couldn't see anything, really, but Big Ray's must be simply *enormous*.

He had an inspiration. "Mr Perkins," he asked, "you wouldn't show us your knives? . . . P'raps we could help with the polishing, Raymond and me."

Big Ray admired his reflection. His strong white teeth and flashing eyes. And the way his red eyebrows shot up and down. This was a face of character. "Show you my knives?" he said. "They're nothing. If you boys are interested, I've got some better things to show you . . . *if* you can hold your tongues, that is. *If* you both know what's good for you." Suddenly he was looking sly.

(In the background Mrs Perkins dropped two plates in the sink, and the crash of the china half swallowed her swearing. It sounded as though she said "Pigshit", but Guy was too absorbed to be sure.)

He took a deep breath. Big Ray had turned to stare at him.

169

"Young Guy," he intoned, red eyes going over him, down to his legs which felt very short and then over his arms which felt thin and bony and lastly a circuit of his head and chest, at this point nodding slightly as if something was decided, "are you what I would call a patriot, that's what I'm wondering. A *pay-tree-ut*," he added, for explanation. "You know what that is, I take it."

"You mean, liking Britain," stuttered Guy, trying hard. "Well yes, I think so. I mean, I do." "*ENGLAND*," roared Big Ray. "In the first place, you wanna start thinking about England. The British Empire, now that's different. The two sweetest words in the language, those are: *Brit-ish Em-pire*," he repeated, with relish, as if he was sucking a thickly-covered bone. "British Empire," gabbled Guy, encouragingly. "Yes, I know about that. British Empire."

"That's *right*," grinned Big Ray, and it might have been sarcastic. Or it might have been friendly, you just never knew. "You're a quick learner, aren't you, young Guy. There's a lot of brains in your family. So we are told, so we *hear*." It was true, of course, thought Guy, looking pleased, with Angela and George in his family. Though no one had ever thought *he* was brainy. But possibly this was his chance. Big Ray was bending over now so you could hear his heavy breathing. It was the sour smell of beer, though it smelled different on his father. Beer on his father was pathetic, but beer on Big Ray was strong. You could see the red hairs in his nostrils, too. His grin definitely *did* look sarcastic. It was very uncomfortable and very exciting, that leaning bulk of black leather.

"I'm just wondering, see, if you've got a few more brains than your sister," he hissed, taking Guy's shoulder in his huge freckled hand. "Yes," gulped Guy, but he answered at random, trying to smile with his teeth gripped tight with tension, staring at the furry red hair on those hands, staring at the bulging blue veins. "Because from what I hear," continued the butcher, taking in his son with a swift reddish flash, "your sister Miranda has got some funny friends. Got some funny *brown* friends, know what I mean?" He squeezed Guy's shoulder, pulling him closer, then released him with a chuckle, so Guy's neck snapped back hard.

"*Angela*," he gasped. "It's not Miranda, it's Angela. She hasn't. She wouldn't, Mr Perkins. She hasn't. She hasn't got any friends at all, Mr Perkins." His sense of injustice drove all the words away.

170

Raymond had gone rather pinker than usual and was giving his father meaningful looks. "No, Dad, it wasn't, that was ages ago. And anyway I might have got it wrong. In any case, it's not *his* . . . hasn't got anything to do with . . . what I mean is, *Guy's all right*."

"He is, is he?" leered Big Ray. "I'll take your word for it, son." He straightened up elaborately, to Guy's sighing relief, and moved in a queer high-kicking walk back towards the mirror. There was a muffled explosion from Mrs Perkins, who had come and stood in the door. Big Ray swung round towards her. "Atchoo," she said, very distinctly.

Pushing out his jaw at the glass, Big Ray repeated his word. "A patriot, is he? The lad says he's a patriot. Well, we're in need of a few patriots, these days." A fine spray of spittle caught the sunlight as he spoke. "What do you think of the Germans, eh, young Guy?" Guy thought quickly. He was a patriot. "They're our enemies," he said. "I mean, they were. In the War."

Mr Perkins sighed pityingly, and crinkled up his brow for the mirror. He was much more pleased than angry. Guy had made the expected error. "That was the opinion of *some*," (he used his debating manner). "Much . . . mis- . . . *presented*, our German brothers have been." He had a feeling he'd got the wrong word: a glance at Guy's habitual sneer was enough to confirm the impression. In fact Guy was just feeling puzzled that he'd got such an easy question wrong. "You've got a *funny face*," Big Ray snarled suddenly, leaning over Guy again.

Guy started to feel very unhappy. He had thought they were going to get on. "*Dad*", protested Raymond, shifting about on the sofa. "Leave him alone. He asked to see the knives. I'd like to too."

"So he did," Big Ray admitted, straightening, pirouetting, "so he did," and Ray's voice had the sudden liberality of the drunk. "You know who the enemy are, young man? I'll tell you this for free, and don't ever forget it. You got them in your schools, you poor little sods. If you're smart you can help us get rid of them too," he added, confidentially, white man to white man. Guy thrilled. It was going to be all right. That was settled, then. He was a patriot.

"We got 'em in the shops and the pubs and the schools and we got some in the next-door street! . . . and it won't be long before we got 'em on the bleeding doorstep, if we don't all wake up our ideas. *Over my dead body*," he declaimed at the mirror, gritting his big teeth and pricking his nostrils. That made him look like a bull, and the red hairs inside them showed.

"Do you two boys know what niggers are? And Pakis and jewboys and wogs and coons?" "They're the same thing," said Guy, unwisely, just trying to show he was smart. The great hand descended once more on his jacket, the great pink pores of Ray's face pushed close. "And what is *that?*" the big beery mouth demanded, pouring out gusts of hot breath.

Before Guy could answer (his mind had shrunk and frozen, a rabbit entranced by the smell of the fox) Big Ray answered for him, pushing him back against the sofa with every word. It was just Ray being emphatic, but Guy's shoulder tingled days later.

"They're *vermin*," he said, "that's what. They're the enemy within, that's what they are. They're the rats in the cellar. Dirty, greedy. Want to eat us out of house and home. Want to take what's *ours*," he insisted, releasing Guy suddenly, pointing to himself. "I know about rats. I'm a *butcher*. They have to be got rid of. Quickly. They have to be put down. Your father," he said, jabbing the air towards Raymond, with a virtuous nod, "your father, and others like him, have worked all their lives to make a decent living. Make this country a place to be proud of. And the streets safe places for decent women. Like your mother," he added, conversational, to Raymond.

Raymond looked doubtful. That was going too far. Even sex-crazed Pakis wouldn't try and rape his mother. She was fussing with the plastic flowers on the sill. Her face was turned to the window, a pudding of cold grey stone. It had sometimes occurred to Raymond that his mother had a damaged brain.

(She was staring out at the sky, the ache of the afternoon. It didn't answer your question, that kind of heavy grey sky. Would they always go on like that, would life always go on like that? If life was left to the men, she was sure life wouldn't go on. *Stupid old bugger*, she thought, as his voice droned on, *all acting*. A tide of pure resentment filled her: that they always had the power. They were just like babies, men. Inventing battles and fighting. It was pigs like him started wars. Then everything came to a halt. How dared they take them away, her secretive peaceful pleasures. Shopping in the market each week, the lovely bright polishy fruit. Stopping for coffee with Emily. Playing with Em's little girl. Going to bed very early, hot water bottle and library book. Asleep before Pig crashed in. He had left her alone, of late. She hoped had found someone else. Some fool would find him attractive. She would love to be on her own. Just as long as life could go on . . . those buggers, playing at armies. There was going to be a storm.)

all that we need is time   *people escape in time*

"And now," Big Ray was back on the attack, thunderous with drama, staring all round him, the black seas beating at his island throne, pacing up and down though the clutter was against him, two clicking paces forward, looking fierily over his shoulder, two clicking paces back, that funny stiff-legged walk. "If we don't make a stand, they'll be crawling all over us. Cocky, they've got. Commy lawyers sticking up for them. And white girls who ought to know better, smarming round them. And bloody vicars—and students—and" (spittle in a stream and a rubbish-emptying gesture of his hands) "*social workers*. . . trying to give them our jobs. And our national health. And our pensions. . . ."

Big Ray stared out of the window. Silence reinforced his power. The two boys sat wordless and waiting on the sofa, not so much as jiggling the springs. Big Ray stood square against the afternoon light, and his back said "against" to it all. His great leather bulk was very black against the glass, waiting and brooding, a man against the storm. Out there in the grey it was England: his garden, threatened, but home.

Guy was mesmerized by that back. The man was gigantic, a hero. His heart's tiny pocket bulged with love.

With the timing of a bar-room orator, the still hunk suddenly swung round. His voice was a machine-gun hammer. "We got to unite!" he blazed. Staring fiercely from one to the other. *It's me that he means*, thought Guy. "It's up to us now. Are you yellow? Raymond, my son: *are you yellow*?" Raymond wriggled a bit but his answering gaze was intense, without humour, and he shook his head violently.

(Mrs Perkins was sneezing again in the doorway, her big hand covering her mouth. "Don't you want no coffee?" she said to her son, but no one was interested in her.)

"Boys," he rallied his audience. "My boys. It's time for you to join us. Raymond," (his tone changed to a clipped, stern urgency, a man behind enemy lines) "go and put on the fire in the

173

workshop. And tell your Mum to make a pot of tea." There was a formal chain of command. She could have heard him perfectly well.

In the kitchen Mrs Perkins shuffled to do it, her corn-plastered toe showing clearly. Big Ray had bought her new slippers for Christmas, but she threw them away by mistake. "What's he on about?" she asked her son, voice as flat as ever, no hint of a question. Raymond didn't answer; he was busy. He was putting chocolate biscuits on a plate.

"You don't want to take no notice," she said, sounding almost alive. "He don't know what he's talking about." For her this was quite a speech. Raymond stared. His mouth was full of biscuit. Struggling to speak, he spat out crumbs. "What would *you* know," he said. "Were these for our tea? We're having them now."

"They *were* for your tea. I suppose you can have them. Only don't stuff them all on the spot. They cost money." The kettle had boiled, but she wasn't getting on with it. Her grey marbled face had a curious look. Sort of hanging on the edge of a life of its own, hanging on the edge of thinking. His mother was a fixture of the kitchen. There was something up. Her insides had gone funny. Perhaps it was the menopause thing they went on about, the horrible thing that old women got.

Her big hand was clutching at a tiny spoon with a blue crest of Margate on it. She pushed it through and through the sugar in a circle, and spilled some over the side. "You're rude," she said. "Like your father. Don't think I don't notice. Because I do notice."

"You don't notice much," said Raymond, untroubled, choking the second biscuit down his throat.

"As for what I notice," said his mother, taking her time. She switched off the kettle, turned round, and stared. She fixed those heavy dead eyes on his, long greyish whites under bulging eyeballs. Heavy dead eyes like poisoned fish. It wasn't comfortable, being stared at. A crumb had got stuck in his tonsils, and he coughed as vilely as he could. "As for what I *know*. You're right that I don't know much, my boy, and that's healthy. It's safer not to know too much about some of the things going on around here. And if you were as smart as you think, you'd take my advice, that's all."

"I think you've gone mental," Raymond said calmly. "Want to watch out. If me Dad heard that . . . if you can't even make him a

174

cup of tea, me Dad'll get fed up of you. You wanter watch out."

She watched his great back marching out of the kitchen. It was horrible, him growing so tall. She never wanted *that*, a great tall thing like Pig. She couldn't remember why she had him in the first place. She was sure she would have a nice girl. The first was a boy, stillborn at six months. And Pig had felt cheated, since he married her for that. As a girl she had planned to marry a vicar. But she had liked . . . *the other*, she had to admit. Till she got in the club, and got married, like a ninny. She supposed she had found Ray attractive, then. He was younger and slimmer, didn't have his own shop. But she never liked the way he *enjoyed* that job. It was something deep inside him that wanted to hurt. The bodies of dead animals didn't fight back. Once she found out his spitefulness, she kept very quiet. He liked dead bodies, so she offered him hers. He had plenty of those, so he wouldn't cut her up. But sometimes she wriggled, when he wasn't really looking. He'd got sloppy recently. She wriggled quite a lot.

Moreover, her sense of her husband had changed. She used to see him as a private torment. For the last two years though it wasn't just that. He was actually wicked: and barmy as well. He hid funny magazines under the tool-chest in the workshop. They were cruel and appalling, to do with whips and chains. She'd never dared refuse him but she tried to be repulsive, after she glimpsed what it was he really liked.

Their *minds* were so revolting. Men's dirty minds. And it was all to do with that, going on about darkies. To do with turning live things into bits of flesh you hurt. There probably *were* too many coloureds here, but all the same, they were people. The ones she'd met in shops and things she'd always found quite pleasant. But the British Empire lot were a bunch of dangerous loonies. She knew a lot about their plans, from listening in doorways.

She had *her* plans too, for when the boy was grownup (the excuse was getting weaker: he couldn't grow much bigger). She would pack up her things, and go to her sister. Her sister lived in Ireland which was far enough away. Then she'd go to the police and tell them all she knew: the things they would do to the coloureds. It must be against the Law. She believed in the British Law. Or send an anonymous letter. Or at the very least, run away and have no more to do with them. Nor her son either. They were welcome to each other. . . .

175

The menfolk thought she was stupid. *I know who's stupid*, she thought.

(But was she really so bright? Women hiding their secrets. Letting men go on cutting things up, hiding their pity and rage. Letting men eat up their lives, while they get weaker and older. Calling their passiveness patience, calling their weakness cunning. Letting their lives be stolen away in little slivers of yielding. One day there's nothing left: nothing inside that is living

   one day finally nothing left   died in the dark, still hiding)

Big Ray, in fact, had a bit on the side that he half intended to marry. She was tall and curvy, a dental nurse, and had long blonde hair, rather brassy. She spoke like an elocution teacher, except for when she forgot. She told him her hair was natural. That gave her hell with peroxide, bleaching the hairs down below.

He was hopeless in bed, as it happened. If anything his cock was small. Guy would have felt quite let down, if he'd seen Big Ray in the bedroom (on the other hand, Martha would have turned Guy on: the air hostess of his dreams). It wasn't just sex though, between them. As Big Ray explained to his pals. "She's got an inkling, has Martha. Never trust a woman with plans, but . . . you need a strong woman behind you."

The truth was, Martha knew everything. Big Ray had to impress her. Someone had to listen to his plans for the world, since he lived with a moron at home. Martha found his talk very boring, but she much preferred listening to sex. She had cultivated a listening face, both (plucked, bleached) eyebrows flying. She had two breathy exclamations, which she used more or less in turn. "*Ree-ly*," she would say, with wooden amazement. And 'Oh . . . Ra-ay . . . you're *ama-zing!*"

At first the money wasn't regular, but later he got into a pattern. Ten pounds under the daily paper, which she always left on the table. "Buy yourself something to turn me on," he would say, with a parody leer.

Everything fell into a pattern. Bleak little loveless patterns. Sex once a month in an oblong flatlet which smelled of hairspray and breakfast. And the ten pounds never went up. What were girls to do about inflation?

Guy with his longing for air hostesses was already part of that pattern. And the women, watching and waiting and counting their notes or their secrets. Bleaching their pubic hair and laughing out in the kitchen. Because the women escaped the men, because they were oddly evasive, the men felt frightened and chilled. It seemed they were on their own. Alone, in a hostile presence. But *whose were the cold eyes watching*? Who could the enemy be? Who made them feel so diminished? They must pin the enemy down.

In the sitting-room Guy could hardly breathe with excitement. A feeling of great things in the air. He tried to sit there without moving, afraid that something would go wrong. After all this time he had some friends. He got asked inside their house. There was something that for once he would not be left out of, something very thrilling going on. His hero stood staring out of the window, the bulk of a brave sea-wall.

"Young Guy," the big man intoned, "I can see you're a lad with ideas."

Guy knew he must be scarlet: blood pulsed in his temples. He felt he would burst if he opened his mouth. He had never been so happy. He clenched his fists tight.

Opening the door at that moment with the news that tea was ready in the workshop, Raymond stared at his friend very hard. "You all right?" he said. "You look as though you're going to have a fit." "I'm just hot," said Guy. "All the same, you look peculiar." "You boys interested or not?" snarled Big Ray over his shoulder, a sulky eighteen-stone prima donna, as he shouldered his way through the door. "Just comin', Dad," said Raymond. He would follow his father to hell. . .

or else they would all go to hell   screaming and burning and falling
black bodies, white bodies, male and female   all would burn equally well

Big Ray showed them his trophies. This is what they saw, in order: a dozen flick-knives, various, beautifully honed and oiled and maintained, every millimetre of shaft and handle shining, with adaptations, personal to Ray, each one explained in detail. Things which would stay in Guy's dreams. . . . A device for peeling back fingernails. It wasn't ostentatious, you wouldn't have guessed. "I haven't tried everything, of course," its owner confessed, with an air of shy pride.

Item, four coshes, lead-loaded. They made Guy gasp at the weight. "You'll be needing that Bullworker, lad, if you're going to be any use to us!" Big Ray's roar wasn't unkindly; he had taken quite a fancy to Guy. For today, while the six pints lasted. Item, cat-o'-nine tails, plaited leather. The lashes twirled out like human hair. "That's genuine Rhodesian," said Ray, as the boys watched it whistle through the air.

Boys will always love toys, and the best toys maim and kill.

The Japanese loved their swords: the samurai always wore two. The blades were elaborately lovely, razor-edges on soft metal centres, black *shakudo* on the sword-furniture with relief sculpture in gold. For centuries Japanese custom had said that menfolk should not wear jewellery. They could not decorate their own pale bodies but they painted and gilded their swords. Their swords were better than their bodies: their swords were all male power. The most beautiful were called *Kiku-go-saku*, stamped with the imperial chrysanthemum. Hard and sharp and bright as the sun, the grain of the metal gleaming. . . .

Against such blades, what armour would serve? The *oyoroi*—"great harness"—huge pantomime horses of numberless strips of steel and toughened cow-hide, laced up with silk and leather, wide-skirted, with antlered helmets and free-flapping arms. They made the men into lurching giants, emblems of force beyond harm. Every item of their decorum was written in the book of time. They were all religious men, and God was their Emperor. Behaviour had all been listed. No room for invention or error.

The Japanese Army went into Nanking with instructions from General Matsui. In their siege of the city they must "sparkle before the eyes of the Chinese . . . and make them place confidence in Japan".

Books of decorum go wrong, though weapons and armour look seamless. Commander-in-chief Asaka had an empty machine inside him. He sent out secret orders that all captives should be killed.

The men who had built Nanking had a special regard for departures. They dreamed of a city with ten great gates, and their names read out like a poem. There was the Water Gate, the River Gate, the Sun-Yat-Sen Gate . . . Gate of the Mountains, Radiant Flower Gate, Gate of the North Star, Gate of Tranquillity. Lastly, the Gate of Great Peace. So many gates to escape from, and so much time for the poem. But the cleverest plans go wrong, the most beautiful names disappoint you.

By the time General Matsui got to Nanking, all that remained was the horror. A war machine had run mad. All human machines had been shattered. There were five old men, berserkly weeping, in the French missionary compound. The wild dogs had recently grown very fat. The city was a smouldering ruin.

He could never reconstruct the Great Crime, never live down its shame. In the Japanese Army the siege of Nanking would be known as the Ten-Year Shame. But the shame of the Japanese doesn't matter. What matters is every scream.

Little junks and sampans trying to escape were picked off in a Japanese 'duck-hunt'. The killers were full of *sake*, making the little birds run. Watching the blood-stains spread on their chest, the dirty red waves on the water. Water Gate, River Gate, Mountain Gate, none of the Gates would open.

General Nakajima Kesago was "in charge of the public peace". He told the Chinese to surrender to "the mercy of the Japanese Army". Terrified, hoping their terror was stupid, they surrendered to this great mercy.

They were trussed with telephone wire. They were put in pens by the river. They were used to test Japanese weapons, those perfect, shimmering weapons. The weapons had grown more perfect, plainer, more fierce and streamlined than ever. Flesh for the bayonets, for samurai swords to shear through. The mangled and dripping survivors were prodded into great fires. There they fell on the blackened bodies of those who were burning before them.

The weapons had grown more perfect, but pain was impure as ever.

There were many weapons to test, and the military victims ran out. The Japanese soldiers grew bored, and boredom falls short of perfection. And so to regain their interest Kesago invited civilians to join them.

The Japanese buried them up to their necks, borrowing from Chinese history (Prunella should have warned them: *Be done by as you did*). Confucian scholars in 3 B.C. were treated the same way. Their heads endured kicks and catcalls till the bodies wasted away. But the twentieth century's not patient. We like our deaths sudden and bloody. Some of them were jabbed through with bayonets, some of them were trampled by horses. Some of them were doused with boiling water, some of them crushed by tanks.

The heads of most of the bodiless men were still when the maggots reached them.

The women were treated more kindly. They were taken away to be questioned. They were tied to beds as permanent fixtures and probed by hard male organs. They didn't have anything to answer, except "Please help me, please no." Even horror can't last for ever. They grew weepy and diseased. When they were too torn to be fun for the men they were taken away and killed. Only stupid and wicked fantasy says the stabs of real steel were kinder.

By the time Matsui went into Nanking two hundred thousand had died. Twenty thousand women were raped. Most women were raped many times. In the end all the nubile women were gone so they raped the old women and children. Women over seventy, girls under twelve, broken and screaming machines.

(But they only *act* like machines, repeating over and over. They don't have the luck of machines. They never stop feeling pain.)

The General's revulsion was total, but sometimes words can do nothing. The screams could no longer be counted, the mourners had died with the mourned. His army had turned into a rabble, cackling with drunken laughter. *But this was the perfect army, the perfect fighting machine . . . .* He could not believe he was hearing waves of obscenity blurring the *banzai*. He hailed their glorious Emperor according to the Japanese custom: "Great Field Marshal on the Steps of Heaven, ten thousand years of life." Then it came, the wave of derision, the mess belching out of the machine.

Next morning he made a statement, the statement of a sad old man. It did not help one victim, yet saying it may have been something. "Now, in the winter, the season gives time to reflect. I offer my sympathy, with deep emotion, to a million innocent people."

In the same way I make my statement. These things have happened, will happen again (*or else the worst thing will happen, and nothing will happen again*). Telling the story does nothing, for nothing can be undone. Children will never run back, who we last saw running and screaming. Those screams still hang on the air, those screams float in through my window. But hearing the scream does nothing. "The season gives time to reflect. . . ." Nothing can make the air quiet, nothing can make the air clean.

(Nothing can make the plot simple. *My* Japanese have been gentle. My Japanese have been victims, surviving another Great Crime. And that is some of the truth; in peace-time they mocked at soldiers. "What use are spurs on a tram-car?" "Big swords *do* get in the way . . . ." Then suddenly it was war-time, and the fighting machine followed orders.

The principals at Nanking were rewarded with silver vases, silver vases stamped with the Imperial chrysanthemum. The emblem of the Great God, the emblem of the Great Leader, the emblem of the one who speaks "from above the clouds, like a Crane". *The symbols are quick to read: they are greed and glitter and lying* . . . . Not very far offstage, the leaders controlling the lighting.)

These are the empire-builders, and these are the dead they build.

This is the Chapter of Empire, this is the Chapter of Lies. Butchers are laughable, until the laughter dies. . . .

Big Ray loved all his machines. With them he was more than just human. He became a machine himself, something that could mow through flesh. It was what he wanted with Martha: to be a great purring machine. Going on smoothly for ever, as she moaned and gasped underneath him. That was what he liked to remember, replaying it on his own. Him hard, and her creaming and melting. Moving like a knife through liver. . . .

What Martha remembered was quite different. She remembered him panting and squirming. She remembered not feeling anything much, since she couldn't really feel small cocks. He always talked to himself like a madman, "Do you like it, oh, I'm giving it you. . . . ." She was glad that his teeth were buried in her neck, so he couldn't see her expression: she was sure it must show, her discomfort and boredom as she whispered "ooh yes" and "oh darling," as she cried "Oh Ray, you're fantastic" and "Give me some more, Big Boy."

The smoothest machines go wrong when they are kept going by lies. In his dreams, he drove through his empire, carved through its soft cowed curves.

181

By daylight he left a clutch of used notes, and the Emperor had no clothes.

By daylight he left Martha yawning and scratching and ringing a girlfriend to giggle. "I would have rung you back before but *he's* been here again. Yeah—the same as usual. I know. You have to laugh, it's pathetic . . . he could put you off it altogether, though. Thank God Jimmy's coming round later. . . ."

Jimmy, a West Indian bouncer, was the man she liked the best. Jimmy was what Ray called a nigger. Jimmy and Martha used to laugh a lot about Big Ray's plans for the future. Martha laughed more than Jimmy. Jimmy took it all in. Jimmy organized the raid one night which reduced the shop to chaos.

When they'd finished, it looked like a massacre. Everywhere blood and crushed meat. The attackers left feeling sick, though all they had smashed was corpses.

All butchers' shops are a massacre, neatly distributed corpses. No one can see the dismembered limbs because they are called *fresh meat*.

Big Ray was dead drunk next door, as he was every Saturday night. Young Raymond was staying with a friend: next day the Party had a rally. Mrs Perkins swore she'd heard nothing. "I'm a Hevvy Sleeper," she said. But she sneezed a lot, the day after it happened. They thought she was dumb. She was not.

Big Ray placed his faith in muscles, but muscles get turned into meat. Enemy laughter can slice it to bits. There, growing dark, on the table.

Empires also grow dark. The sun setting over the Empire. They wanted to build more crimson blocks, building it higher and wider. As Britain grew smaller and smaller, they thought they could swell it by shouting. They stuffed its dry entrails with huge machines, penises stiff with poison.

They shouted that they were strong (growing smaller, growing weaker). They went out with chains and knives, encased in creaking black leather. As they grew smaller, their armour grew bigger, beetles in tortoise shells. The island would bear its "great harness", its great false belly of missiles. They were trying to hide their shrunken hearts in gigantic tanks of tin. But the armour clanked and rattled, and the enemy laughed in the darkness.

And the island sinks in the water as the dead weight bears it down. . . .

Starting to see a world too late that death can come from within.

Little men scared of the Flood . . . the Punks, the Commies, the Darkies. The Flood was coming, Darkness was coming, draw up the lines and fight. . . .

But darkness comes when the missiles will it, driving us into the night.

The Japanese knew they were little men so they built huge shells of armour. They planned on Empire for decades, plotting and growing and building. . . .
And then the Empire of Thunder came in only a fractured second.

In the end there were only the Blind, in the Empire of the Dead.

10 Second Chapter of Brothers

Families pose for the camera with the children shoulder to shoulder. Outsiders see them as all of a kind, under the family banner. The kids stick by each other: *after all, family's family*. Brother fights beside brother, brothers-in-arms to the end. "*Of course* my kids get on—you do ask funny questions." That is Lorna still telling her lie, just like everyone else does.

And the camera tells one little part of the truth. Guy pulling George's hair. Out of the lens's vision, a sharp toe aims at the ankle. Pain going deep in the bone. This is all just childish fun, looking back on it twenty years later. But it wasn't fun at the time. It was all that they knew of hatred.

Sisters are just like brothers. Lorna's sisters never loved her. She was spoiled and pretty and Daddy's pet, and their big brother Guy adored her. Later she was slatternly and dirty and all her kids looked a sight. She didn't seem to make any effort. You couldn't really ask her out. Clarissa and Melissa loved each other best when they both got talking about Lorna. No one else realized how hateful she was. It was lovely to have each other.

Though none of their lives turned out in the least like the rules they were given, they mostly ignored what happened instead of ignoring the rules. Because Lorna's sisters were hateful, she didn't stop trusting sisters: she just attempted (and failed, by the rules) to make her daughter a sister. When Henry's tremendous brotherly love got smashed on the rocks of death, he didn't give up the idea of brothers, lifting you over the void. He wanted to make his own sons brothers who would never lose each other. He knew Guy wasn't very lovable, but he wasn't Guy, just "a brother". He wanted their love to hold through time, strong hearts beating together. He hadn't a clue how to do it, and the phantom heartbeats faded. "*I* used to really love *my* brother George," he told Guy, wistful, worried. Guy's small mean eyes scampered away, he was scribbling LIES on something. "Your brother is a very good boy. There's nothing quite like a brother."

Guy heard what Henry was saying very clearly, clearer than Henry himself. His father was saying that George was good, that his brother was a kind of a hero. Only he knew that George was soft, and weak, and mad, and a coward. It made him burn with fury that Dad should say George took after a soldier. *He* was the soldier in the family. *He* would be hard, dead hard. His father would be sorry in the end, when Guy was old enough to show him. His brother would be more than sorry. He would . . . send his brother to Siberia.

However far Guy sent him, it couldn't be far enough away. For as long as Guy remembered George was breathing his air, sharing that tiny little bedroom. Sleeping five feet away from somebody you hated. Hearing him snore and whimper. Watching him grow as tall as Alan Quinn while his own legs seemed to grow shorter.

His brother was cunning, as well. Guy knew how much George despised him. *Of course* George must have despised him for not being bright and for having great spots on his forehead. George certainly despised him for masturbating. He didn't think that George *did*. He had sometimes lain there listening at night, but he never did manage to catch him.

George probably despised him for his friends. George said he couldn't stand the Perkinses. (In fact, he only said it when pushed. Guy had asked him to come to a meeting. "You might be quite frightened," Guy said, very grand. "They're real hard men, in the Party." He wanted to make George sit up, show him he had powerful contacts. But when George knew it was Mr Perkins, he just said he was a *loony*. Big Ray a loony! Guy lay in the dark, planning a thorough revenge. It had hurt all the same, right under his ribs, that George didn't take them seriously.)

The cunning came in the silence. George pretended not to take any notice. He never said anything nasty to Guy unless he was needled and needled. He never admitted he despised him, which just made it harder for Guy. You could see it in George's blue eyes, which never looked right into his. You could see it from the way George stared out of the window when he tried to bring things out in the open.

He was sure George and Angela talked about him, when they went off on their own. Otherwise he couldn't see why they did it—she *couldn't* like talking to George. But she took him with her on boring walks or to boring peculiar films. The only reason was to make him feel bad: they guessed he would never go with them. He imagined them walking in boring Kew Gardens, discussing what was wrong with him. Or sitting in the cinema before the film started, whispering about him, laughing. When George came back from these expeditions he always looked particularly smug. He had a sort of holy, fake happy look, those filthy blue eyes on the ceiling.

One evening they were both upstairs, after one of George's outings with *her*. Guy was doing his maths homework. He couldn't understand it at all. It made him feel as though his brain was full of razor blades, cutting the connections as soon as he made them. The stupid unfairness of not being able to do it, the stupid unfairness of being left out. *They never meant it when they asked him.* They only did it to annoy. His brain felt criss-crossed with scratches, scratches of pain and rage. *Unfair, unfair, unfair.* For his brother everything was easy.

George lay on his bed pretending to read the programme from wherever they had been. But Guy was watching him from under his lids. In fact he was staring at the ceiling. He hadn't even got his bedside lamp on, so his side of the room was quite dark. Staring up above him with that horrible look, like a stupid pink angel from a painting.

"You're not really reading that programme. I can see you, you're only pretending. I bet you didn't like it, whatever you saw. I bet you it was really boring. I bet you pretended to *her* that you liked it. I've found you out. You're a phony."

"Didn't go and see something, actually," said George, with a stupid kind of sigh. Whenever he wanted to drive Guy mad, he would *sigh*, as if he was too good for quarrels.

"You're not telling me what you did on purpose," said Guy, in a well tried tactic. The best way of making George join in a quarrel was telling him *he* had started it. Then he would get all indignant, and join in twice as fast.

"She *asked* you," said George. "She *asked* you to go. It was an anti-bomb thing actually. It's not a programme, it's a leaflet. "N' I wasn't reading it, anyway—I was lying there *thinking* about it."

"Yeargh," said Guy, very loudly, the most horrible noise he could make. "You're a horrible creep, that's what you are. You just copy what Angela thinks. I bet you told her you thought it was marvellous. They're mental, the people she knows. My friends say she's probably a communist."

"She is your sister," said George. "You don't want to listen to them." He knew what Guy's new friends were like. Guy shouldn't go talking about Angela.

"I expect you'll start making banners, now," Guy sneered, sitting up on his bed. "I expect you'll have to drag round after her, putting stupid announcements through doors. I expect you've fallen in love with the Russians. You were always a . . . coward, in any case."

That meant the argument was serious. He suddenly felt afraid. Last time he called George a coward, everything between them changed. It was about this revolting kid in George's class who had his hair like a girl. Augustus was a nigger, of course. There was only one in George's class, where all of the bright boys were. They were all taking O-levels early. People kind of respected them for that. But Augustus Jackson was different. That hair, and big teeth, always laughing. They were hardly human really. And his body, kind of wild, not connected. He was a very fast runner, which made it more annoying, him always doing well in the Sports. It wasn't quite convincing when they called him *Augusta*, since he could beat most of them at running.

One Sports Day he went too far. Raymond Perkins had always won the sprints without effort, though the margin grew less every year. Then Raymond started to put on flesh, on his thighs and his chest and his stomach. Augustus was the merest liquorice-stick man when he stood at the start by Raymond. Raymond grinned down towards the finish. He saw it in a haze of gold. It was his yearly injection of innocent pleasure, thrashing the others to pieces. He turned to Augustus in the lane beside him. "Would you like a start, Augusta?" Augustus laughed wildly, like he always laughed. Darkies were soft in the head. But the starter called them to order, and the gun turned them into machines.

Human machines aren't like any others. Performance cannot be predicted. A word, a gesture, a joke—any little thing turns the wheels. Augustus had gone into overdrive, a berserk long black set of pistons. He flew down the track like an oiled Jesse Owens, and screamed with laughter at the end. He had beaten Perkins by yards. Raymond knelt on the floor, red and gasping. Next day he was waiting for Augustus by the bikesheds, with Guy and some of his friends.

Gus usually came down on his own to collect his brilliant blue bike. It was a stupid colour for a bike, but typical of Augustus. That evening however he was with three mates. The fight was long and exhausting. In the middle, George walked past, not even holding a satchel. Guy was trying to get both knees in the balls of one of those bastards. But *he* had Guy by the throat and was calling him a motherfucking bastard. Guy's friend who was holding him down couldn't stop the filth spewing out. Then Guy glimpsed George. His *brother*. "Hey George," he panted, "come and help!"

George stopped and stared for what seemed a long time but might only have been a few seconds. Then he flung up his hands, in a funny way Guy had never seen before. His face had gone red, Guy supposed with fear. Then he walked away. "You're a coward!" Guy yelled after his brother before he got back to the fight. That night they ignored each other till Henry and Lorna went out. They were going round to Mrs Eames next door to drink the health of her baby. As soon as they were gone Guy started. "Who's yellow?" he called up the stairs. "I know someone yellow round here. Who wouldn't stick up for his brother?"

He was quite surprised by what happened. George came downstairs looking white. "Do you really want to fight?" he said, with his eyes somehow sunk back inside, and his voice gone squeaky with anger. Then Guy was really frightened, for the first time ever of George. It was frightening when someone went different, someone you thought you knew. George's fists were clenched by his sides. He had never really seen George angry. For the first time ever he saw that his brother really wanted a reason to hit him. A queer nerve pulsed in his stomach. The house had gone very quiet.

He grinned, but it didn't feel right, and pretended everything

188

was normal. "I wanted you to fight this after*noon*," he said, in a don't-care voice. "But don't worry, we beat them in any case." And he backed out into the kitchen, and pretended to put on the kettle.

He stood there feeling—peculiar—till George's feet went back upstairs. It wasn't true that they beat them. In the end, Guy had run away.

It changed the way he thought of George. Before, it was hatred pure and simple. And disgust left over from when George was fat and everyone called him Porker. But now it was tinged with half-forgotten fear, a razor edge on the hatred.

Perhaps he knew it would have to come out. Perhaps he found it exciting. He didn't mean to call him a coward again, that day when he'd been to the meeting. It just slipped out of his mouth, and at once he knew it was dangerous.

But George didn't move from the bed. He put the bit of paper on the floor. "You don't know a thing about what I think. You *presume* I agree with her. As a matter of fact I don't."

Thank God he didn't feel like fighting. Guy knew how *big* George was.

"You're keen on foreigners, aren't you? Darkies and Russians and things. You think we ought to hand it all over to them. That's what Angela thinks. She told me."

"I bet she never said anything like that. Your trouble is, you're a liar." George was sitting up, and looking at him. Guy waited, half pleased to have taken effect, half scared of what he had started. The brothers looked at each other. They knew each other's faces too well. Guy was too used to detesting George. Nothing would ever get better.

George was taking him seriously, suddenly, Guy could see. "If you ever say anything about Angela to those . . . beasts who go round with the Perkinses. If I ever found out that you had. Just listen to me. I'd kill you." He was poised on the edge of the bed, a very big shape indeed, hands on his muscular thighs, his jaw jutted forward at Guy. George never looked at him directly, but now he stared heavily, eyes like . . . *something*. Frightening beams coming out of the darkness. Cutting through the distance between them.

"I thought you were s'posed to be a whatsit, *pacifist*." Guy was breathing fast, but he tried to sound cheeky. "Don't think Angela

189

would like you killing people. *She* thinks we ought to let the *Russians* kill *us*. It doesn't make sense. It's barmy."

George liked to think things out. He sat back just a little. Guy could see him thinking. You could never have a proper argument with Porker. He always started thinking, so you couldn't get mad. This time it was half a relief, however. That look in his eyes when he talked about Angela . . . it made the little hairs on Guy's arm stand on end. They were *still* half on end, though George was looking at his feet.

"Your trouble is, you don't try to understand. You never read books, or talk about things. The whole point is, you *assume* I'm like her. Well I'm not. I don't agree about nuclear weapons. I think it's stupid to chuck them away."

That was typical George. It drove you crazy. Wriggling out of it, never agreeing. Deliberately twisting what you knew was true. Guy had got it worked out that he was wet like Angela. It stood to reason. You never saw him fighting. He was biggest in his class, and not fat any more. But you never saw him sorting people out, like Raymond. He was . . . sort of soft-centred. Not *exactly* a coward, not *obvious* coward, as he had found out on the day he fought Augustus. All the same he was yellow in a funny twisted way. Of course he was a pacifist. Of course he liked Russia.

So Guy pressed on, but he watched George carefully. "There are camps in Russia where they kill . . . writers and people. Like Angela. Or you. They'd kill both of you if you went to live in Russia."

"I'm *telling* you. I don't *want* to live in Russia."

"If we don't have weapons, the Russians'll come here. They'll walk right in and build camps everywhere. And niggers too. The Russians like niggers. *Her* lot would let 'em just take England over."

"You don't ever listen. You're not worth talking to." George hit the eiderdown in exasperation. He saw Guy flinch as his fist came down. That rather shocked him, so he tried once again.

"She's *romantic*, Angela. That's not so bad. I'm not romantic. Because I'm a boy. They're just *there*, aren't they. You've got to face facts. I mean, you can't just wish weapons away. And I think you should . . . stand up for things, you believe in. I *love* my country. You've got it all wrong."

"You say you do, but you wouldn't join the Party. I *asked* you to come to that meeting, but you wouldn't. It's all *in theory*, you loving England." The phrase that he loved was running through his brain, the phrase that always brought the blood to his forehead. "I'm different, see. I would . . . *die for the cause*. That's what we all promise. To *die for the cause*."

George listened to the little throb of furious emotion. He'd never heard Guy sounding so worked up. It was sort of parroted, most of what he said, un-thought out, said just to annoy you. All the same, he believed it, this *die for the cause*. He felt sorry for Guy, and that wasn't easy.

"That's because I don't approve of your party. That's not *England*, the New Empire Party. Joining *that* can't be standing against Russia. That'd be joining something real, like the army."

(What George didn't know was that *that* was what Guy wanted more than anything else in his poor thin world. He had read up the brochures in the Public Library: coloured pictures of strong brave men.

> You'll find you have new mates as soon as you join the Army. Your first posting could take you anywhere in the world . . . within the regiment there's certainly plenty of entertainment . . . sports, discos, and Christmas parties for the children . . .

(Guy had never even had a *birthday* party, grinding his teeth as he read)

> Your equipment will include the most sophisticated modern weapons: self-loading rifles, hard-hitting machine guns, formidable anti-tank weapons and mortars . . . You will go into battle by high-speed aircraft, helicopter, parachute, or perhaps the latest model of armoured personnel carrier.

Guy's eyes glistened and he licked his lips. The mates and the uniform. The travel and the girls. Knowing who would back you. Knowing who you were. Belonging somewhere, *absolutely and completely*. . . . And then on leave, he would work for the Party. He'd know about discipline then, from the top. He could help to train men: *hard-hitting, formidable*. The Party would respect him— they didn't much, at present. They saw him as Raymond Perkins' little hanger-on. When he was a soldier, everything would change.)

191

He wanted to just say, "I'm *going* to join the Army," but he couldn't tell him, that would spoil everything. He tried another tack. This was almost unbearable, *George* pretending to be on the same side. "You're going to be something like a teacher or a scientist. Seeing as how you always come top. *You* wouldn't ever do anything for England. *You're* the last person who'd go and join up."

There was another annoying silence. George was thinking, heavily, again, pulling at the knees of his trousers. "That might be true, what you say." Then another of those sighs, heavy breath. The heaviness of his brother was not just a matter of flesh. It was always pretending to be virtuous. Guy hated it, if this was goodness. Give him badness, any old day. You couldn't have a quarrel on your own. The acid taste of unfairness.

The last year was a long nightmare, being in the no hope stream. They were just wasting time till they could leave. The teachers couldn't control them. It was nice giving trouble to the teachers, but all the same Guy felt vague shame. He felt he ought to be sorting things out, sorting out the world he lived in. He had got too old for screwing up teachers. He wanted a *real* enemy. He wanted to be someone big in the world, not a *bloody nasty little drop-out*. That was what someone actually called him when they heard him calling names at some girl. The names that he called her were true. She *was* a filthy fat slag. People said she was *anybody's*. Anyone but Guy's, in that case. *Naturally* Guy had to get her. And then they came down on him! It was a very funny world they lived in, if you couldn't call a sperm-bag a sperm-bag.

And smarmy-voiced poofter of an English teacher got away with calling *him* a drop-out. They were worse than the niggers, the ones like that. Henshaw was known to like niggers. He put Johnson's poems in the School Magazine. How could a nigger write poems? He had even read it to make sure. They didn't have a rhythm, or rhymes. That was it, if you were a nigger. People made things easy for you. Whereas everything felt hard, for Guy. *Unfair, unfair, unfair*.

Things always *were* hard for Guy. People are not born equal. Some babies look like sweet little dolls, some look twisted and queer. And people born looking ugly are sometimes born stupid as well. And people born ugly and stupid may miss being loved at all. Guy's soul never grew lovable because it didn't get any love. Nothing can grow without sunlight. In the dark it grew shrivelled and small.

(And this is a problem *for novels*, the writers and readers of novels. But others are born who soon look hungry, whose bodies grow shrivelled and small. Things are harder for some. Soon they are little dead dolls. They lie on the page of this novel. I hardly think they fit in.)

Guy's insides grew like his outsides. No one saw anything in him. He couldn't see very much in himself but he had to find something to love. So he fell in love with his penis, the Army . . .

and later the Space Machines.

He discovered them in his last year at school, on the long cold days playing truant. That year he was only a tourist (next year love would grow serious). It was called *The Happy Land*, which struck a sad chord in Guy. At first he sneered and looked distant: later he came to stay.

In the dim arcades, he felt somebody. Wholly controlling the screen, until his money ran out. He was good at *Missile Command*. He would soon have the world in order. (There were hardly any girls in here, which made his mission easier.) Smash away mess and weaklings, until his luck ran out. The machine made everything clear:

SMART MISSILE	125 PTS
KILLER SATELLITE	100 PTS
BOMBER	100 PTS
UNUSED DEFENSIVE MISSILE	5 PTS

Suddenly things seemed fair, and everything might get better.

He didn't feel ugly, here. Nobody cared about his face. Fluorescent light thrown up from the games made all of them look like corpses. Whirling unearthly minor chords and tense electronic bleepings turned the whole place into somewhere else where you didn't have to be human. Nobody talked or listened, so no one could think he was dim. Everything seemed to get better. He was part of a great machine. And the words were powerful, exciting:

193

ALPHA BASE
DELTA BASE
OMEGA BASE

STARGATE
MORTALS
IMMORTALS

Holding the gate against the aliens, beating them back on his own. Practising to be in the Army, waiting for the end to come. . . . Guy was in command of the missiles. *Things would come right in time*.

Things would get worse for Guy. Things would get worse for many. "Things'll look up," Raymond Perkins said, as the future loomed towards them. He was really shocked to find Guy crying one day in the disused Nissen hut. They used to go there to smoke and make plans and read *Hot and Wet* together. They hadn't planned to meet that day, a few weeks after both left school. When Raymond heard the sound of sobs from outside he started to feel quite cheerful. It must be an intruder in there, and a weed, not just an intruder. He would really enjoy making sure the intruder never came intruding again. The scruddled-up face on the floor, however, turned out to be Guy, all streaming. His face was swollen and red, and shining with snot and tears. He couldn't get his breath for ages, tried to crawl away like an animal, dragging himself into a corner of the hut where he could just die or hide.

At first Raymond thought that the niggers had got him. His face looked completely misshapen, as if he'd been beaten up. They would sort them out together, thought Raymond. With his Dad, perhaps, and the dogs. Guy finally stopped crying long enough to try and explain what it was. He had been turned down by the Army. He was tall enough, just, it wasn't that. It was the medical. You couldn't argue with that. They said that he had a weak heart.

At first Guy didn't believe them, after they explained what it meant, the horrible stupid-sounding Latin word that they only used to annoy him. "You've confused me with somebody else." "I'm afraid that we haven't, Mr Ship. We're scrupulous about our records." Guy couldn't believe what he was hearing. It was just like everywhere else. Smarmy-voiced people, on the inside, telling him he couldn't get in. For reasons he just couldn't quarrel with because he didn't know the secret. Because he didn't have the brain. Now his heart wasn't right as well.

There was nothing for Guy but the Dole. He couldn't bear to think about the future. He had already been to sign on, and it somehow all seemed familiar. As if it had always been waiting for him, as if he had always known. He would have to stand in a mean hot room in a queue of backs for ever. Filling in forms he couldn't understand, answering stupid questions. The worst thing of all was the niggers. The office was full of niggers. There were even some behind the counter, but the worst were the ones in the queue. Looking at Guy with friendly contempt, asking to borrow his *Sun*. It was folded in a tight wodge of anxious pages and pegged into place by his elbow. "I'm *reading* it," Guy ground out, desperate. They thought he was just like them. He would *prove* he was not, in time. . . .

Stargate, Mortals, Immortals. Alpha to Omega Base.

He hadn't tried to talk to his mother in ages. He knew she didn't care about him. She was too tied up with his horrible father, trying to be all lovey-dovey again. Which was very disgusting however you looked at it. His father couldn't have any pride. He knew perfectly well that she'd been with someone else. He would have knifed her if it had been him.

However, Guy was only sixteen. He had to have someone to talk to. Bad enough being found crying that once; he wouldn't try Raymond again. He brooded and went off his food. He sulked and waited to be asked. He stood on the bathroom scales and discovered he was seven pounds lighter. Seven pounds lighter in just ten days. They would have to ask him what was the matter.

But no, no one cared about Guy. George was relieved he was quieter. Ange didn't live at home any more, and Henry only thought about Lorna. (Something horrible was happening to his father. He was going soft in the head. He didn't get drunk so much, and he bought her revolting little presents. Pot plants which cluttered the window ledge. Guy wanted to smash them all. Once a huge bar of chocolate, which for some reason made them giggle. *Horrible, horrible, vile.* Grownups behaving like children. And they *didn't offer him any.* He was starving, and nobody noticed. . . .)

In the end his mother did notice. He was getting on her nerves in the kitchen. He stood by the cupboard as she put away the cups, narrow shoulders hanging, mouth drooping down. He was staring at the tiles on the floor. She scraped his plate clean of dinner. "You might like to help, not just stand there. Or get out of my way till I've finished. I needn't bother to cook . . . *what's the matter with you at the moment*? I mean are you sickening for something?"

The cruelty of that sharp voice! And she was supposed to be his mother! No one in the world would be kind to him, if he couldn't rely on his mother. Guy stood and stared at the dirty tiles. Not even real tiles, but lino. There was *nothing* in his life that was good. He was stuck in this dump for ever. He was poor, unemployed, and ugly. He hadn't enough money to play the machines. And even his mother didn't care. Self-pity welled up like a fountain. "Want to tell you something," he said. There were tears breaking into that statement. Jaw dropping, she put down her plate.

"Oh, God, you haven't been shoplifting. . . ."

That was his mother. His mother! All the same, he told her his story. (Inside, he was almost glad. One more to cross off his list. That last little bit of softness, that lingering wish to be good . . . . It got easier and easier, in some ways, the more he saw life as a whole. Linked by the blaze of unfairness, his longing to burn and kill.)

He forced her to listen to his story, and she pretended to be sad. But she kept on looking at the sink as if she preferred the washing-up. "You poor boy," she said, in a solemn voice, but it sounded like acting to him. "I'm *not* a boy," he said firmly, but inside he knew that he was.

"What's this about your heart, in any case? There isn't any heart trouble in our family." Lorna put her hand on her heart. She hoped that she hadn't strained hers. She might have done, over Jack Latham. She peered very closely at Guy, which she never usually did. She was surprised to see how unpleasant he lookde, with dark hairs growing under his long twisted nose and horrible spots on his forehead and chin. Why should he be so ugly when the others looked all right?

"What're you looking at?" he snapped.

"I was wondering who you took after, me or your father. Not that you look like either of us much."

"Thanks very much," her son said.

"I don't mean because you're not good-looking," said Lorna, with ready tact. "It was your heart I was thinking about, silly, wondering if it was mine or your father's. I haven't been feeling so well, you see, lately. I try to keep going, but I *have* felt weak."

"I'd better go out," said Guy, standing up. That was it then. His mother only cared about herself. He had always known it, but he was glad to have it proved.

"Don't you want to talk then?" Lorna said, relieved. "I mean you shouldn't get broody. The doctor said that to me."

Guy turned on his mother his most withering look. "It's *women* get broody. *I'm* not broody."

She was already back at her sink with the mop. The withering missed her. Her voice was quite perky. "I don't mean broody. It's Ange who's good at English. I just mean they tell you not to bottle things up. Still if you're going out. . . ." She made a great effort. She turned back towards him and made her face queer. "Look at me, Guy. I want you to remember. I will always listen. I am always . . . your mother."

"Yeah," said Guy. He wanted to throw up. In the cold on the way to *The Happy Land* he grimaced and muttered to himself. *Sodding stupid women. Sodding selfish cunts.*

The machines looked clean and masculine.

SMART BOMB
THRUST
FIRE

The other one came home for the weekend. She was different since she'd been to college. Glossier, neater, more distant. He supposed he felt a little bit scared. She wasn't just his sister any more. He'd got quite proud of her too, now she had nice hair and make-up.

He had thought one day she would have to respect him, once he was a colonel in the Army. Of course they would never agree, but at least she couldn't ignore him. Or pretend he was just a little boy, not even worth arguing with. He might even . . . take her out to eat one day, in one of those expensive places. He would wear his very best uniform, and explain the work of the Army. She would have to listen to him, and slowly she would start to see sense. "I was very young at the time," she would tell him. "I understand you were right. I only hope . . . you can forgive me." And after a while he forgave her. They were both eating . . . *After Eight Mints*. A waiter . . . *in tails* hovered dimly. By that time chocolate wouldn't give Guy spots. He would offer her a minor post, as something like . . . an *Army Writer* (everything seemed to get written about, so the Army must be too). "It's wonderful to have a brother," she said, overcome with emotion.

He sat at the kitchen table after all the others had gone. Remembering that stupid little horrible dream. Could he ever have been so pathetic? Could he ever have believed that something would go right, when it was obvious that everything went wrong?

Angela came back into the kitchen. The others were in the front room. He could feel her looking at his bent head, but he wasn't going to bother to look up. He hated them all so much. Going off without him, as usual. Now she felt guilty, as well she might. She could try and make it up to him, then (and another part of him was prickling with pleasure. She had come back to talk *just to him*).

As soon as she started he half guessed what had happened. Her voice was all throbbing with warmth. "Would you like a polo?" she said. (*You poor little Guy, you poor wimp.*) He could hear it perfectly clearly. "Why should I, I just had me tea."

"You always used to like mints."

"Well I've changed my mind. I'm a grownup now . . In case you didn't happen to notice."

That didn't put her off, however. She came and sat down on the table. "How're things going?" she said. Ch-rist! She had never asked him *that* before. As if he was the next-door neighbour, or a kid she was going to teach. (That was what the brainy ones did: she and George would both be teachers.)

"What do you mean, exactly?" he said, making his voice very posh. *Her* voice had got much posher ever since she had gone to college. But *he* knew everything about her. She sighed, a long tired sigh. It was really in the family, sighing. He was the only non-sigher about.

"I mean, you having left school and things. I mean, it's not easy at the moment."

He was sure he could detect something funny in her voice, a tremble of pity, a hint of contempt. His stomach was suddenly burning with acid. His cow of a mother had told her, then. That would mean that his father and . . . *George* would know. That would mean he would have to . . . *murder* them all. Or leave home, at once. Or die. . . .

(Guy still thought the future was up to him. Getting shorter now, coming closer.)

"She told you what happened, didn't she? I'll kill her. I told her not to." Angela flinched, which proved it was true. "Told me what?" she said. Her voice sounded phony as anything. They were two of a kind, she and Lorna. All women were the same, all messing around, trying to make men feel silly. Trying to make them feel small. He would sort them all out, very shortly. When he got one all of his own. She would soon understand. He would show her. She would have a lot to make up for.

"Me being turned down for the Army. I mean, as if you didn't know . . . ." But the world never left things simple, because she looked genuinely shocked. So maybe his mother hadn't. Or else she was *brilliant* at acting. He remembered her pretending not to like *Sexus*, all those years ago, when he caught her. And pretending to love him, *one hour per year*, on his birthday. . . .

"with all my love . . ."

So he couldn't ever be quite certain. *Yeargh*. It didn't really matter.

"Well if you want to know it's true. And I really wanted to, *so*. Is that all you wanted to know? So you could go and discuss it with Porker?"

The light in the kitchen was bright fluorescent. All their quarrels were soured by that light. She stared at him now for the first time in ages. He wasn't a pretty sight. His attempt at a moustache crawled all over. Long limp and rare black hairs. On his chin there were two gigantic spots, red and angry, with flaky white caps. But it wasn't *that* that was horrible. His whole self was somehow crossed. His eyes weren't level, and they couldn't meet yours. His mouth was pursed ready to hate you. His long pink nose looked spiteful as a shrew but also curiously vulnerable. Under the horrible glaring light you could see pink scalp through his straggling hair. And Guy was only sixteen years old. Imagine that face, going bald.

She shuddered to think of his future (*she should have thought of her own*). None of them loved him, not really. No wonder he'd turned

199

into a monster. Imagine that face, going bald and thin. An ageing thug in Acton.

The pity tugged hard at her stomach. She wished she felt nothing for him. You could never quite escape from your family; knowing too much was the problem. You could never quite cut yourself off. The soft knotted roots of your growing. You couldn't see Guy as a thug, *whoever* he chose to go round with. She always saw Guy as a kid: a nasty, unhappy kid. And how could you draw the line properly between *looking* and *being* nasty? You *did* prefer cleverer people. And people with gentle faces. Even when George was so fat he had those beautiful, thoughtful eyes.

Whereas Guy's were lopsided and shifty and a pinkish shade of brown. Reddish whenever he got angry. He got angry again and again. But who was to say what was anger, who was to say what was pain?

He turned away from her scrutiny, the glare of the spiteful light. She thought he was hiding his feelings (in fact, he was hiding his spots). So instead of going back to join the others, she said "Look, I'm really sorry. I mean, about you and the Army."

His head snapped round and his red eyes glared at her, furious with disbelief. "What do *you* know about the Army? You're a liar. You can't stand the Army."

If she sighed once more he would . . . *kick* her. "Oh Guy, for goodness' sake. I mean, I'm sorry for *you*. Not sorry about the Army exactly . . . it makes it a different *thing*."

But Guy heard nothing at all after "I'm sorry for you. . . ."

"Oh *thanks very much*," he sneered, his twisted nostrils flaring. The fluorescent of his face pushed right up to hers. "When I want your pity, I'll tell you." His breath was coming like an engine, fighting to get through the tunnel. "You make me sick, as a matter of fact. Who do you think you are? You're only a . . . *stupid fucking girl*. . . ." *Getting louder, coming closer.*

HYPERSPACE

SMART BOMB

THRUST

In time, since everything's told in time, she did tell George about Guy. Guy's stupid fucking sister talked to his fucking stupid brother. George and Angela no longer agreed as much as they used to do. She couldn't help being irritated when that closed look

200

came on his face. She was used to his large bright eyes lighting up when she told him things. But now his pupils slipped to the left and fixed very hard on the floor. (He didn't want to be seduced. He wanted to think about things. Some of what she said made sense but some of it jumped all the barriers. The sensible barriers were still there, long after the flash of her leaping. When he was little he had never noticed, watching that flying gold hair.)

He didn't like not agreeing with Ange because he could see that it hurt her. An ache had begun between them, the weight of his *I'm not sure*. His eyes refusing to laugh into hers, the grave clenched set of his eyebrows.

At first he didn't believe her. "Did he really? The actual army? With him going round with those other loonies I shouldn't have thought he'd've bothered. . . ."

"That's not the point. I mean I was surprised. But the thing is, he didn't get in. Mum says it was all he ever wanted. And he never told any of us."

"It's funny . . . he did once say to me I wasn't brave enough to get in the Army. Because I was talking about not liking Russia. . . ."

Angela felt sharply betrayed. "I didn't know you ever talked to Guy. For heaven's sake, he's a maniac. You don't want to talk to *him* about Russia." She had a sudden vision of them lying there, *her brothers* planning a world war.

"It was only once. We were quarrelling. Anyway, he said I was a coward. And I couldn't talk about . . . loving England . . . if I wasn't prepared to fight."

She did a little grimace of distaste. "Talking about *loving England*?" It suddenly seemed hopeless. How did you connect them, the child she remembered and this six-foot man? She wanted to tell him to *come off it*, she wanted to make him grin. But she wasn't quite sure she could do it. They weren't alike any more. People moved away, became different. Events moved on too fast.

The thing she had told him had gone in deep, deeper than she ever imagined. George had a big soft heart, although he was learning to hide it. That was one way they were still alike; a family of overgrown hearts. Hearts which descended from Henry's heart locked away in its cage of branches. Hearts which descended from Lorna's heart, held in her arms like a baby.

A family of overgrown, overwired hearts which did not make

201

living easy. In the end Rose could only bear to look at hers through the smoky glass of a bottle. Frank's heart was so full of thwarted desire that he hid it on top of a mountain. Lorna's was born without enough skin so she couldn't control her feelings. Once she discovered how to love other people as well as herself it was worse: her heart was a busy hotel but the locks on the doors all burst. She couldn't protect anybody, and she had to absorb their pain. And the guests weren't always so friendly. They rejected her, they were busy. (Nothing would matter in the end: her heart would be full of Henry. . . .)

hearts didn't matter in the end   *flash-fried lumps of offal*

Guy had a heart as well, though most people didn't believe it. It was a heart as twisted and raw as his face, as his thin body falling, his thin mouth screaming . . . as twisted and raw as his body would look, splayed on great runners of steel . . . the world had stamped on Guy very thoroughly before his heart stopped hurting. Before his heart stopped beating in shock and the world turned foreign and black.

The brothers hadn't been out together since they were little boys. When they were only four and five the last photograph had been taken. They were holding hands for the camera, with golden-haired Ange behind. The sun had blanked out their faces to a neutral, whitish shine. Two little brothers smiling, big sister's arm on their shoulders. At the back was the charmingly rural touch of two of Henry's sunflowers.

That photo would become important to their parents long after it had been lost. Lorna, her face all skewed with weeping, would search for it for days. As she searched she swore to herself, scooping out papers at random. She couldn't ever find it though. It was slipped in a book for safekeeping. She didn't know where to look, not knowing she lived in a novel.

(All of us live in a novel, and none of us do the writing. Just offstage there are grim old men, planning to cut the lighting.)

George was a serious boy who went quiet and did his thinking. Angela knew he had a big heart but about his head she knew little. After he heard about Guy and the Army George went quiet for ages. He started reading a lot of books which were not connected with school. Books about military tactics, books about the Second World War. Books about Soviet Communism, books about nuclear deterrents. The complexities were exhausting. He got behind with his homework. George needed *certainty*. The simplest logic seemed best: "THE JOB . . . and the men to see it through." Brightly coloured, finger-marked pamphlets. Someone had been reading them before him.

> The British people have always expected great things of the British Army . . . their training and equipment is the finest in the world . . . always in the first wave of assault, getting to grips with the enemy . . . or manning the final line of defence . . . fast, efficient and united . . . stand up for what you believe in . . . if you've got what it takes, the Army is the place for you . . . it's a Man's life in the British Army . . . courage . . . commitment . . . the JOB . . . and the men to see it through.

Stand up for what you believe in . . . final line of defence . . . . George started writing something that sunlit day in the library. In the end he had got it more or less right. He posted it, and cheered up. For the first time for weeks he walked round at home without brows sagging with worry. He even managed to talk to Guy. "Any luck with jobs?" he said. "Go fuck yourself," said Guy. ALPHA BASE : DELTA BASE: *KILL.*

George was accepted by army recruitment without a shadow of doubt. His heart beat perfectly, *bom-diddy-om*, his O-levels shone from the paper. He wasn't an unemployment statistic trying to get out of the pond. He was tall and athletic and a patriot, and he *actually chose to be there.* "It cheers you up, getting ones like that," said the officer, after he went out. "There are still good lads," said the other one. Then they both looked stern, and proud.

The family weren't so inspired. Angela, of course, went mad. She didn't take it in at first, and then they had a quarrel where she cried. "I just can't believe it," she gasped, trying to keep her voice steady. "Everyone says how clever you are, and you're going off to play soldiers!"

"What's it got to do with it, me being clever?" he grunted, dark-faced, uneasy. "Just because people are clever, they still have to do what's right."

All this seemed so fiercely important, to all the Ship family. Waking in the morning the shadow was there, the sense something awful had happened. Lorna worried about it to Henry, and Henry ached inside. Angela raged about it to John, and Guy writhed in fury and envy. He and George never said a word to each other. His mother, as usual, told him.

"Do you know what your stupid brother has done?"

"Finished my lager?"

"I mean it. He's chucked up his studies, his whole career, and gone off and joined the Army. I don't understand it, he was never like *you*. He seemed such a *peaceful* boy. . . ."

A speeded-up film of that family house would have seen them swarming like an anthill. Running wildly from room to room, consulting each other, rowing. George tried to stay right out of the way but his presence drew the others like sugar. He didn't give a damn what any of them said. Everything was already settled.

Everything was already settled, but it wasn't settled by them. It all seemed so fiercely important . . . it wouldn't be important for long.

Guy's hatred and jealousy wouldn't last long, the words that burned in his brain. HE WOULD KILL HIM, EVEN IF IT KILLED HIM. Despair this time as well as hatred. This must be the final unfairness. He wished the whole lot of them were dead. Himself, as well as his brother.

And indeed death would take him in his brother's arms, brother holding close to brother. They were moving back towards the last snapshot, too late to catch the lost sun. Lorna looked and looked, but couldn't find it. Little boys lost, moved on.

They never went out together, but they went to the same small home. Chance plays enormous and complicated games and the best are with space and time. Two years before space ran out of time it brought the brothers together. The setting wasn't glamorous, but had its own drama: Piccadilly Underground, Piccadilly line. George was in uniform, coming home on leave. It was only the second time he'd been home. He looked tough and impressive in his uniform. It was Saturday afternoon. There had been a big demonstration, a big anti-nuclear march in Hyde Park. Guy and the Party had meant to disrupt it, but arrangements had gone very wrong. Most of them hadn't turned up at all and the rest hadn't bothered to dress. No wonder only twenty or so of them found each other: everywhere they looked there were commies.

They'd arranged to form up in Bayswater but it wasn't Bayswater any more. It was a solid wall of people, the kind of people you detested. The worst thing of all was they *smiled* at you, just lots of vague smiles like loonies. Assuming you were on their side, assuming the *whole world* was.

Guy had his leathers and his boots on. You didn't get much chance to dress up. His pride in his leathers was enormous. He had saved to buy the boots from his dole. The jacket he had got after that trouble with the Army—his repulsive namesake in Australia had sent him a money order. He was sure it was something to do with his mother. She looked smug, when he told her, and said "He's very kind." By now he was *relieved* he hadn't got into the Army, they were mostly pansies, in the British Army. It stood to reason, if Porker got in.

(Yet his chest had nearly burst with confused emotion the first weekend that George had come home. Jealousy and hatred, the usual things. But something else, though he swallowed it hard. Pride, because it was his brother. Looking so tough in that uniform. The boy who had shared his room. Even though inside he was a . . . *hateful, hateful* . . . . There were things Guy didn't understand. How could he feel that stupid swelling feeling about his horrible brother?)

It would trap him again on that grey afternoon as the future came colder and closer.

The others had drunk a lot of beer at lunch-time in the overflowing pubs near Marble Arch. There were so many of the anti-nuclear berks that you couldn't even lift your elbow. It was hateful, seeing how . . . *happy* they looked. And all those good-looking girls: sort of shining, laughing and shining. Wasting themselves, like his stupid fucking sister. Somewhere in the Park she would be there. . . . He would take them and retrain them, compulsory. But sometimes it just seemed like . . . theory. Just stupid theory, like Angela had. It was cold and grey and empty.

Only five British Empire in the pub. And the others had disgraced their uniform. (Not that they were dressed up properly. It just made a mockery, some of them in jeans, one of them with dyed blonde hair. One of them wearing a poncey wet-look shirt with "HITLER LIVES" on the front. His proper name was Keith, but he said to call him "Kim". He appeared to have eyeliner on. . . .) In any case, Hitler wasn't the point. That sort of thing put off the

205

public. Whatever Big Ray said about "our German brothers", Guy wasn't happy with Hitler.

It was even more humiliating that no one took a blind bit of notice. *Their* lot, the peace lot, were such a mixture that p'raps they couldn't see any difference. They had gone to shout down the speeches in the Park, but twenty people couldn't do much . . . and most of them had sloped off quickly when they saw how many were there. Guy wished *he* could have sloped off. Gone to the *Happy Land*. Though the Tube had got so expensive that his money had nearly run out. . . .

Things lining up against him. It was as if the world had gone crazy. People said there were hundreds of thousands of them, all mad keen to have peace. And some of them had brought little kids along. It wasn't decent, involving the children. Guy felt extremely virtuous. *He* would never have done that. Getting kids mixed up with weirdos and commies (if only they *looked* more weird . . . anyone might have been fooled they were normal, seeing them all in the Park. There were even some really old people, grey-haired people with banners. There wasn't any hope for England if grey-haired people were against it. "You want to be careful, grandpa. You want to watch your glasses." The way they had glared at Guy and his friends, you would have thought *they* were the yobbos!) Guy placed his hopes in the helicopters, humming high over the Park. Efficient and steely and *always there*, he just hoped they'd got good cameras. Science was marvellous these days. Perhaps they could take one giant photograph, then find out all the names . . . perhaps they could all be got rid of together, with obvious exceptions, of course. Then someone said they were just TV. In that case there was no hope. "I expect they're Army *disguised* as TV," he insisted, but it sounded empty. The whole afternoon had turned chill and grey, the sour thin grey of disappointment.

Things only went wrong for *him*, of course. His life had been fixed to thwart him. He kept expecting his luck to change. Life couldn't go on like that. . . .

"Could we 'ave your glasses, your glasses, please. Come on gentlemen, haven't you got a home to go to?" Guy listened to the question, for once. He *didn't* have a home to go to. You couldn't call the dump where he had to live home. A *home* would be somewhere . . . *peaceful*. Somewhere where people . . . quite liked him, anyway. Somewhere where he could feel somebody. He hardly existed, at home. If he'd died, they would all have been glad (but a vengeful little voice said just the opposite: *if I was dead, they'd be sorry*). In fact, he had never existed, until he had joined the Party. Today even that felt like nothing. So where did he belong? *Don't you have a home to go to?*

Voices outside crying no

(Human bodies go home in the end even if they don't know how to find it. There would always be room for the bodies, places for them to fall. In the end they would home on each other, lie there smoking, unburied. . . .)

Voices pelting my window   *voices outside crying no*

The lads were singing a football song as they came down Oxford Street. The speeches were still going on in the Park but people were leaving in droves. It was the cold grey drizzle that did it, the cardboard placards curling over. But the groups of protesters were loud and excited, bright water on smiling faces.

The lads were neither shining or smiling. Their knees were groggy with drink. Of the five of them trying to sing the song only Guy wasn't totally drunk. He had felt too low to enjoy himself, and anyway he was too poor. And if he couldn't pay his round he couldn't join in the drinking. He couldn't accept any favours because he was never secure. Even here he was never quite one of the boys, not unless Raymond was there. They would call him a scrounger when he went for a leak. They would call him a mean Scottish bastard. So he said he wouldn't have any more when he'd just got the taste of the beer.

Watching them swaying along the pavement he despised them, belching and hugging each other. When you were pissed yourself you didn't see it, what you must look like, pissed as a pig. All the same, it was lonely, not being pissed. Boring, and things dragged on. People said the same things again and again as if they were weak in the head. He had really looked forward to today for months, but now he wished it was over. *They* were too drunk to feel lonely, or sad. For them time passed very quickly (and the future was rushing towards Guy now: he was wishing his life away. . . .)

Once they **were** underground their voices sounded even louder. One of **them** wanted to be sick, and the others were laughing and swearing. In a minute he *had* been sick, a great foul-smelling pool of yellow. Some of it had got on his clothes. That seemed even funnier to the other three, but Guy just wanted to curl up. They were supposed to be representing *England*. They were supposed to be keeping it decent. He stood a little way off from them, conscious of the emblem on his back. Today just hadn't been serious. No chance to get really stuck in. He had thought there would be masses of coloureds and trash, in with the ban-the-bombers. But mostly they had been white, so you couldn't really get at the coloureds. You needed to get them off on their own, but they were mixed in with the others. He wished he could get one now. He could *still* show what he was made of. He stared down the bleak grey platform, getting smaller and smaller as it stretched away. Perhaps he would never get a proper job. The jobs had been taken by coloureds. The rhythm his aching head beat out was *unfair, unfair, unfair*.

The echoing tunnel got suddenly louder as some ban-the-bombers stamped in. They were carrying the placards horizontal now and their banners were folded, hanging like scarves, but they acted as if they owned the place, taking up the whole platform. Guy and the lads had gone down the front to jeer at two lesbian women. They were ten foot tall and they curved up the wall, long white thighs locked together. It was really an advert for tights. Guy would never have women like that. That advert had got it right: women conspired together. Conspired to make you feel little, conspired to lock you out. There were lots of women with the ban-the-bombers, and you couldn't say they were ugly. But what were they doing with trash like that? Tall white impossible women. Guy stared down the platform with vacant hatred, and then he caught sight of—*No*. Coming on to the platform with a bulging kitbag, turning sideways to get through the throng. It was George, and before he had thought about it he felt glad and proud he was his brother. Not . . . drunk like this little lot he was with, not poncey and stupid like the ban-the-bombers. He looked very tall and big indeed, and pale and grownup in the glare. With his hair cut short you could see the bones of his head. He seemed to have got even thinner.

"George!" shouted Guy, too late to swallow it, and ran a few steps towards him. He was thirty feet away and there were people between them, vague bright flashes of colour. . . . Guy was focused on the little precise patch of bone and flesh that was his brother: on top of the tower of khaki, the face he had always known . . . but even as he moved towards him, his heart within him changed. Where did he think he was running? George might not want to be with him. He didn't think much of the Party . . . he supposed he didn't think much of *him*. What if George cut him dead? He hesitated, straining to see what the pale face said. . . .

Then someone charged him from behind. It was Kim and one of the others. They'd heard him yell and seen him move forward and thought he was going for the ban-the-bombers. They were much too drunk to think about it or realize they were outnumbered. Kim had got his arms round Guy's shoulder and squeezed it and then he was screaming "Kill!" "Wha . . ." Guy started, trying to keep George in focus, then something else caught him: the flash of a very long, very thin knife in Kim's other hand. It began. It began as if he had always known that this was the way it would happen. He almost stumbled as he was plunged forward and into a heavy body. It was someone quite old, a lined angry face, that silly little badge was in focus, and then the bloke yelled "You nasty little fascist" and something snapped his jaw back, hard. "George," he shouted, punching at his balls, but his voice came out breathless, hopeless. He shouted again as he tried to get far enough back to get his boot in. His brother, his brother would come. Then the bastard hit him in the stomach. They were rolling together on the ground: it was hard and hurt, and the noise was getting worse, something warm trickled down from his nose . . . you could hear women screaming and screaming (he wished he could see Kim cut them), but he couldn't see any more, just the face of the man all contorted with rage, not a human face, something vile which hurt him, the pains getting worse, and a train must be coming, a throbbing, a humming growing louder and louder or else it was his heart now a-hammering, HAMMERING (stop the machinery . . .) and now there was nothing but *pain* and *PAIN* as his poor soft nose was crushed into the stone (he couldn't see George who was pushing through the panic, he was big, he was strong, he would have to sort it out, George who was pushing through the crowd in agony, it couldn't have been Guy though, he must have imagined it) his brother was coming, George 'ud help

209

11 *Chapter of Loss*

This is the chapter of loss. When Guy was lost, no one much mourned. The worst thing about being Guy was that only Guy really loved him. As soon as Guy had been killed, there was no one left to be sad. His family were shocked, of course, felt guilt and surprise and sickness—flesh of their flesh, grown up in their house, lying bruised and cold in a tunnel. What was living shoved down in the dark.

"I wish he'd been cremated," said George. Perhaps he had lost the most. He couldn't work out what he felt. He had shared a room, after all, nearly all his life, with that body. It seemed morbid, having him buried. A body as young as his own.

It was as if they'd rolled up all his memories of Guy, Guy bent to the mirror, his ribs sticking out, Guy pulling on his trousers, down on the beach, with sand on his short bow legs, Guy sniffing with the drop on the end of his nose—all those snapshots shoved down in the mud, growing dark, soaking up the brown water.

Yet he hadn't lost a brother, exactly, in the way people thought of a brother. He felt bad when his mates looked grave and important and grunted their sympathy. He had never explained about Guy, of course, and they just knew "Ship's brother's dead." And some of them assumed he agreed with it all, that fucking awful silly little party.

"He died for the cause," one said, with a wink at the back of a black. "Well he didn't *want* to die," said George. "I know, because he was my brother." He had hardly ever said that before, hadn't thought of live Guy as his brother. That day on the platform was the very first time he had said it like that, *my brother*. He was just the other half of the room, the person he most nearly hated, the person who breathed his air and picked quarrels and left the wrong hairs on his soap.

Yet George came nearer to loving Guy than anyone else did, because it was his nature to love. There was an aching sense of a lack somewhere. Some finger or toe had been severed. A dark space there where—*his brother* had been, something awkward that wouldn't come back.

But George had other things to think about, sitting far away in Berlin. When he decided to join, the decision had felt *inspired*. He knew he was doing right. But the blaze of certainty faded. Now he was losing ground, now he was losing heart.

Joanna had lost her brother too, over sixty years before. A life of intrigue piled on top but the shape of the loss remained. When all the jostling bodies had gone, the flesh fell away from the bone. Joanna shrank to her loss, the missing shape of her twin.

Now nearly a hundred, she sits here, shrivelled, weeping in a small hot room. The tears run black down her cheeks: it is never too late for glamour. "That's twice it's come, in my lifetime. There was so much *sun*, as a child. We used to go out all day in the fields on a Sunday, later. I remember the giant daisies . . . he always adored me, Joseph. You couldn't have a better . . . brother. And then it all had to end. Just going off and dying like sheep. They go off and die like sheep."

The light of all the dead boys was still like thin sunshine, unchanging, a day before 1914 in the arched pale bones of her head. They are waving from photographs, still, lined up on her grandchild's sideboard, calling their distant survivors, the faces too faint and too far . . . is it love, or regret, or a warning? The point of their loss was lost.

This is the chapter of loss. There are greater losses, and smaller.

And this is perhaps the greatest loss that those in the Great War suffered: loss of the stupid boyish hope that this war would end all wars. *Loss to stop other losses*. Instead it forewarned, foreshadowed.

Which losses seem to be greater, to peaceful folk in a fiction? There was Mervyn's loss of a daughter, say, when Lorna ran off and got married. That was a loss as big as all Wales, as big as all Mervyn's Welsh heart. Too large a loss, and too late. Mervyn's ration of loss was used up. It was ultimate loss, for Mervyn, since Lorna was life for him. So great an absence bred evil replacements, cells which spawned under cover. Once the signal *despair* had been given, the pain ran wild after dark. He felt he was eaten alive, lying in the dark thinking *Lorna*. The loss ate into his bones every night and the cancer gnawed at his liver.

She was punished twenty years later, when Latham treated her like dirt. (*No one is punished, never: their faces shine over the earth.*) But she suddenly felt it was punishment, knowing what a fool she'd been, knowing how much she had loved a man who didn't think anything of her. She had lost her long glossy curls by then and the quiet milk of her skin. "I'm thirsty," Mervyn had kept on saying as he lay in the final ward.

It wasn't milk he wanted, though the nurses brought him that. It was love he wanted, of course: the return of his golden daughter. She came in the end, but changed. She came in the end, wouldn't meet his eyes, couldn't bear all the love that was in them. Came with a frightened peaky face and an impossible bulging belly. "You look wonderful, girl, just wonderful," said the love in Mervyn's heart. Came in the end and went without looking and he had to die without her. He had his dream of her, though: stick-thin, bright-eyed and balletic, dancing around in the thin cloak of sunlight, her spread rays of hair falling gently over him, yes, she was here, she had come. . . .

Her loss perhaps was the greater, though she did not know it at the time. She had lost her father, which might be normal, but they never come again. She had lost the glowing sense of her future which shone for her in him. There was only Henry to turn to, and Henry had been a comfort. A husband wasn't a father but he doted on her in his way. For years she turned to her husband and felt the warmth of his light. And then the warmth started fading, and Henry's light went out. He became the dull shade of the past, and Lorna had to escape him.

He had never been dull before, but Jack's flame burned him to nothing. She lay in bed with her husband and wondered where he

213

had gone. She once used to worry so much about whether he really loved her. It was as if all her nerves had died, as if her heart had lost feeling.

(Some losses aren't for ever . . . bright rings turn up in the garden, yellowing love-letters flutter from books and hearts start beating again.)

Maybe all Lorna lost with Jack Latham was his beautiful heavy body. Bodies don't come again. Rewrapped in their clothes, redirected. Will strip off his clothes for others, show them what were her secrets. Show them the parts she touched, his long thighs covering hers. The curve of his neck and shoulder.

Those times and dreams in the storeroom, in dim creamy light, the high window. The burning red of his genitals, burning excitement and pain. Bodies don't come again, they have passed down the line to others. Skin touching skin seems for ever, but skin doesn't let love through. Her love never bled into him, and all that she got was friction.

Those weeks of seeing him after the break in the shop each day as a stranger, his clothes wouldn't muffle the pain: not thick enough to protect her. She wanted him swathed in layers of cloth, so the blaze of need would be less. Each time he passed her, their eyes not meeting, her bruised flesh swelled and burned. She could feel her loss as a weight of hot blood, pushing her back towards him.

It was not the shell others looked at. That managerial suit. Italian-looking and cheap, she had never really liked it. Those creases straight as cheese-wire. His stomach bulging the waistcoat . . . and yet those curves, his thick blood beating, were hers (*were no longer hers*).

He had held her close so their hearts knocked together, and she said so, licking his arm. "They can't be together, you silly," he said. "They must be on different sides." And him, of course, on the management side. The stripes on his suit were like bars. Years later, she would tell Henry "He wasn't worth half of you." But people aren't weighed like ham. Her loss could not be made good. One single human body, the loss of one detailed world.

This is the chapter of loss. There are greater losses, and smaller. But no one can ever be sure that the thing they have lost doesn't matter.

Maybe we should have been swans, all swans, necks curving

214

together for ever. (But some would have been left out: how could their loss be measured?)

Voices with nothing to lose. Voices which pelt my window.

If Lorna had not lost Jack, what would Henry have suffered? He thought he would lose his Lorna to that ham-like, stupid man. Each time his mind wound round that rail it stopped, stuck dead, in pain. It refused to go any further, consider a time to come. He couldn't live without Lorna: they had lived their lives together. And Henry didn't feel lucky. A lot of things had gone wrong. On the whole he noticed that once things *started* to go wrong they never got better. He had almost made that his rule. Once you got that sinking feeling . . . the ship would just go on crumbling and rustling down to the dank cold bottom.

Some people get what they want, long paths lead to their longing. Hope began to come back, a faint bubble, when she came home one day red-eyed. She refused to answer his questions or mend his shirt for tomorrow. Instead of going to the pub for a drink and coming back brave enough to hit her, Henry thought behind his lenses. A definite tiny bubble. He went to the drawer he had never opened and found a packet of needles. He took the shirt down to his workshop so she wouldn't think he'd gone mad. It wasn't very easy, sewing. No wonder she used to complain. He was still out there with his oil-lamp sewing at nearly half past ten. He had started to enjoy it by then, the delicate mesh of the stitches, dark threads wooed back into their place, nothing escaping or fraying. . . .

He was tying a final knot when he heard something scratch at the window. It was Lorna timidly scratching at the glass. "Are you *all right*, Henry? You haven't had your cocoa. . . ." She could see his face swimming in the lantern-light like a sun coming up through water. Things can come right in time, the deepest wounds heal over. The slender fish swam round him again, a rainbow of reds in winter.

But Henry would suffer another loss that no Lorna could make good. And because she did not understand him, quite, she made that loss more bitter.

The child or poet in Henry had never accepted his role. That he was a man, and a father, and *fathers must knuckle down*. That the

215

future would be no different: that they worked until they were old. He hadn't minded the Brewery because that was just marking time. His real self lived in the coils of the springs of Ken Minder's clocks and watches. Going there every evening, helping him out and learning. Learning to work with a three-haired brush, the eye-glass held in his eye by willpower. . . . Magnified wonders seen through that lens. The world was windows on windows. He left the Brewery, leaped through the pane, when the job came up in Acton. Ken Minder's uncle was looking for someone to handle the Repairs side of things. His eyes weren't good any more but his tongue was as sharp as ever. Henry could bear it. It wouldn't be for long. He was marking time again.

And he had his vision of life to come, a stadium packed with faces. The faces were gentle, silver, gold. He could feel the flutter of their quiet hearts beating. They held out their hands towards him, in final recognition. Henry would be their protector, he would heal them, polish them, find them new lovers. HENRY R SHIP: TIMEPIECES. The shop would be his own.

And the shop did become his own very suddenly, when old Mr Minder died (he had a soft spot for Henry, and he wanted to spite Mrs M).

But the dream of freedom went wrong. Henry tended his shop seven years. Businesses weren't about time and its magic. The wall-clock was huge, electric. It hummed in mindless spurts. He never quite bothered to change it. If you took that ugly thing down from the wall, there would be a torn hole behind it. The clock was telling him something with its surges of manic humming. "TIME IS MONEY, Henry. Have you realized, TIME IS MONEY." Shops were all about balancing books, as Mervyn had found to his cost. All over sinking England the little shops sank too. A nation of sinking shopkeepers. The black sea of paper, rising . . . National Insurance, VAT, Ingoings, Outgoings, Profit and Loss. . . . Lorna felt faint and sick when Henry mentioned the books. What if he got like her father? What if she got like her mother? Too many of his customers seemed to be friends and friends didn't want to pay. *Outgoings, outgoings, loss.* In the end there was nothing but loss.

Lorna couldn't bear to watch him. "You think you're too good to make money. You act as if that place is a church. Well it's not, Henry Ship, it's a shop—a fiddly little unsuccessful shop." Then she sniffed and begged his forgiveness.

Everything slipped away. The electric hum got louder. Patterns of loss were imposed from outside (*England, darkening, sinking*). Just before the end he had a spasm of activity, painted the sign of his dreams . . . nailed it up in a fever instead of the mean small facts (*Minders', Clocks and Watches: Sales and Repairs, No Credit*).

The new sign was very different. The letters were big, flying skywards. The background was exquisite deep rose, a beautiful colour, she told him, over her forehead the deep lines worrying *but is it right for a shop*? The letters were elegantly fluted and curled in a leftover pot of old gold, skinny gold long-legged spread-feathered birds flying over the ache and the darkness.

"There's an artist in Henry," Lorna said proudly to her next-door neighbour Mrs Eames. Mrs Eames had eyes like stitches and her mouth pulled in to a button. "Well *I like it*," said Lorna, pugnacious. From a distance, though, she looked back: you couldn't read a glimmer of the words. HENRY R SHIP: TIMEPIECES. FORMER GLORIES RESTORED. Not that it mattered, who'd understand it? It looked like a sunset, old gold and old roses. The sun had gone down within the year, a computer firm bought his vision. For Henry, loss became final, drawing a line at the end. Staring at those homeless faces, the still cold hands that remained.

After eighteen months on benefit, living on eggs and potatoes, he found a job in a bar, in a small hotel in Chiswick. You *couldn't*, not with three kids . . . he had to be the father of the family. But *every* night, in *that bar*. . . . The cash register with its stupid ringing, the fag machine's endless slam. The smell of the chef frying old black steak for the drunken fools who were hungry. The TV blaring just out of his view and the bursts of senseless laughter. Next door the swing-doors crashed all night and each time he burned to run through. . . .

But Lorna went mad with joy. He'd have a proper wage, he'd have holidays, stamps . . . she lashed out on a bottle of wine. She was sure that rosé was nice. She set it out with two glasses. When Henry saw *that*, his face closed down and his hopes closed down as well. He must work until he was old. The future would be no different.

To keep the shell of himself afloat he started serious drinking. But something lived in that shell. He still had the kids, and Lorna. If he could hide and just keep going, things would come right in time. *Lifers crossing off days in the dark break into light one morning.* . . .

No one quite knows what they've done. No one knows what

they're losing. Mervyn didn't see that the loss of his shop would lead to the loss of his daughter. Lorna didn't see that the loss of Latham would lead her back to her husband. Henry didn't see that the loss of his freedom would lead to the drink, the bruises. . . . 'They could none of them quite keep hold of their lives, so we have to follow behind them. They mostly looked after the small things and somehow lost the big. The list of things we have to pick up would fill a capacious novel. And none of them tried to save their lives . . . *if only a novel could help them*. All written off as numbers in a bigger, colder fiction'.

George felt sorry for his father but disgusted by him as well. Could someone like Dad, whom he loved and admired, turn suddenly into a coward? *It was cowardly hitting a woman*—rules you learn early on. George's life hadn't been easy, for a boy not twenty-one. He had tried to do what was right, which is not what everyone else does. He never quite learned that rules are random, keeping them a lost cause.

At first, doing right wasn't terribly hard. The things to do were *certain*—always coming top in maths. Always telling the truth. Loving his sister, his mother. Loving their hair, and the patterns in things. Proving elaborate theorems. Seeing the light in geometry. Trying to understand. . . . Trying to do the same things in life, work out the rules by numbers. . . .

Failing to understand. *Sometimes* knowing the truth, *sometimes* telling the truth. Trying to understand, in time, the darkness which smeared the paper. As he grew older the darkness grew and began to make rival patterns.

The colour of goodness had once been blue, though Angela wanted a rainbow. He liked the phrase *true blue*. He loved his model policemen. But the blue paint peeled and chipped very quickly. Life wasn't all it was painted.

Inside George grew a special kind of ache, a pain which was also a pleasure. The ache was striving for perfection, no longer believing in perfection: after he had ceased to believe in the future perfect tense. Just out of reach was a perfect fit between wanting to be good and achieving goodness . . . beyond that high bare horizon, at the top of the steep little road. There it would be, the one word GOODNESS, the eagle upon the blue. The skin of the sea and the sky made one single taut meniscus. The fit for a moment was perfect. The dreamer's joy, complete. But the dream and the ache grew distant as those clear colours faded. . . .

As you grew up things were harder. Things would get worse in time.

He did understand that the harder things were the more you should probably do them. Loving Guy, for example, and not being charmed by his sister. Trying to look at the facts behind the bright swing of her feelings. You didn't have to look at her hair: you had to look down at the floor. The loss of closeness was hard but it helped him be *free*, and *fair*. Logic belonged to men. He could work things out by numbers.

The hardest thing of all was deciding to join the army. When he thought of killing or hurting people he had to close his eyes. The blood beat hard in his temples. (Blood in the roots of trees . . . his uncle had died in France, but the pain lived on in George.) Still he had to stay in, for Guy. Or his brother's life would be wasted. He had to stay in, to prove that he meant it, you had to stand up for freedom. Keeping the peace was simple: you showed you were ready for war. It was the hardest way of thinking, so he trusted it all the more.

To help other people be free, he had to give up his freedom. He had to give up the beauty of maths, his glittering hopes for the future. He lost the country he loved. . . . Angela cut him off. All this George could accept, though his eyes and mouth grew different. . . .

We always lose more than we know. Very soon, George would lose hope. He realized that logical thinking had led him into a trap. The world was heavy with logic, a creaking graveyard of hardware. Battened in West Berlin, so far from the sea, the sky. All round him were barriers, checkpoints, wire. Control towers, sentry posts, tanks.

The machinery wasn't just machinery, logical, factual, neutral. He had watched for a very long time, and his thoughts had circled, painful. In the end he couldn't deny it any more. They were all in a cage together. All those millions of tons of steel converted in seconds to murder. Their purpose was bursting and spilling flesh, animals weeping and crawling. That was the only talent they had, those logical great machines. They were packed away to look clean and safe but when George looked close he could see it. They weren't just *now*, sitting cold and still, they were hideous skinless futures.

He tried to talk to the other soldiers. The lids came down over their eyes. Their silos were packed already, the fate of their lands was decided. They no longer wished to remember what was once living there. Lids closed down on the floor. You should keep away from the nutters.

(And yet they were secretly thrilled, understanding, when there was an outbreak of joy-rides. One man, another, a third took tanks, rammed the barriers, revved through the city . . . adrenalin roaring mad through their veins, human again, on their own . . . using a killing machine at last to do what it was meant to, kill. Their raging unhappy hearts in charge of the steel again. Crashing it through the slow cold plan, slamming it through the waiting. . . .)

George discovered the steel of logic had penned him up with the mad. They were all entirely surrounded. The weight of machinery, humming. Humming all through the night, whispering impossible numbers. Numbers that dreams would convert into sheets of lost names, smashed faces. He longed for somebody normal, *just to talk about things.* . . .

The other soldiers weren't normal, boasting and boozing, nervous. Small overwound alarm-clocks which suddenly shrilled and fell over. They kept their eyes as close as possible up to the gleaming dials. The bones of their foreheads touched the chrome so the humming dinned into their brains. That way they didn't have to think about things. Ship was a nuisance, a weirdo. The sympathy he got over Guy disappeared. They had probably *both* been weirdos.

There weren't any girls out here. With them you could sometimes be normal. Try and talk about your feelings, talk about things that mattered. Looking for the sequence of their thoughts, every factor unknown, mysterious. They flashed to answers by instinct, a great deal quicker than George. But George was top of his class. George had to stick with the facts.

And now he was stuck with hard facts, the hardest facts of our dying. The numbers marched in formation, marched to the final sum. Too much respect for *what is* and the terminal facts press down. Metal lines tightening, closing. On the air a faint smell of burning. There *must still be some way out*, but smoke was confusing his view. He would find the equation soon, but the hum ate into his brain. . . .

Before the final addition came he would mourn the loss of his

220

goodness. He thought he could fly like an eagle . . . trussed like a waterlogged chicken.

Christmas is coming, the bird is getting fat. Wire-trussed, glistening victim.

George did write to his sister, but he could not write what he felt. Angela never wrote back. So he wrote to his mother and father: lies about *sausages*, landscape. He always said he was happy. *Never upset the family* . . . one rule he still heard clearly.

Angela would have learned in time that a brother is more than a theory.

"I just can't bear it," she said to John. "It makes me too ashamed. I mean, my own brother in Germany."

"Well he *is* your brother," said John. "And I mean, he must've loved *you*."

"And *I* loved him!" she wailed. "But I mean, my *brother* a soldier. And he really hurt my feelings. I spent *so much time* on George. . . ." In time, she would have grown kinder, as her mother did before her. But time didn't last long enough, so the loss of their love was final.

But this is the chapter of loss, where every loss is recorded. Nothing need ever be lost as long as one moment held it. Here in a dusty pile lie all the forgotten objects . . . things that slipped out of the story, things that were missed by the camera. Patiently waiting to be picked up, stroked and put back in our pocket. Stockings and rings and hankies: those must belong to Joanna, left in a hansom cab, sprawled underneath a sofa. . . . Ghostly names from a diary. Those must belong to Prunella. She wrote in her boyfriends in pencil, mostly too brief for ink. Fish Mervyn left in a drawer; belly-up under these pages. They wriggle at last and reappear in a rainbow blaze of colour. Queer bricks lost by Henry, dim in the pile of days. Back in the end in glory, building the end of the story. Photographs laid aside, then missed, then frantically looked for . . . Lorna had rows on her sideboard, but some were removed by her daughter . . . Angela kept the one of the boys, though she wouldn't write to her brother.

Persons are lost as well. What of our missing person? Grandfather Ship, eyes veiled, on the move, determined to quit this story?

Frank will be found again. Print can track down a man. Frank

221

will be found when we least expect it, bold on the page of the mountain. . . . Frank will be found with his own kind ghost and his happiness, the white fountain.

Some things cannot return. Our certainties about goodness. *My* Japanese were so gentle. They lay in the park without sound. Cranes flying blind for the darkened sun, their mayfly-legs perhaps broken. Chrysanthemums on a kimono, shapes which burned on the skin. The Emperor was a marine biologist: small pale pearls, mute fish. And the Japanese loved children. Their gentle children would die. Two hundred thousand victims: so many gentle children. . . .

All of us know too much. Numbers play evil games. Two hundred thousand people were also killed at Nanking. The Japanese were the killers. The killers were not very gentle. Their orders turned them into machines, machines which killed one by one. The worlds of novels burst open, and stinking insides pour out. Entrails were draped by the purple yard down the sides of the road in Bataan.

The Japanese were inventive, and not just with decoration. Bombs of plague-germs in fleas and rat-poison fell like rain over China. The Emperor *was* a biologist, but his greatest love was disease. Tissue-cultures of botulism, encephalitis, yaws.

The Japanese adored children. *Everyone knows that is true.* But it wasn't true in China. Japanese dealers flooded Manchuria with heroin, opium, morphine. There were canvas booths on street corners where children got special rates. The Chinese children paid less than a farthing, stuck their thin arms through the canvas. The needle shot into the vein, and nobody saw their faces. Perhaps that is just as well, since the Japanese adored children.

Some things cannot return. Our certainties about words. Japanese Emperors choose the name that their reign shall have in history. Young Hirohito decided that his reign would be *Showa*, "Peace".

Perhaps only God was lost. The Emperor's god-like cunning. Perhaps it is only ever our gods who understand what they're doing. Emperors, princes, generals . . . glittering tinpot gods. . . .

(Staring down over our story, watching how far we are going)

Japanese metaphor housed the Emperor "above the clouds, like a Crane". But the Crane saw down through the clouds. The Crane had elaborate plans. The Crane-God had his bunkers, six miles of underground tunnels. Up on the surface under the sky the Japanese waited to suffer. Most of them gentle people, women, old men, and children.

After the atom bomb fell, the Crane had something to say. "The war situation has developed . . . *not necessarily to Japan's advantage*. . . ." The Crane voice sang of his *not necessarilys* blazing with gold chrysanthemums. Cranes and chrysanthemums change, speckled with human sin.

> Something returns in time, a different wholeness, a pattern. New life came to Hiroshima, new leaves covered the scars. Gaps which are healed by the thing we learn, gentle and careful darning.

> Nothing was lost which was written down . . .

> . . . *until the Chapter of Burning.*

12 *Chapter of Smoke*

The summer that Guy was lost it was clear that trouble was coming. The city was boiling hot, and no air came in from outside. Every factory in London was burning its engines, running on throbbing heat. There wasn't any oxygen any more; they were breathing fumes of poison. Every pavement in London was packed at lunch-times with people who didn't know how to cool down, standing pressed together in the heavy sunlight, mouthing *it's lovely, being outside*. Buses roared past, blue fumes. Pigeons sat flat on the pavement.

Barmen in pubs were bad-tempered. "We ran out two days ago." "Could you wait a minute, sir, *please*. I've only got one pair of hands." By the time they cleared everyone out, every pore was a frying-pan, gleaming. "*Time*," they yelled, with a last hoarse energy. "*Time*. Would you *please* go 'ome?"

In Japan, August is *O-Bon*, the Season of the Dead. The Japanese are good children. Nearly all observe the season, visiting their parents' homes to pay tribute to the dead.

They kneel at small wooden shrines and pray for the souls of their ancestors. They burn small clouds of incense and watch the smoke blow back.

It was only chance that the Thin Boy came to Japan on the sixth of August. Summers are hot, intensely humid, fireworks, incense and grief. The papers are full of senseless crimes, murders and suicides. And the atom bomb came to join it, the Season of the Dead.

Angela hated August. It was the very worst part of the year. Too hot to think and too hot to work. Too hot to keep yourself separate. She felt swallowed up by things, by the sticky heat and the grey. The newspapers seemed to grow larger, insistent, the News blared out all day. She woke in a sweat every morning, too early, brain buzzing with worry. John would be lying there breathing heavily, innocent and strange in sleep.

She had only moved in with him in June and she hadn't got used to him yet. It was different him being there *always* from him being there when she chose. It was hard to bear his regular breath when she was sleepless and edgy. . . . She felt stifled by all the unfamiliar objects nestling close to her own. Their attic was crowded with love, two lives crowding together. His books interleaved her books: his shoes piled up over hers. In the bathroom, their toothbrushes got confused. "I *know*, but mine is much newer."

She felt all angular fretfulness in the face of his slow still ease. And he never looked hot, with his thick pale skin and slow balletic movements. Her own thin freckled skin was permanently beaded with moisture, even the roots of her hair felt damp. The drops on her forehead grew so enormous they felt like rain or blood.

"My God, I'll die if we don't have a storm. There's no air at all in here." "Well all the windows are open. If I left the front door ajar. . . ." "Don't be stupid, I wouldn't feel safe," she snapped, her hand going over her heart. "What's the matter, Ange," he said, coming over, taking her tired damp hand. "You can't feel frightened when I'm here with you." "What do you mean, I *can't*. I *am*, I'm always frightened." "But what are you frightened *of*? I'd never let anyone hurt you."

He was kissing her hair very lightly, and she started to relax in his arms. "Oh John, you're . . . marvellous . . . I'm sorry. It's just that . . . well, I suppose . . . I've always been a fearful person. It's . . . well, it's just the whole world."

"But you also say you're *reasonable*, and you know that you're safe with me. I mean, it *was* scary, where you used to live, with all

225

those nutters downstairs. And no proper lock on the door. And you never used to draw your curtains."

"That's cos I hate feeling . . . *all locked up*. I sometimes feel I can't breathe."

"Are you saying that's how you feel with me?"

Ange knew she *was* saying that. All the same she didn't want to hurt him. She kissed his bare arm, and said "Dafty". But he went and stared out of the window.

"We shouldn't have got this attic, I suppose. It's bound to be hot up the top."

"No, for goodness' sake, I've always loved heights . . . seeing all over the city." (True—coloured lights, cars floating, tiny boats full of dreams . . . you couldn't see the horizon. The night turned into the world.) "After all, summer won't last long. It just *feels* as though it's here for ever."

"Let's open a bottle of wine."

"I don't want to. I've got a headache. And lots of work still to do. That might be part of the trouble. . . ."

She was two years into a Ph.D. and knew it was all a mistake. There wasn't the time to waste on all that: her heart said time had grown urgent. Sirens were wailing below, alternate blares of distress. She had to inscribe her urgent self on whatever white space she could find.

But writing frightened her too. How could she dare to write? Her writing made her wince with embarrassment, seeing herself in a mirror. She wanted to stare right over the city, take in the whole strange world. Herself just a tiny part of the pattern . . . but there she was, misting the glass.

She couldn't show it anybody, not even John, though he asked and she liked him asking. (Ange never asked about what *he* did: so boring, to be in computers. "I shouldn't be moaning about my work when I know how boring yours is," she said one day, after spending two hours describing the snags in her writing. "It isn't boring at all," he said mildly. "Look, the whole world's on computers!" She didn't hear what he said, staring down at her paper.)

It added to the stockpile of poisonous fears, the fear that she hadn't any talent. The fear of just being nothing and nobody, ant-like under the table . . . and ants can be easily crushed, so easily, even if they curl together.

It was terrible being so stupidly young, with everything left to achieve. If she died only John and her family would miss her. She would leave nothing behind. She needed ten years, or twenty years, or at any rate one cool winter. . . .

This horrible sulphurous summer it seemed there was no time left. Flying ants swarmed outside in the heat, which had never happened before . . . or else it was planes, that faint humming of insects, more coming over than ever . . . stirring unpleasant memories, setting the little limbs whirring. . . .

Some time after 11.02 a.m. on that boiling August morning, Tatsuichiro Akizuki stared out of his glassless window. His consulting room was high up, had a view all over the city. Not only the glass but the wooden frame had been blown completely away. He told himself *it is morning*. But the sky was black as pitch. Under the swirling darkness hung a heavy yellow-brown fog. And beneath, the whole earth was burning, flames bursting up from the ground. Black, yellow and scarlet bands of inferno pressed down over the people. They were running, running like ants, but some of them crawled, were broken. They ran like ants going crazy with fear, with nowhere left to escape to. *Perhaps the planes had sprayed gasoline*. How could so much be burning?

Thirty minutes ago the all-clear had sounded. *Can the world end without warning?*

Ange hated the stupid wail of the sirens more than anything else on earth. It was worst when they couldn't get through the traffic so the dissonance blared for hours, calling for help abortively, uselessly, hearts must be stopping inside. Or people being murdered a few blocks away with no one coming to save them. . . .

"You don't want to take any notice," said John. "You really do work yourself up."

"You're so bloody *calm*," she said, but quite friendly. "I think it's quite sane to be worried."

"Look, if you don't want a glass of wine, let's just have a cigarette. Come and lie down and be cuddled, and we'll smoke just one cigarette."

227

"Come and lie down and get cancer."

"Oh *God* . . . come *on* . . . just ten *minutes*."

But the siren was sounding again, from further away, less urgent, more sad, as if the patient had already died and someone was playing a dirge. She let herself stretch out along his firm body on the low line of cushions by the window. He kissed her neck, very gently. "Well anyway, Ange, I adore you." He took out a cigarette, his fingers as graceful as ever. The thick strong line of his neck like a panther, a friendly, dreamy great cat. He was beautiful, and she *did* like that. His black-fringed eyes always calmed her. She stared at them now as he sucked on the tip, their deep soft greyish-brown centres. Close up, human flesh looked so real and solid, it would never change or vanish. Fear became stupid here in the animal warmth of his closeness. The tip began to glow red as he sucked and the smoke curled out round his mouth, untidily, then on his second deep draw blew out two neat dragon-gouts from his nostrils.

"You haven't lit one for me."

"No fear, if it's giving you cancer. Anyway, I thought you would have half of mine. Then we'll have another one after."

He put the tip very gently between her thirsty lips. "You're a terrible woman," he said, mock-Irish. "But not too bad to look at." His eyes closed over her, tender. Normally she loved the way he gazed at her; this evening though it was too moist, too hot.

"Don't look at me, I feel stifled," she said. She shifted away and blew smoke in his face. It was only meant as a joke, but he coughed until she felt guilty.

"The truth is maybe I'm barmy. I shouldn't be living with anybody. Maybe I shouldn't be living at all, not in this horrible century. You talk about being reasonable. Well being terrified *is*. What do you think he was really saying, that man on the bus last night? *Cheer up, it may never happen*. What do they mean by *it*? I feel it *is* going to happen. I feel we're all going to die."

The smoke curled gently, elegantly through the growing space between them. "What's that got to do with being scared *now*, and it being so hot, and the sirens? The thing about war is quite different; you know I'm behind you on that. I mean, I wasn't so hot till I met you, but now I go on every single bloody march." He paused, drew the smoke in deep. "Look, let's just be practical, Ange. Let's just *do more about it*. We never go to local meetings, we never write

228

letters to the Press. Let's . . . go down to one of the Peace Camps when I have my next week off. Lakenheath might be nice . . . I mean *sod* them, *sod* their missiles."

But her eyes were as tense as ever, the grooves like her mother's deepened. "I'm *not* going to go on a Peace Camp. You ought to know me by now. I mean, it would drive me crazy. There are just *too many people*. Demos are bad enough. . . ."

"*For Christ's sake, Ange!*" he exploded. "You know there aren't *half enough* people."

He sounded so self-righteous that she cut across him, very sharp. "Look none of that's really the point. It's happening *in my mind*, do you see. All involved with the heat and the city. . . . If you don't understand how it all fits in then you're probably right not to understand. But it does fit in *to me*, that's all. I just have the sense things are ending. And it just makes everything so *pointless*. I mean, loving you, and writing."

He rubbed his cheek against hers when she said that bit about love. It was always like that with Angela, coming when you least expected it. The feel of his rough warm cheek was so good that her hands slipped down to his fly. Then the feel of his bulky cock under denim was so good that she pressed against it. Just as she did so however there was a sudden smell of burning. "*Ange!*" John yelled, in sudden panic, and she realized it was her hair . . . hideous smell like burning rubber, the smell of something not meant for fire. They fell on the floor as they panicked and beat at it, pressing her head on a cushion. The smell was horribly sharp and heavy and she ran and looked in the mirror. Only a section of fringe was singed, but she promptly cried, the tears streaming down, streaming and streaming as she stared through the window, hot thick tears which were not for her hair . . . but it made her feel better, and they went to bed.

You had to wake up the next morning, though, and the burning smell was still there. When she leant out of the window to see the weather the black smell hung on the air. And the siren was howling again, unutterably weary and boring. They would never leave her alone. There would never be time to escape them.

It was hard to remember a time when the smoke of fear was not there. Ever since they explained to them at school about the bomber-planes in the War. After that whenever a plane came over she'd felt the same sick fear. The whine of the engines getting

229

louder and louder, it would never start to get less. Lying in the darkness, helplessly waiting, unable to see the mad bomber.

Sometimes she thought they must be circling above her as she lay in bed with her knees clutched tight, counting to ten then twenty, praying God would send them away. It was definitely spite that they stayed so long . . . either spite or a warning. Perhaps she was chosen to feel that fear, chosen to hear the warning . . . the worst thing was not knowing what was happening, whether it was normal or not. Would anyone tell them if it was the bombers? Did anyone else lie and wonder?

Smoke didn't clear from the sky, after *pikadon* came. The sun showed red in the early afternoon, glowing and fading through the layers of smoke. Worse things loomed in the darkness. The sound of planes had returned. The planes droned over again and again, and those on the ground were blind. The smoke wrapped tightly over the light and increased their helpless terror. Every time the droning came closer they all felt sick with fear, and those who were able to move scuttled for some kind of shelter. Brave men trembled and cowered. If *pikadon* came again. . . . All through the terrible night which followed the terrible planes droned on. (In fact, small clean observer planes were trying to see what they'd done.)

The Japanese were not warned, not the humble folk in those cities. They did not stubbornly choose to die, shaking their fist at the heavens. *Pikadon* fell from a clear blue sky on Japanese eating their breakfast. Eating their rice and pickled plums, heating their thin pale *miso*. Even war became normal . . . until 8.15 a.m. That was the first explosion, the first time the earth was shaken.

When the second great blue-white flash ripped out over Nagasaki, the smoke had begun to seep through. Wild rumours of a new kind of bomb, of a light which put out the sun. *They have done this thing in Hiroshima. They will not do this again.* . . .

And the skies took pity on the ant-like people and veiled them with a thin shade. Kokura was saved by a pall of smoke from its hot machines that morning. The little plane wheeled and came in again. The centre of Nagasaki, also, was saved by a faint skin of haze.

They finally dropped it off-centre, and the little fish swam down. Swam through forty seconds of silk, small silver fish, milk sky. . . .

Beauty is also confusing. Beauty of the fish swimming down. The dazzling power of all metaphors to blind us to *what is*. Churchill said of the British Bomb, "It went off beautifully."

Blood seeping through the pages. The chaos after the beauty.

Angela lay with her knees curled up in the dark and thought about thinking. Most people didn't think much about *anything* except their own little lives. Her mother, for example, what *she* thought about was whether she could pay for her shopping. At least that was what she talked about most, and she never answered real questions. And Guy just thought about upsetting people, and her dad just thought about watches. Well, he thought about her mother and her as well, but he wasn't any good to talk to.

One day she'd caught him coming in from the shed where he sat and examined his watches. The sky was a painfully lovely blue: on the little black tree, the apples were growing. "Dad," she said, "can I ask you something?" He was in a good mood. "Of course you can."

"Well I just want to know your *opinion*. Do you think—there'll be another world war?"

"What on earth put that into your head?" He stared down at her hard for a moment, uneasy, his eyebrows shooting up into his hair. The sun shone brightly on his pebble-thick glasses. She couldn't really see what his eyes were doing. She was sitting on the step so he couldn't go in. She was desperate to have an answer.

"Well, it's just we've been doing it a bit in history. We asked Mr Gillingham things. He told us. He said he was a pilot in the air force. He told us about dropping bombs. And the very big bomb, one very big bomb, that killed thousands and thousands of people. I think it was a Japanese bomb, that they went and dropped on America. And then all the babies died."

"The trouble is, you don't listen," said Henry. "It was all the other way round. It was the Yanks went and dropped the bloody Bomb on Japan, and since then they've made a whole lot more.

231

They've got too much money and too little sense." It was a real speech for Henry.

Lorna called through from the sink, where she was noisily washing some lettuce. "What on earth are you doing putting *that* into her head? Don't you listen to a word of it, Angela. Of course there won't ever be another war. That's why we had to fight the last one. In any case, you don't want to worry about America. The Americans are our *friends*."

It was her "being-a-mother" voice. It never sounded convincing.

Angela was only thirteen, but she always had a strong sense of logic. She didn't argue with her mother, but she thought about what she had said. If the world had fought a second world war to prevent there ever being a third, they would probably have to fight a third, to prevent there being a fourth. And if they used those special big bombs, she supposed that the world would end; and people her age would never grow up. The hairs on her legs all prickled. (Mr Gillingham said all the children were poisoned, and the little girls' hair fell out. . . .)

A vague dull ache settled over her life like a headache from reading too much. Reading a story that she'd been told not to, in case it gave her bad dreams. And life didn't let her forget. The papers were full of wars starting. And things that proved men were wicked. Husbands would stab their wives. Mothers would strangle their babies. And Guy was cruel to insects, and cruel to people as well. And her parents might not be wicked exactly but their quarrels were part of the pattern.

Inside her head was another kind of world where everything was different, perfect. She lived there with George and her best friend Clara till she found out Clara didn't like her. And then she lived there with George, and it felt rather cold and lonely. Still that was the *real* world, she knew it, and the other bad world was a dream. But the dream grew solider as she grew older and the dull ache dragged and stayed. The vision of goodness in her own mind faded, she saw it was just invention.

She thought a lot about dying, as well. You had to, of course, in the end. Though everyone pretended you didn't, but Biology said that you did. So it seemed quite sensible to work it out, the way of dying that was best. She soon found no one would talk about it: it was something grownups called *morbid*. And *morbid*, it seemed, was bad. Why that should be so wasn't clear to Angela since TV was all about dying. People being shot or stabbed or poisoned, and grownups loved to watch that. But it was only fun if it happened to others, they didn't mean to die themselves. Which just showed how stupid grownups could be, Ange thought, making plans very gravely.

She didn't want to die of a *disease*, not with spots or swellings or fevers. She didn't want to die of a stroke like Mr Adams, sitting shaking and red in a wheelchair. She didn't want to be murdered . . . the terror before you died . . . she didn't want to fall off a very high building, seeing the concrete rush up to meet her.

She didn't want to die in a battle. She didn't want to be a lady soldier, not even a brave one like Uncle George, who had died in the Second World War. (In any case, she wasn't convinced he was brave. That was just what Daddy invented. She bet no one knew what had happened out there, in the mud and muddle and darkness. . . .)

That was the thing with grownups, the reason not to believe them. They pretended that things were clear which would never be clear at all. They asked things like "Are you happy?" or said people were "happy together". Then when you met this couple who were "happy", they didn't seem happy at all. . . .

She was sometimes so happy for a second or two that she felt her heart was a fountain. But that wasn't what they meant. And most of the time she felt worried, but she wasn't allowed to say that. She was supposed to say she was happy, and everything was all right.

What was more, she thought *they* were the same. They were all just as worried as she was. Mum had two lines like the side of a ruler growing up straight from her eyebrows. Dad's lines were ruled straight across, not vertical, but he nearly always looked sad. And yet when she heard them talking to their friends they always said they were happy. "Oh yes, love, Henry's just fine." "Lorna? Oh, fine, just fine." "Oh, everything's fine at work. . . ."

So why did her father stare at the door when he should have been reading the papers? As if something might get in, something he could not fight? Why should she find her mother crying on the crazy-paving path in the garden?

someone else had asked questions like that
                    childish, harrowing questions
things weren't real, that the grownups said
   (BUT IF GROWNUPS DECIDED, YOU WERE ALL DEAD . . .)
they kill things easily   put them in fridges
   stare at the bodies in small clean packets. . . .

Not until Ange was away from her mother could she hear the small girl crying inside her, glimpse little Lorna shivering with fear, *no, I won't eat it, it looks like liver*. . . . Voices weaving in love through time, likenesses weaving slowly together. But haste is stretching and tearing the weave . . . *yes, coming near, coming nearer*.

That day she found her mother on the crazy-paving path, her arms raised up as she hung out the washing. It looked like an old-fashioned kind of prayer, but her cheeks were flooding with tears. It was a fine bright day, and sun splashed in the water. At first she thought it was water from the washing.

So everything wasn't so fine after all. "What's the matter Mum?" she shrilled at the line. "Be quiet, your father will hear you." And so she went to Clara's, and worried all day. Mum had looked so thin and tiny and cold, with her arms stretched up to the sky. Staring up at the brilliant sun, her fixed face running and running.

The Bomb burned shadows on granite where something had shielded the stone. There were people printed on stone, vague shadows of running people. The concrete was stained with a light reddish tint except where the bodies ran . . . dim lost bodies imprinted for ever as living flesh charred to darkness.

This camera was not selective. It caught whatever was ordinary. Final extremes of pain and horror change everydayness to beauty. Three thousand metres from the centre of hell a washing-line shielded a wooden wall. White shadows here where the wood had burned dark.

Great luxury . . . standing and hanging out washing . . . if only that world would blow back again, the gentle shape of the blowing washing. . . .

Ange saw the heat-flash photos years later when she'd nearly forgotten that day. In her mind they melted together; small women, the huge raw sky.

(As a matter of fact all Lorna was thinking was *help*, *getting older*, *time's slipping away* . . .

    help   *time slipping*   *slipping away*)

She had started to smoke like a bonfire, every since she had Guy. The yellow smoke hung like a headache in the kitchen and seemed to soak into Mum's skin. It took on the colour of an autumn leaf, lightly crinkled, too red and too yellow. Angela concluded it *must* be the smoking when Mum's hair turned yellowish as well. It was hair that still looked lovely from a distance; from a distance she looked like a girl. She had permed it "to get back the curl, you sometimes lose it with babies". Then she thought the colour was fading, and went on and on about that.

"Tell me the truth, Ange, will you. Do you think it used to be more red?" "Not sure," said Ange, since she *wasn't* sure whether "being more red" was good. "There you are," her mother muttered, staring in the mirror. "I knew the colour 'ud gone." Then she tried to put it back, with some red from a packet, which came out the colour of brick. Henry and she had a quarrel when he wouldn't say whether he liked it. But Angela said she did, telling lies like everyone else does. And the brick-red faded after three shampoos, smoke-grey and smoke-yellow blew through.

And her mother's worry blew up through the house like the anxious smell of cheap cigarettes; her mother's sorrow (which no one understood) hung trembling above them like the sound of the planes . . . the sound of the planes criss-crossing the hot low sky of their dreams in summer.

Later perhaps Ange did understand, making her pilgrimage backwards. Living away from her parents, she met them again in dreams. Once they were not labelled *mother* and *father* she could start to visit, start to bring flowers, see them as separate and marvellous selves, linking her self to history.

When she was living at home, all she could see was difference; now she could see how the patterns of likeness wove through the years like incense. Seeing her adoration of form in Henry's passion for watches, seeing her parching thirst for affection in

Lorna's grabs for love. Seeing her parents' love for each other as something stronger than quarrels, something stronger than her mother's horrible shaming affair with Jack. Hurling her body down through the air into that cruel warm water. Thinking it was the ocean, not just a small stale pool . . . for Lorna the worst of it must have been meeting the six cold eyes of her children. Standing on the edge, for once united. Naked and tired, crawl past them. Living it all again, Ange knelt to the suffering form of her mother.

> *if there had been more time*   *patterns come clear in time*
> *time to go back and explain*   *next time yes she would do it . . .*

Even as a pale sticky child, Angela never liked heat. It was *always* too hot in summer. Things throbbed and thrummed and ached as she played on her own at break-time. And sometimes the throb was rhythmical, going too fast, coming closer. The planes coming over more every year, she was sure, but nobody noticed. . . .

It wasn't easy to ask. Making friends had never been easy. You couldn't really *talk* to people once they thought you were queer. She confined herself to *is it French conversation*? or *could you lend me your pencil*? Inside her the questions she wanted to ask ached to find other answers.

After the great explosion, a five-year-old's voice in the darkness. Little Miyeko Nakamura kept asking the same old question: "Why is it night already? Why did our house fall down?" Five-year-old girls don't understand. "Why is it night? What happened?"

Angela went to the library with the faint smell of smoke in her nostrils. And Angela's life split in two

> *as the world might crack, split, later*

—the things she read about two world wars shattered life's normal surface. How could they tell you to "look on the bright side" when they knew what had happened to the Jews? And why weren't people more *grateful*, that they were safe and alive? Why didn't people seem to feel *anything*? Her father had lived through the last one. He didn't want to talk about it. "Look, it's history, isnit," he grunted. But he looked uneasy and his eyes had crept years and miles away under the lenses. Keeping what he felt under glass. So perhaps that was what they *all* did.

But what was she supposed to do with the turmoil under her ribcage? It made her weep with pity and rage, alone in her tiny bedroom. Crying till there was a silly dark stain on the pale pink candlewick bedspread. Silly because she felt guilty crying when she was so safe and warm; curled round her kind hot-water bottle, full of her mother's warm cocoa. She didn't know what else to do but cry; no one had warned her, no one had confessed. No one had mentioned what the world had been up to, two decades before she was born

no one would warn them, no one would teach them how to go black and burn . . .   why is it dark already?   why did our house fall down?

Lorna edged into her bedroom one day and found her reading as usual. "What're you reading, Ange?" she said, making the words a reproach. "*The Diary of Anne Frank*," said Angela. "About a Jewish girl in the War."

"You're *obsessed* with war," her Mum said, almost angry. "I can't understand it, what's the matter with you? Why can't you be like other girls your age? Go out and get yourself a boyfriend?"

Her voice rose almost to a screech as she asked that stupid question. She regretted it as soon as it had shot from her lips, but it was too late for regrets, Ange half sat up on the bedspread and her pale-lashed eyes blazed with hate. "You chase enough for us both," she said, very quiet (because of her Dad). But the quietness was poisonous fury, and her face was white and strange. "Don't talk to me about boyfriends. Me brothers are ashamed of you."

The room was silent and electric. They stared at each other, helpless. Words which should never be said, wounds which can never be healed.

Then Lorna did what Ange knew she would do, and her sense of unfairness deepened. Tears flooded up like a tap turning on and spilled over her sharp worn cheekbones. Ange *would not* say she was sorry. Her mother had started it all. But as the thin back jerked out through the door she was torn with pity and guilt.

Then she looked at the book in her hand, the sallow young face with its formal curls. Smiling as if nothing was happening, just before the end of her world. Why should Ange feel sorry for her mother, when life held so much worse? But the guilt cramped down hard on her stomach. She wanted to be gentle and good. She wanted to be on the other side from all that was cruel and evil . . . but the hatred was in her as well, the burning impulse to hurt. She threw the book on the floor with a sigh and went down to look for her mother.

Sat in the kitchen smoking, smoking, working at it as if she wanted to burn, as if she could make herself burst into flame by sucking and blowing, blowing and sucking. She didn't look at her daughter. Smoke and water, smoke and grey tears. But what she said was a surprise. It came slowly, not acting, for once, through the puffs.

"I'm sorry, Ange, to go on at you . . . why shouldn't you read what you want to . . . It's not my business, is it . . . it was just that I wanted to *talk* to you. . . ."

"*Please* don't say sorry, Mum, I can't bear it. I came to say sorry to you."

"Won't you have a cigarette? Just this once. Go on. Your father's out in the workshop."

(So again Ange had to say *No*, and the guilt intermixed with resentment.) "It's no good Mum, I don't like it . . . it always makes me feel ill."

"Well I thought just this once . . . oh well. You've always got your own ideas." She looked up at her daughter suddenly and a smile began on her own, as if it had got there by accident, a loving, cheeky smile (that was it with Mum: she was totally wretched, then that beautiful two-year-old's smile). "When you get to my age, you'll get selfish too. You get so many worries you can't think about . . . you know. It's right you should though, at your age. I just don't want you to get depressed. I used to be your type exactly, seeing all the bad in the world. Only now I've got so many worries of my own I can hardly think about . . . *those things*."

The relief of seeing her mother smile. Ange nodded so hard her head nearly fell off. "Did you really used to worry then, Mum? Just about . . . all the cruelty?"

"You'd laugh at me if you knew all the things I worried about," said Lorna, enjoying Angela's interest. She didn't get that very often. "I used to worry about killing animals. That's why I hate the butcher's. Even now I don't like it, and it's years and years. They took me to a farm one day. It was like seeing through things suddenly, and this was what we were like really. Gobbling all those baby animals, keeping them in horrid little cages. I know it sounds funny now . . . And then when me Dad got cancer. It seemed like a horrible world. And you being born. It scared me stiff. They never explain that things hurt you."

"That's not the sort of things I mean," said Angela, biting her nails, disappointed. "I'm thinking of things in history."

Lorna felt very put down. For once she had thought they agreed. She flushed, and tried to strike back. "Well, that's what *you* think, my girl. If you think all that stuff is *history*. . . . There's enough bad things still happening. There's enough that could do with changing." The moment of intimacy blew away as the smoke blew up to the ceiling. Angela sighed. You couldn't get it right. Just when you thought you'd got through . . . her mother's voice made her cringe with embarrassment, trying to sound wise and tough. Overacting, always overacting.

"That's not what I meant," she sighed. "Oh well, I'll get on with my reading."

"You've done your homework, haven't you Ange?" said her mother, unnaturally firm. A last-ditch attempt to get the initiative, be in control, the wise mother.

"Yeah," said Angela, not even bothering to keep the contempt from her voice. "I've always done my homework, remember. That's not what we're talking about."

Silence and smoke and the long acid light. They were locked in their own tight worlds. They loved each other but they could not talk, too busy fighting each other.

Of course, that was the point, what her mother had said, though she'd somehow got it all twisted. It wasn't just history that was bothering Ange. You could only mourn for history. What bothered Ange was the future: what history meant for the future. What would happen to the mad cruel streak in men, what would happen to those horrible weapons.

For instance, the enormous bomb really existed, Mr Gillingham's giant bomb. The thing he had told them about in History and scared them to death up at school.

There were two bombs as bad as each other, in fact, and two hundred thousand people had died. In cities with fairy-tale names. Hiroshima, Nagasaki. Hard to make it real, that many people. Trying to imagine them laid out in rows. Except that nothing was tidy; sprawling on top of each other.

239

Sitting in the library feeling sicker and sicker. Tidy pink faces gleamed all round her. If this was all true, how could people just sit there? How could life just go on? For none of this could be forgotten. She was reading about their future.

What the book said was that they weren't so big, the bombs that were dropped on Japan. In fact they were really quite tiny, *compared to what they had now*. The bomb that was dropped on Nagasaki was 200 kilotons. Big enough to smash a city flat, and kill 100,000 people. You'd think that was big enough. But the new bombs being built were *five times, twenty-five times that*. Longing not to believe it . . . but she sensed it was all quite true. She couldn't be a child any more, being told bad things didn't happen. Staring at the chart, it can't be, *one hundred and twenty-five times bigger*. . . .

There was a bomb called the SS 9 which was one hundred and twenty-five times bigger. *One hundred and twenty-five times the explosion that utterly ruined a city*. . . .

That wasn't the end of it, though. There were nearly 300 of those. And altogether, the Russians had 2,275 missiles. (What did they think they were doing? You can only kill everyone once.)

Silly childish questions . . . *why is it dark this morning*?)

(Whatever the Russians were doing, the Americans were doing it worse, according to a table of figures from the US Air Force Journal. The figures were for 1975 (*they would grow more monstrous later. Figures for a year in her hopeful teens, pressing her into her future*.) They fell in straight cool columns; her eyes went haywire, trembled. She read the sentences again and again, trying to make them less dreadful. (Worse than the horrors in Auschwitz somehow . . . there you could see who was wicked. You knew who was doing it, at least. Whereas this wasn't . . . personal . . . at all; it tried to sound perfectly neutral.) She wanted to scream and beat the desk, wake all those heads dipped neatly all round her. Why did they never look up at the sky . . . *why is it dark this morning*?

There was something called *lethality*, a way of measuring bombs. Lethality fell from the sky. (And her eyes fell from the page. The normal floor, the bright window. She wanted so much to live to be old, staring through the glass at the bright trees waving. Suddenly pain in that green and gold.) Dragged her eyes back to the table. Death, lethality, falling so logically, out of that clear blue sky.

> . . . the lethality (k) of a nuclear warhead depends on its strength or 'yield' (y) and the accuracy of delivery (CEP) . . . So lethality is increased with powerful bombs (i.e. large y) and high accuracy (i.e. small CEP) the exact mathematical formula being $k = y^{2/3} / (CEP)^2$. . . .

Somewhere between these hard-edged figures the mess and the pain were bleeding. Somewhere between these logical characters smoke was fogging her thoughts. Fingers white on the cover, trying to keep the print straight. She would get it straight in a minute: work it out in the end. She wouldn't be blown away like dust, blown to dust by the whirlwind. . . .

coming   the end was coming   glimpsed through the smoke of fear

The Americans had a much greater "total lethality" than the Russians. What could you do with such "total lethality"? What could be more than "total"? The same book said that 400 weapons were all that either side needed: that would smash two-thirds of the other side's industry, kill sixty million people—"excluding subsequent deaths from fallout, social disruption, starvation."

The numbers turned into tiny black skiers falling regularly from the snow. The dazzling whiteness of these new facts. *Sixty million dying, excluding.* . . .

And that was 400 warheads. If you added the weapons together, there were nearly 10,000 warheads. They were falling in waves of black tears off the edge of the world, which shook. . . . She took a deep breath, tried to stop. If all the weapons exploded (she would have to go out, have to get some fresh air . . . but how could she walk on the pavement . . . under that mad blue sky? *At night it's black, but it's blue when we fall . . .)* If all those weapons exploded, more than a *hundred and fifty thousand million people* would die . . . *excluding* subsequent deaths from fallout, social disruption. . . .

There couldn't be (*no, it cannot be true*) that many people in the world. She sat there staring at the people round her through shiny bands of tears. In her head, the whole world had just died. They were living at the end of time. The sky itself should be weeping. Her stomach lurched and turned.

"Can I help you?" the librarian said, as a white-faced teenager pushed straight past her, breaking into a tottering run as she neared the door to the cloakroom.

The Reverend Tanimoto ran to the top of the hillock in the rayon-man's garden. From there you could see the whole of Hiroshima . . . *except it wasn't there any more*. The buildings he recognized through the murk were streaming with thick grey smoke . . . and clumps of fire began to push purposefully up through the general miasma. He couldn't understand what had happened; all this from a silent sky. *Surely God will take pity on us . . . my wife, my baby, my people* . . . all the little people running like ants, flickering ants through the darkness. . . .

When the drops of water began to fall, as huge and heavy as marbles, he thought for a second God wept. And then his heart lightened a little; it must be from firehoses fighting the blaze, *someone* was helping them, *something* survived. . . .

Help us, pity us, Father.

If it was God, he sent poisonous water down from the clouds above them, black from the tower of atomic dust still boiling over the city.

Angela was sixteen, and a lot of life lay ahead. But the shock of that information changed something deep inside. She had usually trusted facts. They usually helped with fear. There were helpful facts about cancer cures or how few planes ever crashed. But this information was different. It seemed to say they were all dying. Smears and stains from this terrible knowledge spotted all that she wanted. Dreaming she might be famous, live in a flat in Paris . . . horrible to think of that silver-grey city smashed before she had seen it. Wanting to be happy, wanting . . . loving other people's writings . . . longing to have read them all. Dazzling windows of pages. Glimpse what being alive had meant for the living ghosts inside them. The miracle which drew tears of joy as she thought *I see you I hear you . . . thank you, I feel you breathing . . .*

crushed to blind ash in a second. Ashes of writers inside their readers, turned to dead information

why were the books all burning   where have the names all gone
dreams where everyone dies at once and the dead die over again

Waking, life had changed colour. She had to rewrite the future.

When she tried to make a speech about it, in Current Affairs at school, the emotion got too much for her and her sentences got confused. The boys who were there, who hated her, because she had always ignored them, made stupid jokes about bows and arrows and handing Britain over to the Russians. The teacher tried to intercede. "Now boys, it's a serious matter. . . ."

Miss Tucker stayed at the end of the lesson for a word with Angela Ship. "Of course war's a horrible thing. But we have to have faith in our leaders. There are thousands of experts working . . . I always think it's a comfort. So many clever men. They want what's best for us all. Things will come right in the end." But Angela looked depressed. Miss Tucker beamed on her kindly. "You are such a *clever* girl. Only don't take things so personally. Next term we'll go to the House of Commons, see our leaders at work."

But the giant fiction with the giant bombs was not being written in the Public Gallery. Clever men thought in small locked rooms, clever and grim old men. And sometimes the adjectives slip. Clever and mad old men.

Defense Secretary James Forrestall was one of these clever leaders. (The story, alas, is true, although it all seems like a novel.) Two months after retirement, he jumped from the sixteenth storey. This was the man who had to defend the rest of the USA. Forrestall was an expert on the evil plans of the Russians. The Russians moaned in the pipes, the Russians creaked in the plaster. Lying in bed in the middle of the night he heard fire-engines down in the street. The clever, expert man ran out in pyjamas screaming. "The Russians are coming! The Russians are coming! Help! Help!" After such nights of fear, the terrible peace of his jump. Falling past so many stories . . . he could have ended them all.

Though Miss Tucker was a teacher, she didn't teach Forestall's story. She patted the child on the arm. "Imagination's a dangerous thing. Even adults can get things out of proportion. . . ."

An ache of fatigue near the ache of tears began in Angela, choking. Outside the window, the bright blue sky. They didn't believe what she told them. They thought she was making it up. She hadn't been able to believe it either, that terrible day in the library, sitting there raw and shocked among the miles of polish.

Adolescents lack skin. "You're too thin-skinned," said her mother. Her mother also lacked skin. And this is the language of novels.

people lack skin   we shall all lack skin   skin will hang like gloves
skin hung like gloves   as the wounded walked in a living chain from
the burning city of Nagasaki   dragging themselves in a dying chain
out of burned and blasted Nagasaki   some of them blind
all of them skinned   creeping together with their skin hanging down
searching for water in which to sleep
searching for water in which to drown

Angela couldn't stay young (though she wouldn't ever grow very old). She grew layers of careful skin to protect her, she grew other needs and desires. The knowledge of death never left her but life planted seeds on top. Life was a garden of grateful pleasures, once she escaped from grey Acton. . . .

But as soon as she reached the garden she knew it was late in the year. The garden couldn't stay young. Time pressed on faster and faster. The growing seasons would soon freeze hard, bringing the pain of winter. Digging deep into the roots of trees, closing down hard on the buildings. Silting the air with invisible pressure, time pressing on, pressing faster. . . .

The college she chose was in Regent's Park in the middle of the shrieking city. The garden waited to greet her, a bowl of light and green air. Horse-chestnuts, beeches, birches breathed their oxygen into the sky. It was the best bit of sky for miles around if you stood right out in the centre: no buildings biting at the sky's deep lake which reflected the duckpond, the river. The beds of flowers were more orderly than the rich wild ones in her head. But their beauty was intense and delicate, new life planted tenderly week after week, a few lucky workers in sensible boots spared from making weapons to plant and dig.

Ange watched the beds bloom according to the month, plants

which were over replaced by others, delivered in batches, already in flower. The men popped them neatly into soft soil, like the small bright candle-holders Mum used to pop into the birthday icing on the shop-bought cake . . . small sweet pleasures, things that were gone.

On the eve of the Day of Peace in the Peace Park, people brought bunches of flowers. Bundles of incense smouldered. They crouched on their haunches to pray. Smoke drifted over the Park. Fans of thin scented paper fluttered against damp skin. Priests chanted, a huge bell tolled. An old man wept without sound.

They were selling coloured paper lanterns to float down the river tomorrow evening, each one bearing a candle, shining for one lost soul, burning red yellow or green till at last they sank down in the water, bearing the efforts of those still alive deep down in the darkening water.

In the early 1950s, new life had begun in the city. The munitions plants started working again on machine-guns, assault craft, pontoon bridges. The fighting forces in Korea placed huge orders with the bombed city, and Prime Minister Yoshida rejoiced, calling it *manna from heaven*.

So the atom bomb came from heaven and the manna of fine new wars. Only tears didn't come from heaven. The tears were left to old men.

Inscribed on the Peace Memorial, carved hopefully on the grey granite:

> *Rest in peace. The mistake shall never be made again.*

There was plenty to do and Ange did it quite cheerfully, but no one understood what was happening below. She tried not to look, not to think too often. There were lectures to go to, exams to pass, tutors to flirt with, hate, grow out of. There were friendships to make, there were bodies to lie by . . . naked bodies, a new hot luxury, strange sharp bodies to count and enjoy

> *bodies would lie side by side   uncounted*
> *bodies stripped naked to the blue blank sky*
> *. . . at night it's black, but it's blue when we fall . . .*

She worked long and hard at revising the texts, texts from past centuries she must learn by heart, texts she would keep on the shelves of her brain

> unless the smoke leaked into the library
> LEAVE WITHOUT PANIC IN ORDERLY FASHION
> ACCORDING TO INSTRUCTIONS IN YOUR FIRE
> DRILL MANUAL

To escape from ignorance, escape from Acton, wander the infinite city of words. Her visitor's ticket to the British Library. Visiting the sea under the pale dome of stars, sitting there suspended, surrounded by whispers, listening hard to the low tide of voices, whispers of pages in dead men's books . . . the whispers wove her in living language and they asked live questions which were not in the index, not on microfilm, sibilant questions, questions which swam in the dust on the sunbeams, questions woven from golden smoke . . .

> will you protect us   will you preserve us
>   are we all dying   dying in formation
>   must we all die   dying information
>   must the leaves burn   and the great dome crumble
>   peopled with shadows   feeling for light

Don't ever trust to a city of paper. Pages smoulder and people stifle.

She walked to lectures across the Park. For a year she made the journey three times a week, always the long way, when she wasn't late, along the river and over the bridge. Muscovies and moorhens, mallards and swans and the ordinary seagulls and pigeons above them . . . a miracle of living things locked among the buildings, flashes of feathers like shooting-stars, movement not directed by policeman or maps, flutters and chases on sun-riffled water. Life in the Park was marvellously improvised, swans arabesquing their gestures of love, thousands of starlings descending like dew. . . .

But other, heavier feet were moving, organized or desperate, working to a plan. The joggers were different, with an end in view.

> keep on running for the end is coming   keep on running
> the end is in view

Face after face, pink and glassy with effort, beat blindly past her, breathing like trains, eyes on the path which stretched heavy before them, strapped to big watches with gleaming dials. She filed endless snapshots of faces in extremity, caught as they fought for the perfect body, the bone of the nose-bridge nearly bursting through, limbs which were waving with the fury of a lifetime, fury at the clock ticking AGE in their bones, limbs thrown starward from the earthbound centre and their little hearts beating a drum against death for they *will not* stop running, *will not* grow old. . . .

Brave little bodies half raw in the cold with their sharp knees turning a kaleidoscope of colours as the blood does a crazy tattoo underneath flooding crazy pigments into lost tight veins, the rebellious outlands of the living body. The white plumes of triumph blew rhythmically up from their red fish mouths, boastfully spouting up into the blue but all arcs have an ending, the blue will survive and the white plumes vanish like feathers from birds and the innocent birds be blown from the heavens and fall as heavy and crippled as men

(I ought to feel more for the men, but the fate of the birds disturbs me. For the birds and the fish and the flowers the world will go suddenly crazy. I hate to think of their terror, out in the blazing Park. There is so much sky in the Park, and the whole incandescent with pain. The intent bright struggle of each bird's life against wind and the weight of its body, shattered to stupid soot, become part of the stupid darkness.)

The men run on in the blaze of the morning, run for their lives as if they could save them, running as if they might live for ever, running till their muscles work pistons of bone and their hearts pump blood like a factory boiler, running till their lungs blow up like balloons *oh if only their lungs could blow up like balloons which would lift them away into the far free sky*. . . . But their exercised sinews, their red glossy hearts, their thick tuned muscles hang close to the ground

> *can such fine heavy meat be reduced to powder?*
> *dust of dust on the howling wind*

Ducks on their still pond dipped and dived, sly quick fishes plopped up and sank down, surely the garden would go on for ever. . . .

But the stray dogs barking had an anxious sound: leaf after leaf fell away from the trees, she was late this morning, a faint bell shrilled . . . telephone bells bringing bad news, surely . . . the runners ran faster, getting smaller in the distance, flailed past the zoo where something is howling or the bald rose-garden, thorns like barbed wire, zooming past the great glossy frontages of stone, white-painted stone with patched-up gods sitting snug in their alcoves staring blind over London, our leaders behind them, our leaders inside them, white-painted eyes not seeing the warning . . . panting at last (as the phones grew louder) back home, now a burst for the wife, back home. . . .

One quiet morning no runners will come.

Ange heard rumours all over the city, talk growing loudest in the endless summers though the smoke hung on in the deepening cold. The sirens knitted a tightening net of worry between her eyebrows. The rumble of underground trains shook on through the roots of her nerves on the surface. Always the taste of her death, on waking. Though the dentist had said "Well, we're doing splendidly, nothing to worry about, keep flossing. . . ." There was drilling, by horns and engines, finding the holes in her bones. Memories of drills, reflections of pincers; bowls full of blood, and the last bowl spills. . . .

There were scraps of messages passed on furtively, torn scraps of messages hanging on the wind. . . .

Angela heard things on Tube trains, jamming in the dark under London. When the horror happened to Guy, it merely confirmed her feelings. Down in the blackness, herded like rats. . . . At first though she tried to use them. Some of the lines were bearable, half of the track above ground. If you could sometimes look at the sky, it was almost an ordinary train . . . and yet the doors were so different: designed to seal off water or light

(or fire, perhaps   thick smoke in the darkness)

One day she was enjoying the rattling sunlight before they plunged back into the night. Then a man with a big red face started talking, addressing her CND badge.

"It's tanks you got to fear, not bombs. Bombs stop tanks. You can't argue with that. That's why they call it a nuclear umbrella. Keeps off Russian reign. R-E-I-G-N, geddit?" His big red face exploded into laughter, getting the bored blank carriage on his side but at last subsided, no one had heard him.

Angela had heard him. Swallowed, said nothing. In the loud silence they shot into the dark. The sunlight shrank to a glass full-stop.

She heard things on buses, too. Buses were nice, or used to be nice, but the smoke seeped down from the upper deck. . . . Two women, fat under sweaters and mackintoshes. One woman's thigh spilling into the aisle.

"It's crazy having bombs if you're not gonna use them. *Say* you're not. They're like a bad dream . . . *I* never voted for them, nobody asked me, *I* never saw 'em, *I* shan't be asked. If I want them used. And nor will you, either."

"Give over, will you. You're depressing me. This is my day out, *supposed* to be. I don't know what's got into you, honestly. You weren't like this before you met Reg."

"Don't start about Reg. Oh let's not argue. Have a peppermint, love, go on, take two. It's no use starving ourselves if we're all going to. . . ." Silence. The sentence ended in a rustle of sweets. For the rest of the journey they talked about Christmas.

Christmas was coming   crackling paper   and the smell of fat the chicken-fat burning

Half of Angela was helplessly spinning. She turned like a leaf on the seasons changing, sensing the flux of the world all round her, tuned to the numbers shifting underneath, the ticking of a clock going faster and faster. . . .

Yet a novel about Ange would have had its events. The plot of her life proceeded in order. She lost her virginity, she started an 'affair', she got a First (a whole glittering chapter . . .) She no longer got spots or ate too many biscuits, she didn't get depressed or write long formless poems, she had broken with Andrew, she was living with John. She no longer dressed like the dummy in Oxfam. She learned to take lovers, learned to make friends; learned smiles suited her, learned to be charming. She had half escaped from the worst of her family.

On the inside Ange had changed too. She had found the best of her family. The peace of the roots going back in time, neither good

249

nor bad but the quiet plait of fact. No longer being angry with her mother's acting. She grasped at last that all being was acting. They were close again with an easy closeness, sitting in the kitchen gossiping and laughing. She learned what death was when Guy was killed, learned you could weep as you stood with your family though you weren't a Christian and you hadn't loved the dead. . . . She had learned how much she loved John, though she still loved herself much more. For so long, in her teens, she was forced to love herself, it took time to adjust to new habits of loving. . . .

She had learned a few wise rules of thumb for living (as her mother had learned how to love other people on the long steep road from her golden girlhood; or Henry, learning to hide it away, the jewelled movement of lost desire; as George had learned that following goodness leads to a bunk behind German wire, but didn't have quite enough time to cut free, climb down out of the Army . . . as Frank on his mountain learned to be happy, made his own rules and learned to be happy . . .). The shell of her fiction was coming on nicely, chapter-plan full of bright event, internal monologue showing her growing, pushing her on to the final pages. . . .

But something inside her never changed at all, something was connected to other things entirely. Rules of thumb didn't get you anywhere, learning to live didn't help you here. Smoke was erasing the triumphs of the characters, all they had learned was to live in a novel . . . learning to be 'human', learning to 'survive'.

These gentle lessons would not survive. Meat is not gentle, nor the cooking heat.

Survival was a matter of other things entirely. Another narrative. Numbers, machines. Something in Angela was listening obsessively.

Digits mounting on distant screens.

Endless conversations between grey-faced statesmen.

Generals shouting in small hot rooms.

Slow wheels shifting far away in the night. . . .

An outer shell so much bigger and darker than the little bright mosaic of narrative pieces.

Inside Angela, fear smudged desire. Smoke blurred the rubric controlling the chapters.

Inside Angela grew outer darkness.

They were just irritations, the fingers on her pages, turning them remorselessly, not far to go. . . .

There were others listening to the same muffled messages, searching for clues, not wanting to find them.

Item, the planes. There were always too many but something was different now. These planes were smaller and grimmer and sharper, razoring light with their wings. At night the engines bore down through their dreams, shook them awake, swooping up too late so they lay there clutching the ache of the hum and twisting the sheet and the ache in their spines, yellow as wax in the censored light leaking in from the street at one in the morning.

When the hum was over, they waited. The yellow whites of their eyes. Lay and sucked hard on old worries, old nicotine and sour wine. John on his back beside her was sleeping the sleep of the just. She stretched away from his peaceful breath to the far flat slope of the sheet.

Very cold out here, getting colder.

At night, she lives quite alone. Lives with her fear of dying. Cold as death, getting colder. . . .

Noises have changed their meaning, or perhaps her hearing has changed. All public clocks threaten news. They once had simpler functions. But now they are marking our futures, ticking away from our pasts.

As Big Ben's clockwork shuddered, global anxiety mounted; programmed hands all over the world reached out for the radio switch. With a crackle, fear blared into action. The pips squealed briefly and died.

"Good evening," the voice intoned, and millions of hearts beat quickly, straining to hear in the voice what kind of news lay ahead. But the voice was always the same, round and inscrutably solemn, comfortably holding the weight of the world, the pain of the night inside. And the news was always the same, news of talks against tension, news of talks about talks and tension which always rose.

When things were worst, she would get up quietly and leave him, creeping next door to the sofa with the alarm clock, her pillow, the radio. Pulling her old fur over her, lighting his cigarettes. Drawing the poison into her lungs she knew the bleakest of comforts, playing the dial with her other hand, searching for others still wakeful. *If somebody would watch with her*. . . . But she doesn't want to disturb him.

Japanese children loved fireflies, *hotaru*, which live for two weeks in summer. They chased them singing like lovers: "Please come over here, firefly! That side of the water is bitter. but this side of the water is sweet! Please come over here, firefly. . . ." They loved them for bringing light. Darkness made them feel lonely. If someone would watch there with them. . . .

If they could catch the fireflies they put them in tiny cages, glowing beneath the deep green mosquito-net's border of dark red silk.

> *firefly, shine on the dream*   *keep this child from harm*. . . .

Summer burns into autumn, short lives burn in their cages.

> *Why is it dark already?*   *Why did our house fall down?*

At times when the fear was greatest, *to know* was the only comfort. You had to wait for the hour for news, doze and wait for the hour. Scraping the wheel round the dial through sudden barrages of music.

Impossible dreams and triumphs were recounted somewhere in Russian. Somebody sad and bored said prayers in what might have been Dutch. Far underneath, in incomprehensible anguish, the dark globe muttered and howled. It was strange that anyone slept through all those agonized voices. Smell of the wireless metal, her own vile saucer of ash. . . . Setting the clocks and sighing, time to shut off the light.

> *not much left of the night*   *please slow*   *please wait*

Spring was appalling, too hopeful. Green growth promising nothing. Summer of course was the worst, every summer the worst. Machines running wild all round us, heavy with heat and terror. The city burning already, south of the dirty river. Autumn was a brief bright poem   *remember what you loved*. . . .

Remember that things die, that growing time is over. Final reds in the garden, leaf-bodies dancing, feet running. Smoke or fog or the sun asleep, the closing of the light.

The truth is seasons don't matter. Normal clocks don't matter. We only use them as poems, metaphors for our fear.

But the fear that gnawed at Angela had nothing to do with poems; her fear was written in numbers, the numbers of the dead. The missiles down in their silos were unaware of the seasons. Listening to numbers ticking, the codes for *Rest* or *Alert*. Midges on radar screens replace the slow-flying stars. It is out of date, unwanted, the time that could run for ever.

The time we are living by now is measured back from the darkness, measured back from the launch-on-warning, ticking towards that edge. We are all the same age today if electric time slips forward. . . .

The blue-white flash of eternity knowing neither night nor morning.

What does she want, poor Angela, nervously sucking and blowing? Suddenly an old woman, yellow, ear to the acrid metal? Dead smoke yellows her fingers, the waxen lid of her eye. . . .

Doesn't want much, poor Angela. Time to finish the pattern. Just wants not to be woken, told it is time to die.

Yet at 8.15 next day, she lies dreaming sweet as a baby. Washing white endless sheets, the snow light blowing and floating. . . .

13 Chapter of the Miracle

"Worry about a pension? Jesus, you must be joking! . . . any of *us* reach pension age it'll be a miracle. . . ."

Only a miracle will save us now, thought George, staring out at the wire. But miracles sometimes happen. Miracles can be made.

At Greenham Common, at Lakenheath, the wire was wrapped round with bodies. Women, no longer gentle, were out in the freezing open. Women slept out in the freezing winter under the freezing rain. They lay in front of the missiles, wrapped the barbed wire in flesh. The policemen carried the bodies away but the women kept on coming. Maybe when so many hoped together it wasn't quite so cold.

Their hands were white and lifeless after a night in the open. But blood came back in time . . . they would stop the missiles in time. Metal will bend in time, if thousands of hands can join them. Some things cannot be measured and yet they must be told.

Frank reached pension age, far beyond the reach of a pension. Frank made a life of his own: a world of his making and choosing. Could a world of such long hard making ever be burned away?

Frank was a clever man and he soon knew everyday German. But some German words didn't come: for *death* and *longing* and *love*. His longing was always for freedom, which seemed to be spoiled by love. He had tried not to feel much love, but the word for freedom escaped him. Escaped him in England, also.

Now *he* had escaped from England. And perhaps he was closer to the things behind the words, in the cool clear air of the mountains. *Some things the heart can measure, although they cannot be told.*

He would find the word for a miracle, right at the end of his life. It was not until then that he saw the pattern and glow that *miracle* meant.

At first he didn't want to learn German because of what they did in the war. Then he realized it wasn't *that* German, there were lots of other Germans, the language stretched wider and longer than wickedness in uniform. There must be German poets without any wickedness in. There were German names for rivers and trees and stars and rare wild flowers. And sausages and cheese and delicious milk chocolate. German in that case was cows and tongues, slow lappings of milk and sugar. *Milchschokolade*, you just ate it—war couldn't make those things evil. So he learned enough to be friendly, and get the things that he wanted. He learned to describe the weather, and the face of the physical world.

But he never learned enough German to describe his new kind of happiness: he never learned enough German to catch the dance of his blood. He never learned enough German to say that each day he felt free.

Most people would have called his room in the hotel a rabbit-hutch, with its high narrow bed on which the bedding bulked up (but to him, like waves on the sea). The walls were plain white, where you could see them, but most of them were covered in maps. Frank Ship had the world all about him, and the silent singing of names. Some of the maps were the fine old-fashioned kind where the mountains were drawn in relief, long delicate scrolls of minute shadowed shells stretching up to the ceiling above him. Since the Himalayas canopied his pillow, he floated through millions of miles.

He would close his eyes in the morning, in that precious half-hour on his own, and change the scale so he swept down close and saw the sun on the pine trees: or sometimes he stared at the white of the pillow and saw the immortal snows. Rose had never been there to spoil it, the whiteness was only his own. There were slopes which had not been trodden, where the brilliance would never melt . . . suns rose, swept over and set. She *never would* come here to spoil it. He lay as the day grew brighter, listened to his steady heart.

Inside his own head, of course, Frank didn't need to use German. He often didn't exactly use language at all, in there. He didn't think that much of language: Rose had used plenty of language. Words sometimes seemed to him to be a way of killing a thing.

And yet they are also essential, to promise and to record. He would need them to claim a meaning, in the silence before he died.

But for now he had pictures inside him, of seas and sunsets and faces. They were often more films than pictures, films which swept over the world. He felt he was right at the top, in his little room on the mountain. It was a flying boat, a glider, and the window looked down over nothing, over curtains of mist and miles of air, which meant it looked down over everything.

When the mist rose in the morning the mountain peaks looked so clear that he could have reached out and touched them, electric under his fingers. Yet the valley stretched blue and veined with sunlight between himself and the ice. But behind the hotel were the nearer peaks, and the snow which was walking distance.

There were slopes for every mood; snow which had not been printed. The light that shone from unprinted snow was blinding, intent and silent. Some things were still beyond him, still made him feel like a child. But a child who ached with wonder. The silent, turning world.

There were the sweeping slopes they skied on where the ski-lifts dipped and dived. Black wires skated across them, making fantastic patterns. People were tiny, ant-like, each detail carved upon white. Again and again they tumbled and again and again they climbed. Always beginning again. Frank watched them, marvelled, smiled. The sky above was the blaze of blue that grew bluer before night fell. . . . Nights were more total than English nights. Their grip on the snow was so frail.

At night it's black, but it's blue when we fall. . . .

His night-time visions were peaceful.

In his time off he would walk to the snow, to dip his hands in the whiteness. To him his hands looked very old, much older than the rest of his body. But dipping their ridges in the agonizing snow

256

there was a sense of mysterious rightness. They still felt things, those hands. They were his, they were still alive. Through them he had felt the world. Their freckles and lines were deserved. Perhaps they only looked old because they were so far from his centre. Your hand could lie on the pillow, a hundred miles from your head. You felt you could watch what happened to it, instead of living inside. From watching his hands Frank knew he was eighty, eighty-one, eighty-two, eighty-three. . . . Soon, perhaps, he would die. But the messages actually *felt* by his hands told him all that was a lie.

They liked touching linen, clean linen, and his linen was changed every week. They liked fresh bread in the morning, the crust and the softness beneath. They liked the first dribble of water to wash in before it gushed out too hot. They liked the grass by the side of the road as he eased himself down for a minute. He liked to sit with the void in front of him, the track slipping down in deep tongues like a snake, the thin clean sun on the back of his neck, his hands clutching on to the grasses.

They liked being hot inside gloves when his cheeks were freezing in winter. They loved the soft cheeks of Frieda, stroking them (now growing looser and softer). It was strange such hands should look old. You could almost see the mechanism through them: the bones and the veins and the muscles like string, and the brown freckles clumping together. One day, Frank supposed, he would be no more, just the mechanism, dumped on the earth. But he didn't, in fact, believe it. He lived in some far free centre where feeling things proved they were true, and he felt he must live for ever, in the fierce high winds from the snow.

If he'd been in England, he'd have been dead. That was clear, because the family would have killed him. He would have been a grandfather, going down the pub, flashing his teeth at his cronies. He would have been glad enough to die, to escape from that marital bed. The smell of her cheap sweet perfume, and sometimes stale menstrual blood. And her teeth clicking horribly at night. He would have to have aged to order, so they could recede side by side. To the back of the family picture: Grandma and Grandpa Ship.

Because Sally was the type to have children, lots of horrible children. They'd have taken after her and Rose, he'd have had to pretend that he loved them. They would have been fat and greedy and squawled for TV and icecream. They would have grabbed all the attention and had birthdays four times a year, and ripped open their presents with red greedy hands and dropped the insides on the floor.

They would have thought that he didn't have a life, that he was just an extension of theirs. A narrow, old-fashioned corridor where the windows were rarely opened. In the end it would have come true: he would have moved out of the light. Rose was too stupid to have minded, to her growing old would seem right. Though she might have stayed lively in bed . . . (in the safety of his own, Frank shuddered). Rose winking as the grandkids gorged cake: "*if they guessed that only last night. . . .*"

And the boys would have turned into men and taken him down to the pub. As a jolly favour to Grandad. "We shan't let him out of our sight. . . ." And in fact they'd get drunk on his money, and laugh at their own crude jokes. They would have thought their visits brought the summer. Sun in the corridor. They would have said "Poor old geezer" when he was at the bar buying drinks.

Frank hated those imaginary grandkids, all those thousands of miles away. They looked like those big Belgian tourists who made all the fuss at breakfast. He was sweeping the bar out one morning, as a favour to Frieda, the cook. He should really have been down in the fall-out shelter, shifting up the crates of beer. It was a laugh, the law that all buildings had a shelter. Once they had got them, they used them. They would have looked stupid trying to shelter among stacks of toilet rolls, crates of beer. In England, he used to worry about all that. He felt invulnerable, here. He smiled as he swept up the fag-ends. But voices were raised next door.

They had come down five minutes early, after drinking Schnapps all night. Their eyes were red and pig-angry and their heads were stupid with pain. They started to shout at the maid.

They wanted some ham or some cheese. They wouldn't eat shit for breakfast. Bread on its own was pig-food. The hotel was full of robbers. They would pack their bags and leave.

They were sure only they had feelings: the maid had no life of her own. She was cut out of tin, tin trembling, a cut-out target for hatred. Because their great stomachs were empty they were trying to kill her with words. They would turn the maid into meat and then they would eat her for breakfast.

Frank had an inspiration. Their German was worse than her

own. He was wearing his uniform jacket, and his plate was already in. He put down the broom very quietly and inspected himself in the glass. The manager was off for two days choosing wine far away in the Valais. He made his feet stamp on the parquet as he moved across the bright room.

"Good Morning, gentlemen," he said, and his bearing was pure British Army. "You will please not insult this young lady. Your bill is almost prepared. The management wish that you leave. We shall now be requiring this table. Vacate by midday, if you please." His eyes were electric with hatred, and his eyebrows stiff and white. The biggest one swore in Flemish, but they staggered to their feet.

The girl was not very bright, and her mouth fell loose with surprise. Then abruptly she started to giggle, and one of the louts turned angrily. Shambling, not lurching out. When the door crashed to, Frank was sweating. But you learned how to deal with grandchildren, here in the free far mountains.

He would sometimes wake up sweating, not sure what country he was in. The window was in the wrong place, and his head wouldn't move on the pillow. His freedom was only a dream. Then a knock on the door: it was Frieda. "Would you like some coffee?" she called. He could move again. "No, thank you."

The offer was only a ritual. He hadn't had coffee for years. When he first came to live in the Paradise Alp they had taken their coffee together. Frieda was fifty and married with a daughter she adored. Her husband was a postman, a kind cheery man who worked unsociable hours. She described her husband as "good", which to Frank meant *kind* and *cheery*. Frank wanted to think he was *stupid* and *weak*, but she was too honest to let him.

Her body was pale and warm and firm and her smile all tiny white teeth. At the back, three flashes of gold. And she was too fat to be pretty exactly, and her legs were bandy and short. What he loved about her was her laughter. She laughed all the time, and said little. Her laughter was better than talking: she laughed to show she was pleased. She laughed to show it didn't matter, when he was shy at the beginning. He was nearly sixty-three, after all, and he feared his nerves would insult her. But she laughed with pleasure that this brown-skinned, white-haired foreigner wanted to make love to her.

That wasn't exactly what Frank wanted. He just didn't want to be alone. He wanted to be on his own but he feared a total aloneness. The Matterhorn could bear it, but he was only a man. He didn't want to lie there and think that no one would ever touch his body again. He'd looked at his hands on the back of the seat as the train brought him up the mountain. That sense that his hands had grown old. They wanted to touch something living. And when he met Frieda at the Paradise Alp there was so much life in her laughter. She laughed at his English German and offered to teach him some more. But she hadn't a clue about language: what were verbs? what were nouns? what were adverbs? "I touch . . . the hand . . . gently," she said, "for example," then touched his hand. He needed to learn to ask questions, but Frieda simply said *Yes*. It was easy to understand. They managed without much talking.

Compared to the standards of his grandchildren, the phantoms he so much hated, that lovemaking in the mountains would not have won many prizes. Frank felt so happy in those firm arms that at first he came very quickly. Then later he felt so happy to be held he just wanted to lie there quietly. Frieda liked to have orgasms so she'd give herself them with his hand. He loved the feel of her hard little bud, the silky seams which enclosed it. To him she felt young as a baby, not ten years younger than him. And the gasps and cries she gave at the end were another refinement of laughter.

But he smoothed out the rough, looking back. The new life wasn't always perfect. At first he was scared of Frieda. She would get like Rose. She would cling. She would want him to say he adored her, and jump through hoops like a goat. She would want him when he didn't want her, and taunt him if he couldn't do it. She would tell him he was getting old, too old to appeal to her. She would go to Herr Leitz, the owner, and tell him to throw Frank out. She would say he was stealing from the market produce that he had to deliver each day. At first her green eyes seemed cunning, looking and then looking down. And there were other things, little things, spoiling it, things which made her a stranger.

She didn't know any of his habits, so he felt she would never *get* to know. He would stay on his own in his strangeness, in a maze of dry dark wood. The old bark twisted around his tongue: he would not be understood. It was cold, and joy would vanish. Old fools shouldn't hope for joy.

He suffered intensely, childishly, the first year she went on holiday with her family. No one brought him treats any more, and his sheets weren't changed in three weeks. He pretended to grouch about *that*, but really he felt she had left him. He loved his own company of course, but *what if she didn't come back?*

She laughed at his short-sleeved vests: he had brought a dozen from England. She laughed at most things, of course, but that time it made him feel old. She bought him a "nice new" toothbrush, though the old one had done him fine. His back teeth were seeing him through, and he didn't like too much cleaning. You could rub yourself away, and he wasn't ready to go. Stung by that bright red brush, yapping on the edge of the basin, he told her English women wouldn't dream of it, having gold fillings like her. Instantly her bright smile vanished. "You don't like me," she said. "You think I am too old to be pretty, yes, because I have not perfect teeth." That was typical woman's logic. It was *her* who started about teeth! Still, better unfair than critical. He gave her a lordly cuddle.

The other little problem was the garlic, and he knew that he wasn't being fair. In the course of his travels round the world he had grown to love the taste of garlic. Of course he'd never got it at home. Rose wouldn't have known what it looked like. Frieda, who cooked like a dream, was addicted to the fierce little bulb. The silly thing was that he loved the taste but it smelled unpleasant on her! But he told himself it couldn't smell bad on her when it didn't in the steam off the soup. Many times he stopped himself saying anything, many times he swore he would. In the end the unpleasantness lessened, and he realized it wasn't just garlic.

It was foreignness, strangeness, something foreign on her flesh, something proving she wasn't his home. And however much *he* loved travelling, he wanted a woman to be home.

That was sentimental, he knew it. And a lie, which was worse than that. Because Rose had been home, and a prison. And he never told lies about Rose. No matter how icy the nights, he never imagined he missed her. . . .

(Though he sometimes remembered, quite separately, a girl with frizzy blonde hair. She roared with laughter as girls should not, and her eyes were bold and knew nothing. They were going for a walk by the canal, and as they walked under the bridge, she hugged him. Before they were out in the light, she had kissed him, a present, three times. In the sun she had flushed bright red, and her hair shone almost white. Three kisses he married her for: what impulse had made her do it? But it wasn't Rose who had done it. In the shadows, a young flushed girl.)

Such girls never smelled of garlic, and their teeth were not filled with gold. *And such girls would not come to your bed, Frank Ship*, he told himself, lying there thinking. And those flashes of sun in the shade or the dazzle, they weren't what girls were about. They had wants and needs and greeds and plans, and futures which weren't very girlish. Girls turned into hooks and lines, and the hook would be barbed to pierce flesh. They wanted to turn into greedy machines which cooked and gorged and had babies.

He didn't understand why it was so, he had never understood why it was so. He had never met a woman like he was, longsighted, wanting to be free.

Yet he believed his own mother must have been that way, he was sure that was why she had done it. In middle life he thought of her less: when the kids were young, not at all. He hadn't had freedom to think, when the kids were growing at home. Once Henry had asked if his Grandma had died, and Frank just told him yes, she died just after he was born. "I don't want to talk about it." Henry didn't say anything much, and went off to do his homework. But when he came down for his tea, he was quieter than usual, thoughtful. (It was hard for Frank to think about his son, even half a lifetime later. Those solemn, piercing blue eyes. You could not hide them away.)

She'd left him on the rainy steps at the door of the Seamen's Mission. "What kind of a woman would do that?" was what Rose said, derisive. He wished he had never told her. But *he* didn't feel like that. He wondered if she'd been like Frieda, a bit, though Frieda loved her own kids. But something in Frieda was independent, she didn't *belong* to her family. And she didn't want to hook you either; she wanted to wrap you in laughter.

Frieda had a sense of the marvellous, which made her marvel at Frank. He had always felt himself interesting, with the map of the world in his head; with the dazzling sweeps of distance, the close-up shots of bright waves. His eyes were still bright as waves as well from the pictures he kept inside. Veins of sun in the iris like the sun on sea or on leaves. And Frieda saw it and danced, Frieda saw it and laughed, Frieda saw it and loved him, didn't want to put the light out.

His mother had left him before daylight, they reckoned, wrapped up in blankets and an oilskin. She must have crept away into the sun coming up with the freedom pushing at her chest. He was sure that his mother had loved him (just as Frank had loved Henry, hadn't he?) And she would have kept the picture inside her, she would have still thought of him at night. She must have been a wanderer like him, he was sure she would never have married. His father was obviously a sailor, which was why she chose the Mission steps. And they named him Ship, not original, really, but 'Sailor' would have been worse. Imagine trying to chat up a girl if you had to say your name was just *Sailor*!

It seemed natural to go for a sailor, as soon as he was out of Barnardo's. The windows in the Home had been small, and the walls impossibly high. In the middle of the sea who would care about the past? There no one had fathers and mothers. But when he got his first berth, he found that a ship wasn't freedom. The windows were little round holes, much worse, and the walls reached up to the sky. The sea was just something beyond you, where lucky birds flew for the cliffs. And the wonderful countries they went to, of which he had dreamed for so long—if you only had eight hours ashore they remained as confusing as dreams. In fact, the ship was a prison, a tiny Barnardo's of tin. It was dirtier and the smells were worse and the officers more cruel. And he wasn't supposed to be a child any more, there was no one there to protect him. At least in the Home there were cleaning women and his bright blue eyes made them pet him. He was only fifteen, and frightened. The men didn't mean to be cruel perhaps but they always picked on the youngest.

Beauty was always outside you then, something you could never quite reach. He would stare at the wave curling over, the lovely free fall of the light. Near land the birds hovered over the waves and their white wings beat at his heart. "Are you 'aving a kip," asked a shipmate satirically, "or is that seagull your mother?" He was wrong about sailors being orphans, more or less: they boasted non-stop of their wives and sweethearts, their parents, their pets and their kids. One day after two nights' ration of rum he had told this man what had happened. Ever since then he had made stupid jokes, and each time Frank winced and turned red. At least in Barnardo's people didn't make jokes. He vowed he would *not* be a sailor.

263

He went on shore with the little bit of cash he had earned while they were at sea. As soon as he stood on the land again the ships looked as lovely as ever. But he took his money into the pub and bought himself a bottle of beer. He could have danced for joy just to stand on firm ground, no iron walls jostling round him.

A paper was lying on the leather seat which might have looked dull enough to others. Evidently left by a customer. Not even a local paper. The *Wolverhampton Gazette*. Still, anything was interesting after being at sea, and he opened it up like a luxury. The pages rustled like chocolate, and he sucked down his cool strong beer.

What he found was a job advertisement: Trainee Wanted, 15–18, Keen Boy for General Work. Which might have looked hard enough to others, again, but Frank was a young Keen Boy. And the work was for Great Western Railways, and the town was far from the sea. He spent all his money on getting there, instead of sending a letter. He didn't trust words, or letters.

He hadn't used trains much before: Barnardo's boys don't travel. He loved the station with its foreign faces and life rushing off all ways. When he got to the other end, the Station Master was kindly. Frank looked a bit like his son. When he heard how far he had come from, he gave him the job on the spot. And the ride had been pure adventure. Toy villages, gardens, woods. Passing brilliant little moving figures you would never come close to again. There must be some kind of pattern: that paper, left there for him. The sense that life was ahead, that each bright toy window opened. . . .

But Rose was ahead as well, in the shade of that distant tunnel. She gave him the thing he wanted—three kisses, a moment of grace. In return she gobbled his freedom, became his Barnardo's Home. In the mountains he saw it more clearly, saw way back down over Europe. He saw over hills and valleys of years and he saw how life had got trapped. Caught between wanting tenderness and wanting to be left alone. Caught between chasing his mother and running away from Rose.

He lay in his high cool bed, smoothing the sheets of the past. And the more he thought of the pattern, the less the garlic mattered. Or if it mattered at all, perhaps it gave him the clue. He focused upon his mother. She was brown, he imagined, and lean. Not at all like cushion-round Frieda. She stared at the sky, and laughed less. She looked foreign, and yet she was English. . . .

(They told him she'd left him a note, and it read like natural-born English. No one recalled what it said. He would write that note in his head, and every time it was different. That note had made words unreal; whatever she said hadn't reached him. She must have thought it important, but it hadn't changed things a jot.)

. . . his mother was his oldest memory, the memory that seemed to be home. He didn't feel angry with her, just as long as she'd *thought* about him. He'd probably travelled the world already, a red-haired kid in her brain. She would have been proud to have met him, in Iceland during the War. She would even have envied him, maybe, his last high berth up here.

She would have had big white teeth (Frieda's were tiny, imperfect). She would never have cut her hair. She wouldn't have looked like a mother, less like a mother than Frieda. But the closer he got to her phantom, half closing his eyes, almost there . . . the clearer her image became, and his sense of a wound was lessened, his sense of a distant emptiness, back in the blue sea air.

Like him, and like home, she was English, his mother, not foreign, not *quite* like Frieda. But in the end he was sure: the smell of garlic was there.

He had to learn *this* was home, this strange flying home in the mountains. He had to believe Frieda loved him, although she just came and went. He had to believe it was shyness, when her thick white eyelids dropped. He had to believe that her kind of cleverness walked the maze without words.

He remembered the kisses Rose gave him, before she turned into Rose. Three kisses. He gave her his life, although in the end he reclaimed it. And Frieda gave hundreds of kisses, for love and wonder and thanks. Now out of the tunnel, the kisses. Those tender garlicky kisses.

At first she came to him three times a week in that room with its maps and its mountains. They lay there tiny under the world and lifted its corners with laughter. Frank always knew how small they were, though their bodies felt solid together. He knew the maps would outlive them, that this wouldn't last for ever. (*He didn't know everything though, had forgotten what blackens paper.*) It was far too good to be true that he should have found love now. He felt she was here on a visit, that she must get tired of him . . . all the older customers flirted with her when she got dressed up in the evening. He wasn't a ladies' man. So why was it him who was chosen? At first when she had made love to him and then got dressed and gone home, first straightening his sheets like a chambermaid and winding his clock for him, he would lie there stroking his body where she'd been and wondering if it was a dream.

But she knocked on his door every morning, and her firm flesh wasn't a dream. And as he got older and his body less sure, Frieda was ever more tender.

The word came to him one evening, as he watched the light on the peaks. He was thinking about that light, and then he realized he wasn't. He was thinking about all light, the beauty you never expected. As a kid he knew it was there but he thought he would never reach it. He experienced light as an ache.

Now each evening the peaks were a glory, each evening the joy was a shock. Each morning her knock did the same, the fact it all wasn't a dream. Like the view plunging down into the valley, and the slow sure ascent of the train.

He knew so well what could happen, that life could plunge like a stone. He knew that hatred could come, either in one heart or between you. He knew that he might have been trapped in a box of a house with Rose. He knew that his tough old body might suddenly let him down. He knew that nothing was certain. He guessed he would die on his own.

But none of that was true at that moment, with the peaks in that deep rose sun. He lived alone and was loved. He'd had twenty-five years of freedom. His hearing was getting bad but he still had wonderful eyes. The air he breathed was white wine. His skin still prickled with pleasure. The light wind played on his forehead and he stretched out his palms for joy. He was standing at a bend of the road, with low rocks between him and the drop. There were harebells and aconites going to sleep in the last pale gasp of the daylight. A plane hummed gently in the distance, like crickets on a summer night.

The word that was growing was *miracle*. His life in the world was a miracle. He was eighty-six years old, and he wanted to live for ever.

(What Frank couldn't know was that "miracle" was a word that his mother had used.

266

As I write this note I am crying. I love my little boy. But I just can't give him a life. And so I am leaving him here, and hoping God will be kind. Whoever finds my baby, *please please* will you keep him safe. I believe that there can be miracles. Please may he know he was loved.

His mother sounds sentimental, but then she was just sixteen. And God may have read it, but no one made sure that her little boy knew what she'd said. Frank never knew enough words, didn't even know what he was missing. But words are a record, and a warning. They tell about love, and death.)

Frank bought the English papers only once a month, when he went down to the city. He usually chose the *Telegraph* though he'd always voted Labour. It had so many stories to read, an occasional feast of newsprint. The names meant nothing to him any more, nor the gravity, nor the outrage. It was sometimes nice just to know those voices still droned on in London. The fact that the leaders still droned on made it surer that he had escaped. The swarm of black words lacking meaning made the few words he had more real.

It was *love* he had found, and *freedom*, and a *miracle*: they combined.

The miracle of Frank's freedom. He found it before he died.

But he didn't know how to read the newspapers. Muffled feet stamping the pages. And he didn't quite know the miracle of living as long as he did. There were people of only twenty, who longed to cross the bright seas. There were people of only fourteen, who longed to know sexual love. There were children of only five, who longed to be praised by their mothers. There were children of only one, not knowing the word for pain. They would scream for the things they'd wanted, finding the world going dark.

Frank thought he'd escaped the papers, except as a souvenir. All the world except here seemed theoretical: miraculous snow in the silence. But the newsprint was creeping towards him, crows' feet printing the snow.

267

The word for miracle melted, when it came to the final violence. The word for miracle melted, the maps of the world all burned. The earth he had loved turned black, when it came to the final violence.

Some losses cannot be measured because they will not be told.

14 *Chapter of Burning*

US TELLS RUSSIA: BACK DOWN

The house seemed suddenly empty, with all of the family gone. There were letters from Ange quite often, and she visited at weekends. Henry and Lorna noticed each other very acutely, moving about in the empty rooms. It was almost embarrassing. What they said was all that there was. It didn't just float out easily into the sea of tangled voices.

Letters thumped on the floor, made much more noise than they used to. Even George's thin airmails from Germany echoed for the rest of the morning. At least he was happy, and he liked the food. But he never really *said* anything . . . missing his real live presence. He had been a good boy, George.

Since Henry worked nights in the bar they were there in the day together. But they couldn't settle down to enjoy it. They weren't sure they *would* enjoy it. It was frightening being alone together after all these years of being crowded. They started to plan family visits which they'd always put off before. "We'll go up to Wolves for Christmas," said Lorna, looking quite bright. "We haven't seen mine since August and we haven't seen yours since March. We don't have to stay with *either* of them, to make sure there aren't any quarrels. I suppose we could stay with Melissa. She's not been so nasty lately. Or else we could go to a guesthouse and then it'd be

269

like a holiday. But I ought to go and see my mother, at any rate. I mean, she won't last for ever. And Grandma." (Joanna was still alive: Joanna was nearly a hundred. Tiny, erratically painted, she still had vermilion hair.)

"Your mother doesn't care if we go or not," said Henry, which was more or less true. Prunella was living in a world of her own, with a face of her own she'd invented. The world had a crimson fish for a mouth and purple flashes for eyelids. It moved on legs of black liquorice which supported its creaking body. She used to have ordinary legs. The new fish-net legs were still exciting. She could only vaguely remember her daughters, except on fortnightly visits. With Lorna living so far away she was hardly alive at all.

And yet her mother still dreamed about her, a child with sheets of gold hair. Making up fibs so she wouldn't have to eat, making up to her father.

"You can't say that about *yours* though," said Lorna, smoking her biro. "She wishes she could come here. For good, I mean. She said it last Christmas, when you were out."

"She was joking," said Henry, face dropping down. "She'd be better off with Sally. At least old Sal's got some money now which might help pay for the booze."

"I never used to like your mother, but now I'm sorry for her. She never got over your Dad. *I* wouldn't, Henry, if *you* did."

He stared at the table as he usually did when Lorna made him happy. It was almost too strong to bear. To feel, again, she might love him. He'd thought it was gone for ever, but things come back in time. . . .

if there was time, my darling   *if there had been more time*

"Do you think she was ever good-looking? I mean she looks awful *now*. I sometimes think I don't blame your Dad. Like a sort of overboiled pudding."

"She always looked just the same." *If only he would talk more.* After twenty years of marriage, she still wished he'd make himself talk. But in fact, he was merely thinking.

". . . There was a photograph, though. I could never believe it was her. They took it down by the canal. Of her and me father courting. They had their arms round each other, and she looked sort of . . . different."

"Well *go on*, Henry, for goodness' sake."

"Just young, I suppose. She was young. You can never believe she *was*." Behind his glasses, his eyes peeped out. Behind old men's glasses, young. Sometimes he broke her heart. They wouldn't be young again.

He made a tremendous effort. "She was . . . so much thinner, and lots of hair. It looked white in the sun, white-fair, I mean . . . not . . . pretty exactly, but *merry*." Lorna stirred her tea in wonderment, visualizing Rose like that. "It used to be on the sideboard, behind the plate with the oranges." (It was supposed to be *decorative*, that plate, so they stayed uneaten in the dusty front room. The oranges sat till they shrivelled and dried before she remembered to change them. He used to go in and sniff them: they smelled of abroad, of sun, of wonderful spicy forgotten things, though their skin was a sad dark brown.) "But of course, it vanished when he did. I suppose she . . . hid it. Or burned it."

"Maybe he took it with him." There were things she would never understand, he thought.

"He hated her. I bet he never looked back. Never gave us another thought."

"Well I wish he *had* taken it with him. You can't . . . just wipe out the past."

US SENDS PEACEKEEPING FORCES
RUSSIA CONDEMNS US MOVE

(She had done her best, as a runaway girl, when she left her father to die. You could never manage it though. Echoes blew back to find you. You knew in the end you would have to turn round and go and see what you'd done. As she grew older she made queer penance for trying to break the pattern. When Prunella moved to her tiny flat that would somehow seem all bedroom, she gave her daughters a chest of drawers, a wardrobe and a sideboard. Lorna got the sideboard, and the sideboard became a museum. Photographs, letters, old birthday cards, birth certificates, holiday postcards. Wrapped cubes of sugar in dusty paper proving the few times they had been "out". But the photographs were what mattered the most. Nearly all of them family. "I wish we had a photograph with all of us on, everybody together," she said to Ange one day, trying to straighten the row. Everyone was there more or less, but every photo was different; different sizes and different ages, and nothing quite connected. "There probably *is* one somewhere," said Ange, not meeting her

271

eyes. She had quietly removed half a dozen of the photos, the year that she left home. The ones she especially liked. No one liked them as much as *her*.)

"And *if* he didn't take it with him, I wish you'd have kept it, Henry." As she was talking, the second post thumped through the letterbox in the hall. "I'll go," said Henry. "You drink your tea." It made him uneasy, thinking of home. Bruises that never stopped hurting. You never dreamed, when you were a kid, that things would still matter at fifty.

It was the weekly letter from Rose. Left to himself, he would never have opened them. It was Lorna who always ripped open the envelope, five per cent of her never quite believing that everything would always be the same. One week Rose would suddenly write and say she'd come up on the Pools. Or met a nice man, or was happy. In fact, you couldn't tell the letters apart, especially as she didn't date them (time didn't matter to Rose; it didn't put an end to mourning).

Each one was folded by Lorna and put away on the sideboard, shoved into a wooden stand which had once held mats, long gone. She pushed more and more of them in, till the rustling became a creaking, a solid mass of words, most of them miserable words.

Dear All

I hope you are well and eating properly don't "cut down" in this kind of weather Lorna. Has George written he never writes to me Ah Well I suppose he hasn't got time to write his granma. Angela doesnt either still give her my love and hope she isnt starving herself and tell her I'm at the same address if she wonders, maybe I'll see her Christmas more likely I wont. I suppose you dont know what she's "up to" either. Are they getting married yet its embarrasing when people ask. Though he seemd quite nice a bit soft maybe but it doesnt do to critise they dont listen.

My legs are awful at the moment in this weather and of course Mrs Cribbins hasnt bothered to come round though I did ALL the shoping for her when she was laid up with Shingles "thats life." The Doctor wont come says I can get round there myself if I want to thats the "National Health". I dont know honestly how much longer I can go on managing on my own Ive never complaned but in the end family's

272

family. If you cant turn to your own Family who can you? Sally does her best shes a good girl but you cant expect her to have me not with two still at home. She says you never write she cant hardly remember what Angela looks like I told her skinny like her Mother but not bad looking. Please send a photo you dont seem to bother sending snaps any more like you used to.

Has Lorna sent back the kettle with the default its no good hanging about. Their theives, the kettle people. I never let myself be cheated it doesnt do being to soft.

Your loving Mother

Rose

PS did you get my last with the Recipe that would do Henry good Lorna. Tell Angela Marks have got lovely warm tights this weather but an awful price maybe her chap would pay its no good expecting her granma to.

"She thinks I don't look after you," said Lorna, as she always did. (Women were meant to look after people. Not just *one* person, but four. She'd never quite felt she was up to it . . . someone should look after *her*. . . .)

"She doesn't think at all, she just says it," said Henry.

"I do my best," said Lorna. "The kids have grown up all right." As soon as she said it, the great gap yawned. George and Angela, they were all right. They seemed worlds away, they were both a bit—queer—but still they were both good children. But Guy. You couldn't get round it. Pretend that he hadn't been there. His growing up had just failed; all those years, and he had just stopped. Which meant he would never leave home. She imagined she heard him moving about, shuffling feet like leaves. It wasn't a friendly ghost. It was worse now that George was gone.

RUSSIAN BEAR GROWLS AT WEST
US: "NATO STANDS FIRM"

Henry didn't reply. He was miles away on his own. He was thinking of Rose and Guy, the chains you could never escape from. And money was part of it too. You always had to make money. That awful bar every evening. It wasn't the booze so much, he had almost stopped that now. It was having to go where he didn't want to, five nights a week, seven hours a night. Having to be friendly with the customers. Wasting words, and he didn't have many. Wasting time, and he didn't have much. *Wasting his life*—unbearable words which offered themselves in the silence. But no, it was *not too late*. He still loved life and he still loved Lorna: the world, when he suddenly remembered to look, was still . . . a miracle, yes.

(Dad had taught him the word years ago when he was just a young kid. Frank handed the word to his son, just before he himself forgot it. They had gone up the Rec one Sunday afternoon to watch the bigger boys playing football. Each different gang had its game. The moon was already there, floating. Around it the balls swooped up and then plunged. When he asked his Dad why it didn't fall down, Frank stared for a very long time. "It's . . . well, I suppose it's a miracle. Something grownups call a miracle. How would you like to go up there? One day we'll go. I'll take you."

RUSSIAN TROOP MOVEMENTS REPORTED
SOVIET COUNTER-CLAIMS

Inside, Henry still felt young. Hidden inside, buried not so deep, he *minded* everything just as at first, and the world was miraculous. But *never let them see what you feel* (if you love someone they'll go away and they won't ever take you with them. . . .)

The transparent, nervous self within caught each changing pulse of colour. It quivered at each faint note of distress from Lorna, the neighbours, a customer. It yearned for the exquisite finned and red-fringed things that floated past him. . . .

. . . *in the deepening blue*. A change in the current. The whole world seemed to grow darker. They were floating just out of view. Was it happening then at last? Would he have to grow up, get older?

He'd thought he could stay completely untouched by hiding himself underground. But the layers of habit, the layers of wood, grew heavier, thicker, coarser. Five nights a week in the gleaming cell with the great bodies pressed against it. Shouting at him all at once. Ordering him to go faster. Growing more lordly and stupid as they drank more and more. No wonder he drank himself at first so *he* could be stupid, not mind it. "Time, gentlemen, please." (*Timepieces . . . timepieces.*) He told himself he was saving up to start with the watches again. *In time he would climb up into the light in time they would all be free.* . . .

Lorna put this very carefully. She looked at him quizzically, under her lashes, looked at her hands, looked back. "I sometimes wonder, Henry. Do you ever think . . . do you ever *imagine* . . . what I mean is, I sometimes think one day we might somehow hear from your Dad. A postcard with a view of somewhere exotic. Mountains. Palm trees. The desert."

"He's dead," said Henry, briskly, taking his cup to the sink. "He'd be dead by now. Don't go bringing him up. He'd be eighty-six. Don't be silly."

He was gone before she could say any more. She read Rose's letter again. The *Recipe that would do Henry good* . . . after all these years, did she know him?

Walking down the crazy-paving path to the shed, Henry thought about freedom. Frank had done it, made himself free. He hoped his dad had been happy. He must have been too ashamed to come back, even if he ended up lonely. The thought of him dying in a Home somewhere, surrounded by strangers, not speaking the language . . . but *mountains, palm trees, the desert*. His father must have had guts. He realized that Frank had made his break for it when he was *his* age now. But that thought made him break out in a sweat, in the chill of early October.

He would never abandon Lorna. All the same, he couldn't let life go by. He needed the roses, the watches . . . space where his heart could feel free.

A week later Lorna sat down with a frown and a biro which felt like lead. She was writing her monthly letter to Rose and for once there was news to give. Henry had come up to bed around one in the morning, and woken her. Put on the light, which he never did. At first she thought he was drunk, but he was wildly excited and sober. "I just gave notice," he said. "It's done. I'll be free in November."

How could she say it so Rose didn't worry, so she didn't think it was a failure. Lorna had surprised herself by not making a fuss, not moaning about the money. She was worried about money of course but at least there were only two mouths to feed. The main thing was Henry's face when he told her, the look in his eyes, sort

275

of . . . *naked*. He never looked quite like that, except in the seconds just after making love, or waking up Sunday mornings when he wouldn't work again till the Monday. It was a look of joy blazing out so fierce she could hardly bear to meet it. "I just gave notice . . . *stuff them*." Her first scared thought in the sudden brightness was that he'd been caught on the fiddle. But no, there was nothing: *listen to me: it's not right for me, just not right.* They would get unemployment benefit and he'd make a bit from odd jobs. Mend clocks and watches for money. You don't need a shop to do that. "I shan't have to worry how much they pay me if the Dole is paying the bills."

"I'll go back to work myself," said Lorna. "I know you hated the bar. I shouldn't have let you go on."

"Do you want to go back to work? Go on Lorna, be honest."

"Well, I wouldn't exactly say that. But for *you*, I'd . . . well, do anything."

It was a new, exalted Henry, his eyes and his cheeks ablaze. He knelt on the floor beside the bed and kissed her cheeks and her breasts, very gently. It made her want to cry with happiness. *Never before, perhaps never again*. Movements and moments that come just once. Inside her a voice said *thank you*.

They started to make their plans. To anyone else they would have sounded like kids. They thought of all the things they could do, now they didn't *have* to do things. They'd go to evening classes. It was cheap, if you weren't working. "We shan't be really poor," said Lorna. "So many things don't cost money."

Would have been, would have been poor. But the plans were rich and happy.

Rose sent the letter they expected, ominously fatter than usual.

I just hope you know what your doing Henry you never did settle I wasnt surprised that the Shop didnt work. The Brewry was steady you cant deny it but there you go again it didnt suit you did it. What do you think of it Lorna. Just as long as he finds something solid quick theres the morgage remember and hes no "Spring Chicken." Its a pity you couldnt of made him think twice for a moment but whats the good no one listens to me. . . .

Lorna giggled as she read that out. "What's she, I wonder, if her

276

son's no spring chicken? Don't look so gloomy, Henry. It really is quite comical."

"She used to kill chickens, out at the back," said Henry, not sure he would let himself smile.

"Well at least she *thinks* about us," said Lorna. "That's more than you can say about mine. I don't know why I bother to write. I'm sure she never reads it."

"Ma's just worried she won't get a Christmas present," Henry said grimly.

She went on 'thinking about' them for the little time they had left. The morning they were going to Kew Gardens, another letter arrived.

> Has Henry got another job yet, he doesnt want to lose the habit that can happen Lorna they get used to it. Maybe the Hotel would still take him back if he asked after all "Pride doesnt butter any Parsnips". Especially these days and with Christmas coming to . . .

US SENDS PEACE "FEELER"
USSR "SUSPICIOUS"

Henry had other plans; shimmering, long-term plans. They would travel, the world would open.

He also had short-term plans which were all about staying at home. Staying in the heart of his home, in the shed in the garden, working. Never ever having to go anywhere he didn't want to again. Staying in bed with Lorna. That was blissful. "No reason why not," said Lorna, uncertainly, hopefully.

They lay and cuddled and dozed, and she talked, and he listened and tried to talk, and the trying became less hard. "This takes me back," she said, lying curled with his thin careful arms around her. Those days in his flat, when they were first married, and only had each other. . . .

"Do you remember the chocolate, Henry? How I used to think it was *food*."

He looked so young this morning, lying there without his glasses. His face still softened by sleep, and the reddish glow from the curtains. "Uhnn," he said, but he was stroking her, stroking her, thin warm hands which loved her. His hands moved round to her belly, firm on the softness there. She thought, *I must be so*

277

different . . . from when we did this before.

"It's weird about kids," she said very slowly. "You know, you start with just two of you. And it's sort of perfect like that. Like going out to play, but you think it's for ever, you never have to go home. We *were* like kids, you remember."

"You were so. . . ." Henry mumbled. He was going to say "pretty", but stopped. It sounded as if she wasn't now.

"Then all of a sudden you're pregnant. And somehow you end up with three. And you're *never* the two of you, never. Did we ever stay in bed, *even once*?"

"Well, Boxing Day . . . '78," said Henry, thinking very hard. "We all slept in till ten."

"That's not what I mean," sighed Lorna. "Listen to me, will you Henry? Then just as suddenly the whole lot go, and you're left in the house, all *empty*. You're a two again like you were before, only . . . you've got old. You're older."

"I don't feel older," said Henry, so firm and loud that Lorna jumped. "I don't, I don't, I mean it. Lorna, let's not be old. We can be whatever we want to. We can do whatever we want. We only have to think about *each other*, now."

"I love you Henry," said Lorna.

She knew it would never be entirely true: the spaces were full of voices. They lived on their own in the house in Acton but also in other brains. Wherever people were thinking of them, threads stretched out towards them. You never escaped your family. You didn't want to, entirely. It would be so awful, to be forgotten, as if you had never lived.

PEACE TALKS "CONSTRUCTIVE" SAYS RUSSIA
HOPES OF SETTLEMENT RISE

Lorna still thought of everybody. The strangest people, grown small, admittedly, wandered about in the park of memory. Ange's friend Clara . . . her own friend Maisie . . . Grandpa Cleaver with the gin in his hand . . . Guy's friend Raymond, bulking black and menacing (it wasn't nice but you couldn't just forget them) . . . Latham of course, her Jack, even now. Going over it all it grew less painful . . . and then not painful at all, in the end. Whatever he was, and perhaps he wasn't much, it was part of life, it was living. At least she wouldn't have to go to her grave thinking she'd only had Henry. Henry was all that she wanted, Henry was

278

who she loved. But she wouldn't have known that, would she, if she hadn't tried with Jack? Her brother Guy in Australia, making all those piles of money. She never cared for him much as a kid, but well, he'd been loyal to her. Every Christmas there was a parcel, and a money order as well. And he sometimes phoned up on her birthday, sounding more Australian every year. But under all that was the gawky boy who still called her Lollipop. Henry said she was a hypocrite once when she was talking about her brother.

"What I thought then isn't what I think *now*," she said, but a bit ashamed. Why shouldn't you change what you thought of people? Life seemed kinder, and people changed. The further away you were from things the more you could understand. The longer you had to think, the more it seemed part of a pattern. Perhaps by the time she was ninety she would understand everything. And never feel sad any more . . . never feel sad, or frightened.

RUSSIA CONDEMNS US
GENEVA PEACE TALKS BREAK DOWN

Life *was* more frightening, lately. But *she* refused to be frightened. They were going to give up the newspaper, now Henry had left his job. *He* didn't really want to: Henry enjoyed his reading (*they always enjoy it more, those who come late to the garden*). But the headlines stamped on her morning, brought in a chill of fear. And TV had got scary too, and even the radio. They didn't want to be scared. She *would not let them* be scared. They'd decided to have a good time, they'd made plans for how to be happy. It was trouble with Russia again. Lorna was sick of Russia. Henry insisted it wasn't their fault, but she didn't take him seriously. Of course it was Russia's fault. You couldn't let them walk all over you.

"That's why George is in Germany," she told him, reproachfully. "Otherwise the Russians would just come and take us over."

"Why should they want to do that? It's a very long way, for nothing." That was quite hard to answer. It was obvious England was poor. She tried another tack. "You've always had a thing about America. What's so bad about America? One day we ought to go there. If me brother leaves us some money."

"I've got no time for them."

"Well go on, you must have a reason."

But he wouldn't, couldn't answer. It was all too hard to explain.

(He saw them as everything bad . . . all flash and money, gimmicks and gadgets. Things like digital watches. Everything bigger and better. Watches without any hands . . . horrible, ugly, inhuman things. Time was what life was about. Light and darkness were real. Coming in stripes, they were beautiful. And the changing light in a day. They could hold those things in their hands. But who needs gigantic great cars and freezers and time without hands or faces. . . .

> there was one enormous bomb
> > lately the hum had got louder
> the Japanese bombed the Americans Daddy. . . .
> > your trouble is you don't listen. . . .)

US GIVES NEW ULTIMATUM
RUSSIA WILL NOT BACK DOWN

It was the nearest they'd got to an argument since he'd left the hotel. "Well *I* don't want to know anything about it until it's all died down," said Lorna, switching off the gloomy voice of the newsreader right in the middle of a sentence. "I'm going down the shop to stop the paper, and *that* can go off and stay off." She couldn't stand it, those tight grey faces, bearing her back to old terrors. Killing and crushing of gentle things. Bad things that couldn't be mended. She was going to be happy with Henry. They were starting their life again.

The day they set off for Kew Gardens was the first of the outings she'd planned. Her plans were all for outings. So many places to see. He was secretly hoping it would be too cold; it seemed mad to go in November. But the day dawned sunny and mild. The sky was as blue as summer. The leaves on the trees glittered yellow as coins, rare coins on the long road down. "It's good for us having a walk," said Lorna. "Don't look so long-faced, my darling." The *darling* made him cheer up, and her pushing her hand through his.

The road was very long and noisy all the same with lorries like great sprinting houses. Sometimes he felt they were such little people, both of them. Shrinking almost to nothing. Getting smaller as they got older, just two of them now and the world so large. . . . That sense that he ought to protect her. It had always tormented Henry. He had taken her over from her father, but had he done all that he should? Men must look after women (but who would look after him?). Now they would both grow old, and sometimes there seemed too much that was evil, too much you could not understand or control . . . and they were out of date, old-fashioned. Dispensable, if you liked. Pieces on a chessboard that was growing and changing and he didn't know what the rules were . . . they were bound to fall off, they were much too small, they had slipped too far from the centre . . .

all the little people falling like ants
> *at night it's black but it's blue when we fall. . . .*

"Just look at the blue of that sky," said Lorna. She was looking at everything, bright as Guy's buttons. "The *King's Arms. Courage*" (reading things out). "And it's good for you, this wind. The gate's only just round the corner. Aren't you glad for once not to stick inside?"

"I'm not complaining," said Henry.

In fact it was nice to be out of the house where the silent radio spoke in his head, saying worse things he was sure than the truth, and the dead grey screen meant horror. They delivered the papers by mistake, but she threw them away unread. "We agreed to please ourselves what we did. Let's please ourselves and not be frightened. I'm going to put a record on." If they were pleasing themselves, of course, she could hear Carla Wing at breakfast. . . .

The earth is trembling/beneath our feet/ See the blue sky . . . darken and fall/ . . . Stayed in bed with you my love, close all morning/ Passing the time/ Watching time passing/ Is something wrong? tell me, darling/ Is it too late/ too late for loving/ tell me, love, is it ending?

It was easier when we did *some* things normal, thought Henry, swamped in music. The chords went oddly with marmalade. It sounded like midnight in the early morning. And it sounded sad, as well.

But she made chicken sandwiches, and looked at the map. "Ange said it was nice in the glasshouses. We never had time to go in, that day. We could have our lunch in there. If they let us. Or else by the lake, it was beautiful there. There's a famous Pagoda, *we* never saw it, I'd like to do that, have lunch in a Pagoda. I've never seen a Pagoda, except in pictures, of course."

"One day we'll go to Japan," said Henry, without any truth. "We'll go to Japan, or China." The rising sun of his dreams. And so they walked to Kew Gardens, hand-in-hand till they paid at the gate.

Inside, the world suddenly got much larger, and the light poured down in a blaze. It was very quiet in the Gardens, they thought for the first few minutes, grinning at each other in shy pleasure as their quiet feet pattered on the path. Half-naked trees flanked the walk, in extravagant attitudes, foreign: asking them something, begging them something, fantastically graceful, with a few yellow leaves. There were miles of brilliant sky, and the cars had melted away. It felt as if this was their garden. He took her hand again.

Then the humming began and changed to a roar. A plane came over so low and slow they could see every detail of its body. The slowness seemed to be on purpose so the horrible noise would last. "It's near Heathrow I suppose," said Henry. He wanted to say "I'm sorry." He wanted to apologize if anything wasn't perfect. This was the very first outing of their new life together.

"You feel you could reach out and touch it," said Lorna, dropping his hand, reaching her small one skywards.

Such a frail drying-up hand he saw in the knife-sharp light of the sky. Light as a leaf with the veins showing through. But beautiful: light and gentle. He loved her lightness, her quick light voice. She was life and light to him. If she had left him for Latham . . . *things had come right in time*.

"Wouldn't *want* to touch one of those things," said Henry very firmly indeed. "They're . . . an aggravation." But the aggravation would come again and again. Each time it scratched a little path in contentment, a wound on the music playing . . . until their own music played so loud that they could not hear the warning.

The Orangery hadn't got oranges, which was a bit of a disappointment. It was a beautiful building though, white as snow, with postcards and guides and maps inside. There was a radio bussing in the background like a fly caught under a lampshade. "They shouldn't have that on at work," said Lorna, but then they forgot about it. Henry was quickly absorbed. "D'you think I should buy some of these?" "Why not?" said Lorna. "It's an outing."

Henry bought factual things: a booklet on the Alpine House, a General Guide Book, a map. Lorna bought some postcards which caught her eye, the brightest ones she could see. There was one of "Flowering (or Japanese) Cherries and Daffodils at Kew in springtime". There were actually narcissi too, and pine trees dark in the background. There was one of rhododendrons in summer, lush pinks and reds, even yellow." South West China, South East Tibet . . ." "It's a wonderful world," said Lorna. A flamboyant autumn scene with sun through golden leaves; you could see each ray coming separately, as fine as hair, like hers used to be. "Leaf Fall of the Sweet Chestnut." The leaves were a bright pure gold. There was one very pretty but somehow unreal, which she realized at last was a painting. It showed the top of a purple-snowed mountain peeking out of snowy mauve cloud. The sea and the sky were pale turquoise, and the view was framed by blue-purple flowers. They looked like upside-down lupins, hanging and weeping and trembling. Turning it over she saw it was a "Painting from the Marianne North Gallery, Royal Botanic Gardens, Kew. Distant View of Mount Fujiyama, Japan and *Wistaria*."

What a beautiful name for a flower. It made you think *wistful* and *mysterious*, and was right for that still mauve winter. She could have looked at these all day. "Don't you want to go and see the *real* things?" asked Henry, ready to pay. "I'm looking at *Paintings*," said reverent Lorna, so he waited for her outside.

Everything was real to Lorna, everything imaginary. Paintings were photographs, and long-ago things were still here. The last card she chose she wasn't sure about, if it was a *fact*, all the same. It was a photograph, though, not a painting. "Have a look at this one, Henry," she called as she came through the door.

It was a photo taken at night of the giant glasshouse they'd glimpsed in the distance. Inside there were blueish lights, and outside a great crowd of people. The sky was an amazing tasselled trail of white and crimson flame. In the black lake under the people, everything shone in waves, the fireworks, the glass and the great blueish lights. The card didn't really explain. "Palm House Promenade Concert Firework Finale," it said, full-stop. "Catch us going to a concert," said Henry, but he didn't sound glad. "Point is, no one ever tells us, do they. Our sort wouldn't get in."

"We've got in now though," said Lorna, brightening, "and we've only paid 10p! But they weren't very nice to us in the shop. As if they couldn't be bothered. More interested in the radio."

"More fool them," said Henry.

The Palm House was different by daylight. It was huge, all those panes of sun. It looked like the whole of the nineteenth century, to Henry, who knew about History. Elaborate, like chains of waterfalls, water running for ever. At first they couldn't open the door, but he wouldn't give up, they got in. The warmth and the moisture hit you in the face, and a smell which was intensely familiar. "What's that smell?" she asked. "Lovely, I know it ever so well. Oh you know Henry. Go on, *smell*."

He was puzzled. The warmth was as dense as a flannel, the smell was both sweet and rough (she wished he wouldn't screw up his face like that; today he was supposed to look handsome). Then she realized.

"Henry, it's *summer*. It smells of *summer* in here. Not summer now, all fumes and things. It smells like summers once used to." As they walked, she was floating back. It was Grandpa's greenhouse, of course. Grandpa Cleaver's greenhouse. She didn't like him and his hairy hands but she loved the rich warmth of the greenhouse. The tomatoes growing, tiny tomatoes with colours from gold to green. They looked like fruit, not vegetables, which the little girl found confusing. It meant you didn't know anything (but that was exciting, too . . .).

The Palm House was more confusing, and she was a child again. Lots of things that she thought she knew, like coconuts, sugar, bananas, were here in another disguise, giant plants with enormous leaves. Everything seemed very big and fleshy and Lorna felt very small. Then Henry persuaded her to climb the white wrought-iron staircase to the gallery, and she found that when you looked down on those great jungly things they turned back into a pattern: most of them spread from a centre like fountains, tight green fountains or flowers.

"It's wonderful how everything fits together," said Henry, deep in thought. Why had he stayed inside so long? Why had he never been here? It was a wonder equal to his workshop, equal to his maps of the world. His father's maps of the world whose power he had always kept chained, hidden deep under the TV seat with the mad thought that *one* day, *one* day . . . but being here seemed as

284

good as the world, it *was* the world, in a garden. Without the worst of the world. All *that* couldn't get them here.

Usually he didn't like walking, but today they walked all over: eager as children to see it *all*, though they planned to come back tomorrow. "We could come here every day for a week," said Lorna, squeezing his arm, red-cheeked from the wind and the walking.

They went into the Water-lily House. There was a slight silver sound of water. Sun in skeins in between the creepers, where purple convolvulus climbed. Everything here was so peaceful, no movement, no people to spoil it. The name of the water-lilies for some reason made Henry think of Lorna. *Nymphaea Rubra* which was pale sugar pink, and another *Nymphae, "Blue Beauty".* *Nymphae* ought to be mermaids really, or sweet blue flying-fish flying. Lorna was round the other side of the pond, looking at some Loofah plants. But wherever he looked he saw Lorna, in the lacy, delicate light. Lorna was the red fish darting and floating between the stems of the lilies. Lorna was the blue fish flying in his brain, making faint high sounds of laughter. *Nymphaea Lotus* was another Lorna, could life be pleasure for ever. . .?

They went to the Aroid House, which was Greenhouse Number One. Lorna thought it would be even better than the Palm House because of that Number One. It was duller, really, but still smelled of summer and the noise was beautiful, a slow drip drip, water splashing and beating on thick heavy leaves like summer. *They would come back every day for a year, every day of their lifetimes.* Henry's glasses steamed up and he took them off to wipe them. "Bend over, Henry," she said, and he did, and she kissed his eyelids one after another; very gently, like little waterdrops tapping, kissed each one and then laughed. She didn't say anything, he turned away and they walked on through the green temple.

There was a plant which was more exciting than the others with red-striped leaves on long straight stems and lovely long crumbling tails of flowers, deep pink with bright yellow stamens. "It looks like love-lies-bleeding," she said, but she hoped it wasn't, it would be a bad sign, the needle scratching, something bad, the plane in the distance. . . . But the label that seemed to go with the plant said *Anchomanes Welwitschi.* "Look Henry," she said, "it's a well-wishing plant, it's wishing us well for the future."

He nodded, his face to the window. When they got outside, she understood. There were tears running down his lined cheeks. But he didn't look sad, he looked so happy that she wanted to kiss him again. "No one ever did that before," he said. "No one ever kissed my eye-lids." So happy he changed the subject. "I'm starving, let's go and have lunch." "Can we go to that Pagoda?" He looked at the map. It was miles away. "Not if you're hungry. We'll go there after."

The rustle of leaves went with them everywhere, quietly saying *sshh, it's all right, sshh, it's all right, sshh, it's all right*. They walked past the Palm House again, and round the side of the lake. They passed two great peculiar grey stone beasts that Henry found out were lions. "Chinese lions, the guidebook says." "Well they're very different from British ones." "We don't *have* lions, dafty." "You know what I *mean*," she said. Away to the right she spotted a thing like a temple on a small hill. It was sparkling white with a little round roof and just the right size for them. At first she thought it was pretty. Then she read what it said on the wall. Not a *factual* notice, but pompous.

> The decoration of the interior incorporates
> medallions displaying the names and numbers
> of British and Hanoverian regiments who
> distinguished themselves in the
> Seven Years' War.

"I wonder when that was," said Henry, interested, starting to unpack the bag. But her mood had changed in an instant. "Ooh Henry, I don't think I want to eat here. I don't want to think about that sort of thing."

She was suddenly imagining George. Turned into stiff gold lettering on someone else's future. A stupid name on a wall, no one knowing it was him. A stranger munching under her son

(if they could stop   stop time)

Uncomplaining, Henry packed up again. "It says on the map there's another little temple, nearer the lake. We could sit and look out."

"I really love our son," she said as they walked, for some reason faster. Hurrying up lest the day run out, although it was only two. "He's got a kind heart, has George. I wish he was out of all that."

Henry couldn't talk about George, not even for love of Lorna. It connected to so many corridors, darkening narrowing corridors. Leading away from this new bright centre of light where he wanted to stay. *It didn't do loving people, in case they were taken away.* . . .

(Yet another sliver of Henry was knitting his life together. Both of the Georges would have loved it here; if they'd met, they'd have loved each other . . . now, in his head, in this garden, they met, and the three men, none of them kids any more, kicked a bright ball from one to another in the rustling leaves where nobody walked, and Dad would be back in a minute, back from the moon to join them. . . .)

Queer how few people were out today. They'd met almost no one, just a boy drawing, sitting bent over his sketch-pad as if there was no one else on earth. He liked to see that, he was seeing himself, himself bent over the watches. Making a world of your own, which nobody could destroy. He wished that he had made Kew. And everyone would come in free. No slow poison would spoil the joy as it did when they never paid him. Wanting to make them a present of it but he couldn't, he had a family. . . .

"It's so hard to think of one of your family all that way away." Her voice pattered on unhappily, not keeping up with her footsteps. "In *Germany* of all places. Well isn't it stupid, Henry. All of a sudden, we're on the same side. For *your* George, they were the enemy."

"That's just the point about the Russians," he said, but her face was blank so he didn't go on.

Under his ribcage a dull pain droned. That was the point, but nobody saw it. *They* don't care, just as long as there's an enemy. So they can make people patriotic. So they can send people off to die. So they can use up those horrible weapons and somebody can make money. Always somewhere else, out of sight, the big decisions were taken. A bigger and better war. A million miles from this garden.

A bigger and better fiction, closing down on my story. . . .

"Come on, I'm starving," he said, and Lorna brightened at once. He loved those half-moon dimples. "You haven't been starving for *years*."

The new little temple looked just like the other one. "Who was Arethusa?" mused Henry. "This one's the Temple of Arethusa, according to this book."

"Don't know, but I like the name," and her voice made that

sudden change to a bird's. "*Enthusiastic*, she sounds. With a name like that. This'll do."

It was smaller and more straightforward inside, but the same dull note of warning. The plaque was of brass, this time, the voice was less boastful, simpler. Weathered metal with smoke in the shadows of the names which were worked in relief.

IN HONOURED MEMORY OF THE KEW GUILD AND
STAFF OF THE BOTANIC GARDENS WHO GAVE THEIR
LIVES IN THE GREAT WAR 1914–1919

Then there was a list of thirty-seven names. Though the metal was almost the same, you could see the bottom half of the plaque was different, that it had been tacked on later. Names of the dead in the Second World War.

"They didn't call it Great, the second time," he muttered to Lorna, feeling the names. "I don't mind this place so much," she whispered, reading, small face tipped up. "It's not that I think they should be forgotten. After all, the wars weren't *their* fault."

Some of the names were like music: *Sgt. John Dear, East Surrey Regt., Sgt. Frederick Honey, East Surrey . . . L/Cpl. Frank Windebank . . .* simple and sweet, like sleep. But *she* hadn't slept well recently; jerking awake quite sure she was falling. . . .

"All the same, it's chilly in here. I think I need a cup of tea. Let's have a cup of tea before we have our picnic." She set off walking determinedly in the direction of the Tea Bar.

It had a green roof skating up in the air like sails of long-ago boats. "We could have our sandwiches in here, maybe," she said under her breath to Henry. There was no one else there, just a faint fly buzzing, and one old woman serving. She had flat black hair like a wig and looked very preoccupied. Henry smiled his rare sweet smile as he paid for their teas. "Thanks a lot." She stared at him, heavy and sour. Then she started to talk, in a flood.

"I didn't expect there'd be anyone in today. There's only me here working. But what's the point of staying away. Where are we supposed to go. You're the first to come in all day."

"More room for us, that's fine," he grinned, not understanding. She looked as if she had more to say, but he turned away back to Lorna. They sat on the bench in the window and the sun poured hot through the glass. It made the tea feel almost too hot. Moreover, it was horribly stewed. The woman had disappeared.

She was out in the kitchen with that buzzing fly and *don't listen to it don't listen*.

Lorna pointed to a handwritten notice. The writing was like dead insects.

No food or drink whatever to be consumed here unless bought on the premises.

"I didn't want to anyway," said Henry, though his hand was in the bag. "Catch *me* eating *my* food here," he said loudly, towards the kitchen. Lorna started to giggle. "Do you think she was wearing a wig?" "You'll never have to wear a wig, Lorna," he said, staring at her. With the sun pouring in through the glass behind her she looked like a girl again: the triangular blur of her small pale face in a cloud of burning auburn.

They didn't drink much of the tea but it somehow filled them up. Looking out of the window, Lorna saw that the sun had gone in for a second. A tiny cloud like a small pale leaf had drifted across the sun. "Let's keep on walking, let's look at everything, *then* have our lunch," she pleaded. "We can eat lunch any old day. *I want to see the Pagoda.*"

"We thank you for your custom and wish you **'A HAPPY DAY'**."

The **HAPPY DAY** was in red. "They wrote that for us," said Lorna.

They started to walk at a good brisk pace. It was cold when the sun went in. They had to reach the Pagoda. It suddenly came into view.

It stood at the end of a long wide path that was specially cleared of trees. It was the shape she expected, with all those little roofs, like a Christmas tree, but regular. What she didn't expect was its colour. She always imagined it red. She was sure that Ange said it was red. It stood black against the sky. They walked down the path towards it, down the long gold carpet of leaves. On the right you could see more enormous glasshouses, snow and ice in the sunlight. "There aren't any birds," she remarked. "Except those geese by the Palm House." A single magpie had swooped across and a pair of enormous ravens. But you didn't see sparrows, or pigeons . . . things like that, she liked town birds. Plucky little things, keeping on against the wind. And the filthy air of the city. They always looked hopeful, their wings making signs, cheeking the great smooth planes.

As you got nearer the Pagoda, you started to see the red. Red glowed underneath each roof, on the window frames, in the door. One side of the building was flaming red where the sun picked out the lacquer. Henry was reading as he walked along, but Lorna was just hurrying, staring.

"*Come on* Henry you can read that later," she called back, echoing, echoing.

It blazed redder and redder as they came underneath till the red was all they could see. On the side of the building under the bright red pillars was a very long notice which Henry read. Lorna just read out the end. It seemed a very stupid notice.

Although the building is soundly constructed
and in excellent condition, IT IS NOT SAFE TO
ALLOW FREE ACCESS TO THE PUBLIC

She felt it was aimed at her, having planned to eat lunch inside. "It's like saying yah boo sucks, it doesn't belong to you. They tell you it's safe as houses then they tell you to keep away."

"Never mind, Lorna, doesn't matter. It's not so good from close up. It used to have hanging dragons, and rainbow glass, it says. It's nothing like what it was."

"What happened to it then Henry?" He didn't say. "Something bad? What's the matter? Why can't we go in?" *Harrowing, childish questions.*

"Look, *we* don't care," her husband assured her, Henry the brave, the jaunty. "It might be about to fall down." She loved this holiday Henry. "There's plenty of other places." He was walking away through the leaves. "We haven't seen half of the Gardens yet." (But it still burned red in the background.)

Lorna called him across. "Come and look at this, Henry, *quick*!"

"What's the hurry?" asked Henry, but still he did hurry, running through the deepening leaves.

The tree she had found was in blossom. It was slender and still looked young. The bark was glossy with a hint of green. Long, graceful arms with sharp angles, in which the blossom clung. The blossom was beautiful, pointed petals which ranged from white to pale pink. Where the petals had fallen the stamens remained, pink from a deep pink centre. Living gold dots of pollen on those little knots of flame.

"Oh Henry, it's like a good whatsit, *omen*. I mean, it looks just like spring! It must be a kind of omen—a fruit tree blooming in autumn!" Through the bent limbs of the cherry, the Pagoda stared at them. "It's a cherry, I think," said Henry. "What does it say on the label? *Prunus* something-or-other *autumnalis*, it says."

"That's better than going inside the Pagoda, me finding that," she bragged. "Don't you think I'm clever, Henry? *You* would have walked straight past it."

But there wasn't any time to waste, although the cherry was lovely. She tried to snap off a twig of it to hide in their picnic bag, but the petals fell off when she shook it. "That serves you right," said Henry. "It's better just to remember." Instead of the cherry she picked up some leaves which were left on the ground as presents.

Half walking, half trotting through the reddening light and the sea of leaves, they remembered. So many beautiful things to cram into one short day. "I wish I could live for ever, and for ever be like today," said Lorna above the scrunch of the leaves and the noise of the wind in the tree-tops. "I'm glad I remembered my coat," she said, although it slowed her down. He could have gone faster if he'd wanted to but he'd never leave her behind. He could have escaped if he'd wanted to but he'd never desert his Lorna.

Running past the small empty greenhouses near the gate, something caught Henry's eye. "Hold on for a minute, Lorna. I think that's the Alpine House." It was shaped like a mountain, with a deep high point, a pyramid of glass flaming crimson. "It looked ever so much bigger in the picture. Let's go and have a peep inside." "Are you sure we've got time?" cried Lorna. "No . . ." said Henry. "Come on."

It was waiting for them as the sun went down, the answer to something, the key. There were other greenhouses all around but nobody seemed to be working: they stared through the glass and the glass behind it and the layers of leaves in the sunset. "Everyone's left but us," said Lorna, sounding half excited, half frightened.

Inside it was very cold. "They have to keep cold, you see," said Henry, clutching his leaflet. The plants shone out from their pebble beds like stars, with a cold sweet smell. The leaves were all silver-greens and greys, the flowers cool mauves and pinks. "This place is a miracle, that's what," he said, his face clenched with effort (he had found more words in the past six hours than in the six days before it).

"That's a lovely word, like water falling," said Lorna, as they ran on. "Isn't it. *Miracle* . . . *miracle*" (running feet jolted it, blurring the syllables, sense being dazzled by the terminal sun).

They would have their banquet at last, they would sit and be calm together. Lorna knew where she was going, but she knew there might not be time. All round the Park the gates would be closing, though first there should be a warning. "When I came with the kids there were men on bikes going round shouting *Closing Time*, she panted. "I don't know what's happened today." The geese sat dazzled, honking.

No sirens could come in the Garden. She was making for one special tree. She had seen it when they left the Tea Bar. It wasn't an enormous protective tree and yet she was sure it was lucky. Lorna believed in luck as her daughter believed in luck: both of them followed the rituals of pattern, sure it would make them lucky. She knew that luck was with her, at least on this one special day: that well-wishing plant in the Aroid House and the notice printed in the Tea Bar. "**HAPPY DAY**" in red capitals, bright red for a happy day. So the sad-faced woman in her wig didn't matter or the black buzzing fly growing louder (but Lorna had read the wrong label, and *Anchomanes* wished nothing . . .).

They were running straight into sunlight, which made everything hard to see. Henry's arthritis had started to pinch but he wasn't going to spoil things. In the bag he had a secret: a bottle of rosé wine. The day that he left the Hotel it had been standing about in the kitchen, as if it was waiting for them. So he slipped it inside his jacket, and walked out stiff as a soldier. It reminded him of something long ago, a pale bottle rang on pale glasses. An error being put right ("Oh Henry, I thought you'd be pleased . . ."). He didn't want to think about that. It was right for today: romantic. She ought to have wine and roses. The way they were shaking the bag it would probably be more like champagne.

Spreading in the wind against the storm of light which joined black distant trees and the sky's blue roof, there was something between a tree and a bird, a tree and a bunch of feathers. It had a long slender stalk stretching up about nine feet high. Then the leaves spread out where the branches should be, as long as arms, fine deep-gold feathers fledging the central rib of the leaf, the whole waving gently like wings, like arms, welcoming, blessing or saying goodbye

come on Henry   *saying goodbye*

Ailanthus altissima, the "Tree of Heaven". He took off his coat, despite the chill wind blowing crimson and fierce now across from the lake, spread it on the ground for them to sit on. Then he took off his jacket, wrapped it round her shoulders, wrapped it round the worn tweed coat already wrapping them. "Have you gone crazy, Henry?" she said. But she understood somehow he had to do it, sit in his shirt and be sure she was warm, protecting her now from long-ago bruises, wrapping her round in his own flayed skin. She rested against him with her eyes on the sky, watching the gold wings curving above them.

"I've got a surprise in here," said Henry. "When we've opened *that* we'll be warm all right."

Distinct and melancholy, the voice began. She looked at her watch; it was ten to four. It was only one voice by the sound of it, one man left to send people home but he'd never find them as the sun went down. . . .

She hadn't brought glasses so they drank from the bottle, raising the amethyst glass to the sky, glimpsing the sun swimming red through the liquid as gentle fire swam down through their throats. *Clo-osing time . . . Clo-osing time.* "Ange 'ud love this," Lorna said very quietly. "She's like me, romantic. I bet she spends her whole life with that John." Pause. She was thinking. Old wounds, old aches. "She's . . . selfish, though, Ange, don't you think so, Henry?" She was rested against him, nested in his jacket, her cheek against his chest and through his thin shirt she could feel his heart beating, fluttering, fast.

Henry said "Uhnn." He was reading his brochure, the brochure he'd bought about the Alpine House.

"Are you listening Henry?" asked Lorna, reaching across him for the half-empty bottle and turning to blow hot mouths on his chest, little wet caves as Henry grew colder.

"You were saying about Ange," he said, uncertain. He made an effort, thought about Ange (it was hard to think straight in this blinding vermilion, the leaves blowing round them, the cold blowing in). "She's a good girl, Ange. I hope she writes her book. I hope it goes well. I hope she'll be happy. . . ."

What can you do? How can you help them? You love your kids but you can't protect them . . .

No more birds in the sky, just leaves. Clouds like red curling leaves on the flame, real leaves spinning like clouds of birds. . . . She still had the leaves she'd collected in her handbag. She pulled them out and put them on her lap. That must be an oak, but the tooth-marks were bigger . . . a *foreign* oak, maybe, though oaks should be English . . . that was horse chestnut, of course she knew that . . . then two beautiful fine leaves with lovely veins on, pale gold and pale yellow, the shape was familiar but what was it, something . . . reminded her of something . . . something in an airline advertisement, was it? . . . flying and falling . . . a sycamore? a plane? . . . it didn't really matter; they were only names. Every tree was different, every leaf of every tree. She didn't envy scientists, seeing things in batches. She did wish she *knew* more, she would *get* to know more, they'd both go to classes like Henry said . . . she'd come away with names coming out of her ears, she'd know so many names that the kids would be frightened . . . but even if she *knew* more, it wouldn't change some things. At least I *see* everything, Lorna thought, gazing. And there wouldn't be a name for a sunset like this. Even Angela couldn't find words for this, and the faint scary edge of the darkness to follow. . . .

darkness to follow   the fearful edge

Facts might be comforting. Nice to know facts. More information, she could do with that. Despite his jacket, the goose-pimples started. "Read it out, Henry, whatever you're reading," she asked him urgently, pulling him closer.

"About the Alpine House? It interests me, but it mightn't you. It interests me because it's all about . . . *the pattern.*"

"What do you mean? Go on then, Henry."

So he read it aloud, in his thin careful voice which age had dried out (*I don't feel older, let's not be old*).

Form and Construction

The complex requirements of the house can be summarized from the architect's brief as allowing a freedom of form as against the discipline of using 60cm wide glass (from which the house dimensions were ultimately derived) . . . on a non-standard structure. Further requirements were: for a scale of house in keeping with the diminutive scale of Alpine plants; a large area of unobstructed glass; good ventilation; a solid peripheral wall; the collection and storage of . . . water . . . supplementary and photoperiodic lighting. . .

She wasn't really listening, she was rustling her leaves, playing a game where she tried to look through them. The sun was so brilliant it ought to be a lamp, you ought to be able to look through them like slides, one over the other, a double exposure like Henry said she did when the photos came out wrong but she thought that it often looked better like that, like a dream where everything happened at once and all of her life could be seen together, everything together in one queer garden . . . but the leaves in their glory stayed quietly separate, each one itself, casting small precise shadows, and *she* was herself and would not be repeated. . . .

His words were drifting through the nets of the trees and the tendrils of wine and content licking through her

The mountain-like form, a crystalline pyramid 14m square and 7m high, has proved an attractive design solution . . . the light steel structure, which achieves . . . minimum obstruction to daylight . . . the moat . . . interconnected to an underground tank and circulating pump . . . rainwater . . . irrigation/mist points . . . Internally, a display panel screens the control equipment required for irrigation, ventilation, refrigeration and lighting . . . stock is continually replenished from the vast reservoirs of pot-grown material in adjoining support-houses and frames . . . Endangered European plants include. . . .

"I want to cuddle you Henry," she whispered, over the rustling leaves.

"You're more wonderful than any machinery," said Henry hoarsely, putting down his pamphlet, staring at his wife in the sun's red glaze, a lit bright carving of living bronze with her hair spreading out in a metal river and the leaves spreading round her as far as he could see, shivering and rustling in the sunset wind . . . how had he, Henry, married such beauty?

It seemed somehow final, this shining Lorna, as if their whole life had led to this moment. "Do you think we should go?" she said, staring sunwards. He didn't answer, but picked up the curling handful of leaves she had laid on her knees. "Aren't they lovely Henry? I could stay here for ever . . . I'm so happy I could die . . . but you're *cold*, my darling. . . ."

His teeth were chattering but *he* wasn't cold, his heart beat fiercely in quickening flurries like small birds stirring though there *weren't* any birds, no birds and no people, just the faint voice calling *clo-osing time   time to go home .*   but *this* could be home, their home in the garden

(he had never quite built the whole that he wanted, the magic building from magic bricks, all different shapes, leaf-reds and yellows, strange clear prisms with small wheels singing but the colours were here, could *this* be the building. . .?)

The leaves in his fingers looked like a flower, a great gold shaggy-petalled complicated flower. Or a star, perhaps, a star which had fallen . . . it might have fallen from the heaventree above them whose long gold arms waved ever more slowly . . . he bunched up the flower and held it to her hair, wished he'd been brave enough to steal her some roses. *In all the expanse of rose-red light he saw no shadow of another parting. . . .*

"What are you doing?"

"It looks like a star . . ."

In the untouched blue at the top of the dome, peering through the wings of *Ailanthus altissima*, the first star shone near the shell of the moon

but in another world long arcs were rising

(no, it was here   there was only one world
despite all those hundreds of leaves of paper   only one
world   and one last picture)

   long arcs were falling into the picture, "We'll never get there,"
said Lorna to the moon, and against the red end of the day they
saw nothing   *nothing would happen*   *they had done nothing*
they did nothing like so many others   locked in the picture as the
long arcs fell

   They were in Kew Gardens   in each other's arms
   skies flashed white and the day cracked open   stories
smashed as all became one   through the glass flaming for a
split-glass second all was transparent, the last light shone
   glass became tears as the picture was taken

   (George in Germany died a little earlier, by some irony thinking
of Guy: still half believing goodness would win . . . half
believing, then not believing . . . STARGATE   IMMORTALS
   MORTALS, MORTALS   ALPHA   *I didn't*
TO OMEGA BASE   . . . Angela and John in the same white second,
half a mile apart, in the middle of a tiff . . . Rose red and bare as in
Frank's worst nightmare, drinking and weeping in her cooling
bath . . . Prunella bad-tempered on a bus to see her mother, *it's
freezing, honestly, what was the point* . . . Ray and his son in the
shop with the corpses . . . Joanna wheeled out in the garden of
the Home, paralysed, staring at the dim lost sunlight . . . Mr
Briggs driving to the nearby churchyard with florist's roses as he
did every week and his wife would not know he would never
reach her, dry flowers powdered as the gravestone
cracked . . . Maisie killing turkeys for the Christmas season,
worrying whether it would ever come . . . Guy and his family
rather later in Brisbane, scorched quite slowly, deprived of
ozone . . . Dr Akizuki giving blood to a patient, *the error shall not be
made again* . . . Frank in bliss on the side of the mountain, the
word for miracle melting to nothing . . .)

Some died instantly, some took time. Bags of skinned organs,
spilling, crawling. A thing called *lethality*, a thing called time. Time
was a measure of terror and pain   *no*   *I can't bear it*
   please stop time

The last light shone with no one to see it. The final photograph made its print. Everything was on it, nothing escaped. The pattern had an unearthly clarity. Melted eyeballs, shattering bone. Miracles of form became crackling bacon, miracles of feeling flashed to hot fat. Bleeding and terrified things pushed blindly against the pain which put out the light. *Some died instantly, most took time.* Nothing was too little for poison to reach it. Mice and sparrows found nowhere to hide. Black burst crusts which were rainbow fishes. Balls of burnt feathers on the burnt black ground. Flakes of ash were once soft moths quivering. Books in their charred skins feel less pain. . . .

All was as if it had never   *tell me*
why is it dark already   *what happened*
why did we let our house burn down?

All was as if it had never been.

Blackening paper, the last leaves burning.

ii ...Against Ending

Waking again from the book you look out of the window at stillness. The sunlight on the pavement lying pale and still as peace.

Stones which lie pale as peace . . . unless you look, you won't see it. Green fronds push through the cracks. Some children crouch on brown shins.

Look at your hand, so peaceful. It lies on the page or the table. That hand has felt the warm sand run slow or fast through its fingers. The flesh looks so safe on the bone.

And the sun looks so safe on the stone. That fringe of green looks designed. It is hard to believe that each frond invisibly pushes on upwards.

(And other things grow the same way: slow steel drives up through the ground.)

Remember that Japanese hands were burned right through to the bone. Remember the mother who, one by one, dug out her four buried children.

She dug with bare hands at the red-hot bricks and the smoking piles of timber. Her flesh was soon cooked to pulp, exposing raw edges of bone. In the days that followed, the children died one by one, and she could not hold them. They lay there, dead in formation, their blind puzzled eyes on the clouds. Then the mother died also, alone.

She had thought such things could not happen. You planned on life going on.

Einstein stirred from his nightmares, the funeral sheets of white light. "We are worse than beasts," he muttered. "Stupid. Stupidest. Stupid."

Our sky is printed with birds. Yet planes bore through at the corners. . . .

My characters died in formation, nearsighted, their eyes on the ground. I loved them all, but they died. I had thought such things could not happen.

To catch the sky in our hands.
                    Endings that must not happen.

Birds, light-bodied and strong on the wind, make signs of love over Europe. Brave on the vast cruel wind, over Moscow, Washington, London.

Words beat on against death . . .
                    Our bright lives beat against ending . . .

Always beginning again, beginning against ending

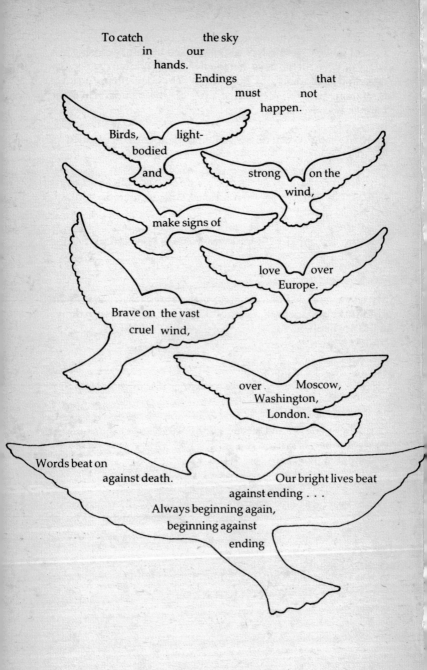

To catch   the sky
          in   our
        hands.
              Endings   that
                must   not
                happen.

  Birds,   light-
      bodied
      and   strong   on the
                          wind,

      make signs of

                    love   over
                    Europe.

  Brave on the vast
    cruel wind,

                over   Moscow,
              Washington,
                London.

Words beat on
      against death.   Our bright lives beat
                          against ending . . .
          Always beginning again,
            beginning against
                    ending